BOOK ONE
CONVERGENCE

BOOK ONE
CONVERGENCE

WRITTEN BY
STAN LEE AND STUART MOORE

ART BY
ANDIE TONG

DISNEP PRESS

Los Angeles · New York

Printed in the United States of America

First Hardcover Edition, January 2015
First Paperback Edition, November 2015

1 3 5 7 9 10 8 6 4 2

Library of Congress Control Number: 2014935029

FAC-020093-15268

ISBN 978-1-4847-5253-1

Visit disneybooks.com and disneyzodiac.com

SUSTAINABLE FORESTRY INITIATIVE
Certified Sourcing
www.sfiprogram.org
SFI-00993

THIS LABEL APPLIES TO TEXT STOCK

DEDICATED TO EVERYONE WHO LOVES
FANTASY AND HIGH ADVENTURE VIA
TALES THAT TITILLATE AND THRILL THE
IMAGINATION. WHEN YOU THINK ABOUT IT,
ISN'T THAT REALLY ALL OF US?
—S.L.

FOR LIZ
—S.M.

FOR STEPH, ZOE, AND BUBBA2
—A.T.

PART ONE
CONVERGENCE

CHAPTER ONE

THERE WAS SOMETHING odd about the

tour guide. She was tall, with long hair, and she seemed to know a lot about Chinese history—as she should, working in a museum. But as Steven Lee listened to her, he couldn't shake the feeling that she wasn't quite what she seemed.

"The New China Heritage Museum first opened five years ago," the guide said. "It was designed to resemble a traditional Chinese quadrangle house, with several buildings surrounding a central courtyard."

Steven raised his hand. Mr. Singh, the teacher, nodded to him.

"Was it always planned to be a museum?" Steven asked.

"Yes," the guide replied. She seemed distracted; her eyes darted quickly around the room. "I mean, no. Maybe. I think it was supposed to be a hotel?"

Steven frowned. *A hotel?* That didn't sound right. And the guide didn't sound very sure of herself.

The rest of the class just nodded.

Steven looked around the room. Its high walls were covered with intricate wooden carvings, stained-glass windows, and stylized artwork depicting ancient peasants with their oxen. A couple of large Buddha statues stood in the center of the room.

"The earliest books were manufactured in China," the guide said, gesturing toward a glass case. "Even before the invention of paper, writing was printed on materials like bone, wood, and, uh . . ." She trailed off.

Steven's friend Harani stepped forward. "And what?" she asked.

"Umm . . ." The guide had pulled out her phone and stood frowning at it. "Uh, plastic . . ."

Mr. Singh cocked his head. "Excuse me, ma'am. Did . . . did you say plastic?"

"Did I?" She smiled distantly. "That's silly, of course. I meant, uh . . . aluminum foil."

That's definitely *not right,* Steven thought.

CHAPTER ONE

"This woman is way off-script," Harani whispered, leaning in close to Steven. Her dark hair was pulled back from her face and she wore a bright orange sweater.

"I know, right?" Steven replied. "And what's she doing now?"

The guide was jabbing at her phone's screen, shaking her head.

Harani smiled. "Maybe she's waiting for a better job offer."

Then he noticed the guide's name tag: It read Jumanne. Steven frowned; the woman sounded Chinese, but the name didn't. Then again, Steven looked Chinese, and his name was American—a fact that had surprised a few of the locals in Hong Kong on this very trip.

Ryan, a friendly kid with red hair, pushed in between Steven and Harani. "Hey, Lee," Ryan said. "You see this?"

Ryan pointed at a display case. Inside it, a very old printed book stood propped open. A few Chinese characters ran down the side, but the page was dominated by an old-style etching, a stylized drawing of a man in robes shooting some kind of lightning out of his hand.

Steven blinked. "We've been over this, Ryan. I don't know what everything here says," he said.

"I know, dude, but it's not that—the guy in the drawing. He looks like a crazy super hero!"

"He looks like that guy," Harani said. She pointed at Steven's chest.

Steven looked from the book down to the image on his T-shirt. It showed a dark-skinned man in metallic armor, his hand crackling with energy.

Steven looked up at Harani in disbelief. "You mean the Steel Mongoose?" he asked.

She shrugged.

"You've never heard of the Steel Mongoose?" Steven continued. "African adventurer Bob Mugabi, who found himself critically injured and built a high-tech exoskeleton that gives him the powers of a cute but deadly wild animal?"

"Is, uh, is he in comic books?" Harani asked.

"No. Maybe, I dunno. He only starred in *Steel Mongoose 3*, the top-grossing film of last year! It was playing on the flight?"

"I like poetry," she said.

Then Harani looked past him and grimaced. Steven turned to see Mr. Singh glaring at them from a few feet away.

"We better cool it," Harani whispered.

Ryan laughed. "You and your heroes, Lee. They're not real, you know."

Harani and Ryan moved off. Steven lingered behind for a moment, staring at the book in the case. The strange image of the man with the lightning bolts seemed to stare back at him, as if it were speaking to him through the ages.

"Hey, Lee," Ryan called. "Take a look at this."

Steven crossed over to the wall. Ryan had stopped

next to a big empty case with a sign reading, in English and Chinese: EXHIBIT REMOVED FOR REPAIRS.

"Sucks, huh?" Ryan said. "This thing must be fifteen feet tall."

Steven peered closer. Inside the case was a small cardboard standup with a picture of the missing exhibit: a large flat disk, etched with a series of concentric circles and lines. The lines formed hundreds of tiny boxes, each filled with one or more ancient Chinese characters. Notches studded the outer part, marked with numbers from 0 to 360. A label read: *Shipan*—Astrological Compass. C. 200 B.C.

"My grandfather," Steven said. "He's got one of those. Well, his is a lot smaller. I think he brought it over from China." Steven pointed. "The markings are the names of stars in the sky."

"I like your grandpa," Ryan said. "He makes those tasty little salty peapods. Yo, we better get moving."

Ryan started off after Harani and the rest of the class, who had gathered around a large Buddha statue. But Steven hesitated. He looked around at the rugs and weathered maps covering the walls. The glass cases holding ancient pieces of bone and pottery. An exhibit of Cantonese opera showing people in bright, lavish costumes. The vast history and culture of China preserved in this place.

Steven hadn't wanted to come to Hong Kong. He liked his home in suburban Philadelphia, his big TV and his Xbox and his Blu-ray collection of superhero movies. But his parents had insisted. "You should see China," his father had said. "You have to *be* in a place to understand it. You need to know where you came from."

It must have been important, Steven knew, because his father rarely spoke for that long. In fact, Steven's parents weren't around much; ever since he could remember, they'd been busy running their company, seven days a week. But grandfather was always around, with his awesome cooking and his warm smile and his long stories about old China.

I should listen to those stories more, Steven thought.

He gazed over at the class. Harani asked the guide another question. Steven couldn't hear the answer, but some of the other kids laughed. Mr. Singh frowned, leaning forward to reprimand them gently.

Standing apart from the class, Steven suddenly felt very lonely, very much out of place. *Just two weeks . . .* he thought. *But I'm already looking forward to getting home.*

He looked down at his shirt again. He stared at the determined, muscular figure of the Steel Mongoose, fists glowing with righteous power.

"Mr. Lee!"

Mr. Singh was glaring at him. The class was marching through a high archway into an adjacent exhibit space. Frowning, Steven started forward to join them.

Then he stopped in his tracks.

The scream was quiet—so faint that Steven could barely make it out. But it felt deep and resonant, and it penetrated right into his skull. It sounded like someone— a man or woman, Steven couldn't tell—howling in agony.

Steven whirled around, trying to locate the source of the scream. It seemed to be coming from the far wall. Two huge ornate rugs covered most of the wall, with a small door between them.

Then the noise was gone.

Steven frowned. *Did I really hear that?* he wondered. He shook his head and started toward the archway—then stopped again as the scream sounded once more.

The class had moved on to the next room. But the guide, the strange woman named Jumanne, stood alone now. She stared intently at her phone, then glanced up at the door—the one between the two rugs. The door the screams had come from.

Instinctively, Steven moved behind a Buddha statue. He peered around the side, watching Jumanne as her eyes flicked from the door back to the phone, and then to the door again. She looked like she was trying to make a decision.

Then she tossed the phone aside and strode toward the door. Her whole demeanor seemed different now; she wasn't awkward or distracted at all. She moved quickly, with purpose. Her eyes were sharp and hard.

Steven ducked from one Buddha to the next, moving closer. The woman didn't notice him.

Jumanne reached out and pushed the door open. Casting a quick, grim glance backward, she disappeared into the darkness. The door swung shut behind her.

Steven looked around again. He was alone in the

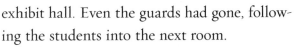

exhibit hall. Even the guards had gone, following the students into the next room.

He sprinted over to the door the woman had passed through. It bore a red sign reading: NO ENTRY. MUSEUM PERSONNEL ONLY.

Steven grabbed hold of the door handle. Then he stopped and turned to look back at the archway. *I should go back to the class,* he thought. *This is a foreign country. I could get in a lot of trouble.*

Then he heard the scream again. It was louder this time, and higher-pitched. *Someone,* he realized, *is in a lot of pain.*

He glanced down again at the image on his T-shirt. He thought of the woman, the tour guide. Was she in trouble on the other side of this door? Or had she gone through to *save* someone who was?

Maybe I should just see if anyone needs help, he thought.

As he pushed the door open, he realized he was smiling.

CHAPTER TWO

STEVEN TOOK a step forward into the darkness. He blinked, waiting for his eyes to adjust. Then he stopped short.

The floor dropped off just ahead of him, descending into a long stairway. It was made of wood, with a creaky old railing beside it. The walls were worn metal, stained and weathered by time.

Steven sucked in a breath. The air was stale and quiet. *Whatever this place is,* he thought, *it's a lot older than the museum.*

Once again, he hesitated. He leaned forward, but he couldn't see more than a few steps down. There was no way to tell where it went, or how far down it stretched.

Suddenly, the scream rang out again, deep and resonant.

Steven pulled out his phone. Shining it like a weak flashlight, he started down the staircase. The steps sagged under his feet, and the railing felt like it might snap off in his hand. The light from his phone illuminated a few steps at a time, but that was all.

Soon he couldn't see the door anymore, either.

I'm headed deep underground, Steven thought, *but sideways, too. I think we're going . . . away from the museum?*

The scream rose to a high pitch, then went silent again.

Steven tried to keep track of how far he'd traveled. But he hadn't thought to start counting steps at the beginning, and now it was impossible to tell where he was.

"Oh!" Steven cried as he stumbled, reaching the staircase's abrupt end. Something lay at his feet, crumpled in a shapeless lump.

For a terrible moment, he thought it was a body.

Grimacing, afraid to look, he leaned down and touched it. With relief, he realized it was just a pile of cloth—a uniform, like the ones worn by the guides at the museum. Something sharp pricked his finger, and he felt a small hard object pinned to the uniform.

Wincing, he lifted the object. It was a name tag.

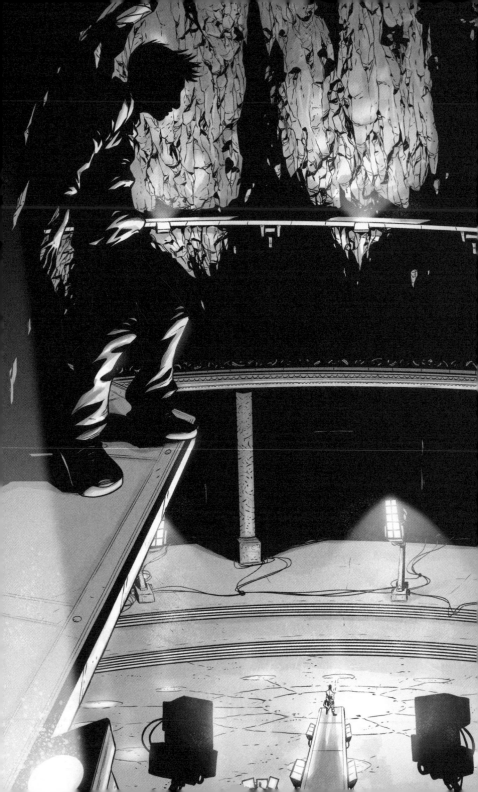

Jumanne.

A million thoughts raced through Steven's brain. Had the guide changed clothes down here for some reason, hastily tossing her old uniform aside? Had she been attacked?

The stairwell was still dark, but Steven's eyes were starting to adjust. Just ahead, a metal door loomed at the end of the passageway. He tossed the clothing aside and felt around until his hand closed over a doorknob.

For a moment, he thought about turning and running back up the stairs. Then he glanced at the discarded uniform, crumpled on the floor. His heart skipped a beat.

If somebody's in trouble . . .

He pushed open the door and stepped forward. Then he gasped.

Steven stood on a thin catwalk running all the way around a large, perfectly circular room. The room was dark, lit only slightly from the floor below.

Steven realized that the catwalk frighteningly didn't have a railing. He stepped forward carefully, peering over the edge. Ten or twelve feet below, a dozen round circles were arrayed around the edges of the chamber, each about the size of a wading pool. Looking closer, he noticed they actually *were* pools, filled with some strange, shimmering liquid. They radiated a pale, eerie greenish light into the room.

The room was quiet. If someone had been screaming in here, they'd stopped now.

Steven looked up. The chamber stretched far upward, several stories high. Its walls were made of metal and tapered, narrowing toward the ceiling like an upside-down ice-cream cone. This gave the room a claustrophobic feel, despite its immense size.

Round holes and old support struts dotted the walls, as if other catwalks had once been mounted there and then removed. And at the narrow top of the chamber, where the walls converged almost to a point, a large flat disk had been mounted on the ceiling. It looked very old, and on its visible side, facing down, it was marked with a very familiar set of numbers and boxes.

That's the—what was it called?—the shipan! Steven realized. *The exhibit from upstairs, the one that had been removed for repairs.*

The one that looks like grandfather's little compass.

Steven sucked in a deep breath. What was going on? What was this room, anyway? What were those mysterious pools of liquid? Why had a valuable exhibit from the museum been installed in such a bizarre place?

And how did the mysterious Jumanne fit in?

In the exact center of the room, a group of lights winked on. Steven blinked and saw a small elevated stage with three people standing on it. The stage was covered with computers, monitors, and technical equipment, all rigged up in a crazy tangle of wires and cables.

The people wore baggy jumpsuits and held clipboards and tablet computers. One of them, a serious-looking technician with thin glasses, looked up, away from Steven. "Sorry, Maxwell," he called out. "Just a minor power glitch."

Steven followed the technician's gaze. Partway across the room, a large figure hovered in midair. He was lit from below by one of the pools so Steven couldn't make out his features; but his body was coiled, his fists clenched. The pool below him seemed to glow slightly brighter than the others, casting long, imposing shadows along his body.

When the man—Maxwell—spoke, his voice was deep and commanding. "Is it repaired now?" he asked.

"Yes, sir," the technician replied.

Maxwell reached out a hand and pointed to another pool. Now Steven could see: Maxwell was astride a one-person hover-vehicle, sort of a crazy, higher-tech version of a Segway. And around Maxwell's outstretched arm— around his entire body, in fact—a greenish glow radiated, a fainter version of the glow from the pools below.

"Then proceed," Maxwell said. "And Carlos?"

The technician cocked his head. He seemed agitated, even a bit fearful.

"I'm counting on you," Maxwell finished.

Carlos nodded. He cast a nervous glance around the

chamber, from the compass on the roof down the sides to the catwalk. His eyes almost met Steven's, and for a moment Steven was afraid Carlos had spotted him.

Then Carlos turned away, issuing a series of orders to the other techs. The three technicians consulted a bank of monitors, their eyes darting quickly from screen to screen.

"Upper stems look good," Carlos said. "Lower branches . . . slight blockage in branch two."

"On it," said the female technician. "Flushing the branch now . . . qi levels returning to normal."

Steven pressed his back against the wall of the chamber, shaking his head. *What are they talking about?*

"All systems nominal." Carlos turned back toward the hovering figure. "Maxwell, we're ready for Position Three."

"No," Maxwell replied, his voice booming through the chamber. "Position Six."

Carlos grimaced.

"I told you," Maxwell continued. "I want the strongest powers first."

When Carlos hesitated, Maxwell swiveled his hover-vehicle to face the stage. Maxwell's eyes glowed a fierce, angry green, and a spasm of pain seemed to pass through him.

"Carlos," Maxwell said. "Your knowledge of the Convergence has gotten us this far. I am grateful, and I would prefer that you complete the procedure." His voice grew cold. "But if necessary, I can bring in someone else."

Carlos shook his head quickly and returned to his work.

Maxwell turned away without a word and glided across the center of the chamber. He came to a stop just above another pool, a few spaces closer to Steven.

"I've got a slight Fire deficit," said another male technician.

"I see it," Carlos replied. "Maria, shunt some Wood energy over to branch five."

"What?" the woman asked. "That'll overload that whole branch."

"Right, uh, my mistake," Carlos said. "I meant branch four. Qi levels compensated; activating *shipan* now."

A whirring noise filled the room. Steven looked up at the source: the *shipan*, the ancient astrological disk mounted on the narrow ceiling. A large bright light flashed on, one of twelve lamps mounted around the *shipan*'s outer edge. The spotlight stabbed straight onto the ground.

The other eleven lamps ranged around the edge of the *shipan* were dark.

"Alignment sequence is go," the female technician said.

With a loud grinding sound, the *shipan* began to swivel slowly in place. As it moved, the spotlight traveled along the floor between the pools.

Except, Steven saw now, it wasn't a floor at all. It was dirt, ordinary soil. That meant the pools hadn't been brought into the museum after it was constructed. The pools were already here, sunken deep in this strange chamber beneath the Earth. The museum had been constructed *above* them.

Steven drew in another, deep breath. *What is this place?*

The *shipan* ground to a halt, directly above Maxwell's hovering figure. Its light shone straight down and around him, focused directly on the pool beneath his feet. Maxwell floated between the disk above and the pool below, caught between the two sources of unnatural radiance.

Then Steven noticed something else strange. Something—someone—was creeping along the ground, in the darkness at the edge of the room. A slim, lithe figure, darting from one pool to another, moving closer to Maxwell's position. Steven couldn't see the figure clearly; it was keeping to the shadows. But something about the shadow's motion reminded him of the last time he'd seen Jumanne, the tour guide, as she'd crossed the exhibit hall to the door.

That's her, he thought. *I know it.*

Maxwell glanced up at the *shipan*, then down at the luminous pool. His fists clenched open and closed on the handles of his hover-vehicle. He seemed to be bracing himself for something.

"Resume Convergence," he said. "Position Six."

On the central stage, Carlos pointed a finger at the female technician. She tapped out a command on her screen.

On the underside of the *shipan*, the spotlight surged brighter. Energy crackled across the surface of the disk, pulsing and gathering. At the same time, directly below Maxwell, the pool erupted with light. When the energy from above met the blazing liquid shooting up from below—

—Maxwell screamed.

It was a deep, soul-chilling sound. Steven recognized it immediately as the scream he'd heard upstairs in the museum and then again in the stairwell. *It sounds,* he thought, *as if something's being ripped out of his body.*

Then he realized: *No. It's more like something's being forced* into *him. Something foreign, alien.*

The energy flared, forming a vertical column. Maxwell's body became a silhouette, a twitching mass still clinging to its high-tech hover-machine. Something else started to form: a second figure, rearing and bucking in the energy-glow above Maxwell. A raging beast, a creature of pure energy, wild and untamed.

As Steven stared into the glow, the beast coalesced into a huge, wild stallion. Its mouth opened wide, and its mane whipped back and forth in a breathtaking display of silent savagery.

Steven glanced over at the control stage. Carlos and the other technicians stood watching Maxwell with clinical, scientific eyes. Carlos flinched slightly, just once, when Maxwell's scream rose to a deafening pitch.

ZODIAC

Steven cast a look down at the corner of the room again, but the "tour guide" had vanished. If she was still here, she must be hiding deep in the shadows.

The energy flared once, then again. Maxwell raised his head to the heavens and howled, even louder, more savagely than before.

Then, all at once, the energy was gone. The *shipan* went dark; the liquid splashed back down into the pool. The glow flashed and faded around Maxwell, taking the ethereal stallion-vision with it.

On the control stage, the technicians rushed around, manipulating touchscreen controls. The woman began to speak, but Carlos motioned her to silence. All three of them turned to stare at their leader.

Maxwell still hovered in midair, wobbling slightly. He glowed more brightly than before, like a coal that had been heated in a fire. Green energy leaked from his eyes, his mouth, his fingertips. Liquid from the pool dripped off of him, drying rapidly.

Slowly he looked up, staring just past Steven. His head swiveled to face the control stage. Then he smiled and spoke a single word.

"*Horse,*" he said.

CHAPTER THREE

STEVEN STOOD for a long moment, almost paralyzed. He struggled to collect his thoughts, to make sense of what he had just seen.

I could bounce, he thought. *The door's right behind me. I could bolt back up that staircase, get back to the class, and make up some lame excuse about getting lost. It'd be like all this never happened. I bet, after a while, even I'd think I made it all up in my head.*

But there was still Jumanne, the tour guide—or whatever she was. And more than that: There was a mystery here. Something very important, something that might even affect the future of the world.

Something a hero would investigate.

Maxwell raised his head slowly as if it weighed a hundred pounds. "Carlos," he said. "Position Five."

"Sir," the female technician said, "are you sure?"

Maxwell glared at her. When he bared his teeth, a bit of green energy leaked out. The woman stepped back, frightened.

"Maxwell," Carlos said. "The Zodiac power—it's not meant to be held by a single person. Especially someone who's not the appropriate sign."

"You're not a Horse!" the woman cried.

That, Steven thought, *is a strange thing to say.*

Carlos swept an arm around to indicate the pools on the ground. "You've absorbed three of the twelve Zodiac signs," he said. "The rest could kill you."

"They would kill a person like you. They will make me the most powerful man on Earth."

There was silence for a moment. Carlos's gaze flicked briefly down to the ground, below the stage.

"Position Five," Maxwell repeated.

Carlos nodded. He turned back to his work, issuing a series of low commands to the other techs.

Above, the *shipan* began to grind once again. A second light flared to life on its underside, blazing down toward another pool.

Maxwell sucked in a deep breath. He glided around the room, moving one space counterclockwise to the newly lit pool. He slipped easily into the spotlight from the *shipan*—moving, in the process, one position closer to Steven's hiding place on the dark catwalk at the edge of the room.

Again, Steven saw a movement down below. He leaned over the edge of the catwalk, conscious of the drop to the ground. It was the woman, Jumanne, still hugging the shadows. She moved swiftly, gracefully, and her hair was pulled up now into a ponytail.

Jumanne crept toward Maxwell. Both of them were converging on Steven's position—but neither of them seemed to have noticed him. Yet.

I should run, Steven thought, once more. But he couldn't. Something held him rooted to the spot.

I've got to see this through to the end. Whatever this *is.*

Maxwell took up position above the newly illuminated pool, just as he had with the previous one. "Begin," he said.

Again, the *shipan* in the ceiling glowed bright. Again the pool surged upward, meeting the blinding light from above in a flare of power. And again, Maxwell screamed.

Steven glanced down at the corner of the room. He could see Jumanne crouched behind another pool, the next one over. *She's using the pool to hide from Maxwell,* Steven realized. And she was pulling something out of a pack, casting nervous glances up at the pulsing column of light.

Maxwell's head whipped back and forth in the air,

flinging drops of the strange green fluid all around. This time, his howl of agony sounded more like a hissing sound. The coiled form of a snake surged into being above him, its scaly head and sharp tongue hissing back and forth in time to Maxwell's own movements.

Steven stared. The motion was mesmerizing, like the rhythmic motions of a hypnotist's watch. The snake's head seemed to turn toward him, its deep red eyes boring deep into his mind.

Then, once again, the energy faded away. Steven shook his head, still trapped by the snake's hypnotic spell. And then, with a sinking feeling, he realized that Maxwell was staring straight at him.

Slowly, Maxwell twisted the handle-controls of his hover-device. He glided across the room, unhurried, keeping his eyes fixed on Steven. Green radiance leaked from his body, emanating from his face, his clothes, his very pores. He stopped just beyond the edge of the catwalk, hovering in midair, his eyes precisely level with Steven's.

Then he smiled.

"Look what's wandered in out of the wild," Maxwell said. "A young Tiger."

He sounded as if he'd just caught something for dinner.

Suddenly Steven remembered something. *Grandfather used to call me that: "My little Tiger." Is this an astrology thing? Something about the year I was born?*

And then he understood. The horse, the snake. The pools—twelve of them. Twelve signs . . . just like on grandfather's compass. He glanced up at the heavily marked disk in the ceiling, then found his gaze drawn back irresistibly to Maxwell's probing eyes.

"The Zodiac," Steven said. "Those are the signs."

Maxwell's smile stayed fixed. He nodded.

Below, Steven could see activity on the control stage. Carlos pointed, and the two other techs climbed down and started off across the floor toward Steven and Maxwell.

"You're clever," Maxwell said. "How did you get in here?"

Steven still couldn't move. "The door," he said, trying to sound confident.

Maxwell turned back toward the stage. "I ordered the Convergence chamber sealed."

"It was," Carlos replied. But his voice trembled.

The two other techs were running toward the catwalk now, swerving around the pools.

"I already have a Tiger," Maxwell said, turning back toward Steven. "Unless you think you're a better choice?"

Steven shrugged. He felt like he was watching a foreign film.

Abruptly Maxwell tipped sideways in midair and swooped away. Without looking back, he gestured at the two techs. "Maria, Fedor," Maxwell said, "remove him. We can't have him interfering with the Convergence." Then he stopped a few feet from the stage and tilted his head back toward Steven. "But hold him. I'd like to continue this little chat later."

The techs were climbing a small ladder now, a few yards down the catwalk from Steven. They'd be on him in a minute.

He looked around frantically. Maxwell had stopped just above the central stage, leaning down to argue with Carlos. Their voices were low; Steven couldn't make out what they were saying. But Carlos didn't look happy.

Above, the *shipan* glowed softly.

The first of the techs—Fedor, the man—climbed up onto the catwalk. He looked a little unsure of himself. *Probably not used to doing guard duty,* Steven thought. Still, Steven wasn't sure he could take two of them in a fight.

But he really didn't want to "chat" with Maxwell anymore.

Another motion caught his eye, just below. The woman from the museum, Jumanne. He couldn't see her clearly, but it had to be her. He glanced quickly back at the two technicians advancing on him across the catwalk—

—and then he leaped over the edge.

He dropped through the air, into darkness, landing roughly on the bare ground. He dropped to his knees and tumbled onto his back.

When he looked up, the woman from the museum was just a few feet away, barely visible in the diffuse light from the pools. She was staring at a pair of round metal objects in her hand. Each was about the size of a baseball, and each had a blinking red light on its surface.

"Come on," she whispered, apparently to the metal spheres. "Comeoncomeoncomeon!"

Steven glanced back up at the catwalk. The two technicians leaned over the edge, peering into the darkness. They didn't seem to be able to see Steven—but then the female tech, Maria, pointed at the winking red lights in Jumanne's hand.

Steven took a step toward the mysterious woman. "Uh, hi," he said. "Are you—"

Without looking up, Jumanne swung her empty hand around and clamped it down hard over Steven's mouth.

"Keep quiet and I can get you out," she said, keeping her voice low. "Just do everything I say exactly when I say it." She shook one of the spherical objects, as if it were a broken remote control. "Come ON!"

"What . . . what . . ." Steven stared at the glowing figure above them and swallowed in fear. "What *is* all this?"

A blinding light washed over them. For a moment, Steven thought it was another power-light from the *shipan* disk in the ceiling. But when he squinted upward, he saw the hovering form of Maxwell, shining a small arc-light mounted on his hover-vehicle.

Maxwell cast an amused glance at Steven. Then he turned to Jumanne, and his expression turned dark.

"Jasmine," he said.

Steven turned at a sound. The two technicians were climbing down off the ladder again, pointing and heading straight for Steven and Jumanne. *Or Jasmine,* he thought. *Whatever her name is!*

Jasmine looked back up at Maxwell, shading her eyes against the glare. "I was hurt, Maxwell," she said, her mouth curling up into a nasty smile. "I'm not on your guest list anymore?"

"It's a private party, Jasmine," Maxwell replied.

"I get it—glass ceiling. Hold this for me, kid?"

Without looking, she tossed one of the metal spheres at Steven. He fumbled, but managed to catch it.

When he looked up, Jasmine was already in motion. She tossed her sphere up high, barely watching as it followed a lazy arc through the air. Then she leaped forward, aiming a fierce kick at Fedor, the male technician. Her foot struck him square in the stomach, doubling him over. The female tech, Maria, waved a Taser at her, electricity arcing at its tip. Jasmine chopped sideways into Maria's wrist; the tech cried out in pain and the Taser fell, sparking, to the ground.

Jasmine followed up with a brutal elbow to the back of the woman's head. Maria grunted and went down. Fedor struggled to rise, but Jasmine took him down with two fierce blows to his solar plexus.

Then she held out a hand, just in time to catch the

sphere she'd thrown into the air. Its light, Steven noticed, was still red. He glanced down at the one in his hands: It was blinking red, too.

Then Jasmine marched back toward Steven, taking long strides. "Kid," she said, shaking her head. "You're killing me here."

She's barely winded, Steven thought. *Who is this woman?*

But before Jasmine could reach Steven, Maxwell's spotlight shone back down on her.

"Very impressive, Jasmine." Green energy radiated once more from Maxwell's hovering form. "But time is short, and I can't let you stay here. Carlos, please—"

A loud grinding noise cut him off. Steven looked up, knowing what he'd see. The *shipan*, the disk in the ceiling, was glowing. A third light blazed to life, and the disk began its loud, slow, circular movement once again.

Maxwell whirled around in midair. "Carlos?" he called. "What are you doing?"

"Jaz," Carlos yelled, leaning over the edge of the stage. *"Now!"*

Jasmine looked down—just as the light turned green on the metal sphere in her hand. She smiled and threw the sphere into the air.

"Game on," she said.

Maxwell wobbled in midair, dodging the sphere. But he wasn't her target. The sphere sailed past him and struck the *shipan*, near its center. On impact, the sphere released

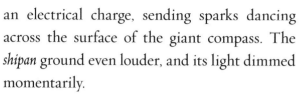

an electrical charge, sending sparks dancing across the surface of the giant compass. The *shipan* ground even louder, and its light dimmed momentarily.

Maxwell had turned to stare at Carlos. "So," Maxwell said. "A traitor at the very heart of my—"

Jasmine leaped up in the air, surprisingly high, and expertly checked Maxwell with the left side of her body. His hover-vehicle whined in protest, tipping perilously to the side. He managed to find his balance and whirled around, lashing out at her. But she ducked, standing her ground.

Then, shockingly, Maxwell laughed.

"Impressive," he said. "And yet, so disappointing."

Jasmine's eyes flashed with anger. "That's what—my *mother* used to say," she said, reaching out to grab Maxwell by the shoulders. "Remember her?"

"Oh, yes."

Above, the *shipan* ground to a halt. Its light was steady again, shining down on yet another pool. The pool seemed to glow in response.

Taking advantage of Maxwell's momentary distraction, Jasmine jumped behind Maxwell and climbed on to his back, grappling with him like a wrestler. She shifted her weight, and the hover-vehicle lurched through the air. She seemed to be steering Maxwell, forcing their combined flight in a particular direction.

"Why are you doing this, Jasmine?" Maxwell asked. "You're like me: a Dragon. We're stronger than all of them."

Then Steven realized where Jasmine was leading Maxwell: toward the glowing pool beneath the shining light of the *shipan*.

"We answer to no one," Maxwell added.

"I answer to my conscience," Jasmine replied. "Ever heard of that?"

Jasmine climbed higher up Maxwell's back. She placed a foot on Maxwell's shoulder, bracing herself. *She's going to leap,* Steven realized. *She's going to jump into the pool. Or into the light.*

But Maxwell grabbed her leg in a firm grip. "Oh, no," he said, his expression deadly. "Never, little girl. Never."

Then Maxwell stopped and glanced upward. He turned in alarm, looking first down at Steven, then over toward Carlos—

—just as the brightest, widest beam of all stabbed down, engulfing both Jasmine and Maxwell in a thick cylinder of light. A matching surge of liquid splashed upward from the pool. The hover-vehicle sparked, shorted out, and fell to the ground with a clatter.

Even without the vehicle, Jasmine and Maxwell hung suspended in the air. They cried out together and rose up higher, held in a cocoon of sparkling, eldritch power.

Steven shielded his eyes, struggling to see. Maxwell and Jasmine were barely visible as silhouettes, jerking back and forth like puppets, suspended halfway between the *shipan* and the ground. As the energy beam held them, an animal figure began to form above their bodies . . . just as it had with Maxwell, before.

But this figure was different. It was blurry, a double image, as if two different forms were fighting to occupy the same space. One figure was lean and sinewy, like a snake, but with sharp, searching claws and a strange mustache-like growth above its gaping jaws. The other was also reptilian, but with sharply angled bat wings that stretched out wide.

The creature flickered and shifted, morphing rapidly from one form to the other. It opened its jaws and screamed, a piercing sound like nothing Steven had ever heard before.

The energy beam held both Jasmine and Maxwell for a long moment, filling both their bodies with its unknown mystic power. Then, all at once, it blinked off.

Maxwell glowed bright now. The energy beast resolved itself into the second, winged form. Maxwell spread his arms, and above, the creature's bat wings flared out along with them.

Jasmine dropped like a rock. She landed hard at Steven's feet, and grunted softly.

Maxwell was still hovering. When he spoke, his voice

seemed to echo off the metal walls. He didn't sound human anymore.

"Young Tiger," he repeated. Power glowed from his eyes, his mouth.

Steven stared upward. His throat was dry. The dark-winged phantasm had wrapped itself tightly around its host. Maxwell shone like a fully charged battery, smiling as if he'd just won every lottery in the world.

"Meet the Dragon," Maxwell said.

CHAPTER FOUR

TIME SEEMED TO stop for a moment in that
strange room beneath the world.

Maxwell stared down at Steven, glowing bright. Whatever the Zodiac was, it was clearly powerful. Maxwell's fists were clenched tight, energy flaring out from them in waves, and he clearly no longer needed a vehicle in order to fly. The Dragon figure hissed and spat, rising proudly above its master.

Steven glanced down at Jasmine. She lay on the ground between the pools, dazed, struggling to rise. The bodies of the two technicians lay still, nearby.

Jasmine and Maxwell, Steven thought. *They can both do such amazing things. And I'm just a kid. I'm helpless—I'm a—*

—a Tiger.

He didn't know what that meant. He didn't really know what was going on in this room, or what was at stake. But as he cast another glance at Jasmine, somehow he knew: *I have to help her.*

He clenched his fists and glared up at Maxwell. *If I jump,* he thought, *I can tackle him. Tackle a big glowing man with crazy mystical powers? Oh, man, this is gonna hurt—*

Then the grinding sound rose up again, louder and harsher than before. It seemed to drill into Steven's ears, filling the room with noise. He and Maxwell glanced up together—just as every light on the *shipan* flared to life at once, bathing the room in blinding radiance.

Steven shrank back, blinking and covering his ears. But Maxwell was already moving, swooping through the air toward the center of the room.

"*CARLOS!*" Maxwell screamed.

Steven peered through the light. On the stage, Carlos moved quickly around, yanking out cords and smashing keyboards. He jabbed his elbow into a glass screen, shattering it. Sparks flew, igniting a low fire that blazed across the array of machinery.

Then Carlos saw Maxwell coming. His eyes widened with fear. He tossed a broken computer display up at Maxwell, and took off at a run.

Maxwell held up a glowing hand. The display sparked as it struck the Dragon energy, then shattered into a thousand pieces.

Above, the *shipan* began to spin. The grinding noise grew even louder; the blinding lights began to whirl, flashing wildly around the room.

"Kid!"

Steven turned in surprise. Jasmine had raised herself to a crouch and was staring at him.

"Throw it!" she said.

He stared at her, baffled.

She held out both hands in a gesture of exasperation. "The *grenade!*"

He looked down. To his surprise, he was still holding the second metal sphere. And the light on its surface had turned green.

Steven reared back and threw the sphere up as hard as he could. It smashed into one of the *shipan*'s lights, triggering a shower of sparks. The light flashed and shorted out.

Then the *shipan* exploded with a deafening crack. Smoke billowed out, thick and black. Shards of glass, pieces of metal and plastic, began to rain down.

Steven raised a hand to shield his face from the debris. "Grenade," Steven said.

Jasmine smiled. "Yeah."

Maxwell swooped up high, his figure barely visible through the smoke. "No," he cried. "The Convergence!"

Steven looked up, past Maxwell. A large crack ran straight through the center of the *shipan*; smoke billowed out of it in thick clouds. Its lights blinked on and off, madly, as the disk continued to spin.

Down below, the pools began to glow brighter.

"Hang on," Jasmine said. "Things are about to get crazy."

Steven stared at her. "Crazier than *this?*"

She laughed.

A light stabbed down. Maxwell swooped through the air, intercepting the beam as it met a matching flare shooting up from one of the pools. Again he screamed, his body glowing bright as he soaked up the power.

In the aura above Maxwell, Steven thought he saw a sinister, long-tailed Rat.

Carlos ran up, waving away smoke. He crouched down to help Jasmine.

"I'm all right," she said.

"Good. Here." Carlos reached into a bag and pulled out three more grenades. All their lights were green.

Above, another light flared bright. Maxwell flew toward it, his scream a constant blare now. When the beam struck him, a smiling, capering Monkey appeared in the energy glow above his head.

Steven gasped.

A look of suspicion crossed Carlos's face. He gestured at Steven. "You trust this kid?" he asked Jasmine.

"I don't trust anybody," Jasmine replied, wincing as she tried to stand. "He's got a good arm, though."

Carlos stared at Steven blankly for a moment. Then he handed Steven a grenade.

Jasmine threw two grenades upward simultaneously. Steven watched as the two spheres whizzed past Maxwell, passing harmlessly through the Monkey apparition.

When the grenades struck the *shipan*, the world seemed to explode. The *shipan* cracked and split in half. One half stayed mounted in place, while the other hung loose from the ceiling like a hinge. Beams flared bright in all directions. Some of them shot downward toward the pools, but they missed their marks, scorching energy marks into the ground. Others blasted sideways, gouging holes in the metal walls.

And above the chaos, just barely visible through the billowing smoke, the *shipan* had cracked free to reveal a sliver of open sky. A few of the disk's beams flared up through the opening, arcing like lightning into the humid Hong Kong night.

Maxwell hovered in midair, staring in alarm at the wreckage. Maxwell's Dragon had manifested again, Steven noticed; it stared along with him, like a pet crouched on his back.

Then Maxwell turned to look down. He fixed green-glowing, murderous eyes on Carlos, and pointed a thick, crackling finger.

"*You,*" he said.

Maxwell swooped down just as Jasmine leaped in front of Carlos, shielding him. Above Maxwell, the Dragon hissed in anticipation. There was a loud crunch from above.

Half of the *shipan*—a massive chunk of bone and metal—crashed down on top of Maxwell. He grunted in pain, flaring bright. Then he fell.

"See? Things got crazy." Jasmine grimaced. "Don't answer, just run!"

Steven followed her and Carlos, dodging around the pools. Maxwell plummeted toward them, the half *shipan* forcing him down with its weight. When they struck the ground, the whole chamber shook.

Up above, the other half of the *shipan* still hung loose from the open ceiling. Beams flashed and flared, stabbing out from it in all directions. Pools erupted across the floor. Some of them intercepted the beams from the broken *shipan*, others splashed harmlessly into the air.

Steven looked over at Maxwell. He lay grimacing in pain, trapped beneath the heavy bulk of the *shipan*. It was lodged in the ground, one sharp end buried deep. Only one light still glowed on its surface, jutting up several feet above Maxwell's figure.

Jasmine gestured at a radiance rising up from the pool behind them. "Uh-oh," she said.

Carlos consulted a handheld analyzer device. "Uh-oh squared," he said.

Steven barely heard them. He found himself staring at the single light on the grounded half of the *shipan*. It seemed to pulse, transfixing him with some strange lure.

"Kid," Jasmine said. "We gotta go."

Steven shrugged her off. The *shipan's* light seemed to expand, to fill his world. He had the strange feeling that it was speaking to him.

Maxwell struggled, craning his neck to look upward at the blazing light. His eyes seemed normal now; the energy had faded from him. Slowly he turned toward Steven.

"No," Maxwell said.

Carlos looked up sharply from his analyzer. "Kid," he said. "What did Maxwell call you before?"

As Steven watched, the *shipan's* light burst forth. It lashed out, arcing up over Maxwell's trapped figure, heading straight toward Steven himself.

Again, time seemed to stop. The energy hung in the air, billowing outward as it drew closer. Steven saw shapes inside it: circles, triangles. Stars and moons and galaxies; sharp fanged teeth and sharper, slashing claws. A long line of people stretching back through the ages, rich landowners and poor Chinese peasants, farmers who worked the soil and kings who ruled other men from gleaming palaces in the sky. The beam seemed to contain all these people, all of them turning to greet Steven as the light reached down to scoop him up inside its depths.

Then the energy struck. Steven felt a cold pain, like a thousand icy needles plunging into his body at once. The

light seemed to reach inside him, penetrating his arms and legs, passing through into his brain and heart. Filling him up, transforming him into something new, something different. Something he couldn't quite imagine.

The last thing he saw was his grandfather. The old man's kindly face smiled wide, his voice cutting through the pain. *It's all right,* Grandfather said. *Something is ending here, but something new is beginning. Just remember me, remember who and what you are. Where you came from, and what you may become.*

My little Tiger.

Then the energy passed, ebbing away like a receding wave. Grandfather vanished along with all the others, the people and the stars and the fangs and claws.

Steven shook his head. The air was thick around him; scorch marks smoked from the floor and walls. He seemed to see everything through a thick green haze.

Jasmine was shakily getting up. It seemed something had knocked her down. She looked at him, her eyes wide. Carlos stood just a few feet away, also staring at him. He started to ask them why, but then a deafening roar rose up, echoing all around. It filled the inside of his head, the room—his whole world.

Jasmine raised a finger and pointed up.

Steven followed her gaze. Above and around his body, haloed in a thick green energy aura, a strange apparition whipped its head from side to side. A fierce, raging Tiger, its sharp fangs and piercing eyes announcing its presence to the world.

CHAPTER FIVE

"HUH," Jasmine said, gesturing at the Tiger form rising up from Steven. "*That* wasn't in the plan."

Carlos aimed his analyzer at Steven. "Almost ninety-seven percent qi suffusion," he said. "Ley-line energy steady . . . stem-branch alignment is—"

The Tiger roared again.

"—he's a Tiger, all right," Carlos finished.

Jasmine rolled her eyes. "Way ahead of you, Doctor Science."

Steven barely heard them. He looked around, trying to clear his head. One of the pools had spilled open, its eldritch liquid flowing out to sink into the ground. The control stage was a wreck, smashed flat by a fallen beam. On the far wall, curving above, a smoking shard of metal hung loose, threatening to fall.

And on the ceiling, the remaining half of the *shipan* disk still flickered—but its beams were fading. Smoke filled the room, but it was starting to clear, dissipating up into the open air.

Maxwell lay still, his eyes closed, legs still buried under the other half of the *shipan*. Bits of green energy puffed out of his mouth with each shallow breath. *How can he be alive?* Steven wondered. *That thing would have crushed a normal person.*

"He won't be out for long," Jasmine said, following Steven's gaze to Maxwell. "We better move."

Carlos cast a long, dour look around at the wreckage. Then he turned, frowning, to gesture at Steven. "What about him?"

Steven clenched his fists. "Hold on. Rewind, restart, respawn. STOP!"

Jasmine raised an eyebrow.

"What's going on here?" Steven continued. "Who are you guys? What is the Zodiac, who is that guy buried under the king-size sundial, and why do I have a *freaking Tiger inside me now?*"

Jasmine and Carlos exchanged surprised looks.

"How do we even start?" Carlos asked.

Steven could only stare at them. He could see and feel the Tiger start to fade away as his energy died down.

"With a question of my own, I think—" Jasmine said. She stopped to gather her thoughts. "What the hell are you doing here?"

"I followed *you*! You were leading a tour with my class and I saw you go through the door and I heard screams and then there was the creepy staircase and your empty uniform and then all this!"

Jasmine stared at him for a moment. Then, unexpectedly, she laughed.

"I never liked that uniform," she said.

Steven stared back. "Are you gonna answer my—"

Before he realized it, Steven was on his feet and leaping. The Tiger roared, stretching its paws upward. Steven soared through the air, landing gracefully several feet away—just as an enormous metal beam tore loose from the wall and slammed down to the ground, exactly where he'd been standing.

Steven stared in shock at the jagged metal beam. Dust rose up around it, settling down in the nearby pools and on the ground. Its far end still hung shakily from the scarred, smoking wall.

I should be dead, he thought. *That thing could have killed me. The Tiger—whatever it is, it just saved my life.*

Jasmine stepped forward and grabbed his arm. "Focus, kid," she said. "What's your name, anyway?"

"St-Steven."

"Steven. I'm just gonna run through this real quick because, as you can see, this isn't a very healthy place to be right now. Okay?"

As if to punctuate her words, the half *shipan* on the ceiling gave out a loud groan. One of its lights cracked loose and fell, shattering on the ground next to the wrecked control stage.

Steven nodded quickly.

Jasmine gestured around. "This chamber here is an ancient site at the center of a bunch of—crap, I can never remember what they're—"

"Ley lines," Carlos said.

"Right," she continued. "Ley lines, qi energy, and a whole bunch of other scientific stuff that I can't understand. *Nobody* understands it except Carlos here."

"I only understand about half of it." Carlos smiled shyly. "Maybe two-thirds."

"The Zodiac influences all our lives," Jasmine said. "And for some reason lost to the ages, its power is concentrated in these pools. Now, every once in a while, a little bit of that energy drifts out into the world. It floats through the air until it reaches someone born in the right year, under the corresponding sign. Then the energy seeps inside that person, enters his or her body."

Steven stared at her. "And that person gets . . . what? Superpowers?"

"The energy is usually present in very small amounts. Somebody contacted by it might wind up being a little bit stronger, faster, or smarter than average. But not enough to make anyone suspect an outside influence."

"However," Carlos explained, "once every twelve Zodiac cycles—every one hundred and forty-four years—the stars line up in a particular configuration. And the power, the energy of the mystic pools, is magnified to more than a thousand times its normal strength. That time is today."

"Carlos calls it the Convergence," Jasmine said, smirking slightly. "He's not so good with names."

Carlos looked hurt. "I'm good with a lot of other things."

"Yes, you are. Of course you are."

Steven blinked. "So . . . you mean . . ."

"It's a lot to take in, I know," Jasmine said.

"I've got the Tiger power. That's one sign of the Zodiac." Steven paused. "You've got . . . something . . . and the rest of the powers are—"

"—with me."

They all turned. Maxwell lay glaring at them, his teeth gritted, power flaring from his eyes. But his legs were still trapped beneath the broken *shipan*.

Carlos held up his analyzer. "I don't think so, chief. Far as I can see, you only absorbed four of the Zodiac signs. Maybe five."

Maxwell's eyes flared green.

"Not only that," Jasmine said, "but you can't hold them very long, can you? Only a person born in the year of the Rat can wield the Rat's power. You might be a Dragon— or half a Dragon, anyway. But you'll have to pass along the other powers soon, or they'll eat you alive."

"You," Maxwell seethed, staring at Jasmine. "Ungrateful girl. You turned my best scientist against me."

"She didn't turn me against anything," Carlos said, a new edge creeping into his voice. "I made my decision when I learned about *Lystria*."

Maxwell squeezed his eyes closed. A snarl escaped his lips. The bat-winged Dragon flared up briefly above him, then faded quickly away.

"Oh!" Jasmine smirked. "I think you hit a nerve, Carlos."

"What's Lystria?" Steven asked.

"I've fought in seven wars," Maxwell said. "I've seen things, made decisions you can't even imagine. This is a hard world, little girl. You're not ready for it."

"I'm not a little girl. Not anymore."

Jasmine reached out her arms, her brow furrowing in concentration. A flurry of energy particles rose up from Maxwell's trapped figure, wafting over to surround Jasmine. As Steven watched, the energy resolved itself into the form of a Dragon . . . but not the winged Dragon he'd seen projected from Maxwell. This was the *other* Dragon— the lean one, with sharp talons and deadly jaw.

Jasmine's Dragon.

She smiled, glowing bright. As she rose up into the air, the Dragon opened its mouth wide and screeched.

Then Jasmine coughed. The Dragon made a shrill noise and faded away. The glow receded, and Jasmine dropped down, shakily, to the ground.

"Oh, Jasmine," Maxwell said. "You think you can steal my power? My birthright, the mantle of the Dragon?"

"We're both Dragons."

"Your mother would be so disappointed," Maxwell said, a cruel smile crossing his face.

Jasmine clenched her fists in anger. Dragon energy rose up from her again. But it was fainter, this time, a ghost of its former self.

"Well," Maxwell continued. "I guess I've stalled you long enough."

Up on the catwalk, the stairwell door slammed open. Four large men in military uniforms marched in, followed by four more. Then another six.

"Crap," Jasmine said. "Vanguard is here."

"You always did talk too much, Jasmine." Maxwell smiled. "Who knew that smart mouth would be your downfall?"

Steven eyed the soldiers, a sinking feeling in his gut. They carried big, high-tech energy weapons and bulky equipment packs. "Who's Vanguard?" he asked.

Jasmine grimaced. "Maxwell's private army."

"Best there is," Maxwell said.

Up on the catwalk, the soldiers stood for a moment, waving away smoke. *They haven't seen us yet,* Steven realized.

Jasmine glared at Maxwell again—and again, the Dragon energy began to swell up around her. But this time, Maxwell raised his head, and a feral expression came over his face. The bat-winged Dragon lunged forth from him, snapping its jaws at Jasmine.

As Jasmine watched, startled, the energy around her started to shimmer, rising up like fireflies in the air. Maxwell's Dragon opened its mouth again, devouring it, breathing it in.

Jasmine collapsed. Carlos ran forward and caught her before she could hit the ground.

Steven heard the Tiger roar inside him again. He turned to Maxwell and snarled.

Then he felt a hand on his shoulder. He whirled, baring his teeth. It was Carlos, with Jasmine standing weakly behind him.

"No!" Carlos said. "You can't fight him."

Steven looked back at the grinning Maxwell. "He's trapped under that thing," Steven said.

"You have no idea how powerful he is. The Dragon is the strongest of all the Zodiac signs. Even *half* that power could stomp a Tiger like a bug."

"Come over here, boy," Maxwell said, baring his teeth like an animal. "Give it a try."

"Besides," Jasmine said, waving her arm upward.

Steven looked. The soldiers had spotted them and were running along the catwalk toward the ladder leading down to the floor.

Steven glanced quickly from Jasmine to Carlos. *Can I trust them?* he wondered. *I don't even know who these people are.*

The clattering of the soldiers' footsteps grew louder. Steven took one last look at Maxwell. The leader was still glowing bright, and grinning from ear to ear.

Jasmine slapped Steven on the shoulder, hard, and ducked under the half-fallen wall beam. Without looking back, she motioned for Steven and Carlos to follow. Carlos took off, and Steven hurried after them.

Jasmine led them across the room, around the pools, past several chunks of debris, to the central stage. It was still smoking, and it smelled like burning metal. Carlos motioned them to duck down behind it.

"We can't hide here for long," Jasmine said, keeping her voice low. She pointed toward the stairwell entrance, up on the catwalk. "And that's the only exit, right?"

Grimly, Carlos nodded. "Jaz, how powerful are you now? Can you . . . I don't know . . . *fly* us out of here?"

"Not right now. You saw what happened back there . . . Maxwell and I share the Dragon power. It's different, more powerful than the others. And right now, he's got the upper hand."

All three of them looked up at once. Steven frowned,

studying the inward-sloping walls of the chamber. They were pocked with jagged metal now, burned and broken.

Eight feet above, the half-fallen ceiling beam slanted over their heads. And past that, above the broken *shipan*, the night sky showed through a semicircle in the roof.

Suddenly Steven noticed that Jasmine was staring at him.

"It's up to you," she said.

"Me?" he asked.

She gestured blithely at Carlos. "*He* doesn't have any powers."

"But . . . but . . . ." Steven paused. "I don't even know you people! Why should I go with you?"

"Are you kidding?" Jasmine asked.

She gestured back toward Maxwell. Steven could see the soldiers clustering around Maxwell, beginning to dig him free.

Steven gritted his teeth. *Guess this is it,* he thought. *Do you really want to be a hero?*

Swallowing in fear, he nodded. He clenched his teeth, willing the Tiger energy to rise up inside him. He tensed himself to leap—

—and then Carlos stepped forward, holding up a hand.

"No," Carlos said.

Jasmine's head whipped around. "What?"

"We can't." Carlos shook his head, gesturing decisively at Steven. "We can't take him with us."

CHAPTER SIX

JASMINE SCUTTLED over to Carlos, keeping low to stay behind the stage. She stared him in the face as if she'd never seen him before.

"What," she whispered again, "are you talking about?"

A loud mechanical hammering noise rose up. Steven glanced around the damaged stage. On the side of the room, the soldiers were using digging tools to break up the big half *shipan* on top of Maxwell.

"Kid," Carlos said. "Steven. How old are you?"

"I'm fourteen," Steven said.

"Fourteen! Yes! That's my point." Carlos turned back to Jasmine. "He's just a kid. This whole thing we're doing, it's dangerous. We should keep him safe."

Jasmine looked back, astonished. "That's exactly what I intend to do, Carlos. That man is a menace. We tried to stop his plan and it didn't work, but we can't give up. This power I have . . . we have . . . it's something we need to figure out," she said. "Besides, what else can we do? You want to leave him here? Leave him with his little friends, so Maxwell can track him down and take him out."

"There's a bigger problem," Carlos pointed at Jasmine. "You took this power. Whatever happens, that was your choice. Maxwell too, for that matter. But the kid didn't."

"That's exactly why we've got to take him," Jasmine replied. "He's one of us now—a Zodiac. And he needs protection."

"Stop talking about me like I'm not here!" Steven cried.

Jasmine turned to him, surprised.

"He's at least got to know what he's getting into," Carlos said. He didn't look happy. "It's got to be his choice."

"Steven," Jasmine said, her voice low and intense. "Here's what's at stake. Maxwell is determined to grab all the Zodiac power for himself. If he gets hold of you, there are two possible outcomes. First he'll try to enlist you in his private army. If you refuse, he'll experiment on you until he figures out how to get the power out of you and into a Tiger of *his* choosing. Someone he can control."

"That . . . doesn't sound good," Steven admitted. "But . . . but I keep wondering . . ." He hesitated.

Jasmine threw up her arms. "Spit it out!"

". . . what would *he* say about *you*?"

She seemed taken aback. "Nothing good," she admitted.

"Maxwell is a monster," Carlos said. There was a dark, hard anger in his eyes now. "He thinks he's the only person who can control the Zodiac power; he thinks he's making the world a safer place. He thinks he's seen enough horrors to know that good and evil don't exist, and that he's the only one who should be trusted with this power.

"The reality? He's a vicious war contractor, a general-for-hire with no allegiances, no principles. He got tired of working for governments and corporations, so he started Vanguard. If he gets the Zodiac power, he'll be unstoppable."

"We've been fighting Maxwell for a long time," Jasmine said. "He has all the advantages: all the toys, all the manpower, all the money. We can't promise you any of that.

"But," she finished, "we can promise you something worth fighting for."

Suddenly, Steven thought about looking at the empty *shipan* display case with Harani and Ryan. It couldn't have been more than an hour earlier, but it seemed like a different life.

He thought about how all the locals in Hong Kong had expected him to speak Cantonese. He thought about the weird looks he'd get from his classmates when he ate the lunches his grandfather had prepared for him. He even thought about the Steel Mongoose, and his endless store of bravery and resourcefulness. The way he seemed to be at ease anywhere.

Now, in this weird subterranean chamber, he realized: Maybe this is my chance. Maybe this is where I belong. Steven glanced up again. The broken ceiling beam arced up at an angle, several feet up. Too far to jump. Too far.

But the Tiger stirred inside, calling to him. *Let me out,* it seemed to say. *I can do this. Let me do this.*

He crouched, feeling the Tiger energy rise up around him. With a roar, he leaped straight up, eight feet at least, and grabbed hold of the half-fallen ceiling beam. He swung his body up, grabbing the beam with both legs and letting his arms hang down.

He cast a glance toward the catwalk. From this angle, slightly elevated, he could see the Vanguard soldiers hefting the pieces of the *shipan* off of Maxwell. He'd be free in a few minutes.

Carlos and Jasmine were staring at Steven. He held out one hand to each of them.

"Come on," Steven said.

Jasmine clasped one of Steven's hands. Carlos hesitated, then grabbed the other. "Is this going to hurrrrrrrrrrt—"

Before Carlos could finish, Steven flipped them both up into the air.

Jasmine reached out gracefully and grabbed hold of the metal beam. Carlos fumbled, unable to get a good grip. Jasmine snatched him out of the air by his belt, grunting as his weight yanked her off-balance. Steven reached down and grabbed Carlos's arm, and together he and Jasmine pulled Carlos up onto the beam.

Steven scrabbled up onto the beam after them. Dimly, he thought: *Every single thing I've just done is impossible.*

"Yes," Carlos said. "Hurting factor: positive."

Jasmine pointed down. "I think the hurting's just begun."

Steven grimaced. Down below, the soldiers had noticed them and were aiming their guns upward.

"Freeze right there!" a soldier called. His long-barreled stun gun, its tip crackling with energy, was aimed straight at Steven.

"Follow me," Steven said.

In a feline-like manner, he took off up the slanted beam at a run. Jasmine motioned for Carlos to follow, and headed in Steven's direction.

Steven heard the weapons firing behind him. With a horrible sinking feeling, he realized: *That's it—we're dead. I can climb like a cat, but those guys are trained soldiers.*

So much for the Tiger's short career.

But then he looked back. Jasmine was edging backward up the beam, facing down at their attackers. As she held out her arms, a powerful aura fanned out to surround her, and the fierce, snakelike form of the Dragon rose up. Electric bolts leaped out from the soldiers' weapons, like miniature lightning—enough to fry a person alive, Steven thought. But when the bolts struck Jasmine's Dragon-glow, they flashed and disappeared.

Down on the ground, another burst of Dragon energy flared up. Maxwell emerged from inside of it, shrugging off the last chunk of the fallen *shipan*.

Steven climbed higher. The roof was only ten or twelve feet above now. The half *shipan* still hung loose, dark and quiet, a silent sentry leading to the open air beyond.

A little too far to jump, Steven thought. *The Tiger might make it, but Jasmine and Carlos wouldn't.*

"There!" he called, pointing at the wall ahead. A line of bolts protruded from it, some of them scorched from the *shipan*'s blasts. Steven reached out and leaped off the beam, grabbing hold of a bolt with each hand.

"You are most surely joking," Carlos said.

But Jasmine laughed. She grabbed Carlos around the waist and jumped. They scrabbled at the wall for a second, then grabbed on to the uneven surface. As Steven climbed upward, they began to follow.

"Don't look down," Jasmine said.

"Not a worry," Carlos replied.

The soldiers seemed to have stopped firing. When Steven looked down, he saw Maxwell yelling at his men, pointing upward. Steven couldn't make out the words.

"Maxwell doesn't want us dead," Jasmine said, still climbing. "He needs the power inside us!"

"Inside *you*," Carlos said. "There's no power in me."

"Just brainpower," Jasmine said, smiling.

"Flatterer. You're just trying to distract me from my imminent demise OH GOD A LITTLE SLOWER PLEASE?"

Steven stopped, breathing hard. The wall ended a few feet above, but the hole, the way out, was just out of reach. The remains of the *shipan* blocked their way: a semicircular mess of smoking metal and broken glass hung precariously by a few thick cables.

Jasmine climbed up next to Steven. "You can do this," she said.

He looked into her eyes. Slowly, he nodded.

Later, Steven could barely remember the next few minutes. Somehow he balanced himself on the wall, grabbing Jasmine under one arm and Carlos under the other; but that was impossible. He leaned forward and tossed Jasmine onto the *shipan*, then took hold of it himself with his free hand, swinging forward with the terrified Carlos under his arm; that was *really* impossible. As the *shipan* strained and creaked under their weight, he tossed Carlos up through the hole, then reached down to grab Jasmine and fling her up after Carlos. Then, just as the *shipan* cracked free and fell, he leaped up through the hole to freedom.

Impossible. All of it.

There was one thing he remembered clearly about the whole ordeal. As he knelt on the ground outside, breathing in the thick Hong Kong air, he cast a final glance down into the now-exposed chamber. Maxwell hovered a few feet off the floor, glaring upward, his winged Dragon-form screeching in helpless anger.

Then Jasmine pulled Steven to his feet. "Nice work," she said.

Steven looked around, dazed. They stood in a cleared, grassy area; trees stretched off to one side, forming a thick forest. On the other side, the brightly colored thatched-roof buildings of the museum rose up in the night. Emergency lights flashed, and local police stood holding back curious spectators, fifteen or twenty feet away.

"Looks like we made a little noise," Jasmine said. "We better get moving before Maxwell gets his strength back. Carlos, let's—"

But Carlos stood a little way off, staring at the sky. Steven followed his gaze and felt his breath catch in his throat.

Above, green energy flashed against the clouds like some unnatural fireworks show. It zipped back and forth, up and down, fanning out in one direction, then another.

"The Zodiac power," Carlos said. He pulled out his analyzer and pointed it toward the sky. "Not all of it flowed into Maxwell, or into you two. When we sabotaged the equipment, some of the power ran wild."

Steven stared. "And it's still up there?"

"I think . . . it was trapped by the warm front blanketing the city. But now that front is moving away."

As they watched, the green energy seemed to flare

even brighter than before. Then it arced away, over the trees, and began to fade.

"Where's it going?" Jasmine asked.

"I don't know," Carlos replied. "This wasn't supposed to happen. I assumed the other powers would just seep back into the pools if they didn't find a nearby host."

"Puzzle it out later. Right now, we better move." Jasmine gestured back down at the hole leading to the strange underground chamber. "Maxwell's weakened, but he's got at least two Vanguard squadrons down there with him. He'll be after us in minutes."

"Steven!"

Steven whirled around. He squinted at the museum buildings, at the crowd held back from the site of the explosions. In that crowd, he recognized a small figure wearing an orange sweater.

"Harani!" he called.

"Steven," Jasmine said. "We've got an exit route. But it's gotta be now."

Harani reached out toward him. A policeman held up a hand, holding her back; she stared helplessly, her hand outstretched. Gathered around her, Steven could see Ryan, Mr. Singh, and the other kids. People he'd known all his life.

His old life.

Jasmine raised a hand and projected a thin beam of Dragon light at the woods. A small path became visible, leading through the orchids and gum trees. When she turned back to Steven, her expression was unusually gentle.

"Say good-bye," she said.

Steven cast a glance at the sky. The faint afterimage of Zodiac energy was just fading. He looked back over at Harani, at her puzzled, questioning face.

Good-bye, he mouthed.

Then he drew in a deep breath and turned to follow Jasmine and Carlos into the unknown.

CHAPTER SEVEN

JASMINE LED THEM swiftly through the forest, past orchids, palm trees, and gum trees. She projected her Dragon energy in tiny bursts to illuminate the path—but with a shock, Steven realized he didn't even need the light. He could see everything with perfect clarity, even in darkness.

"Wait till you see our headquarters," Jasmine said. "It's no luxury hotel, but I think you'll be impressed."

Steven smiled. With every stride, he felt stronger, more triumphant. *I did it,* he thought. *I got us out! Never mind that I don't really know where I got us out of. . . .*

Abruptly, the trees thinned out and the path widened out onto a beach. A battered freighter vessel sat anchored only a few yards offshore. It was heavily loaded down with multicolored shipping containers, and it listed slightly to one side.

Frowning, Steven turned to Jasmine. "Your headquarters is an old *cargo ship?*"

She stared at him, deadpan. "You don't like it?"

Carlos just shook his head.

Jasmine burst into laughter. "Sorry, kid. I'm just messing with you. This isn't really home—just transportation."

"Oh."

He stood staring for a moment, until Jasmine clapped him hard on the back. "Come on," she said. "Let's hit the high seas."

Jasmine led them aboard and handed a big pile of local currency to the captain. He nodded and ushered them down a narrow passageway via a ladder. As they climbed below, Steven could hear the captain issuing orders to get underway.

As soon as they were belowdecks, Carlos seemed to grow agitated. He led the way to a heavy metal door and shouldered it open.

"Take it easy, man," Jasmine said. "We're in no hurry now."

"I am," Carlos replied.

Steven looked around the large, cluttered room. Its walls and low ceilings were made of metal, studded with bolts up and down the sides. A stack of crates sat in one corner, marked with Chinese lettering. There were no windows, and one wall was covered in printed pictures and various clippings.

Carlos hurried to one corner of the room. A worn swivel chair sat before a tangle of computer equipment: tables, keyboards, CRT screens, server arrays. Some of the components seemed very old. Carlos seated himself in the chair and started tapping on a dirty keyboard.

Steven pointed. "Is that some ancient Mac?"

Jasmine smiled. "If it still works, Carlos can find a use for it."

"Could you two talk quietly?" Carlos asked, his eyes darting from one screen to another. "I have to figure out a way to track that runaway Zodiac energy before its trail fades. Which, with this ancient setup, is going to be a bit tricky."

"Sorry," Jasmine said. She walked up behind Carlos and laid a hand on his shoulder. "I'll take the kid to the other side of the room, give him some . . . what?"

Carlos had swiveled around and was staring at her. His expression was blank, as if he were struggling to process something.

Then he stood up and hugged her, hard. Jasmine jumped, startled.

"I thought you were going to die," Carlos whispered. He burrowed his head into her shoulder.

Jasmine pulled away from him and grasped his shoulders. She looked straight into his eyes and smiled.

"Never gonna happen," she said.

Suddenly Steven felt like an intruder.

"Get back to work," Jasmine continued, her voice suddenly soft. "Nobody likes a lazy genius."

Carlos flashed her a quick, uncertain smile. Then he whirled back around and started tapping at keys again.

Jasmine cocked her head at Steven and started across the room. He followed, almost stumbling as the ship lurched in the water. The hum of engines rose up all around them.

"This tub may not look like much," Jasmine said, "but it'll get us out of China. Like I said, we don't have Maxwell's resources. We have to get by on stealth."

As the boat moved through the water, Steven felt his stomach start to churn. He turned to Jasmine, frowning. "Can I ask you some questions?"

"Why not?" Jasmine replied, plopping down on a large metal canister that looked like it might be housing something toxic. "It's not like I'm exhausted or bruised or anything." She pulled off a boot and flexed her sore foot in the air.

"Who are you people?" Steven asked. "How do you know so much about this Maxwell guy? And, uh, if you

knew he was gonna try and grab all that power, why didn't you stop him sooner?"

"That's a lot of questions," she said. "But they all have the same answer: bad timing."

Steven watched her, waiting.

"We keep tabs of Maxwell," she continued. "But he covers his tracks well. I was in India, following up a false lead, when I got a frantic text from Carlos. He said to come to the museum, where he'd set up a job for me under a fake name." She frowned and turned to call across the room. "'Jumanne'?"

"First thing I could think of," Carlos said. He didn't look up from his work.

"So I get there, and for three days, no word. Maxwell had Carlos closeted underground, setting up the Convergence. We told you about that."

Steven nodded.

"I thought Carlos was dead. When I heard Maxwell screaming, it was kind of a relief."

"I heard that too," Steven said. "That's why I followed you."

Jasmine stared at him and a slow smile came over her face. "Tiger ears," she said. "That's cute."

He turned away, embarrassed. When he turned back, her expression was different.

"Actually," she said, "you showing up was quite a coincidence."

With a shock, he realized that she didn't trust him

completely—any more than he trusted her. *Does she think I'm working with Maxwell?*

Jasmine waved her hand, seeming to dismiss the idea. "We didn't have time to coordinate the plan," she continued. She reached into her pack and pulled out a metal sphere, like the ones she'd thrown at the *shipan* back in the museum. "And I didn't manage to get these grenades charged fast enough."

"Not your fault," Carlos called. "I designed the grenades. And I wanted to sabotage the Convergence sooner from the stage, but Maxwell's other techs would have noticed right away."

Jasmine stared sadly at the grenade for a moment. Its light glowed a very dull red. It slipped out of her hands and rattled to the floor.

Steven watched, nervous, as the ship tipped to one side. The grenade rolled past him, into a corner.

"That one never worked right anyway," Jasmine said.

"I still . . . I don't understand." Steven shook his head. "You and me—we were each hit by *one* of the Zodiac beams. Maxwell must have been hit by . . . what? Four or five of them?"

"Six, I think," Jasmine said.

"Seven," Carlos called. "Definitely seven. Counting the Dragon, which struck you both."

Jasmine smirked. "Are you doing any work at all over there?"

Carlos walked over to join them, carrying a handheld

analyzer device. "Actually, I've managed to establish a very slow data link with headquarters," he said. "They're helping me track the Zodiac energy."

"Can we talk to them?" Jasmine asked.

"It's text-only right now."

"Where's headquarters?" Steven asked.

"Greenland," Jasmine said, turning back to face him. "So, yes, Maxwell made contact with, and absorbed, seven of the twelve Zodiac powers. But there's a catch. The only one of those powers he can control—the only one that *belongs* inside him—is the Dragon."

"What about the rest?"

"That's what all the machinery was for," Carlos said. He perched on a crate, still staring at his analyzer. "Maxwell planned to absorb the power of all twelve Zodiac signs into himself temporarily. That would kill a normal person—we all warned him about that. But he was sure he could handle it.

"Right now, he's probably carrying out the next phase of his plan. That involves taking that energy and transferring it out of his body into his own agents. One agent for each sign: Horse, Dog, Monkey, Ox, Rat, and Snake."

Jasmine suddenly stood, walking toward Carlos's makeshift work station. Steven trailed behind her, seeing various photos, notes, and threads pinned to the wall.

"You really have been watching Maxwell for a long time," Steven said.

"He's got an intricate network," Carlos explained, rising. "We don't even know all the people who belong to the Vanguard."

"Not to sound like a broken record, but we *do* know what powers he has, and what powers are left," Jasmine said. "Maxwell and I share the Dragon power." She gestured at Steven. "And you're the Tiger. That leaves . . . wait, my mother taught me this. Ram, Pig, Rabbit, and Rooster." She turned to Carlos. "Those powers—those are the beams that flashed out in the wild, right? Will they just dissipate?"

"I don't think so." Carlos tapped at the analyzer. "It looks like they're seeking out their own hosts."

"People out in the world somewhere, suddenly finding themselves filled with power they can't understand." Jasmine leaned forward, staring at Steven. "Like you. But without us there to guide them."

"Not only that," Carlos said, "but Maxwell will be looking for them, too. He wants that power."

"This is a big change in our mission," Jasmine said, turning to Carlos. "Before, all we needed to do was stop Maxwell. Now there are gonna be more people out there like the kid here, and we're the only ones who can help them." She let out a big, deliberate sigh. "Like it or not, we're about to start a recruitment drive."

Steven nodded, letting the idea sink in. "We've gotta find them."

Carlos gave him a slightly irritated glance. "I'm working on it."

Jasmine cocked her head at Steven. "You said *we*. Does that mean you're in? You're with us?"

"I . . ." He paused. "I think so. But . . . I know Maxwell is a war contractor and all. But is he *that* bad? Why do you care so much about him? What's he going to do with this power, anyway?"

"Anything and everything he wants," Jasmine said.

"That doesn't sound so bad."

Jasmine looked at Carlos. Carlos sat back down on his crate; something in his eyes sent a shiver up Steven's spine.

"It was pretty bad," Jasmine said, "for the city of Lystria."

"You mentioned that before," Steven said. "What's Lystria? I've never heard of it."

"Well, don't go looking for it on a map."

"What?" Steven asked. "What happened?"

Jasmine flashed Carlos a worried look. Carlos sucked in a deep breath and lowered the analyzer. When he spoke again, his voice was raspy, intense.

"Maxwell was a successful war contractor," Carlos said. "He'd fought in several high-profile and low-profile conflicts, and made a lot of money doing it. But he got tired of taking orders. So he decided to start his own company."

"Vanguard," Steven said.

"Vanguard. Their first big job was in a city called Lystria, where rebels had seized some of the government buildings. Maxwell's guys were supposed to get in there, eliminate the rebels, and get out.

"But they botched the job. The rebellion turned into a war, and the war turned very messy. Some of the Vanguard agents were captured by rebels.

"That put Maxwell in a bad spot. Very soon, Vanguard's involvement in Lystria would become public knowledge. That would mean the end of Maxwell's new company, and his employers would be pretty unhappy too. See, he wasn't just working for the local government. There were some shadowy business interests involved, too—people who are *not* used to failing, at anything."

"It was even possible Maxwell himself could have been brought up on international war-crimes charges," Jasmine added.

"At the time," Carlos continued, "I was working for an American company. We specialized in transporting dangerous chemical and biological substances. Maxwell contacted us: he wanted a very specific combination of materials. My bosses gave it to him, and the next thing we knew . . ."

Carlos trailed off, turning away.

Jasmine watched him with worried eyes. "Next thing we knew," she resumed, "Lystria was gone. Maxwell unleashed a deadly bio-plague that killed off ninety percent of the population in less than a day. Then he torched the buildings and sent in snipers to finish off the survivors. Including some of his own people, whom he regarded as casualties of war."

Steven was stunned. "He killed . . . hundreds of thousands of people . . ."

"The entire city," Jasmine said. "Without even thinking twice."

"All those people," Steven repeated. "Just to protect his *business*?"

"He doesn't like to be told what to do."

"What about Lystria? Somebody must have noticed it was just *gone*? What about all those people, their relatives . . . ?"

"Steven," Jasmine said, "sometimes when a crime is so huge, so monstrous, nobody wants to admit it ever happened. Maxwell knew, after he did this, that no corporation *or* government would ever dare interfere with him again."

"I've been to Lystria," Carlos said, his voice dark as the grave. "It's a charred hole in the desert. You wouldn't believe it."

Jasmine forced a smile. "Now do you understand why we're doing this? Why we *cannot* let this man keep control of the Zodiac power?"

Slowly, Steven nodded.

"Good," she said.

He looked up sharply. There was something in her

voice now, some new edge. As he watched,
Jasmine spread her arms. The Zodiac power
began to shimmer and glow, rising up above
her to form the lean, sharp-clawed form of the
Dragon.

"Then maybe you'll understand why I have
to do this," she said.

And she leapt at him, claws bared.

CHAPTER EIGHT

STEVEN SHRANK BACK instinctively. The

Tiger's reflexes kicked in, and time seemed to slow to a
crawl. He watched, all his instincts sharp, as Jasmine flew
through the air toward him, her Dragon form hissing and
snarling in the air above her.

What is she doing? he wondered. *Is she—was I wrong about
Jasmine? Does she want me dead?*

A snarl rose from deep inside him, from the Tiger
itself. He swerved and bounded sideways like a cat, feeling
his own power surround him like a protective suit. Then
he straightened up again.

Jasmine pivoted gracefully in midair and turned to face him. When she grabbed his shoulders, he shivered. Her hands were like Dragon claws, burning like cold fire on his skin.

He snarled and slashed a hand across her shoulder. The Tiger claws cut a shallow gash along her arm. A thin line of blood appeared, and Jasmine cried out.

Carlos glanced at the two of them, shook his head, and stepped away.

Jasmine backed away from Steven, her power flaring throughout the room. When she opened her mouth, fire spewed forth from the Dragon's maw. Steven ducked low, barely managing to avoid the flame.

This is for real, he thought. *She's trying to kill me.*

"Jasmine," he said. "Why—"

She fixed her eyes on him, and the Dragon form turned to match her gaze. But she didn't seem like the woman Steven had been talking with, just a few moments before. This was a deeper, more elemental force. For a moment, he felt it tickling at his brain, like an insect twitching at the base of his spine. Trying to get in.

What had she said, back in the Convergence room? *The Dragon power is different.*

Then Jasmine was moving again. She flew through the air, opening her mouth to spit fire again. *Not fair,* Steven thought. *I can't fly!* He flipped sideways and flattened himself against a wall, watching as she swooped past him. The Dragon flame felt hot against his skin.

Steven saw his chance—or, rather, the Tiger did. In the split-second before Jasmine could turn to face him again, he charged. He ducked down low, ignoring the cold needles of Dragon-energy, and came up between her legs. He lifted her up and tossed her backward, over his shoulder.

Jasmine let out a surprised yelp and tumbled in midair. The Dragon power faded. She landed with a hard thump, out of sight, behind a pile of supply crates.

Steven prowled toward her, his senses still hyper-alert. He cast a quick glance around, looking for Carlos. The Tiger roared within him: another enemy? But Carlos had retreated to his equipment.

Steven looked down at his own hands. The Tiger energy glowed bright, suffusing him with power. He could sense every air current in the room, every faint smell of mold and machine oil. No intruder, no enemy, could possibly take him by surprise now.

He was trapped, thousands of miles from home. And yet, somehow, he felt alive.

Despite himself, Steven Lee laughed.

Jasmine crawled out from behind the crates. Her arm was bleeding slightly, but she was smiling. "Nice throw," she said.

She held out a hand. Cautiously, he took it and helped her up.

She touched the shallow cut on her arm. "Tiger's got claws," she said.

"What was that about?" he asked. "Are you trying to kill me?"

"No I'm *testing* you." She turned to call out to Carlos. "What do you think?"

"I think he's a Tiger," Carlos said. He sounded distracted.

"We knew that already."

"I think tracking these powers is more important right now!"

Jasmine sat down on a crate, and motioned for Steven to sit next to her. He followed her, still wary.

"I won't bite," she said.

"I think you just did."

"Fair point." She glanced again at her arm. "You handle yourself pretty well. Considering you haven't had any combat training."

"Have you? Had training, I mean?"

"Oh yeah." Jasmine looked away. "The neighborhood I grew up in—you had to learn to take care of yourself. And I've had . . . well, I've had military experience, too."

With Maxwell, Steven thought. There was some connection between Jasmine and Maxwell, something beyond the fact that they now shared the Dragon power. But she didn't seem to want to talk about it.

"You're a natural," she continued. "You've got enhanced strength and reflexes. But if you're going to survive, you're gonna need more than that. Maxwell's agents—they'll have all that and more."

Suddenly, as if a switch had been flipped, the Tiger energy receded; the beast seemed to shrink back inside him. His senses grew duller, fading back to normal.

Except it's not normal anymore, he realized. *Not for me.*

And then the enormity of the situation washed over him. He felt scared, overwhelmed. Everything—all the chaos and fighting of the past day—seemed to catch up with him all at once. He turned away, fighting a terrible instinct to burst into tears.

Jasmine watched him closely.

Carlos approached, holding up his analyzer. "HQ has the beams plotted," he said. "Looks like two of them ended up in Europe, one in Africa, and one went all the way to America. I should have exact locations in . . ."

Jasmine motioned him to silence. She laid a hand on Steven's shoulder, and when she spoke, her voice was softer than usual.

"Hey," Jasmine said. "Do you want to call your parents?"

He whirled back around. "Can I do that?"

"Jaz," Carlos said. "That's not a good idea."

"It's better than having them launch a worldwide manhunt for him," Jasmine replied.

Carlos just frowned.

"You can't tell them about this," she said to Steven. "Nothing about the Zodiac, Maxwell, or Vanguard. If you did, you'd be putting them in great danger. Do you understand that?"

Steven nodded.

Jasmine pointed to an old-style, rotary phone mounted on the wall. "That's hooked up to a satellite feed . . . you should be able to get a connection. Just tell them you're all right, and that you won't be home for a while. Tell them . . . well, tell them how you feel, I guess."

With that, Jasmine picked up her boots and started toward the door. "Come on, Carlos," she said. "Let's give the kid some privacy."

"Do we have to go above decks?" Carlos asked. "You know I get seasick."

Jasmine took his arm, smiling. "My brave science man," she said.

"Um," Steven said. Jasmine stopped and looked back. "Thanks," he said.

She smiled a strange, sad smile. "You asked me why I care so much about stopping Maxwell," she said.

"You said. That city, Lystria—"

"It's because of *my* parents. He killed them."

Her voice was very steady. *It sounds,* Steven thought, *as if she's trained herself not to feel anything at all.*

Before he could reply, Jasmine and Carlos were gone. Steven stood alone in the softly lurching room, staring at the cold red phone on the wall.

He closed his eyes and sat down, trembling, on a crate. In his mind, he saw again the whirring, spinning *shipan*—the Chinese compass—its Zodiac rays flashing out in all

directions. He saw Maxwell, swooping and flying through the air, the Dragon power raging all around. And then Steven felt, again, the touch of the Zodiac beam, its icy power stabbing through his body.

With shaky fingers, Steven reached out and started to dial his father's private line. Then he changed his mind, hung up, and dialed his mother instead.

The phone buzzed a rapid-fire busy signal in his ear, not even trying to connect.

What's the country code for the U.S.?

Five minutes later, the line finally started ringing. Steven swallowed nervously. Suddenly he wasn't sure what he could possibly say to his parents.

"Hello?" His mother's voice sounded very far away. "Who is this calling?"

Steven cleared his throat. "Hi, Mom," he said.

"Oh," she said. "Steven."

She doesn't sound very happy to hear from me, he thought.

"Listen," he said. "I just want you to know . . . I'm not going to be home for a while." There was a silence on the line. "Mom, did you hear me?"

"Yes," she said. "I hear you."

"I'm fine. But I'm still in . . . I mean, there's some stuff I have to take care of. I know it sounds weird."

"All right."

Is she even listening to me? he wondered.

"Mom, I . . ." He heard his voice crack, and hated himself for it. "Don't you even care where I am?"

"We heard about the fire, but you're almost an adult, Steven. You can take care of yourself."

"Oh."

"Steven," his mother continued, a strange tone creeping into her voice. "There's something I have to tell you."

"Okay."

"My father . . . your grandfather. He passed away this morning."

Steven felt as if a cold pit had opened up underneath him. The ship lurched, and Steven's stomach churned along with it. He closed his eyes and saw, once again, the vision of his grandfather. The one he'd seen when the Zodiac beam reached out to clutch him in its icy embrace.

Something is ending here, the grandfather-vision had said. *But something new is beginning.*

"It was painless," his mother continued. "He died in his sleep. You'll forgive me, Steven, but I'm a bit distracted now with the funeral arrangements."

His throat felt dry. It was an effort to speak.

"Sure," he said. "I understand."

"You do what you have to," she continued. "I'll let your father know you called."

"Okay."

"Good-bye, Steven."

"Mom." He paused. "I'm sorry I can't be there—"

A dial tone interrupted him. The line had gone dead.

All his life, Steven's parents had been busy with their work. They'd built up their company from scratch, traveling the world to secure contracts. They'd always treated him well, but they weren't around very much. That duty, that role, had been filled by his grandfather.

And now he's gone.

When Jasmine and Carlos came back into the room, they found Steven staring straight ahead. The phone receiver was crushed into pieces in his fist. He'd shattered it without even noticing, leaving little cuts on his palm.

Jasmine touched him on the shoulder while Carlos pried Steven's fingers apart and softly wiped away the blood. Steven turned away, using his sleeve to rub the tears off his face.

Jasmine started to speak, but Steven cut her off. He didn't want her sympathy—not now. He just wanted to get on with his life.

With the mission.

"So," he said, trying to keep his voice light. "Greenland?"

"Ah, no," she replied. "Change of plans."

Steven looked at her, surprised.

"The Zodiac energy has already made contact with its new hosts," Carlos said. "We've got to find them as soon as possible."

"You'll have to wait to see our digs," Jasmine added.

"Okay." Steven nodded. "So where are we going?"

Carlos held up the analyzer. On its screen, a text message from headquarters glowed green against black. It consisted of a single word:

FRANCE

PART TWO

THE RECRUITS

CHAPTER NINE

"DO, RE, MI, FA, SO, LA, TI, DO . . ."

Roxanne leaned over the counter of the small bathroom, running scales to loosen up her voice. She'd locked herself in there for a few minutes to warm up. There were no private dressing rooms on this tour.

Maybe someday.

"Do, re, mi, fa, so, la, ti . . ."

She adjusted her torn T-shirt to reveal one shoulder, then the other. Then she shook her head and reached for a gray hoodie with a black rhinoceros hand-drawn on the front. She shrugged it on, briefly muffling the sound of her own voice.

"Mmo, may, mi, fagh, fo, la, ti, do . . ."

Roxanne was nervous. This was the biggest show her band, *Les Poules*, had played to date. The venue, a converted castle a hundred kilometers outside of Paris, was particularly cool. Even the bathroom had thick stone walls.

"Do, re, mi, fa . . ."

But it wasn't just the size of the show that had Roxanne feeling jumpy. As she ran her voice up the octaves, a sick feeling started to form in her throat. She pushed it away and tried to think of something else.

". . . so, la, ti, do . . ."

That new bass player better get his act together, she thought. *He still hasn't got the latest batch of covers down.*

"Do, re, mi . . ."

Roxanne leaned forward, tilting her head as she peered into the mirror. Her smooth dark skin shined under the fluorescent light. She ran a hand over her cropped hair, squinting her eyes. Too much mascara? It was hard to judge. *It's all about putting on a show,* she thought.

". . . fa, so, la, ti . . ."

The lyrics of her favorite new song started running through her mind: *Mothers don't care. Fathers don't care. Babies don't . . .*

". . . DO—"

As she hit the high note, Roxanne heard a shattering noise. Something whipped her backward, very fast. She stumbled and half fell onto a folding chair, then looked around, dazed.

She noticed the mirror. It was cracked and shattered, falling one piece at a time into the sink.

No, she thought, staring in horror at a distorted image of herself reflected in a hanging shard of glass. *No. Not again.*

There was a banging on the door. She whirled around.

"Roxy? Sweetie?"

Roxanne sighed. She stood up and opened the door.

Roxanne's mother burst into the room, tottering on her heels. "I heard something!" she exclaimed. "Are you okay?"

"Relax, Maman." Roxanne grimaced, trying to disengage herself from her mother's iron grip. "I'm fine."

"I just, you're about to go onstage, and it's your biggest concert ever, and—"

"Maman. Don't make me *nervous* or anything." She rolled her eyes.

"—and I just want to make sure everything's fine." The older woman appraised Roxanne for a moment, her mouth twisting into a frown. "*That's* what you're wearing?"

Roxanne pointed at the image on her sweatshirt. "It dramatizes the plight of the black rhino!"

Roxanne's mom stepped back, shaking her head.

The rest of the band ran up behind her. "Rox," said Paolo, the drummer. "You done hogging the bathroom?"

The new bass player Jaiden pointed past her at the broken mirror on the wall. "Somebody's a temperamental rock star today." Pierre, the second guitarist, snorted.

"Shut it." Roxanne turned back to her mother. "Maman, I'm fine. Really."

But her mom was looking at the mirror now. "You did this?" she asked, turning to Roxanne with concern. "Are you hurt?"

"No, Maman. It was an accident." She held up her hands. "See? No cuts, no bruises."

"Then . . . how . . ." Mom shook her head in confusion. "It's just that I worry about you, dear. Ever since your father left—"

"Maman—"

"I mean, you *know* I support you. I've never questioned your decisions. No matter how much you put off your education to do this, to play in these places, with these people—"

Her mom waved her arms around, vaguely indicating the band. Paolo, Pierre, and Jaiden exchanged a glance, then shrugged.

"—no matter how you choose to dress, the makeup you wear—"

"Maman. I'm *fine!*"

Roxanne's mother just stared for a

moment, a tear forming in her eye. Then she leaned forward again. Roxanne felt the hug coming. Her band mates watched, amused.

Then her mother's arms were around her, and despite herself, Roxanne felt suddenly safer. She closed her eyes and burrowed her head into her mom's shoulder. It was true: Her mother *had* always been there for her. Had always supported her work, her music, her dreams.

For the first time, Roxanne realized: *I'm lucky.*

Then she heard a snicker. She pulled back and glared past her mom.

"You're 'bout to lose those strumming fingers, Jaiden." Roxanne reached back into the bathroom and grabbed her guitar. "Come on, losers. Let's rock this tomb."

The band nodded and turned away, high-fiving each other. Roxanne reached out a hand to touch her mother's shoulder.

"Thanks," Roxanne said. "I, I couldn't do this without—"

Her mom cut her off. "Just go save the black walrus, dear."

"Rhino."

"Whatever." She smiled and turned to go.

Roxanne shook her head, also smiling. But her smile froze as she cast a glance back and saw, once again, the broken mirror. Pieces of her face stared back from its jagged segments.

"Not again," she whispered to herself. "Please, not tonight."

Then she turned and ran toward the stage.

Steven opened his eyes and blinked. A flat, dry plain stretched all around him, barren under the night sky. An unnatural fog rose up in all directions.

Hello? he called.

As if in answer, a low, crouched figure appeared, silhouetted in the fog. As it drew closer, it began to glow. Its eyes flashed, shimmering with energy, as it pawed impatiently at the ashen ground.

The Tiger.

It stared at him, seeming to challenge him with its eyes. And suddenly, Steven felt a surge of doubt. *Can I handle this power?* he wondered.

Then Steven noticed something else. Astride the Tiger, sitting on its back, was the slumped form of his grandfather. His grandfather who had just died, while Steven was off playing hero on the other side of the world.

Grandfather smiled his familiar, kind smile. He pulled on the Tiger's reins, and the great beast came to a halt, roaring in mild protest.

Then Grandfather held out his hand. Steven squinted, and saw a gleaming object sitting in the old man's palm. It was his compass . . . a *luopan*, Grandfather had called it. An old Chinese artifact, a smaller version of the giant whirling disk that had given Steven his Zodiac power.

Impatiently, Grandfather pushed the luopan toward Steven. *Take it,* the old man said. *It's your heritage. It will show you the way.*

Grandfather dropped the compass into Steven's hand. It felt cold, like an old bone.

When Steven looked up, the fog seemed to be closing in from all sides. The old man's face was blurry, and the Tiger was hard to see, too, its low roar rising from the mist.

I don't know the way, Steven said. *I don't know where to go next.*

Grandfather gestured impatiently. He raised a hand and pointed up into the sky. As Steven watched, the sky lit up in a flash of green energy.

Zodiac energy.

Steven squinted. Then he could make out a single pinprick of light shining through the gloom. No—two separate lights, blinking as they crept across the night sky.

An airplane, he realized. *It's—it's chasing the energy.*

Steven looked down again. But his grandfather was gone now. Only the Tiger remained, panting audibly, its breath heavy in the night.

Steven pointed up to the sky. "Is that where I need to be?" he asked.

Slowly, the Tiger's head swiveled side to side.

No, Steven realized. *I don't need to go to the airplane.*
I'm already there.

"Hey, Tiger. You still with us?"

Steven shot upright with a jolt. Jasmine was staring down at him, the now familiar smirk on her lips.

Steven sat up stiffly. He was seated alone in a short row of a commercial airplane, slumped over both seats. The steady thrum of jet engines pulsed in the background.

"Sorry to wake you," Jasmine said, leaning over him from the aisle. "You were kind of thrashing around there."

"He was moving his arms and legs in frantic little motions," Carlos's voice said. "Like a cat having a nightmare."

Steven looked past Jasmine. Carlos sat in the aisle seat opposite, busily cutting something up with scissors.

"Where—" Steven rubbed his eyes. "Where are we?"

"About forty-five minutes from landing," Jasmine replied. "Then it'll be a bit of a drive from Paris." She sighed. "We have *got* to get our own transportation."

"Get me some money," Carlos said, "and I'll get us transportation."

"Details." Jasmine smiled and made a fluttering motion with her hand. "I'm more of a big-picture person."

Steven motioned for her to sit next to him. "And you're sure the girl we're looking for will be there?"

Jasmine pulled out her phone and called up a photo

on the screen. It showed a tall, pretty young woman with dark skin, her hands jammed stiffly into the pockets of a hoodie. The woman was squinting at the camera with a challenging look.

"Carlos has tracked the Zodiac energy very precisely," Jasmine said. "This is the recipient: Roxanne LaFleur, founder and lead singer of the up-and-coming Euro-hip-hop band *Les Poules*. She lives in Paris, but unfortunately for us, she's currently on tour. So this is gonna take a little longer than we'd hoped."

"And we've gotta reach her before Maxwell does," Steven said.

"You got it. First Roxanne, then the other three. As fast as we can."

An image flashed through Steven's mind: the Tiger, with his grandfather atop it. He turned away, suddenly troubled.

"Hey." Jasmine touched his shoulder. "What is it?"

"I . . ." Steven paused. He closed his eyes and clenched his fists, and a flare of Zodiac energy rose up from his body. "I'm just not used to this power," he continued.

"We've got lots of training equipment back at head-quarters, in Greenland. I've talked to our people at HQ—they've already started adapting it for, well, for us." She smiled. "That'll come later, though. Right now, all you need to do is be yourself."

"But . . . but . . ." Steven concentrated harder. The energy swirled and coalesced, forming into the roaring, raging shape of a Tiger—the same Tiger he'd seen just moments before, in his dreams. "What if I can't control it?"

"I think you should control it *now*," Jasmine said. "People are looking."

Steven opened his eyes. A few people in the adjacent rows were pointing and whispering to each other. He shook his head, willing the Tiger energy to subside.

"See?" Jasmine said. "Easy as falling off a *shipan*. Right, Carlos?"

Snip. Snip. Snip.

"Carlos, *what are you doing?*" she demanded.

Steven leaned over to look. Carlos's tray-table was covered with snack foods—peanuts, M&Ms, gumdrops—and the scraps of paper that had once been their boxes and packets. Carlos never traveled without his laptop, but now it lay discarded on the empty seat next to him.

"I was having trouble with a problem," Carlos said, "so I decided to try an old-school, physical approach to it."

Jasmine cocked her head. "And what problem was that?"

"Well . . ." Carlos turned reluctantly toward her. "Remember how you keep saying we should have a name?"

Jasmine groaned. "*One time*, I said our group should have a name," she said. "And ever since then, Carlos keeps coming up with ridiculous acronyms. You know? Like A.I.R.L.O.C.K.S.—Astrological Investigation Remote Locator Operative Central Knowledge Systems."

Steven frowned. "That's kind of un-good."

"Yeah. Not exactly Mission Impossible."

Jasmine was leaning over toward Carlos. "What is that?" she asked. "A clipboard?"

Jasmine grabbed the wooden clipboard out of Carlos's hands and held it up so Steven could see. On a sheet of paper, Carlos had taped the first letters of a column out of candy wrappers: G (from gumdrops), A (almonds), P (peanuts), another P (popcorn), and Z (something called Zappers). Next to them, he'd written out the words:

General

Action

Peril

Posse

Zodiac

Jasmine laughed. "'Peril Posse'?"

"GAPPZ?" Steven asked. "Our name is supposed to be GAPPZ?"

"It sounds like a sound effect," Jasmine agreed. "For flatulence."

"This is why I prefer computers," Carlos said, grabbing the clipboard. "They're password protected."

"Oh, don't be so pouty. We'll come up with a name." Jasmine shrugged her way past Carlos, back to her own seat. "Who knows? Maybe our new recruit will suggest one."

New recruit, Steven thought. He thought of the girl in the hoodie, and wondered what she'd be like. In the photo, she looked confident, even defiant. Would she understand what they had to tell her, and agree to join up?

Or will she tell us to get the heck out?

The seat belt light came on. Steven leaned back and felt the plane tip forward, beginning its descent.

I guess we'll know soon enough.

CHAPTER TEN

THE CONCERT WAS held at a converted castle in the French countryside, nestled against the trees along a quiet road. Steven, Jasmine, and Carlos approached a thick wooden door, framed within dark stone. Above it, on the outside of the building, a modern marquee displayed worn plastic letters: *CE SOIR—LES POULES*.

"'Ce Soir,'" Steven said. "Is that an opening act?"

"I think it means 'tonight,'" Jasmine replied.

"Oh," Steven replied. He felt vaguely embarrassed.

They showed their tickets—which Carlos had bought via Wi-Fi on the plane—and passed through a bar area into the main concert hall. It was dark, with antique chandeliers hanging from a ceiling too high to see. A few small balconies dotted the walls, separated by stage lights and a few huge covered windows. Most of the seats were full—about two hundred or so—and a few people were dancing in the aisles.

Up on the stage, a trio of Asian men danced in formation, stomping their feet. Steven pointed a thumb at the lead singer. "That doesn't look like Roxanne!" he shouted over the music.

Jasmine stifled a giggle. Carlos just shook his head, jabbing at the touchscreen on his analyzer. "She's here somewhere!"

The music built to a crescendo, then stopped. The lead singer raised his hand and barked out several words in mellifluous French. The audience rose to its feet, applauding.

Steven looked at Jasmine. "He said thank you!" she said. "And then he said the main event would be . . ."

But Steven had stopped listening. Up on the stage, a young woman was striding forward. She was tall, with a confident, almost haughty expression, and she wore a hoodie with a picture of a rhino on it. A guitar was slung over her shoulder. She carried it casually, as if she'd been born with it.

The other band members filed onstage behind her, taking their places: guitar and bass player flanking her, the drummer at his drum set. A low rumble of applause rose up as the woman cast her gaze across the audience, a sly smile teasing at the corners of her lips.

"*Merci!*" she yelled.

Her eyes met Steven's—and something happened. He felt the Tiger surge, felt its energy welling up inside him. An aura, faint but strong, appeared around the woman in the hoodie, and for just a second Steven thought he saw fear in her eyes.

Then the other guitarist struck a raucous opening chord—and the moment was broken. The energy faded from the young woman as though it had never existed. She shook her head, turned toward her band mate, and made a quick chopping motion. He broke off playing, puzzled. She leaned in and spoke urgently in his ear.

After a brief, whispered discussion, the band broke into a much softer, quieter song. The woman nodded in approval, but her band mates looked unsure. She cast another glance toward Steven, then quickly looked away and broke into a melodious tune.

"*Jusssss-tice,*" she sang. "*There must be jusssss-tice in the world . . .*"

"Did you feel that?" Jasmine's voice in his ear made Steven jump. He'd forgotten she was there.

"I'm not . . . what?"

"Her." Jasmine cocked her head at the stage.

The singer was pacing back and forth now, rapping in

low, even tones. "*Stop the slaugh-terrr,*" she chanted, pointing with both thumbs at the animal on her shirt. "*Stop the ex-ploi-taaaaaa-tion . . .*"

Carlos pushed in between Steven and Jasmine, holding up his analyzer. He nodded sharply.

Steven remembered the flash of energy, the aura surrounding the singer. He knew what Jasmine was going to say, even before she spoke the words.

"She's Zodiac, all right."

"*Ex-ploi-taaaa-tion . . .*"

Roxanne forced herself to focus on the lyrics. But inside, she was terrified. *Don't let it show,* she told herself. *You're onstage now. Keep the show going. Nothing matters but the show.*

The band, she knew, was baffled by her actions. Pierre had been about to launch into "*Maman,*" the new song. It had a harsh, driving beat and a shrieking vocal, so they'd agreed to open with it. They knew it'd bring the crowd to its feet.

But then Roxanne had seen the three strange people enter: the man in the coat and glasses, the woman with harsh eyes, and . . . and the kid. When she'd locked eyes with him, a strange feeling had run through her. The same sensation, she realized, that she'd felt when she shattered the mirror in the bathroom.

"*Stop the killing. Stop the in-sani-teeeee . . .*"

It had happened before, too—three times over the past couple of days. Whenever Roxanne became agitated and raised her voice, a surge of power seemed to fill her body. And then things . . . well, things broke.

So at the last minute, she'd decided to start off with a softer song, a ballad. The crowd, she could tell, was puzzled too—it was an unusual thing to do. But now the audience was with her, clapping and swaying and rising to their feet to dance gently.

"*My people . . . are your people. Your people are miiiiiiine . . .*"

This song, "*The Killing*," featured a very even, measured vocal. Roxanne had been singing it now for at least two minutes, and nothing had happened. No surge, no energy. No glass breaking.

She glanced out over the crowd. The man in glasses was checking some machine in his hand. The kid's eyes were still glued to her, watching her every move.

Pierre launched into the final chorus, and Paolo the drummer followed. Roxanne finished her last line and lowered the mic, smiling as the applause rose up.

Pierre was looking at her now, one eyebrow raised in question. She knew what that meant: Now?

Forget this, she thought. *Forget jumping at shadows, forget being afraid of things I can't understand. We're young, and we're onstage.*

Let's rock.

She spun around, facing each member of the band in turn, and mouthed the word: *Maman.*

Pierre struck the opening chord, even louder than the first time. Paolo pounded down a drum beat and Jaiden followed suit, laying down the hard, thumping bass line. The crowd let out a crazed howl of joy and release.

Roxanne smiled. For the first time tonight, she felt fully alive. She leaned in hard on the microphone.

"*Mothers don't care,*" she chanted, barking each syllable like it was her last. "*FATHERS DON'T CARE—*"

The room exploded into chaos.

When Roxanne, the woman on stage, cried out the word *care,* her head whipped around. A ripple of sound, like a distortion in the air, seemed to blast upward from her, heading toward the ceiling. At the same time, a halo of energy began to form around her body, writhing and surging outward.

"Look out!" Jasmine yelled.

As Steven watched, the sound-ripple struck a hanging chandelier, shattering it into fragments. Glass exploded in all directions, raining down over the crowd.

People screamed and started to run. Steven covered his head, shielding his eyes with his hands.

Onstage, the band had stopped playing their instruments. Roxanne's eyes were wild now, scared. But sound continued to pulse out of her in short, sharp cries, like water pouring from a pressurized hose.

"*CHILDREN! DON'T! KNOW—*"

With each word, another burst of sound struck somewhere in the room. One blasted a crack in a wall; another shattered a window. One struck a man in the aisle, hurling him backward into a group of fleeing spectators.

"Rooster," Carlos said, studying his analyzer. He pulled his coat tight around him to keep the flying glass away. "She's definitely the Rooster."

Another sound-blast knocked a chunk of the ceiling loose. Panicked audience members ducked and fled.

Steven felt the Tiger rising inside him. *Let me out,* it seemed to say. *This is what I'm here for. This is why I've chosen you!*

He relaxed, letting the energy flow out and around him. He turned toward Jasmine—then stopped.

Jasmine was hovering a few feet above the aisle, oblivious to the falling glass and debris all around. Her eyes were blank, and her whole body glowed with incredible power. The ethereal Dragon figure surrounded her, hissing and spitting, its sharp talons clawing the air in fury.

She spread her arms out, extending the power. She turned to Steven, and her eyes seemed to focus on him for the first time. "I'll

protect these people," she said. "You go get our Rooster!"

Steven's eyes went wide. "Me?"

"You're one of us," Jasmine said. *"Go!"*

Steven gritted his teeth, feeling his own Zodiac energy rise to surround him. The Tiger's energy-mouth growled, fangs flashing. He turned back toward the stage.

Another chandelier shattered. Steven ducked, but it wasn't necessary. Jasmine extended her Dragon power above him, shielding him along with the others.

Up onstage, Roxanne was still singing—but Steven couldn't hear the words anymore. Her power, the uncontrolled Zodiac energy, seemed to have overtaken her. Her entire being seemed to be funneled into those sonic bursts, the sharp deadly shocks shooting out of her mouth.

Steven ran toward her. He jumped over a fallen woman, pausing just long enough to make sure she wasn't badly hurt. He dodged a stage light as it fell into the aisle.

Roxanne had grown her own energy halo now. Its wide, feathered wings spread out from her body, stretching to cover the width of the stage. Above her shrieking head, a coxcombed Rooster whipped its sharp beak back and forth, moving in time to her sonic cries.

Steven leapt up onstage. The band had fled, he noticed, forced back by those vast energy-wings. The last member, the bass player, paused briefly at the curtain, then dashed offstage.

"Hey!" Steven called. "Hey, uh—Roxanne? Rooster?"

He felt vaguely silly, calling her that.

Roxanne turned in response. She seemed to be in shock, unable to stop the sonic assault. Now that she was facing him, a blast of sound caught him right in the chest, knocking him into the air.

Steven gasped, struggling for breath. But the Tiger was already in control. He twisted in midair, whirling around to land on his feet at the edge of the stage.

He cast a quick glance out at the seats. Most of the audience was gone now. Jasmine had narrowed her Dragon shield, protecting the last of the spectators from falling glass and fragments of ceiling. Carlos huddled close to her, still studying his analyzer.

Another sonic blast whizzed past Steven, ruffling his hair. He turned back toward Roxanne and *roared*. The Tiger's cry filled the air between them, a loud primal sound.

Roxanne stopped, shaking her head. The energy around her seemed to flicker and weaken.

"Listen to me," Steven croaked. "Just stop a minute and listen, okay?"

She blinked, clearly disoriented. Then she opened her mouth and barked again. A blast of pure sound struck the ceiling. A heavy curtain rod split in half and clattered down between them.

"Stop it! You have to stop this," Steven said.

She clamped both hands over her mouth, forcing it

shut. Then she turned terrified eyes to Steven and shook her head.

Steven took a step toward her—a normal, human step, small and gentle. He willed the Tiger to recede, forcing the energy back inside. Soothing the Tiger.

Roxanne—she needs to see me as a regular person now, he thought. *As someone she can trust.*

"I've only had this power for a little while myself," he said. "Sometimes I wonder if I can handle it. I need help . . . and I think you do, too."

Roxanne lowered her hands, and a small sonic cry burst forth, high-pitched and frantic. It struck the stage, splintering the floorboards. She clamped her mouth shut again and nodded at him.

The audience was gone now. Jasmine hovered at the edge of the stage, waiting. Her Dragon glow pulsed tight around her, fierce and powerful. Carlos stood behind her, watching.

"Let us help you," Jasmine said.

Roxanne stared at Jasmine, then looked back to Steven. The Tiger energy was gone from him now.

"I need help," Roxanne whispered, keeping each syllable low and quiet. "I do."

Steven smiled and reached out his hand.

CHAPTER ELEVEN

ROXANNE'S MOTHER fluttered around the small hotel room. "Can I get you all something to eat? Or to drink? This room has a mini fridge. Would you like a cola? Or some crackers, a biscuit maybe?"

"We're fine, ma'am," Steven said.

He sat on the little sofa next to Jasmine, with Carlos wedged in on her other side. Carlos was aiming his analyzer at Roxanne, who sat slumped in an armchair. Ever since Steven had helped her offstage, she'd withdrawn, become quiet and sullen.

"I want to thank you so much for saving Roxy," her mother continued. "I *knew* that place was unsafe. It's five hundred years old! I *knew* she shouldn't play there. And I told her not to wear that silly sweatshirt, either. But Roxy knows I support her." She paused, crouching down next to the little fridge. "Would you like me to order hamburgers? Americans like hamburgers, yes?"

"Maman," Roxanne said, not moving her head to look up. "Sit down. You're gonna give me a seizure."

Jasmine smiled. "Thank you for your hospitality, Mrs. LaFleur."

"It's Ms." An uncomfortable look crossed the older woman's face. "*Ms.* LaFleur."

"I use my mother's name," Roxanne said, her voice flat. "Not my father's."

Steven felt a sudden urge to move past that topic. "Ms. LaFleur," he said. "The castle—the concert hall—it didn't collapse on its own. Roxanne had something to do with it."

"What? That's absurd." Ms. LaFleur frowned, and her whole demeanor changed. She marched over to Carlos and said, "What is that thing you keep waving in my daughter's face?"

Carlos looked up. "It's a portable qi analyzer," he said. "We're very close to a ley line here, so I'm getting an unusual amount of interference. But it's designed to detect Zodiac energy, sort it into its five component elements, and measure the relative strength of each branch."

Roxanne's mother just stared at him.

"I've learned not to ask," Jasmine said.

"Sometimes I play Plants vs. Zombies on it, too," Carlos admitted.

"This magic Zodiac energy," Ms. LaFleur said slowly. "You say it's *inside* my daughter?"

"It's inside everyone, to one degree or another." Carlos snapped off the analyzer. "But it's not magic. It's based on elemental forces, the relationship between stellar positions and the earth's electromagnetic field. And yes, there's no doubt. Your daughter now possesses an enormous concentration of Zodiac power."

"She was born in the Year of the Rooster, wasn't she?" Jasmine asked.

Ms. LaFleur shrugged and looked at her daughter.

Roxanne sighed. "Yeah, I was. We did that Chinese Zodiac thing back in school." She turned toward Jasmine with a challenging look. "I hated school."

"You're probably not gonna love this either," Jasmine replied. "But—"

"No. Wait. Hold on a moment." Ms. LaFleur stepped in front of Roxanne. "This is absurd. My daughter is not some superpowered person like in those Steel Aardvark movies—"

"Mongoose," Steven muttered. "Steel Mongoose."

"—she is *normal*," Ms. LaFleur continued. "Why are you here, anyway? What do you want from us?"

Jasmine leaned forward. "We want to help your

daughter, Ms. LaFleur. What happened tonight could happen again, at any time. Back at our headquarters in Greenland, we can train her to use her power safely."

"And," Steven added, "we can keep her safe from this dude called Maxwell. He wants to lock us all up and train us to be super soldiers, or something."

"No. Absolutely not." Ms. LaFleur stared at them. "I may not approve of Roxanne's clothes, or her style of music, or the fact that she left university after one semester. Or the makeup she slathers onto her face, or the causes she latches onto seemingly on a daily basis, or the career path she seems intent on pursuing despite all rationality and sanity—"

"*Maman*," Roxanne said. "The point?"

"*But,*" Ms. LaFleur continued, "I support her right to do these things. To find her own path in life, to follow her dreams. And no fairy tales about magic Zodiac powers are going to stop her from doing that."

There was an awkward silence. Then a sudden light caught Steven's eye. Jasmine stood up, glowing brightly once again. The Dragon energy surrounded her, coiled around her body like a serpent, its jaws gaping wide. When she spoke, her voice was like an amplified hiss.

"The Zodiac power is real."

Roxanne's eyes widened. Her mother froze.

"Jasmine," Steven said. He rose to his feet, alarmed.

But Jasmine just reached out a hand to him, glowing

with Zodiac fire. Before Steven could even formulate a thought, the Tiger within him reacted. He leapt to his feet and loped over to join her.

Then he turned to face Roxanne and her mother. The Tiger energy glowed all around him now, its fierce jaws whipping back and forth, its roar rising up to fill the small room.

"What," Ms. LaFleur said, "what is *that?*"

Carlos just sat on the sofa, a worried look on his face. "No more property damage," he said softly. "Please?"

Together, Steven and Jasmine—the Tiger and the Dragon—stared at their new recruit. Slowly they began to walk toward Roxanne, their energy forms whipping around the room, snarling and roaring.

Steven felt like he was in the grip of something huge, something he could barely control. The Zodiac energy was still new to him, still overwhelming. Jasmine was only using a fraction of her Dragon power, he knew; he'd seen her flare up much brighter than this. But it was still enough to fill the room with light.

Roxanne seemed to shrink back into her chair, watching Jasmine and Steven with terrified eyes. "Mothers don't care," Roxanne whispered. "Mothers don't care . . ."

Steven recognized the lyrics of one of her songs. He stepped out in front of Jasmine. "This is real," he said. "I know you don't want it. I'm not sure if I want it either. But . . ." He held out a hand to Roxanne.

"Fathers don't care," she continued. "Children don't KNOW!"

The sonic blast struck Steven like a truck, slamming him backward into Jasmine. He bounced right off of her powerful Dragon energy and slammed sideways into an end table. His elbow struck a lamp, shattering it in a shower of sparks. Then he toppled to the ground.

The Tiger roared.

Roxanne leapt to her feet, fists clenched, knocking over her chair. Zodiac energy surrounded her, rising up to form the unique shape of the fierce-winged Rooster. Its beak snapped and pecked at the air.

"Oh, no," she said. "Maman, help me . . ."

Roxanne turned toward her mother—who stood perfectly still. She stared at her daughter with a look of utter terror.

Then she backed up into a table, sending it tumbling to the floor. "Stay away," she said. "Stay away from me!"

"Maman?"

Ms. LaFleur's eyes were wide. "Your music," she said. "Your clothes, the makeup, the causes—I can live with all that. But not this." She shook her head in panic. "Not *this*."

"No," Roxanne said. "You can't give up on

me. You can't. I've always had you. I'm—I'm so *LUCKY!*"

The sonic blast struck the wall just above her mother's head, smashing a hole in the plaster. Ms. LaFleur looked up, cast one final terrified glance at her daughter, then turned and sprinted out the door.

Roxanne watched her mother go. She didn't move, but the Rooster energy form raised its head and let out a long, mournful crowing noise.

Then the energy faded, and Roxanne slumped to her knees. Steven rushed forward to catch her. And then, for a moment, the Rooster was just a normal person again. A confused, semiconscious girl.

"I was lucky," Roxanne whispered.

"Music is my life," Roxanne said sadly. "But that part of my life is gone."

"Not gone," Jasmine replied. "You may have to put it on hold for a while."

They sat in a nearby cafe, sipping hot drinks. Carlos had suggested they get out of the hotel room before anyone came to investigate the noise.

Steven turned to watch Roxanne. She stirred a spoon listlessly in her coffee, swirling the milk around.

"I cannot sing anymore," she said. "Not without hurting people."

"We can help you with that." Jasmine took the girl's hand. "We can train you to control your power."

Roxanne squeezed Jasmine's hand. The girl closed her eyes tight and let out something that might have been a sob. "Maman," she said. "She was always there for me. And then . . . the way she looked at me when . . ."

"You were right," Steven said. "You're lucky to have a mom like that. Not everyone does."

Roxanne looked at Steven, squinting as if she were noticing him for the first time.

"She'll come around," he added. "Your mom, I mean."

Something odd crept into Roxanne's eyes. "They are training you, too?" she asked.

"Yeah," Steven replied.

"They will train you to dress better? Not that you aren't rocking that cargo pants look."

Steven stared at her for a moment, shocked. Then Jasmine let out a loud laugh. Roxanne burst out laughing—the first time they'd seen her do that. Even Carlos chuckled.

Steven smiled back.

Man, he thought. *Are all the recruits gonna be like this?*

CHAPTER TWELVE

"I KNOW THIS might be difficult to accept," Steven said. "But there's this thing called the Chinese Zodiac—"

"Aye, sure, I get it," the newcomer interrupted. "Crazy energy, ancient power, an' for some reason it chose me. All good so far."

"Well," Jasmine said, smiling. "At least *somebody's* not freaking out about this."

CHAPTER TWELVE

The newcomer, Liam, wasn't at all what Steven had expected. He was a few years older than Steven but about Steven's height, with thick glasses and a round physique. He didn't look like someone who'd been infused with Zodiac power, or any other power for that matter. And he seemed utterly unconcerned about the whole situation.

But Carlos had confirmed it: Liam was the one they'd come to find. So while Roxanne traveled back to Jasmine and Carlos's hideout, the rest of them headed to find the Ram.

Carlos made a noise, and Jasmine turned to him. "What?" she asked.

"I don't know." Carlos studied his handheld analyzer closely. "I'm getting some sort of new reading. Might be nothing."

Liam waved to a woman, who was just closing up shop for the day. "Oi, Millie," he said. "How's business?"

Millie gave him a sour look, then a quick smile. She turned away.

They were walking down the winding main road of Liam's village, in Northern Ireland. The houses were built low—one or two stories—and a lot of the stores seemed to have gone out of business. The sun had just set, and a light mist was rolling in.

Steven realized that most of the cars parked along the road were compact models. *In America,* he thought, *there'd be a lot more SUVs.*

"This place feels peaceful," he said.

"Peaceful?" Liam turned to him. "Aye, that's one word. Hey, Angus. Crops comin' in?"

"You seem to know everyone here," Jasmine commented.

"I've lived here all my life."

"So," Steven said, "like we were saying. The Zodiac—"

"Mate!" Liam grinned. "I *believe* ye. I already knew something happened to me, you just put the words to it. Here, I'll show ye." He turned to a very large, muscular man, a giant walking by in a T-shirt and jacket. "Mal. Hit me in the stomach, aye? Hard as ye can?"

The giant, Mal, smiled and nodded. He whipped his fist down and slammed it up into Liam's gut. Without a sound, Liam flew up off the ground, soaring several feet through the air. For just a moment, a Zodiac energy form appeared in the air around his body: a raging, charging Ram with sharp, curled horns.

Steven gasped.

Liam slammed into the side of a boarded-up storefront, chipping several bricks on its facade. As he slumped to the ground, the Zodiac energy faded.

Before Steven could make a move, Liam was on his feet, dusting off his stomach. He walked back to the giant, grinning. "Good one, Mal!" Liam said. "You been workin' out, aye?"

Mal nodded, smiling shyly. "Whenever *Downton*'s not on," he said.

Jasmine, Carlos, and Steven converged on Liam. Carlos ran the analyzer across his body, excited. "No damage at all," Carlos said. "But, yes, a considerable discharge of Zodiac energy."

"See you, Mal!" Liam called.

Mal waved and walked off.

Steven felt a sudden sadness, a kind of envy for Liam's life. This man knew who he was and where he belonged. He had friends, routines, and probably family who cared about him. Since Steven's horrible conversation with his mother, since learning that his grandfather had passed away, he felt rootless, unsure where he belonged.

He sure didn't feel as comfortable with the Zodiac power as Liam did.

Steven looked at Liam's gently smiling face. *Is it right for us to take him away from here?* he wondered.

As if she'd read Steven's thoughts, Jasmine began to speak. "Liam," she said. "We were worried that our Zodiac recruits would need training, but I can see that's not a problem with you. You obviously know how to use your power."

Liam shrugged. "I've been brawling since I was six years old. It's just easier to get back up again, now."

"But that's not the only reason we're here." She frowned. "You're in danger. There's a man called Maxwell—he'll stop at nothing to get hold of the power inside you. He, or his agents, are probably on their way right now."

"Aye, so ye say. But nothing can stop me, right? I'm indestructible. So why should I go with . . ." Liam turned as a man staggered by. "Hey, Glenn," Liam said. "You all right there?"

"Right as summer rain, Liam."

Liam watched, an odd look in his eyes, as Glenn shambled off into the sunset. "'Right as summer rain,'" Liam repeated. "You know something? I've had the same conversation with that man, every night for the last ten years."

Then Liam turned abruptly to Steven. "Tell you what, mate," Liam said. "If you can beat me in a fight, I'll go with you."

Steven blinked. "What?"

"In a fight. Fair fight, Zodiac to Zodiac." Liam smiled. "What do you say?"

Steven turned to Jasmine and Carlos, looking for help. But Carlos was engrossed in his analyzer again, tapping at its touchscreen.

Jasmine just shrugged. From the smile tickling at her lips, Steven had the feeling she was looking forward to seeing them fight.

"It . . . it seems like a weird way to decide something important," Steven said.

"Like I said, I've been fightin' all my life." Liam's smile took on a nasty tinge. "Unless you're afraid?"

Steven clenched his fists. Inside him, the Tiger roared. As always, it couldn't resist a challenge.

"Where?" Steven asked.

Liam stopped and gestured at a building with chipped blue paint and a flickering neon sign in the window.

Liam strode forward, pushed open the door, and disappeared inside. Steven hesitated for just a moment.

"Hey," Jasmine said. "Check it out."

He followed her pointing finger to the sign hanging over the pub's awning. In faded, chipped letters, it read: THE RAVEN AND THE TIGER.

Jasmine shrugged. "It's fate."

She held open the door. Steven grimaced and walked inside.

The pub's insides were as rundown as its exterior. Pictures of old men hung on the walls, above tables with missing legs. A couple of bored-looking men and an old couple sat at the bar. Above, a second-story balcony looked like it was about to collapse.

"Not exactly the Four Seasons," Jasmine said.

Steven frowned. "Where's Carlos?"

"Said he'd be along. He wanted to take a few more readings first."

Liam was already clearing tables out of the large central area. The bartender, a wiry middle-aged man, looked on in amusement. "Liam," he said. "Should I be sellin' tickets?"

CHAPTER TWELVE

"I dunno," Liam said, gesturing at Steven. "You think this lad's gonna put up a fight?"

The bartender snorted and started back toward the bar. "I think you'll eat 'im for breakfast," he said. "With maple syrup."

Again, Steven felt the Tiger snarl. He forced it down and walked up to Liam. "Look," Steven said. "I really don't think this is gonna—"

"What's your Zodiac sign, now? The Tiger?" Liam smirked. "That sounds like a right cute little kitty cat."

Steven gritted his teeth.

The bartender stood by the door now, motioning people inside. The townspeople started to troop in, watching the confrontation expectantly.

Liam just kept smiling at Steven. "In fact," Liam continued, "I almost feel sorry for ye. Soft little boy like you wouldn't last ten minutes growin' up around here—"

Steven leaned forward and jabbed his fist twice, very fast, into Liam's face. Liam's head snapped backward, like a bobblehead doll. Then he shook his head, as if he were throwing off water.

"Awww, that's cute, mate," Liam said. "Like a kiss from Grandma."

Steven clenched his fists again. The Tiger energy rose up all around him, forming its familiar energy shape in the air. When he saw Liam's grinning face, the Tiger roared.

Steven charged. He reached out and grabbed both

of Liam's shoulders, slamming the Irishman's body against the wall. A picture frame shattered, and a stuffed fish fell from its hanger to the floor.

"That's more like it!" Liam said.

The two of them grappled for a moment. Out of the corner of his eye, Steven saw Jasmine eyeing the battle. More people were crowding into the pub now, gathering behind her to watch.

Liam freed one arm from Steven's grip and punched him in the stomach. Steven gasped and doubled over. He took a step back.

"Are ye gettin' it yet?" Liam asked.

Steven roared again, a deep, primal sound. Enraged, he ran toward Liam, headfirst. His charge was clumsy, uncoordinated. But when his head struck Liam's stomach, the two of them tumbled down to the floor.

Liam huffed and rolled over on top of Steven. Steven's head struck the floor, and he felt broken glass cut into his ear. He cried out.

When he looked up, Liam was sitting on top of him. Liam wasn't scratched, injured, or even breathing hard.

"I'm trying to show you," Liam said, "there's no way you can beat me. Ye might as well give

up." His voice was almost kindly now. "Nothin' stops the Ram."

Steven's vision was blurry. He looked up, past Liam's looming face, searching for Jasmine. He couldn't see her, but other people were watching. Dozens of local residents, looking to see whether he was tough enough to beat their champion.

"Give up?" Steven spat blood. "Never."

Even as he said the words, he knew they sounded foolish. Steven—the Tiger—was strong, fast, and unnaturally agile. He didn't know the extent of his power yet; this was the first time he'd really been in a fight. But he knew he could hold his own against any normal enemy.

Not Liam, though. The Irishman was right: the Ram was unstoppable. That was the very essence of its power.

Liam shrugged. "Suit yerself." And he reared back.

Steven braced himself for the head-butt, but it still hurt. A lot.

CHAPTER THIRTEEN

THE IRISH TOWN'S winding streets made
Josie dizzy. She trotted down the main road, around sharp
turns, stopping every now and then to check her target's
location on her holographic wrist-computer. She had to
keep pulling up a street-map overlay in order to find her
way.

Once, a man staggered up to her, identified himself
as Glenn, and mumbled something unintelligible. She
frowned and pushed him away. He reeled back, sneered,
and clenched a fist at her.

Then he froze, staring at the air above her. A fierce horse's head, twice the size of a normal creature's, stared down at him with deadly, challenging eyes. When it reared back, Glenn let out a little noise and bolted.

Josie watched, one eyebrow raised, as Glenn rounded a corner and disappeared. *The first test of my power,* she thought. *The next one won't be so easy.*

A few blocks farther on, she spotted the sign on the faded blue pub: THE RAVEN AND THE TIGER. She stopped, staring at it. *Tiger.* Was that coincidence, or luck—what Maxwell called *yun*?

Then she noticed the man leaning against the wall, just outside the door: Carlos, the renegade Vanguard technician Maxwell had yelled so much about. The man who had overseen the Zodiac Convergence process, then deliberately sabotaged it.

Josie drew in a breath and backed up, concealing herself behind a brick wall. Carlos hadn't seen her yet. He was completely engrossed in operating a small, crude, handheld analyzer device.

He's tracking me, she realized. Maxwell had warned her that all Zodiac operatives give off a unique power signature. In a moment, Carlos would detect her presence.

Carlos had no special powers; Josie could take him down with one blow, even without using her new powers. But Carlos was allied with Jasmine, and if *she* were around, that could be trouble. Better to scout out the place a bit more first.

CHAPTER THIRTEEN

Leaning out just slightly from her hiding place, Josie aimed her arm at the pub. With her other hand, she tapped furiously at the wrist-computer. The X-ray imager kicked in, providing a view through the pub's stone-and-brick wall, penetrating inside.

Josie gasped.

A scene of utter mayhem rose up before her. Steven Lee, the young Tiger, grappled furiously with another man whose face was a blur of motion. They tumbled to the floor and rolled up against the wall. The man's round face came into clear view.

"The Ram," Josie whispered.

The two fighters rolled back and forth, climbed to their feet, then knocked each other down again. A crowd of spectators clustered around them, following them around the room, keeping a constant distance away from the battle.

Josie stared at the three-dimensional image projected before her. It looked like Steven and Ram weren't getting along, which could be good news for the Vanguard company. But on the other hand, this was exactly what Maxwell had hoped to avoid: a public spectacle. *If I move in now,* she thought, *things could get messy.*

Josie winced as Liam head-butted Steven in the face. *Messier,* she corrected herself.

She shifted her arm back and forth, varying the angle of the image. She studied the crowd inside the pub, watching them cheer at the two combatants' blows. *Where is she?* Josie wondered. *Where's—*

"Josie," a female voice said. "You been working out?"

Josie looked up from the projected image. Jasmine stood just outside the pub, her hands on her hips.

Josie snapped her arm down, killing the hologram. She stepped out into the street, feeling vaguely like an old-west gunfighter. "Jasmine," she said. "Funny running into you here."

"I don't think it's funny at all."

Carlos had disappeared. *Called in the big gun,* Josie thought.

A few people brushed past them, hurrying into the pub. The drunken man—Glenn—cast a quick glance at Josie, then at Jasmine. Then he scurried inside with the others.

"You know what I'm here for," Josie said.

"And you know I can't let you have it," Jasmine replied.

Josie frowned; despite everything, she *liked* Jasmine. "You used to be one of us," Josie said. "You were working for Vanguard before you turned eighteen."

"I turned in my notice, Josie. The day I learned what kind of monster Maxwell really is."

"He's tough, but he's a good man," Josie replied. "The world's a messed-up place, and we need a person like him. You'll see—the Zodiac powers are a path to peace, Jasmine."

"He's a murderer."

"If you're talking about that city in the Middle East—"

"You have *no idea* what I'm talking about."

A flash of anger crossed Jasmine's face. A burst of Zodiac energy flared up around her, then faded quickly away.

Josie grimaced. Jasmine shared the Dragon power with Maxwell—and the Dragon was the most powerful of the Zodiac signs. That made Jasmine very, very dangerous.

And Josie was still untrained in her new power. Even if the Horse could hold its own against the Dragon—which was doubtful—Jasmine had had precious extra days to practice her new abilities.

I've only got one advantage, Josie thought. *I know she's got Zodiac power—but she doesn't know I have it, too.*

Josie clenched her fists, willing the power of the Horse to come forth. It shimmered into being in the air above her, hooves flashing, its long noble head searching back and forth in the air.

"Give him to me, Jasmine," she said.

Jasmine stepped back for a moment, startled.

My only chance is to take her by surprise, Josie thought. She stepped forward, staring at Jasmine with all the menace she could summon up.

But Jasmine was staring at her now, shaking her head. "Oh, Josie," she said. "I'm sorry."

"For what?"

"I'm sorry Maxwell got you mixed up in this."

Then, like an explosion of fire, Jasmine's own energy form flared up.

Josie's breath caught in her throat. Jasmine's Dragon was different in shape from Maxwell's: sharp-clawed, lithe, and sinuous, a lean mass of coiled, whipping muscle. Maxwell's Dragon seemed ready to crush the world within its bat-wings, but Jasmine's looked like a sinewy whipcord of death. When its head surged forward, hissing, Josie flinched despite herself.

Jasmine stared at her. "You really don't want to do this, Josie."

Josie considered the situation. Jasmine outpowered her, and Josie still hadn't wielded her new power in a combat situation. *And even if I somehow manage to beat Jasmine—*

A thunderous crash resonated from inside the pub.

—even if I can defeat the Dragon, there are two more Zodiac-powered people to face.

Josie forced herself to relax, letting the Horse energy fade. "Another time, Jasmine," she said. "And there *will* be another."

Jasmine just kept staring. "I hope so."

Above her small form, the Dragon let out another loud hiss.

Josie turned and ran. She didn't look back.

ZODIAC

Maxwell won't be happy, she thought, racing down the now dark street. *I've failed him. But there was really no choice. We just got here too late.*

He'll understand. Maxwell will understand.

CHAPTER FOURTEEN

STEVEN FLUNG OUT both arms, pushing
Liam away. Liam staggered back against the wall, and
Steven dropped to the ground, scuttling away from him.

This may have been a bad idea, Steven thought.

The crowd let out a disappointed noise. "Get 'im,
Liam!" a woman yelled. "Pin 'im down!"

Liam turned toward them and raised his arms like a
prizefighter. The crowd cheered wildly.

Then he turned and ran toward Steven, swinging his fists. But that one distracted moment, while Liam was playing to the crowd, was all Steven had needed to get his wind back. He leapt out of the way easily, the Tiger lending him agility and precision. Liam lurched past him, stumbling.

Steven jumped up high and kicked out. His foot struck Liam in the throat, snapping the Irishman's head around.

For a moment Steven panicked. *Did I just break his neck?* But Liam shook his head out almost casually, as if he were drying a towel in the breeze.

Can't let him recover, Steven thought. *I have to beat him. That means letting the Tiger out—all the way.*

Before Liam could turn around, Steven grabbed him by the shoulder, leaping on top of him. Liam grabbed him back, and together they tumbled to the floor again. With a roar, Steven struck out with both fists. His hands felt like Tiger paws, thick, meaty weapons made for pummeling prey into submission.

Liam just smiled. He reached up and slapped both of Steven's ears at once, fast and hard. The blow was deafening; Steven roared in pain. He reared back off of Liam, pivoted on his lower back, reached out with both legs like a wrestler—

—and grabbed Liam's head between his legs.

Liam cried out in surprise as Steven leaned back again,

lifting him up into the air. Liam squirmed around, but couldn't break the Tiger's grip. For just a moment their eyes met, and Liam seemed to nod slightly.

Then Liam went limp. Steven followed through with his legs, tossing the Irishman through the air. Liam sailed over a table and smashed into the wall.

The crowd made a loud "Oh!" noise.

Steven gasped, breathing hard. But Liam was already on his feet again.

Nothing hurts this guy, Steven realized. *I can't beat him—which means I can never convince him to come with us.*

Then he looked at the indestructible figure stalking toward him. The energy form of the Ram blazed up and around Liam, lighting up the dark pub. Its horns whipped back and forth through the air.

Forget recruiting *him,* Steven thought. *Am I gonna survive this fight?*

Liam punched Steven in the chest. Steven stepped back, gasping. He whirled around and kicked out, catching Liam in the stomach. Liam responded with a roundhouse punch. Steven dodged, but Liam managed to land a glancing blow against his side.

Time seemed to stop for a moment. Liam looked into Steven's eyes, judging him. "Not bad," Liam said.

Then Liam took hold of Steven, grappling with him again. But this time when they fell to the ground, Liam twisted himself around to take the brunt of the impact.

Steven rolled, trying to break free, and his shoulder slammed into a table leg. He cried out.

Liam smiled. Keeping his grip on Steven, he rolled them toward the back of the room. They tumbled over and over, faster and faster, gaining speed and momentum. People jumped and dodged out of the way.

Steven saw the back door looming in their path. But Liam crashed into it first, splintering it against his indestructible body. As they tumbled through into the dark, a shard of wood scraped against Steven's arm, drawing blood. He pulled away again, but Liam held on.

"Ride with it, mate," Liam said.

They rolled through a darkened kitchen, caroming off an old, disused stove. They sailed through the outer door, knocking it wide on its hinges, and rolled down three stone steps. Then they crashed to a stop in a concrete garbage alley strewn with metal trash cans.

Steven roared again. He pulled away, tried to break Liam's grip. All around them, the Tiger's energy warred with the Ram's, sharp claws pawing and scraping against fierce, coiled horns.

But Liam held on.

"You're not gonna give up, are you?" Liam asked.

From inside, Steven could hear the sounds of people approaching. "Never," he said.

"Neither am I."

For just a second, Liam smiled. Then, all at once, he

released Steven and flopped down on his back. "OW!" he yelled, rolling around on the concrete. "AH, I GIVE UP! YE GOT ME!"

Dazed, Steven rose to his knees. "What?" he asked.

"YE GOT ME! AYE, IT'S TRUE!" Liam clutched his arm. "OH, ME ARM! YE GOT ME GOOD!"

The first of the locals burst through the outer door. They looked around, puzzled, squinting in the dim light. "ME ARM! ME LEG! ME BUM! AH, KID, YE GOT ME!"

Mal, the large man they'd met in the street, stepped forward. He stared at Liam for a long moment, then turned to Steven with a hard look on his face. *Uh-oh,* Steven thought.

Then Mal reached out a meaty hand and clapped Steven hard on the back. "Good one, mate."

The crowd moved forward, murmuring in agreement. Steven felt exhausted and slightly dizzy. He heard phrases like "Tough kid," "Liam was due for a takedown," and "Best brawl I've seen in years."

Jasmine appeared in the doorway, alarmed. Then she looked from Steven to Liam, still writhing on the ground. She nodded, impressed.

Steven reached out a hand toward her. "But I didn't . . ."

Her eyes widened. Quickly she mouthed the words: *Ride with it.*

Steven shook his head. He looked from Jasmine to

Mal and the locals, then over at Liam. He reached out a hand to help Liam up.

"Good fight," Steven said.

"Aye," Liam said. He leaned in, giving Steven a wink that the others couldn't see. "That it was."

"Move yer big feet, Liam?" the bartender asked. "Got to clean up yer mess here."

Steven and Liam sat on stools, leaning against the bar. Jasmine and Carlos were off somewhere, arranging transportation back to headquarters. All the locals had dispersed, except for a few drunks sleeping in chairs and on the floor.

"So," Steven said, turning back to Liam. "Why'd you do it?"

Liam smiled. He seemed as fresh as the moment he'd walked in the door. *Not like me,* Steven thought, fingering a cut on his arm. *I could sleep for a week.*

"Decide to go with you?" Liam shrugged. "I got my reasons."

"No," Steven replied. "I mean, why'd you tell everyone I beat you?"

"You seem like a good kid. And I'd already told everyone I'd only leave if I lost the fight."

"It's the right thing to do," Steven said quickly. "Jasmine and Carlos—they can explain about the—"

"Mate, mate." Liam held up a hand. "No need for the hard sell. I said I'd go with you."

"But . . ." Steven stared at him. "Just like that? Don't you want to know more about the Zodiac? About Maxwell and the Vanguard company? About how your power works, and what it might mean for the future of the world?"

"I know all I need to know, mate." Liam stared back, his eyes steady. "I know you're a fighter."

They looked around at the toppled barstools, the sleeping drunks, the cracked TV set over the bar. Liam sighed. "I love this town. It's me home, you know?"

Steven nodded.

The bartender nudged an unconscious man with the broom. Steven recognized the man: Glenn, the drunk they'd met in the street. Glenn roused himself just slightly and muttered: "Right as summer rain." Then he slumped down, asleep again.

"But maybe it's time for a change," Liam said.

"Excuse me," Steven said. "I think my TV's broken again."

The flight attendant glared at him. "For the last time, kid. None of these screens work. We told you that when we took off. There's nothing we can do. Deal with it."

"Can I have some gumdrops?"

She rolled her eyes. "We don't have any gumdrops," she said.

"Oh." He thought for a moment. "Do you have maraschino cherries?"

"No."

"Nachos?"

"Kid." The attendant leaned down, glaring at him. "This isn't a restaurant, and it isn't a movie theater. If I get you a couple more packs of cashews, will you sit there quietly for the rest of the flight?"

Steven nodded. The attendant walked away, shaking her head.

When she was gone, Jasmine tapped him on the shoulder. Steven turned, craning his neck around to talk to her and Carlos in the row behind. Carlos was just clicking off his cell phone.

"I hate cashews," Steven said. "And that was humiliating."

Jasmine smiled. "It's called teamwork! You distracted the attendant while Carlos called headquarters."

Steven frowned. "Isn't that dangerous? Making a call while we're in the air?"

"Not with my phone," Carlos said. "It works on a special frequency. But they don't know that."

"Spill, man," Jasmine said to him. "What did they say?"

"Well," Carlos said, "they've been tracking the other two new Zodiac hosts with more sophisticated equipment than I've got here. And they're detecting a rise in the level of Zodiac energy at both locations."

CHAPTER FOURTEEN

Jasmine swore softly. "That's got to be Maxwell. He's already got agents on the ground in both places. We're running out of time."

Steven thought furiously for a moment. "What if we split up?"

Jasmine looked at him. "What?"

"Send two teams. One to America, and the other to South Africa."

She frowned. "That's a good idea . . . we could all change planes in London. But we can't do it alone. We'll have to enlist Roxanne's and Liam's help, and they haven't been trained yet." She paused. "You think they can handle it?"

Steven glanced forward. Two rows up, on the other side of the aisle, Liam sat whacking himself in the head with a thick hardcover book, over and over again. A pair of small boys stood in the aisle, watching him in amazement.

"See?" Liam said, grinning broadly. "Nothin' hurts me!"

He slammed the book against his head again, even harder. The boys squealed with delight.

Steven turned back to Jasmine. "I, uh, hope so," he said.

The flight attendant returned, dropped a dozen packets of cashews onto Steven's tray table, and gave him a withering glance. Then she left without a word.

Steven grimaced at the cashews.

Jasmine laughed and reached out to grab a packet. "Eat up," she said. "You're gonna need your strength."

Grimly, he tore open a packet.

"Hey," Jasmine continued. She gestured over at Liam. "You never told us: how'd you beat him, anyway?"

A slow grin stole over Steven's face.

"I'm the Tiger," he said.

He knew he shouldn't enjoy the look of frustration on her face. But he did.

CHAPTER FIFTEEN

A BRIGHT LIGHT was shining in Duane's eyes.
He flinched, squinted, and squirmed in his chair. He opened his mouth to speak, but all that came out was: "L-l-li . . ."

The woman in the striped business suit, sitting across the table from him, looked up. "Light? Oh, is it bothering you?"

She seemed almost amused. She reached over and adjusted the lamp, swiveling it back and forth. But somehow, when she was finished, it was still in his eyes.

"Th-thanks," he stuttered.

Duane looked around, nervous. The room was small and dark. Two men in police uniforms stood behind the woman, both holding strange looking firearms. The guns were scary, but aside from that, the whole situation felt somewhat familiar. Duane's classmates spent a lot of time shining bright lights at him. Not literally, of course—but that was what it felt like.

A very big man walked in the door and moved over to join the woman. The man wore a suit just like the woman's, but much larger. "Sorry," he said. "Had to drop a crazy big log back there."

The woman rolled her eyes, just enough for Duane to see.

The man sat down next to the woman and made a show of opening a big, clunky laptop computer. Then he leaned forward and stared at Duane with cold, piercing eyes. "So, kid," he said. "You're in a whole pile of trouble."

Duane looked away. "I didn't mean to do anything," he said.

"Didn't mean to do anything," the woman repeated. She shuffled some papers, then picked up the tablet again. "Let's see. Your class was touring the provincial government building when your teacher noticed you were missing. At the same time, the computers registered a massive hacker attack."

"It wasn't an attack," Duane said quietly.

"Soon after that," the woman continued, ignoring him,

"all the computers went haywire. They found you at a terminal in a secure section of the building, and when the guards tried to take you into custody, you panicked. And then all the power went out in the building."

"You're in a big steaming heap of trouble, son," the big man said.

"You told him that already," the woman said. She seemed a little testy.

"I was just curious," Duane said. "I wanted to see the computers."

The man leaned forward, placing his meaty hands on the table. "And what did you do when you saw 'em?"

Duane said nothing.

"Duane." The woman lowered her tablet. "We're here to help you. But we can't do that if you won't be straight with us."

Duane frowned. "Wh-who are you again?"

"You can call him Alpha," the woman said. "And I'm Beta."

"Well . . . Ms. Betty—"

"Beta."

"Ms. Beta! Sorry! The thing is . . ." Duane paused, trying to figure out how to explain. "I've always been good with computers. I can make them do things." He cast a nervous glance back at the armed policemen. "Am I going to jail?"

The man and the woman—Alpha and Beta—exchanged

a glance. Then the woman reached over to adjust the light again. This time, she turned it off.

Duane blinked in relief.

Alpha leaned forward. "Duane, we ain't with the police. We're with the Vanguard company."

Beta slammed a palm into her forehead. "You're not supposed to use the real name!" she said to her companion.

The big man shrugged. "Who cares? He's never heard of it. Have you, kid?"

Duane shook his head.

"Kid. Duane." Beta leaned forward again, with a look on her face that said: *Time for me to fix this mess.* "You've heard of big corporations that hire hackers, people who know how to do a lot of damage to their computers, in order to have the hackers working *for* them instead of *against* them?"

Duane nodded. "My friend Alec got a job like that. Well, he's not really my friend. He's kind of a jerk."

"Yeah. Whatever," Beta replied. "Well, this is kind of like that."

Duane gestured at the policemen. "Why do people from a corporation have c-cops with them?"

"They're here for your protection."

"Th-the cops or the guns?"

Alpha shrugged.

Duane was used to things not making sense. But this *really* didn't make sense.

"You're not a prisoner," Beta assured him. "You can leave anytime."

Duane frowned again at the men with guns.

"Well," Alpha said, smiling nastily. "Maybe not *anytime*."

"You, you want to hire me?" Duane asked.

"Sort of." The woman peered at him. "We know you've been in trouble before, Duane. You've been arrested for hacking more than once."

Duane nodded sheepishly.

"But that's not all," Beta continued. "You haven't told us everything, have you?"

He shrugged.

Beta consulted her tablet again. "A few days ago . . . were you struck by, let's see, a bright light?"

Duane's eyes widened with fright.

"Out of nowhere?" she continued. "A blinding flash, from the sky?"

Duane nodded, very fast.

"And now you can do things, can't you? Strange things?"

The man, Alpha, snorted. "This is the part I don't believe."

"It doesn't matter what you believe!" Beta snapped. "If you're not going to be helpful, just sit there quietly."

As she turned back toward Duane, Alpha made a face at her.

"Duane," Beta continued. "What happened then? After the light hit you?"

"I could make computers do things." Duane sighed loudly. "Things other people c-can't do."

"This is stupid." Alpha lowered his laptop computer and fixed Duane with a challenging gaze. "You can, what, make computers sit up and dance? Prove it."

Beta looked alarmed. "I don't think that's a good—"

"He says he can do things? Let's see." Alpha gestured at the door. "When *she* gets here, she's gonna want proof."

Duane looked up at the faces staring down at him. Alpha's was hostile and challenging; Beta's was cold and now a bit nervous. Behind them, the armed policemen seemed to have tightened their grips on their weapons.

Duane felt himself trembling. Nervously, he pulled his dreadlocks back. All his life, he'd tried to fit in, to hide how smart he was, so people wouldn't make fun of him. Now, somehow, he'd been given something else besides his intelligence—and he *really* needed to hide that. If Duane had learned anything in his seventeen years, it was that people weren't very kind to kids who could do exceptional things.

But the pressure was too much. He could feel it building inside him. And, he realized, if these weird people really *did* want to hire him—not hurt him—they wouldn't let him go until they saw what he could do.

Duane reached out with both hands and let out a tiny bit of the power surging inside of him.

Beta's tablet computer sparked and caught fire. She jumped, let out a little cry, and tossed the computer into the air. It clattered to the table, its screen cracking on impact.

Alpha's laptop was flashing wildly. Smoke poured out

of its top. The big man tried to slam it shut, but it popped back open with a loud electric crackling noise.

The two policemen's guns let out a soft humming noise. They raised the guns and aimed them straight at Duane. Duane felt another stab of panic, and struggled to control his power.

Then he noticed something odd. Alpha and Beta had both risen to their feet, standing just in front of the policemen. Both of them now held small, high-tech hand weapons, too.

"Are . . ." Duane pointed at the handguns. "Are you really from this 'Vanguard' company?"

"Yeah, they are," said a deep female voice. "But it's not the kind of company you think."

Duane looked over at the door and gasped. A muscular woman in combat gear strode into the room. A bright energy glow surrounded her, shimmering upward to form the shape of a fierce, whinnying horse.

That's the same energy that struck me, Duane realized. *The energy that appears whenever I do . . . the things I can do.*

Alpha seemed stunned by the woman. "Whoa," he said. He stepped back to let her come forward. Beta stared at the woman, too, but warily.

The newcomer ignored them both. She placed both powerful arms on the table and leaned forward, studying Duane closely. She seemed to only be concerned with him, not with anyone else in the room.

"Wh-wh-who—" Duane paused, hating his stutter more than ever. "Who are you?"

The woman's face softened slightly.

"My name is Josie," she said. "And my Zodiac sign is Horse. And you . . ."

She paused to press a few buttons on a small computer mounted on her wrist. Then she held up her arm, and as Duane watched in amazement, a three-dimensional image rose from the wrist-computer. It showed a savage, raging boar with two huge fangs, steam snorting out of its enormous nostrils.

". . . you are Pig," she said.

CHAPTER SIXTEEN

ROXANNE looked around at the pier on the Victoria and Alfred Waterfront in Cape Town, South Africa. Yachts bobbed against the dock across from a large market and a field of food stands with white tents over them. It was late, but plenty of tourists were still milling around. A saxophonist, leading a small band, blared a mournful solo into the night.

Not bad, Roxanne thought, missing her band for not the first time since she'd left France.

Beside her, Carlos sat hunched over the picnic table, studying a handheld analyzing device. "I'm reading two Zodiac signatures inside," he said. He gestured up at an ornate red building just off the pier, topped with an elaborate clock tower. "There should only be one. That worries me."

Roxanne barely heard him, her eyes trained on the saxophonist.

"Maxwell must have sent one of his new Zodiac-powered operatives," Carlos continued. "Horse again, or maybe one of the ones we haven't met yet. I was hoping we'd get there before they did."

Roxanne closed her eyes.

"Still, it looks like he only sent one agent. And there's one of you, plus Duane if we can get him on our side right away."

Carlos held up the analyzer. Roxanne glanced over at it and studied the image on its screen: a young man with dreadlocks and large headphones over his ears.

"This is him. Duane," Carlos said. "His sign—the Pig—isn't very physically oriented, so he shouldn't be a threat. That's why Jasmine sent you and me." He grinned, a rare thing for Carlos. "The newbie and the brainiac."

Roxanne stared at the image. Duane's eyes looked scared, as if he wasn't sure why people were taking his picture.

"He's got no immediate family," Carlos continued. "Lives with his uncle, but they don't seem to be close.

Anyway, he's definitely inside the Clock Tower, and he's definitely the Zodiac-powered kid we came to find. Right now he's probably—"

"—terrified?" Roxanne said. "Filled with power he can't understand, with no freaking clue how to use it?"

Carlos lowered the analyzer and looked at her for the first time.

"You keep thinking about it, don't you?" he asked.

She grimaced.

"Jasmine does that too," he said. "She keeps flashing back."

She shrugged. "I signed on for this, man. But I don't have to love it."

Carlos frowned. "We'll sneak in the side entrance," he said. "No powers unless absolutely necessary, okay?"

"No problem. I'd be happy if I *never* had to use my power again."

"I hope that's an option, but I doubt it." He motioned for her to follow him. "Come on."

They left the picnic table, creeping up to the side of the building. A small door was inlaid in stone. Carlos tried the knob, but it wouldn't turn. He reached into his pack and pulled out a small electronic lockpick.

Roxanne sighed. "Let's rock."

"There," the woman called Josie said. "It's just you and me now. Better?"

CHAPTER SIXTEEN

Duane looked up at her. Josie had sent the people in suits away, along with the policemen who, Duane thought, probably weren't really policemen after all. She'd also gotten him a latte, which was normally his favorite drink.

But Duane still wasn't sure about all this.

"Here's the thing," Josie continued. "We *do* want to recruit you. Just, maybe, not exactly the way you were led to believe."

He sipped his latte, not looking at her.

"You're an unusual kid, aren't you, Duane?" Josie stood up and started to pace around the small room. "We're putting together a whole *group* of exceptional kids. Young people who were hit by the Zodiac beams, charged up with this enormous power, before they were equipped to deal with it."

"A g-group of kids," Duane repeated. "You mean like a school?"

"Yeah." She turned toward him, smiling. "A kind of school. A place where you can—"

Then she froze. Motioning Duane to silence, she crossed quickly to the door. Power rose around her: the aura Duane was starting to recognize as Zodiac energy. It formed itself vaguely into the Horse shape he'd seen before, but this time it was dimmer, less fully formed.

With a single quick motion, Josie punched her arms through the wall. She grabbed hold of two people and yanked them into the room, ignoring their startled cries as they tumbled to the floor.

Duane jumped to his feet, knocking over his latte. He looked down at the two figures lying on the floor: a man with glasses and a young woman with short hair wearing a hoodie.

"Carlos," Josie said, glaring down at the man.

The man, Carlos, rubbed his neck. "Josie," he said. "Getting used to your powers, I see."

"No thanks to you." Josie turned toward Duane. "Carlos, here, is the genius who tried to sabotage the Zodiac Convergence."

"You mean I'm the genius who made it work," Carlos corrected her. "You should be thanking me for that extra strength of yours."

But Duane wasn't listening. He was staring at the woman in the hoodie. She returned his gaze. Slowly, a faint energy halo rose up around each of them.

"You're like me," Duane said. It was almost a question.

"Name's Roxanne. And yeah, I guess I am." The woman smiled, climbing to her feet. "Better stylist, though."

Duane wasn't sure how to take that.

Carlos tried to rise, but Josie pointed sharply at him. "Stay down, Carlos. You know I could cripple you in a second." Then Josie

looked over at Roxanne, a smile creeping over her face. "You're right—I *should* thank you. You've brought me the Rooster, haven't you?"

"What's going on in here?"

Beta, the business-suited woman, burst into the room, her gun drawn. Alpha followed behind along with the guards from before.

Alpha pushed forward and surveyed the scene quickly. Then he turned to the guards. "Cover all of 'em," he said.

Josie moved toward him. "You can go," she said. "All of you. I've got this situation contained."

"That's not your call, lady." Alpha stared her down. "You might be one of Maxwell's hotshot new Zodiac agents, but we were ordered to secure this freak."

At the word *freak*, Duane jumped.

Alpha moved in closer, inches away from Josie's face now. "And we don't take orders from you."

A look of rage crossed Josie's face.

Duane flinched. He wasn't good with rage. He'd never been good with crowds, either—let alone crowds of people with guns and superhuman powers.

Roxanne seemed alarmed. Her eyes darted from one corner of the room to another, the Zodiac energy flaring up around her and fading away again, over and over. Instinctively, Duane took a step toward her.

"I'm going to call Maxwell," Josie hissed. "We'll see what his orders are."

"No," Beta replied, "*I'm* going to call Maxwell."

"If anybody moves," Alpha said to the guards, "shoot 'em."

It was all too much. Duane felt his blood pressure rising, the panic growing inside him like a living thing.

"G-g-g-g-GO AWAY!" he screamed.

Someone fired.

CHAPTER SEVENTEEN

ROXANNE WAS NEVER sure where the first blast came from. She saw a bolt of energy slice through the air, and then everyone was moving and shouting at once. The Vanguard agents all seemed to be arguing with each other. Josie was shouting, "*Down! Weapons down!*"

Carlos scrabbled to his feet. He moved toward Roxanne, calling out something, but she couldn't hear him over the crackle of weapons fire.

CHAPTER SEVENTEEN

Then she realized he wasn't talking to her. Roxanne turned to see Duane, the guy they'd come to recruit, standing behind her. His eyes were wild, panicked, and a bright Zodiac aura surrounded his body.

Duane grabbed her by the arm and screamed. Power flashed out of him in all directions, forming the shape of a giant wild Pig.

Roxanne cried out as a burning sensation erupted on her leg. She tried to pull away from Duane, but couldn't break his grip. Wincing, she reached into her pocket with her other hand and pulled out the hot, sparking remains of her phone. She threw it on the floor.

Then she remembered. Carlos had explained that Duane's power could read data directly from electronic devices. But along the way, his power often destroyed those devices.

Roxanne struggled to stay calm. *Carlos warned me about this,* she thought. *He told me about Vanguard and this Maxwell, the guy who runs it. But it's one thing to hear about it, and another thing to have them trying to cap me!*

"Stop it!" Josie yelled. "Do you want to kill him?"

"Don't tell us our jobs, you freak," replied the big male agent in the suit.

"All of you!" the female agent said. "Stand down—"

"Duane," Carlos said urgently. "Listen to me. You have to—"

But Duane's eyes went wide. Energy flared out again,

and two computers on the table sparked and caught fire. The Vanguard agents pointed and yelled.

Roxanne looked down at her arm, still held fast in Duane's panicked grip. *Keep it together,* she told herself. *It's like being onstage. Just keep playing. Keep on—*

With a loud clap, one of the guards' energy weapons exploded.

Roxanne opened her mouth and screamed. A powerful sonic cry shot forth, knocking the two agents in suits off their feet. The energy slammed into the wall, blasting a hole straight through it to the hallway outside.

Duane's grip loosened. Roxanne pulled free, and turned to see him staring at her in shock. Their eyes locked.

"You really *are* like me," he said.

For a moment, everything was quiet.

"Okay," Carlos said. "Let's all—"

Another bolt filled the air, blinding Roxanne momentarily. She felt a burning sensation on her side. She looked down and saw singed clothing and flesh.

Holy crap, she thought. *I've been hit!*

Screaming again, she turned toward the guards, and charged. Sharp shock-cries blasted out of her mouth, dropping everyone and everything in her path. A fierce Rooster shape rose up around her, blazing with Zodiac power.

Dimly she realized that Carlos was right behind her, yelling something. But Roxanne barely registered his presence. All that mattered, right now, was escape.

"Get her!" the female agent called.

Roxanne charged forward, blasting holes in one wall after another, reaching out to clear away shattered drywall and plaster. She reached a wide corridor with a hard stone wall, leaned her head back, and cried out. The wall shook, buckled, and flew apart.

Then she was outside.

She almost slammed into a man, a tourist in a Hawaiian shirt. He gaped at her, staring for a moment at the blood on her side. Then he turned and fled.

Dazed, Roxanne stopped and grabbed at her side. More tourists were fleeing, running crazily along the pier. Others had stopped to stare at the huge round hole in the side of the Clock Tower.

"Roxanne!" Carlos cried, running after her through the hole.

Carlos touched her shoulder and looked down at her side. "Flesh wound," he said. "It just grazed you."

She nodded, relieved. The panic began to subside. Carlos pulled a length of tape out of his pack and started bandaging her wound.

"We've got to move," he said. "They're coming."

They ran a few feet down the pier, shoving a young couple out of the way. "Sorry," Carlos said.

The Vanguard agents burst out of the Clock Tower building. They looked around for a moment. One of them fired straight up into the air, sending a jagged bolt of energy high into the air. People screamed and scattered.

Carlos pointed to a small yacht, tied by a rope to the pier. It looked deserted. He leapt the distance onto its deck, then reached out a hand to Roxanne.

"You're pretty fast," she said, "for a brainiac."

He pulled her onto the deck. "Needs must when the devil drives," he said.

"Is that Bob Dylan?"

He led her to the back of the boat, where a tarp had been tied down over a pile of picnic coolers. They pushed the coolers out of the way and pulled the tarp over themselves.

From this angle, they could just see the pier. The Vanguard agents were running and scrambling around. One of them fired another shot, and people started screaming again.

"I don't think they saw us," Carlos said.

"Yeah."

Then, suddenly, Roxanne felt horrible. "I screwed up," she said. "I panicked. My power made things worse."

"Well," Carlos said, "things were pretty bad already. And you weren't the first one to panic."

She turned away from him, trying not to cry.

"If anybody screwed up," he continued, "it was me. I didn't expect our target's power to be so destructive. And I sure didn't expect this many Vanguard agents. They're not playing around anymore."

Up on the pier, most of the people had fled. Roxanne could see the cluster of Vanguard agents stalking around, searching for Carlos and Roxanne.

"So now what?" she asked. "We bail?"

"We can't. Not yet."

Carlos pointed back toward the battered Clock Tower. In front of it, just behind the Vanguard agents, a bright flare of Zodiac energy lit up the night. Roxanne couldn't make out the details, but she knew who it was.

"Duane," she said.

CHAPTER EIGHTEEN

WHEN THE SHOOTING started, Duane felt

himself losing control. *No*, he thought. *No, don't let it happen
again!* He looked around wildly and instinctively grabbed
the girl in the hoodie. Roxanne.

But it was too late. His power was already flaring,
spreading like a wave across the room. Phones sparked,
lights shorted out. All around him, a cocoon of energy
radiated outward, forming the snarling, snorting form of
a giant boar.

People were yelling—*mostly at me*, Duane realized. Then a gun exploded, and the girl, Roxanne, screamed. But it wasn't just sound that came out of her mouth. Her voice knocked a hole right through the wall, scattering the agents in suits and the ones dressed as policemen.

Except they weren't policemen. Whatever mess Duane had gotten into, it was much deeper than some simple trouble with the law. And he had absolutely no idea who to trust.

Then Roxanne was gone, along with Carlos, the man she'd come in with. Beta, the woman in the suit, pointed after them and started off at a run. The fake policemen followed, gathering up fresh weapons to replace the ones Duane's power had ruined.

"Duane," a voice said.

He whirled around. Josie stepped out of the shadows, moving to stand next to the table. One of its legs had been blasted off, and it tottered at an angle. Josie held up both hands in an "I surrender" gesture.

"I can still help you, Duane," Josie said. "But you've got to calm down." She gestured at her own arm, just as a couple of sparks shot up from a small wrist-mounted device. "Stop using your power, okay?"

Duane stared at her for a moment. He felt himself twitching nervously, the huge energy Pig whipping its head around with every motion he made. *Who,* he thought, *who are the good guys here? The guys dressed like policemen? The girl with the hoodie? This woman who seems to know all about me?*

CHAPTER EIGHTEEN

"I know what you're going through, Duane," Josie continued. The Zodiac energy rose up around her again, forming the raging energy form of a beautiful steed. "I'm just like you. I'm Zodiac."

Suddenly Duane felt exhausted. The energy faded, and he wobbled a bit on his feet. Josie stepped forward and caught him.

"Easy," she said. "It's okay. The Zodiac power—it takes a lot out of you, until you know how to use it." She smiled, and suddenly she looked very tired. "I'm still learning myself."

She started to lead him outside, stepping carefully through the hole in the wall.

"I've got a stealth ship moored just offshore," Josie said. "We can avoid all . . ." She gestured around at the debris left behind from the battle. ". . . all this."

Duane turned away from her, embarrassed. On her wrist, the tiny device had stopped smoking—but now its screen flashed with static.

Josie smiled. "Our electronics have been shielded against the Zodiac power. Your power is a little stronger than we expected, though."

Duane stared at the screen, trying to focus his mind. As they passed through the outer corridor, he reached out a finger. A small flash of Zodiac energy arced from his fingertip to Josie's wrist-device.

A holographic display flashed up from it, showing an image of four people. Duane recognized himself and

Roxanne, the girl in the hoodie. Two others stood with them, two people he didn't know: a short, stout young man in glasses, and another figure that flickered in and out of focus.

Josie frowned. "That's, uh, you don't need to see that yet." She clicked the display off. Then she steered him firmly through another hole, this one blasted through the outer stone wall, onto the bustling pier outside.

People were running around, pointing and shouting in the dim light. Alpha and Beta, the agents in suits, were directing the gunmen, instructing them to search behind buildings and inside boats.

A single blast rang out. Duane flinched.

"This way," Josie said. She led him around the side of the building, toward the pier.

Duane kept thinking about the holo-display. Sometimes his mind worked like that; even though he'd only seen the image for a moment, he couldn't get it out of his mind. As Josie peered around the side of the building, Duane aimed his finger at her wrist-device and fired off another small jolt of power.

Again, the image of the four people flashed up into the air. And this time, display lettering appeared over the four figures. Duane's was labeled PIG, and Roxanne's said ROOSTER in big letters. The man in glasses was RAM.

The last figure was fully visible now. It was a young blonde girl with wide eyes. Her display read RABBIT.

CHAPTER EIGHTEEN

Duane glanced over at Josie. She was creeping around the building, watching for trouble. She hadn't noticed the holo-image rising up from her arm, bobbing and twisting in the air as she moved.

Duane could *feel* the information flowing into him now. It was more intense than just hacking, or reading code. He sent off another jolt into Josie's wrist-gadget, and more lettering appeared. Above his own image, the label appeared: CONTACT MADE. Roxanne's and Ram's both read W/ENEMY. And Rabbit's said AT LARGE.

But the biggest display lettering of all hovered over the whole image now. It read: TARGETS.

"Targets?" Duane asked.

Josie whipped her head around, glaring at him.

Duane felt a stab of fear. Again, energy whipped out from him—a larger bolt this time. The holo-device sparked, flared, and caught fire. Its projected image flashed to static, then vanished.

Josie cried out. She scrabbled at the device, unsnapped it, and threw it, still flaming, to the ground. She clutched at her arm, grimacing in pain.

"Don't. Move," she said, her voice as hard as nails.

Duane pulled away. The fear grew inside him. Josie didn't want to help him; to her, he was just a *target*. He couldn't trust anyone—not the Vanguard agents, not anybody. He was alone, just as he'd always been.

He felt his last shred of control slipping away. The Pig

rose up and took him over, blasting up and outward. On the dark pier, he glowed like the sun.

Josie stared at him. The Horse power flashed up to surround her. But he barely noticed.

People fled in terror. The lights of the pier sparked and went out. Musicians hustled by, scurrying to get out of the area. One of them held an electronic keyboard, which exploded in his hands. He dropped it and ran.

The guards arrived, aiming their guns at Duane.

Beta, the woman in the suit, pushed her way through the panicking crowd. "Contingency Omega," she said, pointing at Duane. "Take him down!"

"No!" Josie said. "Maxwell wants him alive."

Beta stared at her, astonished. "Don't tell us what to do, freak!"

The power was too strong now. The Pig was loose. Duane's energy flare expanded outward, out and up, and all the lights went out on the pier. Then the next block inland went dark. And the next.

Up above, the Clock Tower's mechanism ground to a noisy halt. There was a heavy scraping noise, like stone on metal. Duane saw a quick movement above his head—

—and then the huge clock face crashed to the ground. It landed with the force of an earthquake, shaking the pier. Dust rose; shards of the pier flew into the air. People screamed and ran.

Duane coughed and shook his head. He waved away the dust and looked up. For a terrible moment he thought

Josie was dead, buried underneath the enormous, fallen chunk of the Clock Tower.

Killed by my power, he thought.

Then Josie came sprinting out of the dust. Her clothes were torn and covered with dirt, but she appeared to be unharmed.

"Duane," she called.

Alpha, the big male agent, ran up, his weapon drawn. He cast his eyes from Duane to Josie, then smirked.

"The great and powerful Zodiac," he said, shaking his head.

Beta pushed past him, followed by the armed guards. She pointed at Duane and Josie. "Secure them both. Whatever it takes."

"I don't know what Maxwell's been playing at with you weirdos," said Alpha. "But it's not working. Our mission is to take that kid in, and we're doing it. Without you." They pointed their weapons at Josie.

Josie shot forward, chucking Alpha through the hole in the Clock Tower wall. Before his body could hit the ground, she viciously kicked Beta in the arm holding the pistol, knocking the firearm to the ground. "If you bozos were in charge, we'd have another Lystria on our hands."

Josie whipped around, standing off against the rest of the agents. "I'm the one in charge here," she said, glaring at them. "You follow my orders, or you fly back like these two idiots." One of the agents cocked his gun, and she smiled. "Well, that's one way to do it . . ."

CHAPTER EIGHTEEN

Duane ran around the corner as the Vanguard started fighting each other, when suddenly, firm hands grabbed him, wrenching him around the side of the building. Duane looked up, shocked, and found himself staring at Roxanne.

"We got one chance to get out of here," she said. Behind her, Carlos nodded grimly.

"O-okay," Duane said.

With an enormous effort of will, he forced the Zodiac energy to recede. Then he started off away from the pier, toward the city. But Roxanne grabbed his arm. When he looked back at her, she was smiling. "I got a better plan," she said. And suddenly, Duane knew who to trust.

"She had a hologram, a three-dimensional image of you. And me, too. And two other people she called 'targets.'" Duane glanced nervously at Roxanne. "Is that what we are?"

She reached over and punched his shoulder. "I am no target," she said. "And neither are you."

Duane gave her a shy smile.

They sat crouched down on the lip of the Clock Tower roof, their backs against the stump of wood and stone left behind where the clock face had broken off. Below, police and emergency vehicles swarmed across the pier, emergency lights flashing in the night. The police had searched all around the Clock Tower, but Roxanne had been right: they hadn't thought to check the *top* of it.

"Wh-when can we leave?" Duane asked.

"Carlos is the boss." Roxanne pointed her thumb behind her. Carlos was perched a little higher on the roof, talking urgently into his phone. "But I think we better wait for things to cool out down there."

Duane glanced down at the pier. Josie and the Vanguard agents had fled, leaving the clock face sprawled on its side. Its hands were stuck at 12:48.

"Are you thinking about your power?" Roxanne asked.

He nodded.

"They are going to train me," she continued. "So I can control my power. That's what they say. I guess they can train you, too."

Carlos scooted forward, clicking off his phone. "Jasmine says she and Steven just got to the States," he said. "Hopefully they'll find the last recruit there."

"Rabbit," Duane said. "The blonde girl."

"That's right. She's a blonde girl." Carlos frowned. "How did you know that?"

Duane just smiled, a shy little smirk. Roxanne caught his eye, and smiled along with him.

CHAPTER EIGHTEEN

"Better get comfortable," Carlos continued. "We're gonna have to fly commercial out of South Africa. That means we have to wait till morning."

Duane opened his mouth to speak. "I, I, I—"

"Spit it out, man," Roxanne said.

"I don't think I can go with you," Duane said, all at once. "This is my home."

Roxanne cast her eyes out over the expanse of city, to the right of the pier. A dark city block flared back to life as its power was restored, then winked back off again.

"Hate to tell you this, man," Roxanne said, "but I don't think you have a home anymore. It is kind of broken."

"What's Lystria?" Duane asked.

"Your brain just jumps around like a frog, doesn't it?"

"Lystria," Carlos said slowly, "is a city that Maxwell, leader of the Vanguard company, destroyed. An entire population of people dead, just because—one time—they got in his way."

Carlos's voice was deeper, full of anger. Duane turned away, uncomfortable.

"Maxwell doesn't stop," Carlos continued. "Not before he had the Zodiac power, and certainly not now. If you stay here, he's going to come after you again."

"And next time," Roxanne said, "you might not have Doctor Science and a hot up-and-coming musician to help save your South African butt."

She grinned.

CHAPTER EIGHTEEN

Despite himself, Duane grinned back. He leaned back and closed his eyes for a moment. The night was cool, and he could hear the authorities below, already beginning the work of rebuilding the pier.

Duane leaned back and closed his eyes for a moment. In his mind's eye, he saw once again the dark pier, the Vanguard agents firing into the crowd, the people running for their lives. He felt the power rise up within him, unbound, uncontrollable, blazing out to wreak havoc for miles around. He flinched at the memory.

When he opened his eyes, Roxanne was staring at him with an understanding look.

"That gets better," she said.

He nodded and took a deep breath, letting the night air wash over him.

CHAPTER NINETEEN

MAXWELL'S EYES GLARED out of the holographic display. "So," he said, his voice perfectly even. "Another failure."

"Only because of those idiots you sent along with me." Josie's clothes were still in tatters from where the building had collapsed on her, but more than anything, she was annoyed. With herself, with the other agents, even with Maxwell himself.

Let Maxwell do what he wants to me, she thought. *I don't care anymore.*

"I tried," she said.

In the holo-display, Maxwell leaned back. He was still in Hong Kong, in his temporary office there. He'd had a few weapons brought in to decorate the walls, relics and souvenirs of places where the Vanguard company had fought its private, shadowy wars. A deadly AK-47 rifle stood mounted on a stand atop the desk in front of him. Maxwell ran his hand along the gun, staring at it thoughtfully.

"Did you learn anything at all?" he asked.

Josie cleared her throat. "I got some readings on the subject's Zodiac power. Pig's power, I mean." She paused. "The techs can use that to help us shield our equipment from it, better, in the future."

"Josie," he said, "you know you've always been one of my best agents."

She swallowed.

"If you were me," Maxwell continued, "what would you do?"

She swallowed again, opened her eyes. "Give me one more chance," she said. "I can be in America in five hours."

"No. I've already dispatched another agent to deal with that situation."

"Oh."

"Report back to me here. We'll talk then."

She knew the look on his face. When Maxwell's mind was made up, there was no arguing, no reasoning with him. He was like a force of nature, a storm blowing across the land.

She nodded.

Maxwell plucked the machine gun out of its stand. "Some of us are like bullets, Josie," he said. "And some of us are guns."

He stroked the gun again, as if it were a cat. Then he held it up and aimed, squinting through the site.

"And I," he added, "am the finger on the trigger."

Steven Lee stared at the dark, closed-down fast-food counter. The steam tables sat empty; the sign reading YUMMI NOODLES was dark. The big plastic panda over the cash register was missing one ear.

"So this is America," said Liam.

Steven shrugged. The big food court had clearly seen better days: Half the tables had been taken out, and all the counters on this side of the room were shut down. Some of the hanging lights were dark, and a few of them were missing bulbs.

On the other side of the court, a few burger and pizza vendors were still open for business. Clusters of ten- to thirteen-year-old kids sat at tables around them, gossiping and giggling.

"Elton, Indiana," Liam continued. "You grew up in a place like this, right mate?"

Steven frowned. He thought of his hometown, back in Pennsylvania. He remembered the mall where he used to hang out—where he'd seen so many superhero movies. That mall had a YUMMI NOODLES counter, too, and it was probably lit up and selling food right now. He felt suddenly homesick.

"It's not quite like this," Steven replied.

"Ah, right. The economic woes of the American Midwest." Liam nodded. "I read about it in *The Economist.*"

Steven studied the kids across the big room, trying not to make it look like he was staring.

"You think she's here?" Liam continued, reading his thoughts.

"I don't know," Steven replied. "But we've gotta find her."

"You will. You found me, right?"

Jasmine walked up, frowning. She moved awkwardly, studying a small electronic device in one hand while juggling a smelly fast-food box in the other.

Steven laughed. "The great and graceful Dragon," he said.

She shot him a deadly look. "I don't know how to work this overgrown remote." She shook the electronic device, and a couple of chicken nuggets flopped out of her box onto the floor.

Liam pointed at the fallen nuggets. "Do ye know what's *in* those things?"

Jasmine looked up, embarrassed. "I like 'em," she said.

Steven looked over her shoulder at the tracking device.

Its screen showed a rough schematic of the food court, with a winking, vibrating "Z" wobbling from side to side.

"Is that her?" he asked, pointing to the "Z".

"I think so. But I can't localize the EM reading well enough to tell if she's in the food court, or somewhere else in this mall."

"I don't think there's much else *open* in this mall," Liam said.

"I wish Carlos were here." Jasmine shook the device in the air, as if that would fix it. "Too bad we had to split up."

But Steven had stopped listening. His attention had been caught by a small girl, sitting alone at a table near the pizza counter. She was a year or two younger than Steven, waifish, and blond, in black leggings and a loose shirt. She sat hunched over a slice of pizza, wolfing it down as if she thought someone would come and take it away from her.

"That's her," Steven said. "I recognize her from her picture."

Jasmine looked over at the girl and nodded. She shook the electronic device again and then, with a snort of disgust, threw it into a trash can. Then she rushed over and fished it out again, hurriedly wiping spaghetti off of it.

"Carlos doesn't like me throwing out his toys," she explained. When she saw Steven's and Liam's amused expressions, she stuffed a few chicken nuggets in her mouth. "Shuff upf," Jasmine added.

Steven led the way over to the girl. When she spotted them, a look of panic crossed her face. She looked up and around, frantically. She seemed to be checking the exits.

"Don't be scared," Steven said quickly. "We're, uh. We're from . . . I mean, we're like . . . we're here because . . ."

The girl stared at him with big eyes.

He stopped, helpless, and turned to Jasmine. "How do I explain this?"

Jasmine thrust the box of nuggets against Steven's stomach. He grabbed them in surprise. They smelled awful.

"Kim," Jasmine said. "Your name is Kim Hansen, right?"

The girl said nothing. She didn't even move.

"Something's happened to you, hasn't it?" Jasmine continued. "A bright light flashed down out of the sky, and after that you just had this strange power. Right?"

Kim's eyes widened, just slightly.

Jasmine gestured around. "I'm Jasmine," she said. "This is Steven, and Liam. We're like you—we've all been given Zodiac powers. I kind of asked for them, but they didn't."

"They're kind of cool, though," Liam said, smiling. "My powers, I mean." He picked up a heavy plastic tray off the trash can and bashed himself over the head with it. The tray cracked in half, leaving no mark on his forehead. "See?"

Kim watched his every move. But still she made no sound.

"We want to help you," Steven said. "Thing is, there's

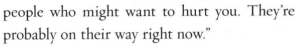

people who might want to hurt you. They're probably on their way right now."

He felt Jasmine's intense gaze, and immediately knew what she was thinking: *Big mistake. Don't scare her!*

Slowly, Kim rose to her feet. Her eyes still looked frightened. But when she spoke, her voice was more confident than Steven had expected.

"Nobody can catch me," she said.

Then she turned away, took a single step— and vanished with a soft *poof.*

Steven gasped. He stared at the empty air where the girl had been just a moment before. Beside him, Liam stood watching too, his mouth open in shock.

"Ah," Jasmine said. She brushed tomato sauce off of the Zodiac tracker device. "Did I mention we think she may be a teleporter?"

CHAPTER TWENTY

THE TRACKER WOULDN'T turn on again.
Steven and Jasmine laid it down on a food court table and unscrewed its cover. Steven grabbed a few plastic knives from a counter, and then the two of them spent five minutes scraping Russian dressing and something that looked like pepperoni out of its circuitry.

"Don't drop this in the trash again, okay?" Steven said.

Liam cleared his throat. "I'm not sayin' I've got second thoughts about joining up with you lot," he said, "but I think yer methods could use some fine-tuning."

"Carlos is the tech expert," Jasmine said. She held up a sizable chunk of meatball on the end of her knife, then tossed it aside.

Snapping the cover closed, she shook the device, and clicked a button. The screen flickered to life, showing a street map of Elton, Indiana. The familiar "Z," for Zodiac, winked on.

"Got her," Jasmine said.

The screen flashed static and died.

"Maybe," she added.

Fifteen minutes later, they stood in the small downtown section of Elton. Like the food court, it seemed to have fallen on hard times. An old market stood vacant. A handwritten sign on the barbershop said OPEN TUESDAYS ONLY.

The only businesses that seemed to be healthy were a convenience store and a bank. With their bright, modern signs, they looked like alien ships that had landed from another planet.

"She's here someplace," Jasmine said, shaking the tracker. Its screen flickered on and off.

Steven looked around. A few people hustled down the street, carrying prescriptions and grocery bags. The old buildings seemed to tilt a little to the side, weighed down with age.

Steven felt an odd sadness wash over him. This whole town seemed so . . . tired. *What would it be like to grow up here?* he wondered.

"Steven," Liam said quietly.

He looked up. Liam cocked his head toward the bank, a couple doors down. At the edge of the parking lot, the girl—Kim—sat perched on a fire hydrant, staring off into the distance.

"Hey," Steven called softly.

Kim turned sharply toward them. Her eyes were wide, haunted.

Then she leapt off the hydrant and went *poof.*

Steven shook his head. Liam looked down the street, searching for the girl. Jasmine shook the analyzer, trying to get its screen to stay on.

"This is gonna be a long day," she said.

They tracked Kim next to the high school, a thick building made of faded orange brick. It was Saturday, so no classes were in session. They slipped in through an unlocked door and started creeping down the hallway.

"There's usually a few janitors around on weekends," Steven whispered. "Watch out for them."

"Mate," Liam replied patiently, "we all went to high school."

They sneaked around the gymnasium, past a line of lockers with chipped paint. One of them had been bashed in. The few windows set into the walls were fogged and dirty.

Jasmine turned sharply, pointing. "What's that?"

Steven looked, just in time to see a large figure dart

past a junction in the corridor. He got a quick glimpse of yellow hair, and then the figure disappeared around a bend.

"What?" Jasmine asked. "Was that her?"

"I don't think so." Steven frowned. "It looked bigger."

Then they rounded a bend, and there was Kim. She stood before a door labeled BAND ROOM, trying to jimmy the lock open with a pin. She turned, startled.

"Okay," Steven said, holding out a hand. "Just listen. HeyjustlistenwhateveryoudoDON'TGOPOOF—"

Poof.

Liam shook his head. "Gone again."

But Jasmine turned sharply to look behind them. "Who's that?"

Steven whirled around. Again, he caught a glimpse of the yellow-haired figure, dashing out of sight around a corner.

The three of them took off after it. They ran around a corner, then another, and a third. "This place is like a hedge maze," Liam said. "Guess that makes sense for a rabbit."

"Either of you get a good look?" Jasmine asked.

"I think it was a guy," Steven said. "And he had a lot of hair—"

They rounded a final bend and nearly collided with a heavyset man standing in the middle of the hall. The man wore a gray jumpsuit, held a mop and pail, and had a huge, unruly black beard exploding from his chin and cheeks.

"You're not s'posed to be here," he said.

Steven grimaced. "I told you. Janitors."

Jasmine frowned. "Is that him? The man we were chasing?"

Liam cocked his head, examining the janitor. "He doesn't look like he can run very fast."

"Maybe not." The man shook his mop threateningly. "But I know how to use this."

Steven watched Liam carefully for a moment, suddenly worried. He knew Jasmine was thinking the same thing he was: *Liam likes to fight.*

But Liam just smiled. "No need for violence, mate." He took a step back, holding up his hands, an amused look on his face. "We just stopped in to pick up me, uh, math book. From me locker, you know. On our way out now."

Kim's next stop was a public park, a few miles away. The park was quiet, with just a few couples sitting together at benches. Jasmine motioned to Liam and Steven, and together they crouched behind a low hill.

"I think she's over there," Jasmine whispered, pointing over unmown grass to the far side of the hill. "But we can't just walk up to her. She'll teleport away again."

"She's fast, all right," Liam agreed.

Steven crept up to the top of the hill, flattening down on his stomach in the grass. On the other side, a few feet below, he could see a playground, its new-looking furnishings already overgrown with weeds. Kim sat on a plastic cartoon snail anchored to the ground by a thick metal spring. She was rocking back and forth, and she hadn't noticed them yet.

Steven shinnied backward down the hill to rejoin Liam and Jasmine.

"I've got an idea," he whispered. "I don't think this girl can just *poof* away when she's standing, or sitting down. Every time she's done it, she's been running or jumping."

Jasmine frowned at the tracker, then shrugged. "Could be. That would fit with the Rabbit."

Liam frowned. "So what are you saying, mate? We need to grab her or something?" He shook his head. "I don't like the idea of attacking a little girl."

"We just need to get her to listen for a minute," Steven replied. "Follow me."

He took off at a run, bounding over the hill. Jasmine shrugged and followed, with Liam bringing up the rear.

Then someone, or some*thing*, howled out loud. Steven turned—just in time to see a mass of fur slam into Liam from behind, knocking him to the ground.

Zodiac energy billowed out from Liam, forming the charging, horned Ram. He rolled along the ground, grappling with his assailant, and began to tumble down the hill toward the playground equipment.

Jasmine stopped, frowning at the tracker. "Unless this thing has too much tomato sauce in it," she said, "that's *another* Zodiac agent."

Liam and his attacker rolled down into the playground, moving toward a jungle gym. Steven still couldn't get a good look at the hairy man, but he watched as the man twisted around so Liam took the brunt of the impact.

Two people leapt up from a nearby bench. They took one look at the grappling duo and ran off.

Liam lay still on the ground about fifteen feet away. The hairy man stood up, towering over his body, and howled again.

Steven stared in shock. The man wasn't just hairy— every inch of his body was covered with fur. Sharp, wolfish ears jutted up from the top of his head, and his bare feet were four times the size of a normal man's. Both his hands and his feet were curled and ended in sharp, animal-like claws.

"What—" Steven paused. "Who is that?"

"At a guess?" Jasmine tapped at the analyzer. "I think it's Dog. Another of Maxwell's newly powered operatives."

"But he's so . . . so . . ." Steven held out his arms. "Tigers are hairy. Am *I* gonna grow fur, too?"

Jasmine stared at him. "*That's* what you're worried about right now?"

The hairy man—Dog—turned toward Steven. His lip curled into a cruel smile, and he let out a low, threatening growl.

Steven had a vision of Dog chasing after the girl, of leaping toward her and whisking her away to safety. "No," Steven said, returning to reality. "Maybe later."

Steven concentrated, allowing the Tiger power to rise up and around him. A halo of energy surrounded him. He turned to face Dog, and felt the Tiger rise to the challenge. Without meaning to, Steven growled in response.

Then he noticed the girl—Kim—standing nearby. Her eyes flashed from Dog to Steven, watching their faceoff. Dog turned toward her, and a hungry smile crossed his face.

Steven felt the ground shake a little. Liam was back on his feet, leaning his head down like a bull and charging toward Dog from behind. Dog had underestimated Liam, Steven realized. A normal person would have been out cold after slamming that hard into the jungle gym—but nothing could harm Liam.

Steven and Liam tackled Dog at the same time from different sides. Liam's head-butt struck Dog in the small of his back just as Steven grabbed the hairy agent's neck, yanking him off his feet.

For a moment, Dog flailed in Steven's grip. Then he jumped up, recovered his balance, and let out another howl. His thick paw reached out and swiped Steven's stomach, knocking him away.

Steven reeled, and the Tiger cried out. He

managed to stop his fall, reaching behind with one hand to touch the ground, and sprang back up again. Dog was raining down blows on Liam—who just stood still, smiling, his arms folded in front of him.

"Keep it up, mate," Liam said. "Tire yourself out. You remind me of my Uncle William. Once he got an idea in his head, he'd never let it go. Once somebody told him tomatoes were really evil spirits, and he sat out in the garden five days straight waiting for 'em to show their true nature."

Steven frowned. Liam told a lot of stories, and some of them sounded pretty doubtful.

The girl hadn't *poofed* away this time, Steven noticed. She just stood at the edge of the playground, watching. Taking it all in.

Steven rushed forward and grabbed Dog again. They grappled, and Steven felt the Zodiac energy ebb and flow, sizzling through the air. His Tiger-form roared and snarled, trading blows with its enemy—

"Dog," Jasmine said.

Steven, Dog, and Liam all froze as a blinding light washed over them. Slowly, as if with one mind, they turned toward the hill.

Jasmine hovered in the air, glowing with power. The hissing form of her Dragon whipped and swirled around her, swiping the air with sharp talons. It lit up the cloudy sky, glowing with unimaginable power.

Jasmine stared straight at Dog with glowing eyes. "Think you can chase the Dragon?" she asked.

Dog struggled in Steven's and Liam's grip. He looked from them over to Jasmine, and then toward the edge of the playground, at Kim. As Dog sniffed the air, that hungry look came over him again.

"*Rrrrrraaaaaaabit,*" he said.

Then he lashed out, kicking and swiping. Startled, Steven lost his grip, tumbling to the ground. Liam fell, too, and Dog took off at a run. He bounded over the hill, incredibly fast, and disappeared into the trees beyond.

Jasmine dropped softly to the ground, her power fading around her. "Pretty soon, they're gonna stop scaring so easily," she said.

Steven shook his head, dazed. The Tiger power was beginning to fade, too. He stumbled over to Jasmine and said, "Can you track him?"

She picked up the tracker—or what was left of it. Its guts were exposed, the circuitry smashed. A single puff of smoke hissed out of it.

"I think he trampled it on his way out," she said sadly.

Liam stood up calmly, dusting himself off. "Like I said: needs some fine-tuning." He looked completely unfazed, as if he'd just woken up and taken a stroll outside.

"Hey," Steven said. "Where's . . ."

But even as he spoke, he knew the answer to his question. Kim was gone again—along with the remaining locals, who'd fled from the odd sight of superpowered combat in their quiet, rundown park.

"Didn't even see her go *poof* that time," Liam said, arching an eyebrow.

Steven clenched his fists in frustration. "We're *never* gonna get her to sit still."

Jasmine walked up and laid a hand on his shoulder. There was a thoughtful look in her eyes.

"Maybe we need a new strategy," she said.

CHAPTER TWENTY-ONE

"WE DON'T KNOW where she is," Kim's mother said. "We don't usually know."

Her husband coughed.

Feeling uncomfortable, Steven shifted on the creaky armchair. A bit of stuffing puffed out into the air.

Kim's parents sat together on their couch, staring at a small TV. Like everything else in the house, the TV was about ten to fifteen years old. The coffee table was littered with soda and beer cans.

Kim's mother looked over at Steven. "Do *you* know where Kimmy might be?" she asked.

Jasmine scuttled her folding chair up next to Steven's, and held up the broken tracker. "Not anymore," she said.

Steven glanced out the window. Night was just beginning to fall. Jasmine had already called back to head-quarters, to Carlos, who had returned there with the newly recruited Pig. Carlos had consulted his own, more power-ful Zodiac sensing equipment, and confirmed Jasmine's hunch: Dog was no longer in the Elton area.

Steven turned back to Kim's parents, who were both engrossed in the muted TV program again. "I've seen this episode before," Mr. Hansen said. "It's funny."

"You, uh, you used to work at the eraser factory, right, Mrs. Hansen?" he asked.

"That was him." Kim's mother jabbed an elbow at her husband.

Mr. Hansen coughed again. "Too much rubber in the lungs," he said.

"Where are my manners?" Mrs. Hansen said. "Can I get you people anything?"

Steven looked at the cans on the coffee table. "How about some water?"

Without looking up, Mr. Hansen tossed him a can of cola.

Jasmine frowned. "Mrs. Hansen," she said, "have you noticed anything . . . odd about your daughter lately? Any strange, uh, abilities or behavior?"

"I told you, we don't see her much anymore." A flicker of fear crossed Mrs. Hansen's face. "Is she into drugs?"

"No, ma'am," Jasmine replied. "I'm pretty sure she's not into drugs."

"She's scared," Mr. Hansen said. "She's always been scared of everything."

"We love her," Mrs. Hansen said. "But the truth is . . . well, there's nothing for her here. You've seen this town; it's dying."

Suddenly Steven felt an irresistible urge to flee. Kim's parents were right: This place was just so *sad*. He understood, now, how Kim felt—why she kept running away, bolting and jumping and *poofing* off into thin air.

He thought back to the places where they'd seen Kim: the mall, the town center, the school, the public park. Where could she be now? Where would a girl like that go?

Liam walked into the room, followed by the sound of a toilet flushing. "I dunno where the girl is," he said, as if reading Steven's mind. "But I think we oughta get her out of here."

"I've got an idea," Steven said softly.

"Hey," Mrs. Hansen said. Something in her voice made Steven turn sharply toward her.

"Yes, Mrs. Hansen?" he asked.

"If you do find Kim," Mrs. Hansen continued. "Just tell her . . . I mean . . ."

"Tell her we're sorry," Mr. Hansen said, looking away. "Sorry we couldn't give her a better life."

Mrs. Hansen stared at Steven with pained eyes, then nodded.

When he turned away, the two of them had turned back to the TV. They laughed softly at something, their hands gently touching each other's knees.

"So that's it," Liam said. "We're goin' after her, right?"

Jasmine looked around at the house for a long, uncomfortable moment. When she turned to Steven, her eyes were very serious.

"No," she said. "Not 'we.'"

By the time Steven got back to the mall, it was just closing for the night. He hid beside an escalator and waited until the lights went out. After the security guard walked past, he leapt, Tiger-like, up the stairs to the food court.

There she is, he thought. *Just like I thought.*

Kim sat alone at a table in the dark, gobbling down a slice of pizza. She ate quickly, looking around furtively between bites. She looked almost exactly the way she had when he'd first seen her, except this time the pizza was probably stolen.

"I knew you'd be here," he said softly. "You've gotta eat, right?"

She whirled around, but before she could vanish, he held up a hand. "Don't!" he said, keeping his voice low. "It's just me—nobody else. Promise."

He took a step forward, then stopped. They stared at each other for a moment, separated by twelve feet of empty mall.

"You're glowing," she said.

Steven looked around in surprise. Without realizing it, he'd let the Tiger out. He concentrated, willing the Zodiac energy to fade.

"I want to tell you something," Steven said. "When I was, uh, when I was five, I asked my father for a Lego set. It was a really nice one, tied in to the first Steel Mongoose movie. It had his headquarters, his beach house, even his high-tech base on the moon.

"My parents, they have their own company—they make a lot of money. Even back then, I knew they could afford the Lego set. But my dad just stared at me like I was a beggar on the street. I'll never forget what he said: 'When you earn it.'"

Kim watched him carefully. She didn't look convinced, but she didn't quite look like she was going to *poof* away anymore, either.

"You've got other problems," he continued. "So do Jasmine and Liam, the people I came here with. There's others, too—this girl called Roxanne. She's, uh, something.

"The thing is: We've all got this ancient energy inside us. It's called the Zodiac, and for some reason, it chose *us* to wield its power. It comes from these pools of liquid in Hong Kong—there was a whole ritual there, and everything blew up. I've been traveling around with Jasmine ever since, recruiting people like you."

Suddenly Kim ducked down under her table. Steven looked around, heard the guard's footsteps, and flattened himself against a column. The guard's flashlight played against the floor, and for a moment it seemed as if he was going to spot them. But he just shrugged and walked off again.

Kim stood up. She took a bite of pizza and flashed Steven a quick, playful smile.

Steven cocked his head at her. "Your parents said you were scared of everything," he said. "But that's not really it, is it?"

She didn't answer.

"You're just good at running away," he finished.

"There's a lot of things to run away from," she said quietly.

"More than you know." Steven sighed. "That big hairy guy, today? He was after *you*, not us. He works for a guy named Maxwell, who's very, very bad news. Maxwell set up the whole Zodiac powers thing, and I guess he's got a whole bunch of Zodiac agents working for him now."

"Dog," Kim said, thoughtfully. "He's a Dog, from the Chinese Zodiac. And I'm a Rabbit?"

"*The* Rabbit," Steven said.

She studied him for a moment. "You must be the Tiger."

"The big glowing cat over my head, before. Did that give me away?"

A smile tickled at the corner of her lips. Then she turned serious again. "So you're saying I should go with you before this Maxwell dude comes after me again?"

"That's one reason. Jasmine and Carlos—you haven't met him yet, but he's this really smart genius guy—they can also train you, teach you how to use your power. And frankly . . . no offense, but . . ." He gestured around. ". . . it doesn't look like you've got a lot to stay here for."

Kim's pizza was just a piece of crust now. She stared at it, thinking.

"The Zodiacs . . . we're all really different from each other," Steven continued. "But we've got stuff in common, too." He ticked off the members on his fingers. "Roxanne—Rooster—she needs training in her powers. Liam needed a change, to get away from his town, like I think you do too.

"As for me . . ." He paused. "I know what it's like when you can't relate to your parents."

Steven looked down for a long moment, thinking about his mother and father. He thought of his grandfather, who'd raised him most of the time. The old man's funeral was probably happening right now. He wiped away a tear, hoping Kim hadn't seen.

When he looked up, she was studying him again with that strange half-smile.

"Did you rehearse that speech?" she asked. "Before you came here?"

"Um," he said.

"How'd it come out? How would you say you did?"

"Pretty good. About eighty, maybe eight-five percent the way I planned." He smiled sheepishly. "Better than usual, for me."

"I'm in." Kim swallowed the last of the pizza crust, then tossed away the plate. "Meet you outside?"

"Great! But, uh . . ." He hesitated. "Did you pay for that pizza?"

She smiled.

Steven heard the guard's footsteps again, and turned to warn Kim. She just lunged away and disappeared with a *poof.*

Steven sighed. He reached into his wallet and pulled out a few bills—then stared at them in dismay. *I haven't used my wallet since I got the Zodiac power in Hong Kong,* he realized. *Jasmine's been paying for everything!*

Steven shrugged and threw some bills down on the table. *Hope they can exchange Chinese money.*

Suddenly he laughed. He felt lighter, he realized, as if a weight had been lifted from him. A wave of excitement washed over him. It took him a moment to figure out the reason:

We've got a team now. A real team.

The guard's footsteps grew louder.

Quick as a cat, Steven ran outside to meet up with his new teammate.

CHAPTER TWENTY-TWO

MAXWELL SPREAD his arms, thrilling to the sudden release of Zodiac power. Even with his eyes closed, he could sense the Dragon form rising, snarling and raging and hissing fire. Its wings stretched wide, growing vast and thin, reaching out invisibly to blanket the entire world.

Now came the crucial part. Maxwell had studied the Zodiac power, learned the ways it flowed and changed. He was not a scientist; he would never understand the ley lines, the electromagnetic flows that made up the power. But he could see it, locate it, track it across time and space.

He forced all distractions out of his mind. *There is no world,* he thought. *There is no self. There is only the qi—the flow, the life force, the vital energy of the Zodiac. That force has leaked out around the world, infused people who were never meant to host it. But none of them can hide from my eyes.*

The eyes of the Dragon.

Maxwell saw the Earth as a pulsing globe, networked with veins across and beneath its surface. Deep in his trance, Maxwell could see them all. All the Zodiacs: his own agents, Horse and Dog and Monkey and Ox, and also Rat and Snake, the hidden stealth agents. He saw Jasmine's group, too: Ram, Rooster, Pig, Rabbit, and, of course, Tiger. They pulsed like lights, like glowing nodes along the ley lines.

But Maxwell wasn't interested in any of them. He was looking for one light, and one only. The Dragon—the *other* Dragon. The pretender to his power.

Where are you, Jasmine?

Plunging deeper into the world-globe, he turned his attention to France. Josie—Horse—had tracked Jasmine there, less than forty-eight hours ago. Maxwell caught sight of Jasmine's qi, and smiled. Now he could see its trail, shining brighter than all the others.

He unfurled his vast energy-wings, reaching out to snare Jasmine. But he knew she'd already moved on. This was the recent past he was seeing, the wake left behind by her passage through the world.

Maxwell dove into the ley lines, wings beating,

churning against the ethereal tide. Following Jasmine's qi.

The trail led to Ireland. Again, Maxwell reached out— and again, she slipped from his grasp. He followed her, in a flash of light, to America, then watched as she dove back into the current once more.

Maxwell smiled. This time, he knew where she was going. And this time—

A clattering of chairs. A clearing of throats. The sound of many heartbeats, surrounding him.

Maxwell opened his eyes. The trance was broken.

"Boss," Dog said. "You wanted to see us?"

Maxwell blinked, looking around. This small chamber where he'd transferred the Zodiac power to his agents had been nearly stripped of its equipment. The two technicians fluttered around in the background, pulling out plugs and lugging computers away.

Maxwell's four assault-team agents stood at attention, facing him where he sat at the head of an old oak table. He cast his eyes across them, one at a time.

Malik, the agent called Ox, was a strong, muscular bald man with thick muscles and a neatly trimmed beard. He'd always been calm in a crisis, and the Zodiac had given him an incredible reserve of physical strength. That would come in handy, Maxwell knew, in the days ahead.

Dog had reverted to his less furry, human form, with only a normal shock of blond hair atop his fresh face. He bore some bruises from his recent battle in Indiana, but he stood at attention, ready for orders.

Monkey—a tall, hunched man with unnaturally long arms—was a problem. He was already fidgeting, looking bored, popping little candies into his mouth with his elongated, prehensile fingers.

And lastly: Horse. Josie stood completely still, the perfect soldier. Her jaw was clenched tightly as she stared at him, her face utterly composed. But Maxwell knew: *She's terrified. Twice now, she's failed me. She thinks she knows what's coming. She thinks she knows.*

"Well," Maxwell said. "We've gotten off to a rocky start, haven't we?"

"Jasmine and Carlos have outmaneuvered us," he said. "They now have all four of the lost powers. That's a problem, one we'll have to deal with.

"But."

He paused dramatically. Ox cocked his head, expectant. Monkey belched.

"I want you to remember three things," Maxwell continued. "First: Jasmine's recruits are no match for you in combat. You were all trained assault and infiltration operatives long before you had Zodiac powers. They're just children.

"Second: by assembling the new recruits in one place, Jasmine may actually have done us a favor.

"And finally: the Zodiac power is new to all of us. We only learn by making mistakes."

He pointed a finger at Josie, and this time she flinched visibly. That made him smile.

"Josie," he said. "Horse. You were right. Putting you in

the field with a normal, non-powered team was a mistake. Your methods are too different from theirs. Neither of you could operate effectively."

She looked up at him, confused.

"I'm promoting you to field leader," he continued. "I want you to take a new team—*this* team—to Jasmine's headquarters in Greenland. I want you to work together, using all your powers, and bring their operation to its knees. But most of all, I want you to *gather up the rest of the Zodiacs and bring them to me.*"

Josie blinked. She nodded, stunned.

"You were right," he repeated. "The Zodiacs should work together. Let's make it happen."

"Yes, sir." She saluted. "Th-thank you, sir."

"Don't thank me, Josie." He stared at her, his eyes steely. "I don't choose tactics based on reward—or on punishment, either. This is a calculated, rational decision."

She nodded sharply. Then she motioned to the others and started leading them toward the exit. When they reached the door, she stopped.

"Sir?" she said. "You're absolutely right—we can handle the recruits. But what about Jasmine?"

Maxwell closed his eyes, visualizing once again the worldwide network of Zodiac energy.

"Leave her to me," he said softly.

Quietly, as if from a long way off, he heard the agents' footfalls as they hurried out of the room. He smiled, savoring the peace and quiet.

Then a crude grunting noise shattered the silence. Maxwell opened his eyes, annoyed. He turned to see the two techs, Maria and Fedor, struggling to unhook a jammed cable from one of the last pieces of computer equipment in the room.

"Get. *Out*," he said.

They turned terrified eyes toward him, then fled.

Finally Maxwell was alone. *Soon,* he thought, *soon I'll be back home, in Australia.* He had real scientists there, brilliant minds working full time on the Zodiac project. Not these idiots he'd brought along to Hong Kong.

A flash of rage passed through him. *I didn't think I needed scientists for the Convergence. I thought I had Carlos.*

Maxwell closed his eyes again, and again he saw Jasmine's spoor. Her trail, the stolen Dragon energy, racing across the world. He followed its path through America, then out over the Atlantic Ocean, angling up to its destination in Greenland.

Again he felt the rage. *The Dragon is mine,* he thought. *No pretender, no traitorous little girl, will take it from me.*

"This is calculated," he said aloud. "This is rational."

He reached out with his terrible bat-wings. The other Dragon, Jasmine's snakelike avatar, flinched away at its touch. But he grabbed hold and held on tight, drinking in its fear and helplessness.

Then he began to feed.

PART THREE

THE SIEGE

CHAPTER TWENTY-THREE

"WELCOME TO GREENLAND," Jasmine

said, holding up four heavy coats.

They'd landed at a small coastal airfield. Now they stood outside on a bare, almost deserted runway. The air was very cold, and the ground beyond the airport looked rocky. Steven could see snowy mountains in the distance.

"Ah, Greenland!" Liam said, as if he were just now recognizing the name. "Where it's always cold as a witch's—"

"—pointy hat," Kim finished.

Liam looked at her, surprised. Kim flashed him a quick, mischievous smile, and he grinned back.

"Let's go, comedians," Jasmine said.

She led them across the airfield to a battered, rugged Humvee with oversized tires. Kim and Liam climbed into the backseat, and Steven took shotgun, next to Jasmine. He barely had time to strap in before she slammed the gas pedal to the floor.

As they drove inland, the roads changed from tar to dirt to snow. The Humvee swerved and slipped a few times, but Jasmine kept it on the road. The mountains loomed closer, and a nasty pattern of dark clouds seemed to be gathering above it.

"Is there a storm coming?" Steven asked.

"Probably," Jasmine replied. "We get a lot of them out here."

Steven wondered how far they were going. He turned around to say something to Kim; he could barely admit it, but he thought she was cute. When he looked at her, she was staring out the window in openmouthed wonder.

Suddenly Steven couldn't think of anything to say.

Finally Jasmine yelled out: "Last stop!"

Steven peered ahead. Just before the mountains, a low plateau rose up, about the size of a city block but rounded and uneven in shape. It was three stories high, covered with ice and snow. It looked like a completely natural artifact.

Steven turned to Jasmine, baffled. "This is the last stop?"

Jasmine steered the Humvee straight toward the icy face of the plateau. Then, grinning, she pressed down hard on the accelerator. As the snowy rock-wall drew closer, Steven gripped his seat in panic.

Just in time, an opening appeared in the side of the rock. It swiveled upward like a garage door, forming an entrance big enough to drive a bus through. As they drove through the dark entrance, the bottom of the garage door slid up. The roof of the Humvee just made it underneath the ceiling. Steven flinched.

Jasmine laughed and pressed down twice on the horn. "Is, uh, is that some secret signal?" Steven asked.

"Nah," she replied. "I just like doing it."

She swung the vehicle around to the left, cutting the headlights. Stage lights clicked on above, revealing a high-ceilinged garage area. The door swung shut again, leaving barely a seam in the wall.

Steven stared around at a variety of vehicles, all designed for difficult terrains: pickup trucks, construction equipment, jeeps—even a dump truck. The room smelled like gasoline.

As Jasmine turned off the engine, a large woman in an oil-smeared jumpsuit ran up to greet them. "Long trip," the woman said.

Jasmine smiled. "Hey, Mags. We brought the Humvee home in one piece."

The woman frowned, running her eyes across the dirty vehicle. "I'll be the judge of that."

Kim crept out of the backseat, looking around the room

warily. Liam followed, shaking his head and grimacing.

"After that ride, I'm *really* glad I'm indestructible," he said.

"See you picked up some hitchhikers," Mags said to Jasmine.

Jasmine smiled. "You wouldn't believe what we picked up."

As they climbed out of the Humvee, Jasmine held up her arms. Energy flared all along her body, rising to form the now-familiar sparkling Dragon shape. The Dragon turned ethereal eyes toward Mags, who raised an eyebrow but didn't flinch.

"Seen it," Mags said. "Your other two power-kids are already here. Still, nice makeover."

"Sorry." Jasmine let the energy fade. "Can't resist showing it off."

Mags shook her head at the Humvee. "This thing is filthy. I'll have to wash it and change the oil. Mind getting out of my way?"

"Come on, kids," Jasmine said. "Let's go. We'll get you settled."

Steven hesitated. *Settled?* he thought. *I don't even know what that means anymore.*

"Nobody argues with Jasmine, kid," Mags said. "You better do what she says."

Steven cocked his head. "She's tough, huh?"

Mags smiled then, and elbowed Jasmine in the ribs. "I've seen tougher."

Jasmine laughed.

Steven looked from one of them to the other. Then he locked eyes for a moment with Kim, who nodded to him, and then Liam. They were all thinking the same thing: the people here regarded Jasmine not just as a boss—or a Dragon—but as a friend. Whatever else might happen, whatever dangers lay in their future, that was a good sign.

So, as Mags started hosing down the dirty jeep, Steven let Jasmine lead him and the others deeper into the rocky compound.

First she took them to a small galley, where a Russian woman brought out soup and sandwiches. Steven wolfed the food down; he hadn't realized how hungry he was. Kim ate two servings, and Liam had three.

Then Jasmine gave them a brief tour. They passed by a library, a small screening room furnished with old car seats, and an indoor tennis court with a half-collapsed net. Everything seemed cheaply constructed, hastily thrown together.

"We don't have anywhere near as many resources as Maxwell," Jasmine said, leading him down a narrow hallway. "But we make do."

Steven peered through a small glass window set into a door. Inside, a couple of women dressed in fatigues practiced their shooting on a cramped firing range.

"How many people do you have here?" he asked.

"Between fifteen and twenty-five. It changes all the

time. Some of them live here all the time, while others come and go."

"And those people do . . . what?" Steven asked. "Plan to stop Maxwell?"

"Among other things," Jasmine replied. "Carlos also has some research projects going. We shelter refugees, too—people with nowhere else to go."

"Where is Carlos, anyway?" Liam asked. "I miss that twitchy genius fella."

"We'll get to him soon. First, let me show you where you'll be training."

The training room looked like an old gymnasium. It stretched up two stories high, its white floor dotted with exercise mats. Jasmine led the group across the floor to the far side, past punching bags with stuffing leaking out of them.

Steven smiled at the sight of a frayed climbing rope, hanging loose from the ceiling. "Where'd you get this stuff?" he asked. "They tear down a playground next door?"

"Like I said, we make do." Jasmine glared at him, pretending to be annoyed. "Nobody likes a smart-mouth Tiger, you know."

Up ahead, a workout was in progress. Roxanne hung gracefully from a jungle gym, swinging herself along from bar to bar. When she reached the end, she jumped down to land in a perfect crouch. Then she raised her arms, calling out in triumph to an imaginary audience.

"Thank you!" Roxanne cried. "*Les Poules, yeeahhhh!*"

Kim leaned over to whisper to Steven. "Who's Less Pools?"

"It's her band," he replied.

Kim frowned. "Does she know they're not here?"

Roxanne ran a hand across her forehead, wiping off the sweat. "Yo, Tiger!" she called. "You done rounding up all the strays?"

Jasmine stepped forward, gesturing. "Roxanne, this is Liam. He's our Ram. And Kim, the Rabbit."

"Hey, girl." Roxanne leaned down to smirk at Kim. "Let me do your hair later, okay?"

Kim peered at her suspiciously.

Roxanne whirled around. "Duane! What else you got for me?"

A tall young man with dreadlocks stood at a freestanding computer display jutting up from the floor behind the jungle gym. He stared at the screen, his eyes moving swiftly back and forth across its surface.

"That's Duane," Roxanne said. "He does not talk much."

Steven studied Duane for a moment. *The last member of the team,* Steven thought. Carlos had warned them that Duane could be very reserved at times. How would he fit in with the others in a combat situation?

A quick smile flickered across Duane's face. He reached out and touched an icon on the screen.

The jungle gym let out a low whirring noise and began to drop down into the floor. When it was all the way down, the floor panel snapped into place above it.

"Better back up," Jasmine said, ushering Steven, Liam, and Kim away. "Let Roxanne finish her session."

Suddenly a small metal cage dropped from the ceiling. It descended straight down, enclosing Roxanne within its bars.

Roxanne looked panicked. She opened her mouth and let out a sharp, loud sonic cry. But it flew wide, diffusing in the air. The bars of the cage rattled noisily, but remained sealed tight.

"Rooster! Remember what we talked about," Jasmine called out. "Pinpoint control."

Roxanne nodded. She furrowed her brow in concentration and fixed her eyes on a single point, then cried out again. This time, the sonic energy struck in one spot. The cage rattled noisily, and a large segment snapped apart.

Roxanne walked out, nodding proudly. "That all you got?" she asked, turning toward Duane.

Duane looked up from his work, just once. Then he returned his gaze to the control screen, his lips moving silently as he tapped out another command.

Two thick metal poles sprouted from the floor. Their tips slid open to reveal Tasers, crackling with electric power.

Liam grimaced. "Got zapped with one of those things a few years back on a dare. It's not what ye call fun."

"They're low power, for training purposes only,"

Jasmine said. "For training purposes only. Though we've juiced 'em up a little bit for Zodiac-power practice."

Both Tasers fired at once, shooting toward Roxanne on thin wires. She watched them come, then let out a quick sonic burst, and another. The Tasers sparked and stopped short in midair, then fell to the ground.

Roxanne smiled, casting her gaze across the spectators. "That is how it's done," she said.

"You'll all be 'doing' here," Jasmine said, turning back to Steven, Kim, and Liam. "Training, I mean. The course is different every time, and we're building new equipment to test each of your abilities."

"Duane, we're through, right?" Roxanne called. "Duane?"

Duane nodded absently. But he kept pecking away at the screen.

Jasmine laughed. "Come on—let's leave these two to their fun. I'll show you the labs."

Steven followed her out of the room, along with Liam and Kim. When he glanced back, Roxanne was under assault from a paintball cannon that had appeared out of the wall. She whipped her head around, blasting two paintballs in midair. But a third one struck her in the stomach, spattering paint across her clothes.

As Steven turned away, he caught a glimpse of Duane's smiling face. Then he heard Roxanne's cry:

"Duane!"

CARLOS'S LAB WAS HUGE. It took up
more than half of the complex's top floor, a sprawling
maze of cubicles, sinks, and private rooms with warning
signs on their doors. Men and women in lab coats sat at
desks, studying computers and bound notebooks full of
notes.

Jasmine gestured at a large open area, where a few scientists stood around something that looked like a large,
humming incubator. "Toys," she said.

As Steven and the others watched, a door labeled CARLOS'S PRIVATE LAB—KEEP OUT! swung open. Carlos strode out, speaking intensely to a dark-skinned man in a lab coat.

"See?" Carlos said, pointing at a tablet computer in the man's hand. "What do you make of that?"

The man frowned. "It could be an atmospheric disturbance. We are due for a storm."

"That's true." But Carlos didn't sound convinced.

He looked up and smiled quickly at Jasmine. He started toward her, tossing something green and metallic from one hand to the other. "Ram, Rabbit, Tiger . . . Dragon," Carlos said, counting off. "Looks like you got all of them."

"*We* got all of them. Nice work in Cape Town."

Kim pointed at the object in Carlos's hand. "What's that?"

Carlos looked at the metallic object as if he'd forgotten he was holding it. "Oh, this? It's a hypo with a strong neurotoxin in it. I just perfected it—might come in handy."

Liam's eyebrows shot up. "A strong—"

"—neurotoxin," Jasmine finished.

Carlos held up the object. It had a sharp metal tip, and its body was clear glass filled with bright green fluid.

Jasmine looked at him as if he were a child. "Put it away, please?" she asked.

Carlos shrugged. He stashed the hypo in his pocket.

"Safety first." Jasmine smiled indulgently. "So what have you boys been up to?"

"Tracking anomalous energy patterns. Show them, Dafari."

The other man—Dafari—held up his tablet computer. On the screen, Steven saw a map of a snowy landscape, with a few red icons winking on and off.

"Does that look like Zodiac energy to you?" Carlos asked.

Jasmine gave an exaggerated shrug. "It could be Tetris for all I know." She gestured at the man in the coat. "Steven, Liam, Kim: this is Dafari. He's one of the finest hackers in the world."

"That is what they say." Dafari smiled, a bit embarrassed. "Jasmine, I have much to tell you about. We have traced many of Maxwell's financial holdings, and identified some key weaknesses in his security systems. If you should wish to launch an assault on his headquarters, I may be able to get you inside."

"I think we're a long way from that," Jasmine said.

Dafari looked disappointed. "Nevertheless, I have accumulated a great deal of information on the Australian outback—"

"Australia?" Steven asked. "I thought Maxwell was based in Hong Kong."

"No, that's just where the Zodiac pools were located," Jasmine said. "Maxwell's headquarters is a former military base in Australia. It's very difficult to approach by land or air."

"He has high-technology devices," Dafari said. "Many more than we have."

"Dafari's entire family was killed in one of Maxwell's private wars," Jasmine explained.

"Ah," Liam said. "Sorry, mate."

"Yeah," Kim added. "Sorry."

"It is true," Dafari said. For just a moment, anger flashed across his dark face. Then it was gone again, and he smiled broadly. "But I do not like to think of such things. I prefer to write my lines of code and play with Carlos's fine computers."

Steven felt for Dafari. He remembered how it had felt when his own grandfather had died, just days ago. What would it be like to lose everyone you loved? And to know that the man responsible was still out there, plotting and scheming?

Liam moved away from the group, eyeing the various experiments. "Quite a spread ye got here, Carlos. This all of it?"

"Well, the real fun is in there." He motioned at the door labeled CARLOS'S PRIVATE LAB, and a rare smile spread across his face. "Want to see?"

Liam nodded. "I dunno if it's the jet lag or sheer disorientation, but I'm suddenly wide awake."

"Not me," Steven said. "I'm exhausted."

"And I'm still hungry." Kim grinned suddenly at Jasmine, then at Steven. "Meet you back at the galley?"

With a soft *poof,* she disappeared. Dafari stood staring, openmouthed, at the spot where Kim had been.

Jasmine laughed. "That's gonna take some getting used to," she said.

Carlos turned to Dafari. "You want to take a closer look at those readings?"

Dafari nodded. "I will be in the War Room."

"War Room?" Steven asked, turning to Jasmine.

"Soon," she said.

Carlos was already leading Liam toward the closed door. "So what've ye got in there?" Liam asked. "Death rays? Cyborgs? Nukes?"

"No nukes," Carlos replied, deadpan.

Across the room, a puff of smoke rose up from the incubator-machine. The scientists bustled around it, putting out little fires.

Steven felt suddenly overwhelmed. *This place,* he thought, *it never stops. And now it's my . . . what? Home?*

"Come on," Jasmine said, putting her arm around his shoulders. "Let's get you settled."

Two floors down, the living quarters were clustered along both sides of a snaking corridor. Jasmine held up a key card in front of one of the doors. Then she stumbled, holding out a hand to brace herself against the wall.

"You okay?" Steven asked.

She nodded quickly. "Guess I'm tired, too." She held up the card again, and the door clicked open.

"The Tiger's lair," she said. "Wash up and change, but don't take long. I think something's up."

The door clicked shut behind her.

Alone now, Steven looked around. The room was small but clean, like a budget hotel room. Clothing lay neatly folded on the twin bed.

Steven picked up the fresh clothes and held them up to the light. Jeans with cargo pockets, a shirt, and a loose jacket. *All exactly my size,* he noticed. He carried the clothing into the small bathroom. It, too, was neat and well furnished, with little soaps and fresh towels.

A strange feeling washed over Steven. This place, this suite of rooms, seemed exactly the right size, as if it had been made for him. He felt strangely at home—more at home, maybe, than he ever had before, anywhere else he'd lived.

As he started to unbuckle his belt, he glanced in the mirror. His face was dirty, tired, with big circles under his eyes. He barely recognized himself.

He leaned against the sink and turned on the tap, then splashed water on his face. He remembered staying up late on school nights, playing games and watching action movies over and over. He'd study the heroes' fighting moves—but even more than that, he was fascinated by *why* they did the things they did. Sometimes he'd watch

the same scene over and over until he dozed off. Grandfather would come in late, gently take off his shoes, and
pull a blanket over him.

When Steven looked up into the mirror, a faint glow
of Tiger energy had risen up around his head. Yellow cat-
eyes seemed to stare back at him.

He leaned forward and *growled*, a sound that came from
somewhere deep inside.

A wave of exhaustion rolled over him. He stumbled,
letting the energy fade. He barely managed to stagger over
to the bed and collapse before he fell into a deep sleep.

Glowing figures appeared in his dreams. One of them
had a snake for a head; another was hunched like a rat.
Steven tried to run away from them, and discovered he
was standing in a giant maze. He darted around one corner, then another. But he could still hear the snake hissing
and the rat squeaking, even though he couldn't see them
anymore.

Then his grandfather was there, standing just ahead
of him in the maze. Just as in Steven's dream on the
plane, the old man seemed to be trying to tell him something. But this time, Steven couldn't make out the words.
The old man's face wouldn't come into focus. His words
sounded like an old tape recording that had been slowed
way, way down.

"I can't hear you," Steven said. "I don't know what
you're telling me."

CHAPTER TWENTY-FOUR

Behind him, the snake hissed again. He felt a moment of terror. He was afraid to turn around—

—then he woke to a banging on the door.

"Kid? You alive in there?" Jasmine's voice came faintly through the door. "Carlos wants us."

"Coming!" Steven called.

He shook himself awake, banishing the dreams. He crossed to the bathroom, feeling once again that this was his room, the place he truly belonged.

As he started to change clothes, he found he still couldn't see his grandfather clearly in his mind. But the rat and snake images lingered. Like monsters hiding in the shadows, waiting for their time to strike.

CHAPTER TWENTY-FIVE

THE SLEEK GRAY aircraft swooped down through the clouds, shaking and quivering in the storm. Heavy winds blew it first in one direction, then another. Ice pelted its sharp wings.

When the plane reached an altitude of five hundred feet, it hovered in midair as a hatch slid open on its underside. Three figures in snow gear and night-vision goggles dropped down on ropes, descending slowly toward the icy tundra.

Josie grimaced as the sub-zero winds blasted against her. She looked around and saw Malik and Vincent—Ox and Monkey—following on their own ropes, just above her. But someone was missing.

"Dog!" she called back up toward the plane. "Shake a leg!"

Her words were almost lost in the roaring wind, but she knew he'd heard her over the cell-radio built into his Vanguard uniform. Vanguard always had the best equipment.

The ground was coming up fast, but still no sign of Dog. Josie turned and yelled upward. "Dog? *Nicky?*"

"He's useless," Vincent's voice said over the radio. "You shoulda put him on a leash." His headgear covered his face, but Josie knew he was smirking underneath.

The wind blew Vincent's rope toward Josie, almost knocking them into each other. "Maybe *you* need a leash," she snapped, smacking him away. "Dog! *Now,* maybe?"

A roar filled the air, audible even over the deafening wind. Dog's howling figure leapt out of the plane, wearing only a combat vest and pants over his thick fur. Unlike the others, he wasn't fastened to a rope. He seemed to stop right next to her for a moment, and then plummeted down past them in free fall.

Josie grimaced, watching as Dog's figure disappeared in the storm. She couldn't even see the ground through the driving ice and snow. She'd heard that cats always landed on their feet, but she wasn't sure about dogs. Or Zodiac-powered superhumans.

"Ox," she said. "Can you make out the ground formations? Are we over their headquarters?"

Malik, the Zodiac agent known as Ox, squinted at a

device on his wrist. "Storm's scrambling the instruments," he replied, his voice calm and steady as always. "I know we're close—the Zodiac energy is still registering. But it's hard to lock it down in this mess."

"Don't trip," Vincent said. "With our powers, we'll have those kids wrapped up and delivered to Maxwell before dessert. Which you promised me, remember. For some reason I've developed a weird craving for banana sundaes."

Josie sighed. She'd worked for the Vanguard company for many years, and seen action in five different countries. Along the way she'd met Malik, and they'd carried out a few combat ops together. He was a loyal soldier, reliable, and easy to get along with. She trusted him, as much as she trusted anyone.

Vincent, on the other hand—Monkey—was a notorious screw-up. In the past, Josie had been sent in to extract him from more than one difficult situation. And Nicky/Dog wasn't turning out to be much better. Josie wondered if they'd ever see him again.

Josie spoke into the radio, pitching her voice low to sound tough. "Zodiac powers don't make you a good soldier," she said. "Concentrate on the mission at hand."

"How 'bout we concentrate on the ground?" Vincent replied, pointing down. "'Cause I think I see it."

Josie looked down to see a sheet of ice rising up to meet them. She swung forward on her rope, let go, and rolled her body up into a ball. She landed on her hands first, galloping forward like her namesake to slow her momentum. An ethereal horse-shape appeared briefly around her, whinnying into the air, then faded as she came to a stop.

Ice pellets rained down on her exposed cheeks. With a shock, she realized she barely felt them. *This power really has changed me,* she thought. *Once we've collected the rest of the Zodiac-powered kids, Maxwell will be unstoppable.*

For some reason, the thought made her uneasy.

Malik landed beside her. He stumbled once, then quickly regained his footing. Vincent tumbled down next, hands over feet over hands, showing off his newfound Monkey abilities. "Look at me!" he said. "Hey, guys, look at this!"

Josie felt a headache coming on. She'd already lost one team member and felt like murdering another one. And the mission had barely started.

"Okay," she said. "You all know the drill: it's a snatch-and-grab. Get into their headquarters, nab all six Zodiacs, and get out as fast as you can. No distractions, no secondary objectives.

"The only one you need to worry about is Jasmine. She's got the Dragon power, and she's had Vanguard training, too. Maxwell has a plan to deal with her, but we can't rely on that. We've got to take her out fast."

"There's civilians in there," Malik said. "What if they get in the way?"

"Don't engage if you don't have to, but the mission comes first," Josie replied. "This should be a milk run, people. Intel says their powers are weaker than ours, and we're trained combat veterans. They're just kids."

Vincent looked around. "What about Nicky? He's probably splattered all over the ice somewhere—"

A familiar roar rose up over the storm. Josie turned in alarm, whipping out her gun, just as Nicky leapt out from behind a rise. The Dog image rose up above him, howling along with Nicky himself.

Josie sighed again and holstered her weapon.

"Dude," Monkey said. "You're alive!"

Nicky landed, light as air, on all fours. Then he straightened up and growled low, scrunching up his features. As Josie watched, his Dog form faded, and the fur receded from his face and body.

"Man, it's cold out here," he said. "Especially without my fur on!"

Josie marched up to him and slapped him hard, across the face. Nicky yipped in surprise.

"You went off-mission," Josie said. "Do that under my command again, and your next assignment will be chasing cars on the freeway. You get me?"

Nicky nodded.

Malik approached, waving snow away from his eyes as he jabbed at the GPS locator on his wrist. "Still can't find anything in this mess," he said. "Sorry."

Nicky grinned. "Well, then," he said, "it's a good thing you've got a bad dog along with your good soldiers, boss. Because I know where their headquarters is."

Before Josie could speak, Nicky scrunched up his face again. Fur started to grow back, all along his body, and Zodiac energy surrounded him. He dropped down to all fours and ran around in a circle.

Vincent laughed. "What's he doing?"

Nicky—Dog—reared up on two legs again and sniffed the air. The storm was still raging; Josie couldn't see ten feet away. Nicky turned slowly in place, then stopped, becoming completely still. He reached up a furry hand and pointed off in the distance.

"*Rrrrrr!*" he growled. Then he took off at a run.

Josie grimaced. She'd been waiting for years to command a Vanguard field team. But this was *not* the kind of team she'd imagined.

She shrugged and pointed after Nicky. "Let's go," she said, and set off into the storm.

CHAPTER TWENTY-SIX

"AND HERE WE ARE," Jasmine said. "The heart of our little operation: the War Room."

Steven gazed around the room. It was wide but low, with a few computers clustered in the center. Wires hung from the ceiling, and a group of old-fashioned desks sat together in one corner. A giant LCD screen covered one wall.

There were plenty of chairs, but only one was occupied—by Dafari, the man Steven had met in the lab. Carlos stood over Dafari's shoulder, pointing at a screen, talking in a low voice.

"Steven!" a voice called. He looked across the room at the old desks just in time to see a figure wink out of existence. A split second later, Kim reappeared at his side with a quiet *poof.* Steven jumped.

"Sorry," she said. "Didn't mean to freak you out. Isn't this place *awesome?*"

Jasmine crossed over to Carlos and pointed at a tablet he held in his hand. As he touched the tablet, large type appeared on the big wall screen:

Z.A.P.P.E.R.S.
Zodiac
Action
Preparation &
Protection
Emergency
Response
Squad

Jasmine frowned. "Another name for the group?"

"That's, uh, sorry." Carlos tapped the tablet frantically. "I didn't want anyone to see that yet."

"I can see why."

The type faded—and then the wallscreen sparked and died. A puff of smoke rose up from it.

Jasmine grimaced. "We really do need some new toys."

Carlos shook his head and walked over to the screen. He yanked out a wire, sending another spark flaring up into the air. Steven, Kim, and Jasmine all flinched.

"Please don't burn down the War Room," Jasmine said.

But Carlos held up a second sparking wire, and smiled. He touched the wires together, and the screen flickered back to life.

It took Steven a moment to figure out the image on the screen. It was a long shot of a blinding ice storm, snow and wind whipping wildly all around.

"Nasty weather outside," Jasmine said. "We got home just in time."

"I'm not worried about the storm," Carlos said, manipulating the display on his tablet. On the big screen, the image zoomed in to show the headquarters exterior, its outline barely visible through the wind and ice. From the top, the place looked like a low, flat hill.

"Tough to get readings," Carlos continued.

"If it was easy, everybody would be doing it." Jasmine smiled. "Not just the Z.A.P.P.E.R.S."

Carlos shot her a quick glare and kept working.

Liam and Roxanne filed into the room. "So this is where y'make the doughnuts," Liam said.

Duane—Pig—stopped short in the doorway, his eyes wide. He walked up to the wall screen and touched the cables leading out of it.

"Duane," Carlos said. "Careful with your power, please? This system is barely hanging together as it is."

Duane nodded absently. He started moving around the room, his fingers tracing the path of the wiring.

"There," Jasmine said, pointing at the tablet. "Those are the energy signatures?"

Carlos nodded and touched the tablet again. Up on the wallscreen, a cluster of icons shaped like the letter "Z" appeared on one side of the headquarters. The icons wavered and wobbled. Two of them winked out for a moment, then reappeared.

"Four Zodiac-powered agents," Carlos said. "Maybe five. But I can't get a precise fix on them in this storm."

"That's what they counted on, aye?" said Liam. "My Uncle Johnny used to wait till his enemies were really drunk, then he'd sneak up and head-butt 'em. They couldn't move fast enough to get out of the way."

"What do you do when this kind of stuff happens?" Steven asked. "Put the headquarters on alert, or something?"

A column of three small windows appeared down the side of the big wall screen. Two of the new images showed pairs of armed guards in heavy winter coats stationed at the outer walls of the complex. The third showed another group of guards being buffeted by wind on the flat, icy roof. Wind swirled the snow all around, hiding the guards from view and then revealing them again.

"All personnel are on guard duty, inside and out of the complex," Carlos said. "That's why the War Room is on a skeleton staff. But these winds are so strong, I don't know if our people would even see an enemy coming."

Steven thought he recognized Mags, the mechanic, doing guard duty on the roof. But it was hard to tell through the thick coats, in the driving storm.

Duane stood at the far side of the room. "What's on the other side of this wall?" he asked.

"The hangar bay," Carlos said. "It stretches up two floors, to the roof. It's where we store copters and planes."

"If we *had* any planes," Jasmine added. "Listen, seeing our attackers coming is only half the problem. The other half is that our people aren't trained to defend against a paramilitary squad of Zodiac-powered agents."

"Ma'am? Isn't that why you recruited us . . ."

Jasmine, Carlos, and Steven all turned at the sound of Kim's voice. But she was gone. Steven heard a soft *poof*, and turned back again to see her reappear in front of the wallscreen.

". . . to use our Zodiac powers?" Kim finished.

Duane and Liam quickly joined her. Roxanne followed, eyeing Jasmine carefully. When they were all assembled, Steven walked over to stand in front of them, facing Carlos and Jasmine.

"Well?" he asked.

Jasmine stared at them for a long moment. The Dragon energy began to take shape around her, fierce jaws and scales forming just above her head. She rose a few inches off the floor.

"No," she said. "You're not ready."

Roxanne threw up her hands. Steven swore he heard her make a clucking sound.

Steven felt the energy surge inside him. Power rippled

across his skin, flaring up to become a raging Tiger. He turned toward Jasmine and growled.

Jasmine winced. Her Dragon form flickered once, and almost vanished. Jasmine gritted her teeth and the Dragon flared back to life, its jaws opening in a silent screech.

They stared at each other for a long moment. Jasmine had told him several times that the Dragon was the most powerful sign of all. The Tiger was strong and fast, but the Dragon was in a whole other league.

Yet something was different now. Some instinct told Steven that Jasmine wasn't as unbeatable as she'd seemed before. The Tiger roared within him, aching to challenge her.

This is how animals act, he realized. *When the world grows dangerous around them, when predators wait just beyond the cave entrance.*

Or when they're competing to rule the pack.

Jasmine seemed to soften. She held up her hands in a placating gesture, and allowed the Dragon energy to softly fade.

"*They're* not ready, I mean," she said. "The recruits. And Maxwell's agents are far stronger."

Carlos walked up, watching Jasmine with worried eyes. "That was part of Maxwell's plan," he said. "He deliberately took the most powerful Zodiac powers first, in case something went wrong."

Steven clenched his fists. "I'm as powerful as any of them," he said. The Tiger energy still flared all around him, begging for release.

"I know," Jasmine said. "That's why we . . . *you and I* . . . are going to be the main line of defense."

"Aw, c'mon," Liam said. "I didn't come here to hide meself away. I've been a fighter all my life."

"I never backed away from a battle either," Roxanne said, holding an imaginary microphone in her hand. "This is just powers instead of mics."

"Why are we here," Kim added, "if not to help?"

"You're here so we can keep you safe!" Jasmine exclaimed.

"Jaz," Carlos said sharply. He pointed at the wallscreen.

Two of the video feeds showing guards had gone blank. As the group watched, the third one winked off, changing to static.

Roxanne stepped up between Jasmine and Steven. "Whatever the plan is, now might be the time."

"The plan is for Steven to take you four down to the reinforced sub-basement bunker," Jasmine said. "Then get back up here, *alone,* as fast as he can."

"And in the meantime?" Steven replied. "You'll take on Maxwell's whole attack team by yourself?"

Jasmine rose up into the air. The Dragon shape appeared above her, glowing and shimmering with energy.

"I'm the Dragon," she said. "Remember?"

This time, Steven could clearly see the strain on her face. Jasmine was putting on a show, displaying her power dramatically for the others. But that power was far weaker than it had been before.

"Are you?" Steven asked. "Really?"

Her eyes flared with anger, mirrored in fire on the Dragon's face. She dropped back to the ground, letting the energy fade away. Then she grabbed Steven's shoulder in a grip like steel and dragged him over to the far corner of the room.

"Um, headquarters, probably already under attack?" Carlos said. "Just a little reminder."

As soon as they were out of earshot, Jasmine leaned in to speak intensely to Steven. "There's no time to argue. The recruits are *not* ready. Most of you haven't had any training time at—"

"I'm not worried about them," he said. "I'm worried about you."

Jasmine blinked.

"I know you're weaker than you were," he continued. "I can tell."

"No, I'm not!"

But when she turned away from him, he knew he was right.

"What's happening?" he asked.

"Maxwell is doing something," she said, her voice low. "He's drawing the energy out of me, back into himself. Remember, we *share* the Dragon power."

"If you fight them all, you're gonna get hurt," Steven said. He could hear his voice breaking. "You can't stop them by yourself."

"I have to!"

Then they both turned at the sound of shouting. Dafari, the technician, was yelling at Duane, who leaned over his console, pointing at the screen. "I am working, Mister Pig," Dafari said. "Leave me alone!"

Duane just shook his head. "But that energy surge. It's *inside* the building—"

The far wall exploded, collapsing inward with a thunderous crash. Dust and plaster filled the air. Steven coughed and ducked behind a desk.

When he looked up, a large figure crouched in front of a giant hole in the wall: Horse, the leader of Maxwell's field team. Steven hadn't met her yet, but Jasmine had described their faceoff outside the pub in Ireland. Horse surveyed the room, waving dust away from her face.

Then the rest of Horse's team approached, gathering behind her. A big man with a mustache; that would be Ox. Then Monkey, and the familiar, yellow-furred Dog.

Four of them, Steven thought. *Four of the most powerful Zodiac powers, all with the same goal: Capture us and take us back to Maxwell.*

He clenched his fists and prepared for the fight of his life.

CHAPTER TWENTY-SEVEN

THE HANGAR BAY was partly visible behind the

Vanguard operatives. They'd entered through the bay,
Steven realized, and burst in from there. Dust filled the
War Room, swirling through the air.

"Steven?" Kim whispered. He turned to see her
crouched next to him, behind the desk.

"Don't be scared," Steven said.

"I'm not," she said, keeping her voice low. "But what
do we do?"

The Vanguard agents were regrouping, slapping dust
off their clothes. They'd catch sight of Steven and the others in a few seconds.

Steven couldn't see Roxanne. Liam was leading Duane around the edge of the room, toward Steven and Kim. Carlos and Dafari were crouched along a far wall. And Jasmine . . .

The Vanguard agents turned in alarm as Jasmine sprinted toward them. She took off into the air like a bird, Dragon energy flaring all around her.

"One chance," she said to the attackers. "Leave this place. *Now.*"

She looked as bright and terrible as Steven had ever seen her. But he knew it was a bluff.

Horse motioned to her team. Ox, Monkey, and Dog began to fan out, forming a semicircle.

"Jaz!" Carlos yelled. "They're trying to surround you!"

She turned in alarm, panic on her face. "Carlos! *Get out of here—*"

Horse jumped straight into the air and grabbed Jasmine by the shoulders, reaching through the roiling Dragon energy. Horse grimaced in pain, but she didn't let go. She started to pull Jasmine down.

Ox reached up and punched Jasmine, hard, in the stomach. She doubled over and fell to the floor, coughing. Her power began to fade.

Then the other agents were on her. Monkey leapt and capered, punching and kicking Jasmine. Dog howled and roared, swiping at her with sharp claws.

Her power's failed, Steven thought. *She's helpless.*

Kim pointed at Jasmine. "They're gonna kill her."

"No," Steven said. "They want her. They want all of us alive."

"Well, that's not an option, right?" Liam asked. "So what do we do?"

Steven turned to look at them. Duane and Liam had sneaked over to join Kim. All three of them stared at him with urgent, scared expressions.

"Steven?" Kim said.

Steven stared back. *I don't know,* he thought. *I don't know what to do.*

He opened his mouth to say something—anything. But before he could speak, a sharp blow struck him on the back of the head. He cried out and fell to the floor.

Through a haze of dust, he saw the calm, looming figure of Ox pointing a handheld analyzer down at him.

"Got him," Ox called out.

Monkey capered up, grinning. "It's fun to hit kids!" he said to Ox. "Isn't it?"

"No, it isn't. This is business," Ox replied. "Do your job—secure the targets."

Steven followed Ox's pointing finger to the other members of his team. They stood watching, frozen and terrified.

"Run!" Steven yelled. "Get away from here!"

Duane and Liam took off, sprinting toward the doors. But Kim lingered for a moment, staring at Steven with worried eyes.

Then Dog, the fur-covered Vanguard operative, bounded up to stare Kim right in the face. She froze. Dog

growled, a long low sound that slowly resolved itself into a single, familiar word:

"Rrrrrrrraaaaabit?"

With a *poof*, Kim sprinted away and vanished.

Dog reached out to swipe his paw through the air where Kim had been just a moment before. *"Rrraabit!"* he said again.

Then he sniffed the air and bounded off, hands over feet, heading for the door.

Horse ran up to join Ox and Monkey. "Get after the last two," Horse said. "I'll find the French girl."

Ox gestured at Steven. "What about this one? And Jasmine?"

Horse glared down at Steven, dismissing him with a look. "They'll keep," she said.

Steven tried to say something, but the dust got into his lungs and he coughed. He struggled to rise from the floor. Ox reached out again, barely exerting himself, and cuffed Steven on the back of the head.

"Just business," Ox said.

As Steven fell, his last thought was: *I've failed. I've failed them all.*

Then he struck the floor and was still.

Poof! Kim appeared in midair, flinching as the wind and ice struck her. Then she fell to the ground, landing awkwardly in a snowdrift.

Great, she thought. *Maybe teleporting randomly wasn't the best idea ever!*

She spat snow, stood up, and dusted herself off. The storm was passing now. Ice still fell from the sky, but the wind was weaker than before. A thin shaft of sunlight pushed its way down through the clouds.

Kim lurched, dizzy. Steven and Jasmine had promised to train her, teach her to use her powers without getting disoriented, to extend her range. But they hadn't gotten around to that yet.

Guess all it took was blind panic. She thought of Dog and shivered, both from the memory and the cold.

The fog began to clear, revealing the side of the ice mound concealing Jasmine's headquarters, about a hundred feet away. A couple of guards lay unconscious near the hidden door. At least, Kim *hoped* they were unconscious, not dead. She crept over to check on them—

—and then the hidden door in the ice rumbled to life, opening slowly upward. Before it was even halfway open, Dog came loping out, sniffing the air and heading straight toward his prey.

"*Rrrrraaaabit!*" he growled.

Kim stopped short. Her first instinct was to run, or to *poof* herself out of here. It was the same instinct she'd had back home, that time when Dad went off his medication and started breaking things. Or every time she saw another old store close down, another park locked up because the town couldn't afford to keep it open.

Like Steven had said, Kim was good at running. And she was careful, too.

She stood her ground, waiting for Dog to come closer. Finally he leapt through the air, his claws raised to strike. Kim smiled, jumped straight up, and *poofed* away.

Dog landed face-first on the ice. He shook his head and looked around, dazed.

"Silly doggy," Kim said, waving to him from a few feet away. "Did you fall on your little pink nose?"

Dog growled and climbed to his feet, shaking snow off his long ears. Kim swallowed hard and glanced backward at the complex. *I can't make it all the way back inside,* she knew. *I'm too weak from that first big jump.*

Maybe I need more training after all.

Dog charged her again.

"You got major self-control issues," she said. "Have you thought about obedience school?"

As Dog's claws swiped out, Kim *poofed* again. This time she reappeared just a few feet behind him. He snarled, turned, and charged again.

Poof.

Poof.

Poof.

CHAPTER TWENTY-SEVEN

Again and again, Dog snarled and swept the air with his sharp claws. And every time, Kim *poofed* out of his reach. But each jump took her a shorter distance.

I'm getting tired, she thought. *If he manages to grab me, I won't be able to teleport—I can only* poof *when I'm in motion. Sooner or later he'll catch me.*

And then what? Will he take me to this mysterious Maxwell dude? Or . . . or will he just eat *me?*

Dog slavered, frustrated, as his prey *poofed* away again. "*RRRRAAAABIT!*" he howled, louder than ever. He whirled around in a circle and charged.

Once again, Kim closed her eyes and went *poof.*

CHAPTER TWENTY-EIGHT

ROXANNE SCURRIED along the wall of the large hangar bay, moving with a dancer's grace past ladders, forklifts, and helicopters. She cast a nervous glance back toward the hole in the wall, the one that led to the War Room. She could hear crashing and yelling, but from this angle she couldn't see what was going on.

She'd fled, hoping to gain time to think. Now she crouched down to hide behind a small copter, her mind racing. She didn't know what to do. Jasmine and the others clearly needed help—but the Vanguard agents were just too powerful.

Looks like I'm a solo act for now, she thought.

CHAPTER TWENTY-EIGHT

Roxanne had two options: fight or run away. She looked up at the ceiling, where a concealed hatchway allowed aircraft to enter and exit the bay. That hatch was partway ajar now—the Vanguard agents must have forced it open, so they could enter from the roof. Ice and snow swirled down through the opening, chilling the room. But the storm seemed to be dying down.

Directly below the hatch stood a large combat helicopter, surrounded by a six-foot-high temporary metal fence. A sign on the fence read MI-17 HELICOPTER UNDER REPAIR / NO ADMITTANCE.

Roxanne turned to a smaller copter, an MH-6 Little Bird with only two seats. Unlike the MI-17, the Little Bird could fly. But Roxanne didn't know how to pilot it, and even if she managed to get it in the air, the hatch above was only halfway open. The Little Bird probably wouldn't fit through.

The only other vehicle in the room was a small vertical-takeoff plane, spread out in pieces along the floor: two giant rotors, a few weird-shaped fins, a thick tubular body split in half. Mags was in the process of assembling it from surplus parts. It wouldn't be in shape to fly for weeks to come.

Roxanne studied the large MI-17 copter, running her eyes up to the roof hatch. *If I can climb over the fence and up on top of the copter,* she thought, *I could escape through the hatch. And maybe I could go for help.*

Then she remembered where she was: way out on the

ice shelf of Greenland, hundreds of miles from any settlement. Where could she possibly go?

She heard a clomping noise coming from the direction of the War Room. Someone was coming.

Suddenly, despite her present circumstances, Roxanne realized she was grinning. She felt energized, the way she always did just before a performance. Adrenalized. She ran around to the far side of the big copter, then leapt onto the fence surrounding it. She grabbed at the top of the fence, but lost her grip and fell backward, landing on her butt.

"Rooster Girl? Is that you?"

The voice was deep and female. Roxanne couldn't see its owner behind the bulk of the copter, but she knew it was Josie, the Horse and the leader of the Vanguard field team.

"You can't fight us," Josie continued. "We're stronger than you, and better trained. We know all about you, too . . . *cherie*."

"I know you, too!" Roxanne yelled back. "Josie, right? You're not so tough without your crew."

Roxanne's voice echoed in the large room, concealing her position. But she knew she sounded scared, and hated herself for it.

"Give up now," Josie replied, "and you won't have to find out how tough I am."

The Horse sounded closer now. She must be edging

around the far side of the copter. Roxanne moved along the outside of the fence. Her only chance was to keep the copter's bulk between her and her attacker.

"Maxwell isn't evil, you know," Josie continued. "He has a plan for the Zodiac powers. In fact, he's the only one who knows how to control them."

Gritting her teeth, Roxanne leapt up again and grabbed hold of the top of the fence. The metal dug into her fingers, cutting them, but she grunted through the pain, vaulted over the fence, and landed on the helicopter's sideboard. She leaned against the copter's hull, gasping for breath.

"What did Jasmine tell you?" Josie asked. "That she and her boy toy Carlos had rebelled against the big bad Maxwell? It's not as simple as that, kid."

Rooster remembered her father calling her *kid*, back before he'd left for good. She hadn't liked it then, and she didn't like it now.

Horse was still on the far side of the room—she hadn't seen Roxanne yet. As quietly as she could, Roxanne began to climb up the body of the copter.

"I think you know I'm right," Josie continued. "Jasmine can't be trusted. How much do you really know about these people, anyway?"

Roxanne stopped dead, halfway up the copter's fuselage. She turned to look down, around the copter, and caught Horse's eye. The Vanguard operative stood on the far side of the fence, next to the jagged hole in the wall.

"You're a hypocrite, *Josie*," Roxanne said, surprised at the anger in her own voice. "Just like every adult I've ever met. How much do you know about *your* people?"

For just a second, she thought she saw a flicker of doubt cross the woman's face. Then, as quickly as it had come, it was gone. "And you, Roxanne, are an innocent," she said, "underneath all that makeup and attitude. I'll give you one chance: come down peacefully and we'll discuss this back at Vanguard headquarters."

Roxanne stood frozen for a long moment. She glanced upward, flinching as a gust of frigid air blew in through the roof hatch. She hated to admit it, but Josie's words had hit home.

I only agreed to come here for training, she thought, *and because Mom . . . she didn't want me anymore. I didn't have anyplace else to go.*

I hardly even know Steven and the others. Is it worth risking my life for them?

But then again . . .

"Maybe I don't trust Jasmine," Roxanne said. "But I sure don't trust *you*."

She turned away and resumed climbing. Above her, the roof hatch gaped open. Just a few more feet . . .

Josie shrugged. "I tried." She stepped back a few feet, then charged forward, the Zodiac energy forming a horse shape around her. She vaulted over the fence in a single motion, as if she were running a steeplechase.

Roxanne climbed higher. She grabbed hold of the copter's top rotor—

—just as Horse landed on the helicopter, a few feet below. Horse leaned back and *head-butted* the copter, very hard. The whole structure shook.

Roxanne slipped, almost losing her grip.

Horse's second head-butt knocked her loose. As Roxanne fell through the air, straight toward her attacker, she had time for a single thought:

Showtime.

Roxanne whipped her head around and let out a sharp sonic cry, the Rooster form flaring up around her. Horse ducked and dropped easily to the floor inside the wooden fence. The sonic assault missed her, striking the fence and splintering a hole into it.

Still falling, Roxanne let out a second cry, then a third. The fourth cry struck the copter, shattering a window. Glass fragments flew into Josie's face, blinding her momentarily.

The next cry hit Horse head-on. She staggered back.

Roxanne twisted around in midair. *Got to land on my feet,* she thought.

But Josie grabbed her by the arms, swinging her around in the air. Roxanne saw the metallic fuselage of the helicopter rushing toward her in a blur of green and black. Then her whole body exploded in pain.

"You've got power, girl," she heard Josie say. "But you

got no idea how to use it. Don't worry, we'll make sure it goes to someone who deserves it."

Roxanne felt a flash of rage. *I didn't ask for this power,* she thought. *I didn't want my career, my whole life, smashed like a guitar onstage. And I sure don't wanna die in* Greenland!

And suddenly there was blackness.

When she came to, Horse was dragging her across the floor, back toward the War Room. Roxanne struggled, but her arms and legs had been tied with rope. She tried to clear her throat, to let out a sonic cry, but she coughed and tasted leather. Josie had gagged her as well.

"I meant what I said, Rooster Girl," Josie said. "You're an innocent. But even innocents make the wrong choices sometimes."

This ain't over, Rooster thought. *You don't know who you just messed with, Josie. When I get out of this, I'll . . . I'll . . .*

Despair washed over her. She was helpless, unable to move.

It's up to them now, she thought. *The others. Steven and Jasmine and Liam and Kim and Duane.*

At that moment, Roxanne missed everything about her old life. Her guitar, her band, her bed with the little flowers on the night table . . . and her mom. She felt a terrible urge to flee, to leave everything here behind and run as far and as fast as she could. But it was too late. With the ropes binding her and the gag blocking her power, she couldn't move.

CHAPTER TWENTY-EIGHT

When Steven struggled back to consciousness, he, too, was bound up in ropes, cocooned in a tightly bound series of cords. Bits of wall plaster and broken computer parts littered the War Room floor. Sounds of fighting carried from across the room.

He struggled and squirmed, but the ropes were too tight. He felt a moment of panic—then stopped, forcing himself to concentrate. Clenching his arms tightly around himself, he thought: *I summon the power of the Tiger.* He paused. *That sounds* super *lame. But it might work!*

Energy rippled through Steven, from his heart outward to his arms and legs. The Tiger energy burned, forming its now-familiar manifestation above and around him. He flexed his muscles and threw his arms wide, splitting the ropes like spaghetti.

Steven leapt to his feet. A ceiling beam had fallen, crushing a bank of computer consoles. Just beyond, Carlos sat crouched down, tending to Jasmine. Steven ran over to them.

Jasmine had cuts on her face and arms. She looked very weak. "The power," she said. "The Dragon power . . . it's gone. I can't feel it at all anymore."

Carlos dabbed at her face with a tissue, wiping up blood. "It's okay, Jaz. Lie still."

"Dafari," she said. "Is he okay?"

"Yes," Carlos replied. "I sent him to the basement, to set up the . . . actually, I need to go, too. It's important. I'm sorry, Jaz—"

"It's okay." Jasmine grinned. With surprising strength, she reached up and grabbed Steven's shoulder. "I've got the Tiger."

Steven reached out and pulled her to her feet.

Carlos looked from Steven to Jasmine, considering. Then he squeezed Jasmine's hand and flashed her a quick, scared smile.

"Don't die," he said.

Jasmine watched him run off, shaking her head. "He's so romantic," she said.

Steven looked around. The room was a mess: fallen wall fragments, smashed computers. The wallscreen hung loose, cracked in half. Strangely, the old desks in the far corner were still intact.

"Looks like I was out for a while," Steven said. "What happened?"

"They trashed the place, tied us up, then went after the newbies. But they didn't see Carlos hiding in the shadows. He untied me."

"The recruits," Steven said. "They asked me what to do, and I . . . I didn't know what to tell them."

The memory came back to him then. The three faces—Liam, Duane, and Kim—staring at him. Begging for guidance, for leadership. For something he couldn't give them.

"Hey!" Jasmine punched him on the shoulder, hard. "Snap out of it."

"What do I do?" Steven asked. "And, ow."

"Go help them!"

"What about you?"

Jasmine frowned and scrunched up her face. As she squeezed her eyes closed, a very faint Dragon aura began to rise up around her body. "Come on," she whispered. "Comeoncomeoncomeon . . ."

Then she gasped, coughed, and doubled over. The Dragon energy vanished.

Steven reached for her. "I'm all right," she said, waving him off. "But I'm not gonna be much help until I can get my power back. It's like a . . . a battle between me and Maxwell, waged across the whole world." She gave a dry laugh. "Come to think of it, that's been true for a long time."

Steven frowned. Again, the thought came to him: *She's got more history with Maxwell than we know.*

"But never mind me," she continued. "You need to pull your head out of the sand and go help your teammates."

"I don't—"

"Steven!" She was practically screaming at him now. "*Help them.*"

He nodded, turned away, and ran.

His mind was racing. The recruits had scattered— who needed his help most urgently? *Ram's pretty tough. Pig has no physical powers, so he's vulnerable. Rabbit is the youngest. But Rooster . . .*

As he dashed out the door, Jasmine's words echoed again in his mind: *Help them.*

There was no more time for doubt. He had to act.

Josie dragged her bound captive across the floor of the garage. The gagged Rooster slid along easily on the oily floor, grunting muffled protests every few feet.

"You know," Josie said. "If you were a Pig instead of a Rooster, you'd be Greased Pig by now."

Stop it, Josie told herself. *You're starting to sound like Monkey. This team is driving me crazy.*

She started toward the outer garage door, then stopped. An electric-powered jeep stood parked in the corner. A thick cord led from it to a large, inductive charging system mounted in a box on the wall.

Josie changed course, lurching toward the jeep. "Change of plans, girl," she said. "Just gotta make a quick call."

She reached into her pack and pulled out a short cord, snapping it quickly onto the analyzer on her wrist. Then she yanked the charging paddle out of the jeep. With the other end still connected to the wall, she plugged the little cord into a tiny port in the paddle.

A hologram rose up from Josie's wrist. It flickered for a moment, flashing from blue static to red, then back to blue. Then it resolved into the hazy, indistinct form of Maxwell himself.

"Horse," he said. "Is everything proceeding as planned?"

"Yes sir," she replied. "I've secured one of the targets, and the other agents are dealing with the rest."

"Then why," he said slowly, "are you disturbing me?"

Maxwell's image flickered. The holo-communicators used up an awful lot of power, and they weren't perfected yet.

"I just, uh . . ." Josie hesitated. "It's about Jasmine. I'm worried . . . is everything going as planned? With her?"

"It is," Maxwell said. "I'm using a variety of meditative techniques, guided by my superior will and intellect, to extract the power from her. In a few hours, the Dragon will be mine and mine alone."

Josie sighed in relief. The others were no problem; even the Tiger, powerful as he seemed, was young and inexperienced. As Josie had told her team, only Jasmine could conceivably disrupt their plans.

Josie squinted at the holo. Maxwell's face was clearer now, and two ethereal images could be seen floating in the air above him. His bat-winged dragon hovered in profile, its wings wrapped tight around a different type of dragon: the slimmer, sharp-clawed serpent that represented Jasmine's power. The two creatures' mouths were only inches apart, snarling and hissing at each other like cats—as Maxwell's dragon, the dominant one, sucked the life force slowly out of its victim.

"At least," Maxwell continued, "the power will be mine *if I am not interrupted again.*"

Josie gulped and nodded. "Understood, sir. Thank you."

She yanked the cord out of the paddle. The hologram flashed and vanished.

On the floor, the Rooster girl let out a sharp cry.

Josie reached out and jabbed a red button on the wall. As the big garage door started to slide open, she smiled down at her struggling captive.

"Save your breath, rock star," Josie said. "It's cold outside."

CHAPTER TWENTY-NINE

DUANE DIDN'T LIKE to talk much. He found that a lot of the time, when he talked, people didn't understand him. Or sometimes they understood the words, but not the ideas he was trying to express.

So when Monkey chased him into the training room, Duane didn't say anything. He just ran across the floor, trampling over the exercise mats, pushing aside the treadmills and punching bags, until he reached the control screen.

Monkey swung around the doorway and into the room—just as Duane activated a half dozen training sequences all at once. Jungle gyms sprouted out of the floor, climbing ropes dropped from the ceiling. Monkey looked at the assortment of workout equipment and grinned wickedly.

"Big mistake, kid," he said, reaching out to grab a pair of exercise rings hanging from the ceiling. "This is what I was made for."

Monkey swooped forward on the rings, almost as if he were weightless. When he reached the top of his arc, he let go and tumbled through the air. He stretched out his unnaturally long feet and grabbed hold of a rope with his toes.

Duane ignored Monkey. He stared at the screen, at the data flashing past his eyes. Duane had always been good at concentrating on a single task, blocking out distractions. That had caused him trouble at school—sometimes he got so engrossed in solving a problem, he wouldn't hear what the teacher was saying. And sometimes the kids made fun of him because he seemed strange and distant.

But at times like this, Duane's ability to focus came in *very* handy.

"You're missin' the show, kid," Monkey said. He swung around the rope in a circle a few times. "Of course, once I take you in, we'll have plenty of time to get to know each other."

Duane frowned. The data on the screen was moving so slowly! He wanted to use his full power, to absorb all the information at once. But he remembered what had happened back in South Africa, when he'd let his power run wild. So he held himself back and allowed the information to come at its own speed.

"Maybe Maxwell will give you to me as a pet," Monkey said. "You ever heard of a monkey owning a pig before?" He chittered with laughter.

Finally—finally!—the Advanced Obstacle Course menu appeared on the screen. Duane pressed an icon.

"Just stand still." Monkey launched himself through the air, straight toward Duane. "This won't hurt muuu-UUUUUHHHH?"

Thick plastic cables dropped from above. They snapped around Monkey's swooping form, plucking him out of the air—binding his arms, legs, and ankles. He jerked upward, caught in midair.

But Duane's victory was short-lived. Monkey looked down at his opponent and grinned again. Then he lifted his arm to his head and, in quick motions, began to gnaw away at the nearest cable.

"Can't catcf a Nonkey in vis kind of frap," Monkey said, chewing madly. When his hand was free, he reached down to untwist another cable from his legs.

Duane turned back to the control screen and tapped another icon, the one for the low-powered Taser gun.

Only one of the Tasers was fully charged. He thumbed up the power on it to full, then pressed ACTIVATE.

The Taser shot up out of the floor. It swiveled around, tracking Monkey. But when it fired off its thin metal wire, Monkey dodged it easily. The Taser shot out to its maximum length, then fell to the floor, sparking harmlessly.

"You're outmatched, kid," Monkey continued, jumping down to the floor.

Duane jabbed at another icon. This was his last chance, and he knew it. The paintball cannon whirred out of the wall—and Monkey took it out with one punch, snapping it loose. As it clattered to the floor, a broken capsule dribbled paint onto the white tile. The paint looked vaguely like fresh blood.

Before Duane could even formulate a thought, Monkey grabbed him by the throat and spun him around. Duane coughed and choked, struggling to breathe.

"I woulda done the same thing," Monkey said. "But it's over, kid. You can't beat Vanguard."

Duane clutched at his throat. Panic began to bubble up inside him.

"You gotta surrender now," Monkey continued. "Otherwise I'm gonna have to keep choking you till you ain't breathing no more."

Ever since he was a little boy, Duane had hated to feel helpless. Now he flailed, waving his arms around wildly. But Monkey hung on to his back, the grip on Duane's throat as tight as iron.

I'm gonna die! Duane thought. *I'm gonna die here!*

Almost without thinking, he let the Pig out of its cage.

Freed at last from its constraints, Duane's power reached out to fill the room. A giant raging energy-boar, larger than he'd ever manifested before, rose up, bucking and snorting. The Zodiac power swept over the control screen, setting off a shower of sparks.

The lights dimmed, flickered, and winked out. The room went dark.

"Wha?" Monkey asked. He turned in alarm, loosening his grip for just a second.

Duane wrenched himself loose and started to run. But before he could take a single step, a heavy weight struck him on the back of the neck. He fell forward, crying out softly.

A bright light shone into his face. When he looked up, Monkey stood holding a flashlight in one hand and the broken paintball cannon in the other.

"Monkeys can see in the dark, y'know. I guess pigs can't."

Duane groaned. He tried to focus his power, to direct it at his opponent—but he couldn't concentrate. His head felt like somebody had just fought a battle inside it.

And he knew: he'd played his gambit and lost. With the power short-circuited, he couldn't use the training room's machines against Monkey anymore.

Monkey pulled out a rope and crouched down. "I'm just gonna tie you up with this now," he said. "Don't fight

anymore, okay? I don't wanna have to bring in a bruised pig."

As Monkey pulled the ropes tight, Duane felt the panic rise inside him again. He turned away, fighting back tears. This time, he really was helpless.

For good measure, Monkey grabbed a stray barbell and hit Duane hard on the crown of his head. Visions of Monkey and the other Vanguard surrounding him and the others, knocking their heads together, swarmed in his head. He didn't know what was real and what wasn't. He only knew that there was no way out.

Liam dashed out of the War Room, skidding a little as he swerved into the long corridor. Alarms rang all around, lights flashed red on the ceiling. He paused at the end of the hall and flung a security door open. Then he took off up the metal maintenance stairway, two steps at a time.

He could hear one of the Vanguard agents following. Heavy footsteps thudded, one after another, in a steady beat. The agent, whoever he or she was, was clearly in no hurry. Sooner or later he'd catch up.

Liam puffed a bit as he reached the first landing. He stopped for a moment, smiling to himself. With his Ram powers, Liam was nearly invulnerable; almost nothing could stop him. He could just let the Vanguard agent catch him and see what happened.

But he had something better in mind.

A crash rang out from below. Liam peered down around the staircase and saw Ox standing at the bottom in front of the smashed-in security door. Liam turned around quickly and started running again.

Ox's footfalls resumed, echoing in the narrow stairwell.

At the top of the stairs, Liam dashed down another short hallway, then pulled open the door labeled MAIN LABORATORIES. Inside, the labs were deserted. Liam ran past cubicles and sinks, experiments left half-finished when the alarms had sounded. He came to the door labeled CARLOS'S PRIVATE LAB—KEEP OUT! and shouldered it open.

Carlos's lab was a maze of desks, computers, and mechanical experiments—and, at the far wall, there was another door. This one was labeled CONTAINMENT CHAMBER. Liam smiled and opened that door, too. Then he got to work.

Five minutes later, when Ox smashed down the Containment Chamber door, Liam was sitting casually inside a large transparent cube. It was about ten feet wide on each side, with an opening on the side nearest to Ox.

Liam held a half-eaten candy bar in one hand and a small tablet in the other.

"Just a sec," he said. "I'm about to level up on Legend of Zook."

Ox smiled and shook his head. He ducked inside the cube, reached out to grab Liam—then turned in surprise as the opening slid shut behind him.

Now they were sealed inside the cube together.

Liam smiled back and held up the computer. "Ah, y'got me. I'm not really playin' Zook," he said. "This is more like a remote control."

He pressed a button. Outside the cube, in the corner of the room, a computer hummed to life. A screen lit up with the words: CAGE MATCH PROTOCOLS—ACTIVATED.

"No Zook," Ox said. He moved up close to Liam, towering over him. "What game *are* you playing, kid?"

"Game," Liam said. "Aye, y'got my number, Mister Ox. I do like games. You know I wouldn't let Steven recruit me to this little circus until he managed to beat me in combat?"

Ox cocked his head. "And how did he do that?"

"Ah, I see what ye did there!" Liam smiled again. "Nice try—but I'm afraid you'll have to find out for yourself. Y'see, Carlos helped me set up *this* little game, right here, to play with Steven. Man's got to get even, you know. But I haven't had a chance to try it out yet."

Ox turned away. He pulled out a knife and began

picking at the seal on the side of the chamber.

"Oh, don't bother tryin' to jimmy the door," Liam continued. "You see, this chamber is now utterly sealed. An' the computer is programmed not to open it again until one of us is unconscious."

"Unconscious."

"Aye. Just like a cage match, see? If ye can knock me out, I'm yours. Bloody clever, if I say so myself."

Ox turned and moved toward Liam. "What if I just take that little 'Nintendo' from you and—"

Liam dropped the console on the floor and stamped on it. It shattered into a hundred pieces.

"It doesn't matter," Ox said. He cracked his knuckles, a loud sound in the confined space. "I'm the strongest person on Earth . . . Mister Maxwell's run the tests. Just close your eyes. This'll be over in a minute."

Ox reared back and punched Liam in the face. Liam's head snapped back, bouncing off the side of the chamber with a loud thumping noise. Then he straightened up, cracked his neck muscles, and smiled.

"Ha!" Liam said. "See, that's what makes this so interestin'. You might *be* the strongest person on Earth—I sure don't remember ever being hit that hard before—but I'm the toughest. The Ram's power is invulnerability, and mate, I'm as invulnerable as they come."

Ox whipped out a small dart gun and fired. The dart struck Liam in the throat and bounced off. Liam scratched his neck, but there wasn't even a mark.

"It's a fascinatin' philosophical dilemma, if ye think about it," Liam continued. "The unstoppable force an' the immovable object."

"It is, at that." Ox paused. He looked around the cube, and at the room visible past its transparent walls. "I think I could bash this chamber hard enough to bring the walls down around us. That would end your little game."

"Aye, it might. But it would probably bring the whole building down too. An' I'm not sure all your wee Vanguard pals could survive that. Are ye sure?"

Ox stood still for a moment, thinking. "I could tie you up."

"That won't end the game."

"No, but I'm gonna have to tie you up sooner or later." Ox reached into his pack and pulled out a length of rope. "Might as well get a head start."

"That's very practical thinkin', Mister Ox. You don't usually see that kind of planning in the muscleman of a gang."

"Well," Ox protested, "we're not just a gang. We're a paramilitary combat unit, and we pride ourselves on our professionalism. Personally, I like to think of myself as more than just a muscleman."

Ox crossed over to Liam and began to bind his arms behind his back.

Liam didn't resist. "Reminds me of my Uncle Seamus," he said. "He was a hard man, no mistake. But he liked to

CHAPTER TWENTY-NINE

do chess puzzles on the side, those brainteasers they used to put in the daily paper. All the other petty criminals made fun of 'im, but . . . well, when you're the best leg-breaker in all Belfast, you can pretty much do what you like."

"I had an uncle like that. Name was Heinrich. He was into word searches."

"Aye, well, word searches aren't exactly yer thinkin' man's puzzle."

"Nobody ever told Uncle Heinrich that," Ox replied. "He wasn't as strong as me, but he was kind of an immovable object. Like you."

"I . . . I got to say, Mister Ox, it's a pleasure to battle to the death against a man so philosophically inclined as yourself. Makes for a refreshing change."

"Likewise." Ox paused in his work, frowning. "My team are good people, and Horse is a very fair leader. But their idea of a good time is a sweaty game of soccer. Which is great, gets the blood pumping and all—but sometimes I crave more cerebral pursuits."

"Aye."

"However."

"However?"

"I can't play your game forever."

Liam squirmed slightly in his ropes. "Have ye figured out a way to render me unconscious?"

"Not yet."

"So you've got no way of actually winning right now?"

"Not in the least. But I know how these things work. Something will come along."

"Huh! I must say, Mister Ox, that's a very deterministic way of lookin' at things. Even, y'might say, *fatalistic*—"

Suddenly the lights went out. The power went off, and the computer displays went dead.

Liam blinked, unable to see for a moment while his eyes adjusted to the darkness. In a flash, he realized what had happened: *Duane.*

Then he saw Ox standing before the chamber door. With the power off, the door had snapped open.

"Game over," Ox said. "Let's go."

Ox tugged on the rope and Liam tumbled off his seat, onto the floor. It didn't hurt—nothing hurt Liam, these days. But he hated to lose, especially because of a bloody power blackout.

"Let's not be hasty," Liam said. "I felt we were developing a bond here. Best two out of three?"

Ox said nothing. He picked up Liam and slung the younger man over his shoulder.

"Well, I tried." Liam shrugged. "Maybe a rematch later? If yer not too busy dissecting me at Vanguard headquarters?"

"Maybe," Ox replied, deadpan. "But it'll have to be word searches."

Aye, Liam thought. *I probably deserved that.*

He settled back and let Ox carry him away.

CHAPTER THIRTY

STEVEN SPRINTED ACROSS the snow, as fast as he could. The storm was almost past; he could see the horizon in the distance. Behind him, the concealed door to headquarters slid shut.

I'm not cold at all, he realized. *Must be the Tiger.*

Ahead, something was kicking up snow from the ground. A low noise carried through the air, like the growling of a frustrated animal. As he drew closer, he spotted the source: Dog, the Vanguard agent. Kim was using her Rabbit power to *poof* in and out, narrowly avoiding his searching claws.

Kim's jumps were growing shorter. Each time, she reappeared a little bit closer to Dog, her Rabbit energy form flashing briefly around her and then fading away. Dog's thick hairy arm sliced through the air again, and Kim barely managed to *poof* away in time.

Steven gritted his teeth and ran faster.

Then he realized that Kim had a strategy. She was teleporting in the same direction, over and over again, luring Dog closer and closer to a high mound of ice left behind by the storm.

Steven stopped and crouched in the snow. He was close enough to jump into the fight if Kim needed him. But he wanted to see what she was planning.

Kim *poofed* in again, right in front of the ice mound, and stuck out her tongue. Dog growled at her, enraged, and leapt through the air. She jumped straight up and disappeared again.

Dog struck the ice mound head-on, cracking it in half. He cried out, a loud sad howling noise, and grabbed at his head. Then he toppled for a second and fell to the icy ground.

Kim reappeared a few feet away. She looked down at Dog's unconscious form, and let out a sigh of relief. She looked exhausted.

"Wow," Steven said.

At the sound of his voice, Kim whirled around, searching the air with frightened eyes. Then she saw Steven and smiled.

CHAPTER THIRTY

He ran up to her. To his surprise, she grabbed him and hugged him tight.

Steven gestured at Dog, who lay unmoving on the ground a few feet away. "That was amazing," Steven said. "You figured out how to use his own strength against him."

Kim pulled away, glanced down at Dog, and shrugged. "We had dogs back home. You gotta be firm with 'em."

Guess I underestimated her, Steven thought.

A sudden gust of wind blew up. Snow swirled all around, and Kim pulled closer to Steven, shivering. "It's okay," he said. "It's only the storm—"

Two oversized fists, clasped together, reached out of the snow cloud and struck Kim on the cheek. She cried out and flew away, falling to the ground.

Steven had just enough time to think, *Monkey*—and then a thick gloved hand grabbed him by the hair. Horse yanked his head up, and he found himself staring into the strangely calm face of Ox.

Then they were all pounding on him. Six fists in all: Horse's and Ox's heavily gloved knuckles, and Monkey's bare, lanky hands. Their punches felt like pile drivers.

"Keep at it," Horse said. "Don't give him a chance to recover."

Steven fell into a crouch, trying to block the blows— but there were too many of them. Despite the Tiger power, he was starting to feel the pain. His face was bruised, and his neck and chest were starting to ache.

"C-coward," Steven said, grabbing Monkey's shirt. "Try fighting me without your friends."

Monkey just cackled back at him. Then Ox spoke up. "This isn't the playground, kid. You're dealing with professionals now."

"And we play to win!" Monkey said, jabbing a punch into Steven's stomach.

Steven slumped to the ground, shaking. *I can't beat them,* he realized. *Not all three of them. My only chance is to get away and catch my breath.*

He looked up, dazed, seeking an escape route. The three Vanguard agents stood over him. *Ox—he's the slowest. If I can get around him . . .*

Then he looked past the Vanguard agents, and his heart sank. Near Dog's unconscious form, Kim lay dazed on the ground. And next to her, piled up like firewood, were the bound and gagged figures of Duane, Liam, and Roxanne.

My team, Steven thought. *I can't leave them here.*

He caught Roxanne's gaze for a moment. She looked completely different from the spirited young woman he'd helped recruit. Her eyes seemed despairing, almost pleading.

Ox leaned down and punched Steven again, four times in rapid succession.

"Hold still, kid," Ox said, pulling his fist back for one final blow. "When this is over, you'll wake up in Vanguard headquarters."

"Maxwell will explain what we're offering you," Horse added, lifting him up by his shirt collar. "It's really for the best."

Steven closed his eyes in utter defeat. *I've failed,* he thought. *I've failed them!*

Just then, a voice cried out across the snow. "Steven! GET DOWN!"

Drawing on some reserve of Tiger power, Steven wrenched free of Horse's grip. But he stumbled down to his knees, too weak to walk.

Get down? he thought, feeling the cold snow under his hands. *That's easy.*

A low hum rose up, filling the air. Steven looked up, puzzled. He couldn't see who had spoken, or where the noise was coming from. But a beam of bright yellow energy flashed through the air above him, heading straight for the assembled Vanguard operatives.

The beam struck Horse first. She stepped back and frowned. She seemed unhurt, but puzzled.

Before Horse could issue any orders, Monkey leapt into the air, waving his arms around. "Whatwhatwhat-what's goin' on?"

Kim crawled over to Steven. She had a cut on her face, but she seemed otherwise unhurt. "Is that Zodiac energy?" she asked.

"I don't think so."

Then they looked up and saw the source of the attack.

Carlos was stalking through the snow toward them, holding up a metallic staff. It looked like a high-tech cane, bristling with electronic switches. He looked like some ancient wizard equipped with a modern, metallic staff. The yellow glow flared out from the staff through the air, bathing the puzzled Vanguard team in its mysterious energy.

Steven glanced at the rest of his teammates. They still lay bound on the ground. The energy beam passed over them, avoiding their bodies.

Carlos manipulated the energy beam carefully, sweeping it through the air. It dipped down briefly to touch Dog's sleeping form.

Kim started to rise, but Steven grabbed her arm. "No. Stay down!"

"Why?" she asked.

"I don't think we want that beam to hit us."

Ox and Horse strode forward. Steven tensed; he doubted Carlos's weapon—let alone Carlos himself—could stand up against those two.

But Carlos just flipped a switch on the staff. The energy flashed off, and the staff went dark. Carlos thrust the staff down to the ground, planting it in the snow. Then he threw his hands up in the air.

"I surrender," he said, then gestured at Steven and Kim. "If you can get past my friends."

The Vanguard agents watched for a moment, confused. Steven and Kim climbed cautiously to their feet.

What's Carlos's game? Steven wondered. *Is he just trying to confuse these guys?*

Kim pointed down at the ground. "Look!"

Steven turned, along with the Vanguard agents, to look down at the unconscious Dog. Something was happening to him. As they watched, Dog's fur seemed to recede, his ears shrinking back against his head. The sharp claws on his fingers and toes disappeared.

Soon he was fully human again.

Dog shuddered and sat up. "Whoa!" he said. "It's *cold* out here!"

Monkey frowned. "His powers . . . did he *lose* 'em?"

Steven studied Monkey for a minute. Monkey looked different too, in a subtler way. His fingers and toes didn't seem to curl as dramatically, and he was shifting back and forth on the ice, as if he suddenly found it cold against his bare feet.

"I think they all have," Kim said.

"What about us?"

As if in answer, Kim vanished with a soft *poof.*

Steven smiled.

Horse turned alarmed eyes toward Steven—just as Steven leapt through the air, unleashing the full power of the Tiger. He'd seen Horse in action before, and he knew she could withstand one of his blows without much trouble. *If* she still had her powers.

He kicked her in the stomach, and she went down.

Ox was already pulling out his dart gun. Steven whipped an arm around and knocked it out of his hand.

Ox winced and shook his hand in pain. His enhanced strength was gone, too.

Carlos was already over by Liam and the others, untying their bonds. "Kim!" Steven called. "Help Carlos!"

Kim nodded and *poofed* away again.

Monkey charged at Steven, swinging his fists. But Monkey seemed slower now, less graceful, without his Zodiac-enhanced agility. Steven dodged his blows easily and chopped a hand against the back of Monkey's neck. Monkey cried out and dropped to the ground.

Then a thick fist slammed into Steven's chin. He grunted and stumbled to the ground. When he looked up, he saw Ox moving forward to strike him again.

"Caught me by surprise there, kid," Ox said. "But I learned how to fight *years* before I got my Zodiac power."

Before Ox could land another punch, a series of loud sharp cries shot through the air. Ox grabbed at his ears in pain and fell to his knees.

Steven looked up to see Roxanne, free of her bonds, stalking toward Ox. She cried out again and again, using her sonic power to force him back. She looked very angry.

Horse and Monkey were helping Dog up off the ground. They all looked dazed, weaker than before. But Steven knew: *This isn't over yet. Carlos's yellow light-beam took away the Vanguard team's powers, but they're still dangerous.*

"Steven. Mate."

Steven turned. Liam stood, shaking off the last of his ropes. Behind him, Kim and Carlos were untying Duane.

Liam pointed at Horse and Monkey, who were huddled together, speaking urgently with the shivering Dog. "Remember the maneuver we talked about back in Ireland?" Liam asked.

Steven looked at him, unsure. "Think it'll work?"

Liam just smiled.

Steven spread out his hands, willing the full power of the Tiger to come forth. Then he reached out and picked up Liam, hoisting him high. Liam curled his stout body into a ball.

"Mind the glasses," Liam said.

Steven reared back and *threw* Liam into the air. Liam drew his knees in toward his chest, pulling his body even tighter together. As he tumbled through the air, the Ram energy took form all around him, sharp horns whirling around like buzz saws.

He struck Dog like a giant bowling ball, sending the Vanguard agent tumbling back down to the cold ice. Liam laughed. "Doggy down!"

But Liam wasn't finished. He bounced off Dog and slammed into Horse, knocking the wind out of her. She staggered and fell. By that time, Liam was already reaching out to head-butt Ox in the face.

Ox coughed and collapsed.

Liam landed roughly, rolling along the ice for several feet. For a moment Steven thought he might be hurt. But Liam just dusted himself off, planted himself in the snow, and glared at Monkey.

"Go ahead, mate," Liam said. "Hit me."

Monkey gulped. He reared his fist back and struck. But his movements were awkward and uncoordinated. When his fist struck Liam's chest, Monkey howled in pain. He whirled around in place, then cried out.

"My hand!" Monkey cried. "My beautiful hand!"

Liam hadn't moved an inch. He pulled off his glasses and cleaned them as if there were no one else around. Then he turned his back on Monkey and marched over to Ox, who lay dazed on the ground.

"Game goes to me, mate," Liam said. "Maybe the unstoppable force isn't so unstoppable after all."

Ox grunted and scrabbled away, across the ice. But when he looked up, Roxanne and Duane were blocking his way.

Josie coughed and rose to her feet. She looked around at the scene. Dog lay moaning on the ground; Monkey was grabbing his foot and hopping around. Ox faced off against Steven's team, who seemed stronger—and angrier—than ever.

"Retreat!" Josie called. She whirled and began to run

off into the wasteland, away from the headquarters complex.

Monkey scrambled after her as fast as he
could, limping slightly. Dog shivered again
and followed, dancing across the snow on his
bare feet. "You guys, did I mention it's *cold* out
here?" he asked.

Ox cast a last, threatening glance at Liam.
"Round three," Ox said. "It's coming."

"I hope so, mate!" Liam called after Ox's
retreating figure. "But *no bloody word searches!*"

Roxanne and the others gathered behind
Steven, watching the Vanguard agents dash
across the ice. A small gray plane flashed by
above, dipping down to follow their path.
Ropes dropped from the plane's undercarriage,
reaching down to intercept the small, fleeing
figures.

"Should we, uh, pursue them?" Duane
asked.

"No," said a female voice. "We can't exactly
arrest them, and we're not equipped to hold
prisoners."

Steven whirled around and saw Jasmine
limping toward them. Carlos ran over and
put an arm around her shoulders, helping her
across the snow.

"Not bad, kids," Jasmine continued. "You might become an actual, for-real team yet."

Kim and Liam exchanged a quick high five. But Roxanne was looking away now, frowning. Duane just looked puzzled.

"Thanks," Steven said. "But what exactly just *happened?*"

Jasmine perched herself shakily on an ice outcropping. "Blame the man here," she said, gesturing at Carlos. "Didn't I tell you he knows more about the Zodiac energy than anyone else alive?"

Carlos pulled the staff out of the snow and held it up. "I sent out a quick pulse that neutralized the Vanguard team's powers," he explained. "It's only temporary. Once they get out of range, they'll revert to their old, powerful selves."

Liam clapped Carlos hard on the back, startling him. "Carlos! Saving the day with bloody *science*! Who's the hero now?"

Carlos smiled. "Dog was the tough one—he was on the ground. It was tricky to get to him without hitting you guys, too. Which would have, uh, defeated the whole purpose."

All at once, Duane started peppering Carlos with technical questions. Jasmine seemed very proud of him, too.

"I would have done it sooner," Carlos said, "but when Duane shorted out the power, all my equipment went dead. I had to wait until the Vanguards dragged him far enough away from headquarters for everything to reboot."

Rabbit *poofed* in next to Carlos. "So does that mean we can un-power those guys whenever we want?"

"I wish," Carlos replied, "but it's probably not that simple. For one thing, we're very close to the north magnetic pole up here. I had to tap an awful lot of EM energy to pull this off—it wouldn't work in most parts of the world."

"I hate to point this out," Jasmine added, "but Maxwell also has dozens of scientists at work, analyzing the Zodiac power. He's probably already figuring out how to shield his operatives from Carlos's pulse tech."

"So we'll come up with something else," Liam said. "You wouldn't believe what this man's got in his lab."

He clamped an arm around Carlos. Carlos winced at Liam's grip, then flashed an embarrassed smile.

"We screwed up," Roxanne said.

Everyone turned to look at her.

"They had us beat," she continued. "Look at Steven's face. They tied the rest of us up, swatted Kim away like she was a fly. If Carlos hadn't pulled his little trick, we'd all be on our way to Maxwell's Zodiac jail right now."

Duane stepped toward her. "R-Roxanne?"

"I've worked with combos before; I know teamwork when I see it," she said to Duane. "This isn't it."

She turned and walked away, back toward the icy headquarters building.

"Ah, she'll come around," Liam said. "Some people ain't used to this sort of brawling—"

"She's right," Steven said.

He could feel their eyes on him, now. But it was Jasmine's look that hurt the most: a look of disappointment, almost betrayal.

"We got really lucky," he continued. "They just used me like a punching bag. Next time, we might not . . . somebody might get . . ."

Suddenly he felt incredibly tired. His face hurt, his feet ached, and his stomach was sore from the pounding the Vanguards had given him. He felt like throwing up.

What am I doing here? he thought. *What are any of us doing?*

"Steven," Kim said. She put a hand on his arm.

But Steven just turned away and stalked off into the snow. He could feel all their eyes on his back.

"We failed," he said, too quietly for the others to hear. "*I* failed."

For the first time since Hong Kong, he felt like he didn't fit in. Like he didn't belong anywhere.

The Tiger power kept him warm, but inside, Steven felt cold.

CHAPTER THIRTY-ONE

IF YOU WERE to start at the spot where Steven Lee was standing and cut a hole straight through the Earth, you'd come out the other side right in the middle of Australia. There isn't much to see in the Australian outback—mostly red sand, withered trees, and the occasional kangaroo.

But in one secret location, hidden in the desert, there sits a strange complex of buildings. From the outside they look like white spheres, perfectly smooth and featureless. Inside, they're the headquarters of Vanguard.

In the largest of those buildings, Maxwell sat in his private sanctum. A classic Japanese garden surrounded him, furnished with waterfalls, wooden bridges, and carefully arranged trays of sand and pebbles. In the exact center of the garden, under a juniper tree, Maxwell rocked slowly on an old porch swing. His eyes were closed, and his legs were folded up in lotus position. The Dragon form blazed over his head, its savage jaws snapping open and closed.

"I am the Dragon," Maxwell chanted softly. "I am strong and farsighted, and I create the future. I am born to rule."

The swing was chipped, covered with peeling white paint, and its metal chain squeaked as it swung. Maxwell had scavenged it from his childhood home back in Indiana.

"Sha Qi," he said, "grant me strength. I accept the burden, the loneliness of power. Help me attain my goals, and bury those who would oppose me beneath the weight of their own weakness."

Above him, a second energy form shimmered into existence. The new construct slithered and whipped around, as if trying to get away. But Maxwell's Dragon turned to it, hissed fire, and reached out for it with sharp-clawed wings.

"Jasmine," he said softly.

The second Dragon—the thinner, older-looking one— tried to shrink away. But Maxwell's avatar clapped its wings around the newcomer, snaring it tight. As it pulled Jasmine's Dragon closer, Maxwell glowed brighter.

"Don't fight me," he whispered. "You can't win."

Then he felt Jasmine's mind, her consciousness, from all the way on the other side of the world. He felt her realization, the knowledge that her power was leeching away. He sensed her defiance, but also her panic.

"There can only be one Dragon," he said. The energy, the vitality, surged through him. "And it will be—"

"Maxwell?"

At the sound of the amplified voice, Maxwell's eyes snapped open.

"The field team has returned, sir."

He darted a glance up above. Too late; his concentration had been broken. The Dragons were gone.

He clenched his fists, then forced himself to relax. *This changes nothing,* he thought. *It might take a little longer, but I will be the only Dragon. Because I understand the price, and she doesn't.*

She still believes she can have friends.

He rose to his feet, his legs aching from the long meditation session. "Acknowledged," he said to a hidden speaker on his lapel. "On my way."

Maxwell's debriefing room was just outside the garden, but it might as well have been on a different world. It was painted white, with low ceilings and fluorescent lighting.

ZODIAC

The Vanguard logo covered one entire wall. It was as corporate as a room could possibly be.

The field team stood waiting for him. They looked terrible. Josie and Malik—Horse and Ox, respectively—were dirty and bruised. Vincent, the agent called Monkey, was shifting from side to side, favoring one leg.

Nicky stood in his non-Dog form, shivering under a blanket. His face was dotted with frostbite scabs.

"I don't see my new recruits," Maxwell said.

Josie stepped forward, grimacing. "We encountered some unexpected trouble."

"It wasn't her fault, sir," Malik said. "We almost had them."

"Nevertheless, I was team leader," Josie said. "I take responsibility."

"Well, I don't," said Vincent.

Maxwell turned to glare at him.

"We did everything we were supposed to do," Vincent continued. "We landed in a sub-zero storm, we split up and secured prisoners and regrouped, just like in all those boring drills you put us through."

Maxwell's eyes flashed with anger. Dragon power flared around him.

Nicky nudged Vincent. "Dude," Nicky said.

But Vincent kept talking. "We would have won," he said, "but for some reason our powers cut out on us. That's not our fault." He pointed at Maxwell. "*You* musta screwed up the Zodiac Convergence."

"*Dude*," Nicky repeated. "Are you suicidal?"

Josie and Malik looked nervous now, too.

Maxwell glanced over at the far corner of the room. A hidden door slid silently open, and a figure glided into the room: a tall, lean woman with a menacing expression, her dark hair swept all the way over one eye. Maxwell smiled. He liked Celine, the Zodiac's deadly Snake.

Celine cast her gaze across the field team, one by one. Her eyes flashed green. A coiled serpent form shimmered into existence above her, its sharp tongue hissing angrily. When her gaze reached Vincent, she smiled cruelly.

Vincent looked suddenly nervous. He took one limping step back, away from the others.

A second figure appeared behind Celine. A short, squat man with narrow eyes and a high collar that almost covered his mouth.

This was Thiago, the Rat.

They took up position on either side of Vincent. He was chittering now, rocking from side to side. He looked to his teammates for help, but Josie just shook her head. Malik glanced away very deliberately, pulled out his dart gun, and started cleaning it.

After flashing Vincent a quick, apologetic smile, Nicky pulled the blanket tighter around his body as if he thought he could hide inside it.

Celine looked up at Maxwell. Vincent followed her gaze, and time seemed to stand still as the others waited for their leader to decide Vincent's fate.

Slowly, Maxwell shook his head.

"Dismissed," he said. "Regroup and prepare. You'll get a rematch against Jasmine and her children sooner than you think."

Malik and Josie saluted. The group broke and began to scatter.

Celine stuck her face in front of Vincent's and *hissed.* Vincent flinched; she laughed. Then Vincent hurried away.

"Wait," Maxwell said.

Everyone froze.

He pointed at Vincent. "You. With me."

"M-me?" Vincent said.

"I won't say it twice."

Again, Vincent looked around for help. But the rest of his team was already gone. Celine and Thiago were just slipping out the back door.

Maxwell turned and started out of the room. He didn't look back, but he knew Vincent was following him. Vincent had no choice.

Maxwell walked through the Japanese garden over a stone bridge that crossed a placid lake. "I find it very peaceful here," he said. "Don't you?"

"Y-yeah," Vincent replied, his voice quavering.

He thinks I've brought him here to kill him, Maxwell thought. The idea pleased him.

"Everything in this garden . . . the pattern of the rocks, the trees, even the temperature-regulated breeze . . . all of it is designed to encourage contemplation. And concentration."

"That's, uh, awesome," Vincent said. He looked down at the floating water, and swallowed nervously.

Maxwell led Vincent to a small wooden gazebo, a covered structure at the top of a low hill, and gestured for him to sit. Vincent limped over to a bench inside the gazebo, and Maxwell sat down opposite him.

"I don't think you've been here before," Maxwell said.

"N-nope," Vincent said. "Listen, I was only jokin' back there—"

Maxwell held up a hand. Vincent went silent.

"You have trouble with authority," Maxwell continued. "That's not a bad thing in itself. In fact, it's why I recruited you. I *want* free thinkers . . . people who are tired of being pushed around by a world that makes less and less sense every year.

"But you don't even know what I'm talking about, do you? You're like a child."

"Uh, yeah," Vincent said, hope creeping into his eyes. "I, uh, I guess you gotta be patient with me."

"True, children have to be nurtured." Maxwell paused. "But sometimes they have to be spanked."

Vincent fidgeted, scratching his neck. "I, I, I don't think you're allowed to do that anymore."

"But you aren't even a child," Maxwell continued. "You're just a screw-up."

"Hey," Vincent said. "I got rights—"

"You've got nothing. You *are* nothing. I tried to free you, to open your mind—but you're still just a monkey in a cage. Aren't you?"

Vincent leapt up, suddenly angry. Maxwell watched his movements calmly.

"I might be different now," Vincent said, "but I ain't your monkey. I'm *nobody's* monkey."

"You can't see," Maxwell said, rising to his feet. "You can't see the cage, all around you."

He clenched his fists, and the Dragon power flared to life.

"That's unfortunate," he continued.

Vincent took a step back. He looked around wildly at the gazebo, at the rolling hills and neatly trimmed grass beyond.

Maxwell stared at his agent. He felt a terrible, familiar feeling, the feeling he had inside when he was about to take a drastic step. For a long moment he considered the pros and cons, weighing them in his mind.

The last time he'd done this, an entire city had died.

"Forgive me," Maxwell said.

Vincent stared at him with frightened eyes. "For what?"

"I wasn't talking to you."

Maxwell raised his hands to his temples. The Dragon power shot forth from his forehead in a sharp, focused burst. Its jaws gaped wide, shrieking like a predator closing in on its prey.

Then Maxwell was inside Vincent's mind. He saw Vincent's childhood self-image: the unwanted youngest son of a large family in Miami, Florida. He saw fear, doubt, and a constant need to prove himself. But Vincent lacked the focus, the concentration, the intellect to break out of his trap. His cage.

And now he was a problem. Maxwell knew his soldiers—he had led them into battle, he had watched them kill, and he had watched them die. He could see the inevitable outcome: Vincent would fail him. The agent had already performed poorly in the field. One day soon, he would actively betray Maxwell.

Maxwell had risked everything, devoted billions of dollars and countless man-hours to the single goal of controlling the most dangerous power the world had ever known. He could not allow that to be undone—especially by one of his own.

He reached deeper into Vincent's brain. Vincent whimpered, trying feebly to push

Maxwell out. But Maxwell was too strong. He forced his way through to the hatred, the resentment, the bitterness that Vincent kept hidden. The bitterness that pulsed like a red star, angry and burning.

The Dragon opened its jaws and *ate the red star.*

Maxwell felt the thrill, the exhilaration, of consuming part of another man. Vincent's hatred, his darker self, exploded inside Maxwell, flashing and scattering to every corner of Maxwell's being. It wasn't a killing, but it felt like one.

You can't be a soldier, Maxwell had often said, *if you will not kill.*

And yet, he knew he'd lost something as well. This was a necessary evil, but an evil nonetheless. The Dragon power was meant for greater, purer things.

Slowly, the red ball's fire faded away. Maxwell exhaled, his hands shaking. He felt spent, exhausted.

Vincent made a little noise. His eyes rolled up in his head, and he slumped forward on the bench.

"Are you injured?" Maxwell asked.

Vincent looked down at his hand, as if he'd never seen it before. He shook it and winced. For a moment, Maxwell wondered if he'd gone too far. Had he damaged Vincent beyond repair?

Then Vincent looked up. When he spoke again, there was a new purpose in his voice, and a new obedience.

"No, sir," Vincent said.

"Good," Maxwell replied, "because I'm going to need you again, very soon. You will obey me now?"

Vincent considered the question for a moment. Then he nodded, firmly and decisively.

"Without question?"

"Yes," Vincent said. "Without question."

Maxwell gestured toward the stone bridge. "You can go."

Vincent stood up and snapped a sharp salute at Maxwell. Then he turned and marched away, all trace of his former rebellious attitude gone. He seemed like a different person now.

In a very real way, he was.

When Monkey was gone, Maxwell stood up. He stumbled and almost fell. He realized he was shaking.

Maxwell had always known that the Dragon was capable of altering men's minds. He'd considered using that power, mostly on his enemies, but he'd vowed to avoid it if at all possible. It seemed like a step too far, even for a man with so much blood already on his hands.

Part of the reason was moral. Killing was one thing: it was a clean, almost purifying act. The person was alive, and then he was dead. Altering a person's mind by force was different. It was a violation, an intrusion into the victim's deepest self.

But there was a practical problem as well. Using the power this way drained Maxwell, caused the Dragon to recede from him. He'd spent a day and a night in the garden, meditating, drawing Jasmine's Dragon power into himself. And now, with a single cruel act, he'd undone almost all of that work.

He walked out of the gazebo and across the pond. He knelt down in a field of sand and traced a circle with his finger.

The garden had always been a place of peace, of escape. But now it felt different. The trees looked gnarled and unnatural, the rocks seemed harsh and jagged in the water. The bridges looked shaky, as if they could collapse any minute.

I've spoiled it, he realized. *By doing what I did to Monkey, I've befouled my perfect place. It can never be pure again.*

Maxwell crossed to the wooden swing and sat down. He closed his eyes and tried to focus the power. Once again, the two Dragons came into view. Maxwell's Dragon held Jasmine's in its firm, talon-winged grip.

No. I did what needed to be done. This is how the world works, and mine is the reaction that the world demands.

But then Maxwell's dragon seemed to flicker, to wink out of existence and back again. Jasmine's Dragon whipped its tail sharply and broke Maxwell's grip. Then it reached out, opened hissing jaws, and lashed out with sharp claws.

Maxwell felt the blow and jumped, startled. Above him, the energy constructs faded away.

More of his power was gone now—into the ether, the link between Dragons. Maybe even back into Jasmine. And he was too rattled, too drained to try again.

Don't get overconfident, Jasmine, he thought. *This is just a temporary setback. I'm still coming for you.*

He reached up to open his shirt, unbuttoning it all the way down to reveal an old, jagged scar. He ran his fingers along it, down his chest to his stomach.

If he couldn't absorb her power from there . . .

. . . then it'll have to be face to face.

CHAPTER THIRTY-TWO

STEVEN PACED AROUND his quarters, gathering up clothing from the desk, the bureau, and the floor. When his arms were full, he trudged over and dropped everything into a suitcase lying open on the bed.

He'd made up his mind. He was leaving.

He started to close the suitcase, then realized the clothes didn't even belong to him. They were all things Jasmine and Carlos had provided. He'd arrived empty-handed from Hong Kong.

Okay, he thought. *Guess I'll leave the same way.*

He caught sight of his face in the mirror. His bruises were fading, healing faster than usual—another byproduct of the Tiger power. But when he closed his eyes, he could still feel every blow, each little defeat in the cold snowy wasteland.

One last time, he looked around the small room—and realized he was going to miss it. It had felt just like home only twenty-four hours earlier. Now, though . . .

. . . now it was just a reminder of his failures.

Something caught his eye: a thick, padded manila envelope sitting on the desk. He couldn't remember seeing it there before. It bore an international postmark and the address:

STEVEN LEE
General Delivery
Greenland

Steven picked it up, frowning. Mags went into town every few days to pick up supplies—this must have been waiting at the post office. But who knew Steven was in Greenland?

He ripped it open and fished around inside. Something cold and hard, nestled between layers of protective padding, touched his hand. He pulled out the object and held it up to the light.

It was a flat, irregular piece of bone, about the size of his hand, almost round but with jagged, worn edges.

It looked very old. Tiny writing stood out, barely visible, gray against the dirty white of the bone.

Steven squinted, peering closer. It was in Cantonese, or maybe Mandarin.

Great, he thought. *Another person who thinks I know Chinese!*

He threw the bone fragment over his shoulder.

"Whoa! Incoming!"

He whirled around at the voice. Jasmine stood in the doorway, frowning at the piece of bone. She'd snatched it out of the air.

"What's this?" she asked. "An oracle bone? Where'd you get it?" Then she noticed the suitcase on the bed. "And, uh, where are you taking it?"

"I'm not taking it anywhere." He frowned. "Can you read it?"

"Sure." Jasmine glanced briefly at the writing on the bone. "It says 'From someone who cares.' You got a secret admirer or something?"

"I dunno." He turned away. "It doesn't matter."

"It does to me. I just spent an hour talking Roxanne off the ledge. She was practically out the door, but I managed to convince her to stay." She paused. "Maybe I was talking to the wrong person."

"I don't need training," Steven said.

"Sure you do. Not as desperately as Roxanne—your power isn't as destructive. But you could be a lot better than you are."

"Guess we'll never know."

He could hear the anger seeping into his own voice. *Why?* he thought. *Why won't she just leave me alone?*

But when Jasmine spoke again, her voice was suddenly twice as angry as his.

"Steven," she said, "we were attacked yesterday, remember? The whole base is on alert—everyone's doing double shifts, repairing walls and equipment, shoring up our defenses. Everyone except *you*. Ever since your little tantrum in the snow, you've been moping and dragging around. We don't have time for that."

"Maybe you don't have time for it. I've got plenty of time."

"Where are you gonna go?"

"I don't know. Home, maybe."

"And then what? What happens when Maxwell comes after you, looking for your power?"

"I can take care of myself."

"You didn't do too well yesterday."

He turned away, really angry now.

"I didn't mean that," Jasmine said. "Steven, what's this about? Why do you want to leave?"

"Because I can't be what you want me to be. I'm no hero."

"Like those guys in the movies you like? Steel Badger, whatever it is?"

He didn't reply.

"Steven, nobody can live up to that," Jasmine

continued. "In the real world, people make mistakes, and they move on."

"Mistakes?" He whirled back around. "Let's see. I wasted time arguing with you when I should have been getting the recruits to safety. Then, when they asked me what to do, I froze. And that gave the Vanguards time enough to get the better of us."

"That's not how—"

"Then, when I had to decide which team member to help, I chose Rabbit. Because she's little, and I, I, maybe I kind of like her. But I was wrong again. She was the only one who managed to take down her attacker!"

"She's tougher than she looks," Jasmine agreed. "That's one of the things we're learning: who's got what skills, and what areas everyone needs to work on. That's why I need you to help train them."

"*Train* them?" He looked at her, incredulous. "I can hardly talk to them. Duane barely speaks, Liam does whatever he wants, and you said Roxanne's halfway out the door."

"Steven, you can't leave now."

"You don't need me. Look at my face! If I were you, I'd get out, too. Maxwell knows where you are now. He's gonna come back with more guys, and next time Carlos's magic trick isn't gonna stop 'em."

Steven flopped down on the bed, sweeping the suitcase aside. He squeezed his eyes closed until he saw bright patterns.

When he looked up, Jasmine was glaring down at him.

"First of all," she said, "the recruits are better than you think. Kim *did* manage to take out Dog. Liam would have trapped Ox, too, if Duane hadn't shorted out the power. And I know Duane could have taken that obnoxious Monkey guy if he knew how to control his power. We've got a good team—we just have to teach them to work *together*.

"As for you: you could have run away when the Vanguards attacked. But you didn't. You stayed and took that beating, because you refused to abandon your team."

Steven said nothing.

"We are *not* leaving this base," she continued. "We've built up too much here, worked too hard to establish things. I've been running since I was seventeen. No more.

"But you're right: we can't just sit around and wait for Maxwell to attack again. Carlos has a plan—he thinks he and I can de-power Maxwell once and for all. But we can't do it here, and we can't do it alone."

She raised her arms and closed her eyes. The Dragon power began to appear around her, shimmering into its familiar, reptilian shape. But another figure formed along with it: a larger, winged Dragon, holding Jasmine's dragon in a thick-winged grip.

Steven recognized the second Dragon. "Maxwell?" he asked.

Jasmine nodded sharply. "He's got hold of me," she

said. "Leeching away the power. And he's—too strong—"

Maxwell's Dragon screeched and squeezed, pressing Jasmine's Dragon tight between dark wings. Jasmine let out a little cry.

Steven felt helpless. Like when his grandfather would burst into a coughing fit, and there was nothing he could do to help.

"I can't lead a normal life, Steven." Jasmine's voice was strained now, her teeth gritted in pain. "I gave that up a long time ago. But you and the others—if we can stop the Vanguard once and for all, you might have a chance—"

Then, all at once, Maxwell's Dragon flickered. Jasmine's eyes shot open, and her Dragon burst free. It reached out with sharp claws and slashed at the larger creature. Maxwell's Dragon recoiled and howled, fire shooting out of its mouth. Then it flapped its wings helplessly and vanished.

Steven stared at Jasmine. "What happened?" he asked. "What was that?"

Jasmine raised a hand to her head. She stumbled, reaching out a hand to steady herself against the desk.

Then he noticed: her Dragon *wasn't* fading. It glowed brighter now, whipping its tail around, slashing the air with its claws.

"I don't know," Jasmine said. "I . . . I feel . . ."

Energy flared out from her in waves. The Dragon seemed firmer, more solid than ever before. Jasmine straightened up and clenched her fists.

". . . I feel *stronger.*"

But something was wrong. Jasmine started staggering around the room, twitching, as her Zodiac glow blazed even brighter. She opened her mouth and the Dragon mirrored her action. Fire burst out of its maw, flaring like a flamethrower.

Just then, Carlos appeared at door. "Hey, I . . . Jaz?" His face had a chance to form a look of concern before he and Steven were knocked backward by Jasmine's Dragon power. Steven squinted against the blinding light. It was clear Carlos was unconscious, and Jasmine's power was growing.

"Too much," Jasmine said. "Too much power. The Dragon . . . it's really strong." She looked from Carlos's limp body to Steven, and for the first time since he'd known her, he saw fear in her eyes. "I can't hold it in!"

Steven leapt to his feet. "What—what do I do?"

"I don't know! Oh, this isn't good. I . . . *no!*"

Again, the Dragon's mouth erupted. Fire struck the wall, charring a hole in the plaster. Steven rushed over to the wall, patting rapidly at it to tamp out the flames.

When he turned around, Jasmine was facing him. The energy seemed to have merged

with her now—they glowed together, as bright as a star. The Dragon whipped its head and tail all around her, like a savage animal.

"Help me," Jasmine said. Her voice sounded small, lost inside the maelstrom of power.

Instinctively, Steven willed the Tiger to rise up inside him. He held out his hand and touched Jasmine's. Touched the Dragon . . .

. . . and felt its power, flowing into him.

Steven had almost become accustomed to the Tiger energy. He was always half aware of it, like a fast heartbeat or an aching limb. Most of the time it pulsed at a low, steady level, flaring up only when he needed to fight someone or punch through a wall.

The Dragon, he now realized, was something entirely different. It burned brighter, hotter, than any of the other Zodiac signs. Maxwell believed he could harness it, bend it to his will. But right now, in its pure form, it was a threat to Jasmine's life.

The power ebbed and flowed, cycling into Steven's body and then back into Jasmine again. The glow around her softened. The Dragon still blazed, but not as bright.

"I'm . . . I'm getting control of it again," she said. "Whatever you're doing, keep doing it."

I don't know *what I'm doing,* he thought. But he held on tight to Jasmine's hand. Her fingers tensed up around his, then relaxed.

The Dragon power settled into a warm, steady glow. Jasmine turned toward Steven, and the Dragon's head turned with her. Two sets of eyes, one real and one made of energy, stared at him.

Then, all at once, the Dragon faded away. Jasmine rushed over to Carlos, who was just coming to.

"Are you all right?" She helped him into a chair.

"I'm fine," Carlos said, searching Jasmine's eyes. "Are *you* all right?"

Jasmine shared a look with Steven. "Yeah, I'm okay now. Thanks to Steven."

"What what *what the what was that?*" Steven asked.

"Something big," Jasmine said. "For days now, Maxwell's been leeching the Dragon right out of me. But something must have happened to him. The power . . . he lost hold of it, somehow. It flowed out of him and back into me."

Steven frowned. "That's good, right?"

"If I can keep it. And if it doesn't fry me alive." She held up a hand, blazing with Dragon fire. "But if I know Maxwell, he won't just give *any* piece of the Zodiac. And I know him better than I'd like."

She turned and stared up at Steven. "You did something there. You reached out and linked our powers, helped me to control mine. You shared your energy with me."

He shook his head, overwhelmed. "Is that a property of the Zodiac power?"

"That must be a property of *your* power. But nobody else's. I'd like to do some more research on this," Carlos said.

Jasmine snapped her fingers. She sat up straight, her eyes suddenly wide. "That might give us the edge we need."

Steven turned away, frowning. "I'm not leaving, am I?"

"That's up to you. But I sure hope not."

"We're not ready," he said, turning to plead with her. "If our team goes up against Maxwell's, we're gonna lose again. We might die."

"Not if we're smart."

Steven walked over to the bed and gazed at the half-filled suitcase. He thought of his father, stern and stoic, and his enigmatic mother. He thought about his classmates, Harani and Ryan, joking and wandering around the museum in Hong Kong. They were all part of another life now, a time that seemed very, very far away.

Then he thought about Jasmine and Carlos setting up this compound because they knew the Zodiac Convergence was coming. He thought about the recruits, Duane and Kim and Liam and Roxanne, who needed someone to guide them. He thought about Maxwell, hovering imperiously above the Zodiac pools, his arms outstretched as if to draw in all the power in the world.

And Steven thought about the world. A world that

now had people of incredible power running wild across it, power like nothing it had ever seen before.

Somebody has to protect that world.

"I'll stay," he said.

There was a soft *poof.* "YAY!" Kim cried, appearing in the air between Steven and Jasmine. She ran to Steven and hugged him, very tight.

"Uh!" he said, surprised. "Um, thanks."

Suddenly, Roxanne, Duane, and Liam appeared at the door and walked inside. Kim pulled away, smiling sheepishly. "We were listening at the door." Then she hugged him again.

"Yeah, mate," Liam chimed in. "We don't want you to leave."

"Not at all," Duane added.

"We need you," Roxanne said, looking him in the eye.

Steven stared at them, utterly surprised that they would care, utterly touched.

Jasmine smiled at the team. "Get back to the training room," she said, "all of you. And, Steven, try out that new trick with the others, the thing where you link your powers together. I'd like to do some more planning."

"Okay." Steven smiled, sheepishly.

Carlos rose surprisingly steadily for having just been knocked out for a few moments. He nodded at Jasmine's questioningly look, and the two of them headed out.

Jasmine paused in the doorway. "We're going after Maxwell tomorrow. Get ready, everyone."

Then they were gone.

Steven turned to the group. "Thanks, everybody. You all go on without me. I'll be right behind you."

Duane, Liam, and Roxanne filed out, while Kim flashed him another smile and *poofed*.

Well, Steven thought when he was alone once more. *I guess I'm staying.*

He still had his doubts. But he felt a strong sense of relief. He had the feeling he'd just been talked out of a very bad decision.

Something on the floor caught his eye, reflecting the overhead light. He reached down and picked up the bone fragment. What had Jasmine called it? An oracle bone?

Now he remembered. His grandfather had told him about oracle bones: they were used in ancient China, centuries ago, to send messages. Some of the earliest examples of Chinese writing were preserved on these bone fragments.

Is that what's going on? he wondered. *Someone trying to send me a message? But who?*

As Steven watched, startled, the Chinese characters on the bone seemed to soften and blur. They moved and shifted, the strokes and lines rearranging themselves into new patterns. When they stopped, the writing spelled out two short sentences in English:

BE CAREFUL, BE SMART. YOU CAN DO THIS.

Steven's hand was trembling. *This is no ancient oracle,* he thought. *Whatever it is, it's got some serious tech inside it. Someone went to a lot of trouble to make it.*

He sat on the bed, staring at it for several minutes. His phone, the phone Jasmine had given him, bleeped. He clicked it on and saw a text message from Liam: WAITING IN THE TRAINING RM, MATE. U COMING?

Steven frowned at the oracle bone, then stashed it in his top bureau drawer. He made a mental note to have it checked out, to see if there was some kind of tracking device inside it. But somehow, he didn't feel like sharing it with anyone else yet.

He ran out of the room, his mind whirling with possibilities.

PART FOUR
DRAGON'S GATE

CHAPTER THIRTY-THREE

"I'VE ALWAYS liked airplanes, you know?" Liam said. "Not like my Uncle Edwin. First time he ever flew, the bloody plane crashed straight into a control tower. Never left Belfast again till the day he died. He used to say, *'If man was meant to fly, he'd have landing gear on his butt.'*"

Steven liked listening to Liam's stories, but right now he had something else on his mind. He mumbled an excuse, unfastened his seat belt, and slipped out into the aisle.

Jasmine had booked them on a series of commercial flights. This was the last leg of the trip, a long flight from Budapest through to Beijing, China. Everyone was tired and stiff from all the travel, and there was still a long truck ride ahead before they reached their destination.

Jasmine had explained the mission; apparently they needed to be in a particular spot in China to pull it off. But Steven still had the strange feeling she wasn't telling him everything.

He walked forward in the cabin. Just ahead, Kim and Roxanne sat together. Kim seemed to be trying to make conversation, but Roxanne was wearing ear buds, rocking back and forth in her seat.

"This is pretty exciting, isn't it?" Kim asked.

Roxanne didn't say anything.

"I mean, this whole thing," Kim continued. "Training to use powers, flying all over the world, going on a mission into unknown territory. Mildly terrifying."

Roxanne made a very faint "Mmmm" noise.

"I just hope we're ready," Kim said. "I think we're really starting to work well together. Don't you think?"

Roxanne raised an eyebrow. Very deliberately, she reached up and removed one earbud.

"Kim, don't take this wrong, but I don't want to talk," Roxanne said. "I'm just here to learn how to use my stupid power without knockin' down walls. That's all I want to focus on."

Kim frowned. "What if you need us? What if one of us needs *you*, to save our lives?"

Roxanne shrugged. She looked at Kim for a long moment, and her expression seemed to soften.

"Then I'll save your life," she said.

In the next row, Jasmine lay sprawled out over both seats, dozing. *She probably hasn't slept for days,* Steven realized. She twitched slightly, as if in the grip of a nightmare.

Steven walked past Jasmine to the next row, where Duane and Carlos sat together. A large laptop computer sat on Carlos's lap, and Duane held a strange cube-shaped machine wired into the laptop with a thick cable. Duane's fingers tapped on the cube's tiny touchscreen, almost too quickly to see.

Carlos looked up, surprised. "Steven."

Steven smiled tentatively. "What are you doing?" he asked.

"Just completing the programming for the procedure," Carlos replied. "It requires a lot of custom code. I was worried about getting it all written in time. But Duane here understood what I needed right away."

Steven watched Duane for a moment, but Duane just kept working, not even looking up. *We all use the Zodiac powers in different ways,* Steven thought.

"Hey, since you're here," Carlos continued, "take a look at this." He pressed a button on the laptop and a logo appeared, with lettering underneath it:

P.I.Z.Z.A.

Private

International

Zodiac

Zero

Assembly

"Another name for the group?" Steven asked.

Carlos nodded.

Steven frowned. "What's a 'Zero Assembly'?"

"Ah, nothing. I think I was just hungry." Carlos pressed DELETE, and the words vanished. "Something else I can do for you?"

"I, uh . . ." Steven held out his hand, allowing a slight Tiger-glow to ripple across his fingers. "I was wondering if Jasmine told you about what happened."

"The power-sharing, you mean. Yes. When we get back, I'll run a full barrage of tests." Carlos tapped at the computer again distractedly.

"Okay. But . . . do you understand it at all?"

"The Zodiac powers operate on a wide spectrum of wavelengths. It sounds like the Tiger can instinctively sense the wavelength of another person's power, and adjust its own to match. This causes a cascading amplification effect." He paused. "That's just a guess, though."

"I don't know how to control it. What if it happens on this mission?"

"I *hope* it happens." Carlos set his computer aside and looked at Steven, very seriously. "You don't understand—none of you understand how powerful Maxwell is. We're going to need every trick, every edge we can muster just to get past his defenses."

Steven nodded, letting that sink in. "And after that? When we get to the, uh . . ."

"The Grottoes." Carlos paused. "Well, the plan is to draw the Dragon power out of Maxwell. Which means it'll all go into . . ."

Carlos twisted his neck around to look at Jasmine, still asleep. Her mouth moved softly, forming words, but Steven couldn't make them out.

He turned back to Carlos. "You're worried about her, aren't you?"

"Yes," Carlos replied. "The Dragon power isn't like the other signs." His voice barely wavered—most people wouldn't have registered the emotion behind it. But Steven was starting to get to know Carlos, and the strange way he and Jasmine related to each other.

"I know," Steven said. "It's much stronger."

"I hope she can handle it. She's so strong and so proud—she hates to ask anyone for help. But . . ." Carlos trailed off, looking away.

For the first time, Steven realized: *He really cares about her.*

Above, the seat belt lights winked on. A voice blared

over the loudspeaker. Steven had learned just enough Cantonese to know it was telling him to take his seat. They were about to begin the approach for landing.

Steven turned and started to walk away. But to his surprise, Carlos grabbed his arm.

"You saved her," Carlos said, his voice intense. "When the power threatened to overwhelm her, you helped her. You may have to do it again."

Steven nodded solemnly.

"Help her," Carlos repeated.

Steven trudged back to his seat. The plane began to tilt forward, descending toward the ground. And Steven felt the weight of yet another burden resting on his shoulders.

They disembarked from the truck and walked across a long stone bridge spanning the Yi River. Carlos was toting a big satchel full of equipment, with Duane and Liam carrying smaller bags. Jasmine ushered them all forward, like a drill sergeant. Other tourists fell in next to them on the bridge.

Duane, who had barely said a word the entire trip, suddenly started talking non-stop. "The Grottoes are one of the greatest historical treasures in China," he said. "There are more than two thousand caves in all, built over a period of four hundred years."

A series of high arches, built into the side of a mountain,

marked the entrance to the caves. Jasmine ushered the group in behind a commercial tour, and soon they were inside the mountain itself.

The path sloped downward, leading them underground. The cave walls began to display a wide variety of carved figures, animals, and landscapes.

"Thousands of examples of Buddhist art are contained in these caverns," Duane continued. "Since very few ancient temples on the surface have survived, the Grottoes have become even more historically important."

The cavern widened out into a big hall. Straight ahead, a cluster of gigantic statues, built into the walls, stared down at the visitors. Each statue was at least eight times as tall as a man. In the center, a Buddha sat serenely. It was the largest of all.

"The Buddha is the most important image in the caves," Duane said. "He's usually depicted, as we see here, with his followers. These statues were carved almost fifteen hundred years ago."

Roxanne rolled her eyes. "If I wanted the Wikipedia entry, I'd read it."

Duane looked puzzled. "I gathered a lot of data on this place during the trip here," he said. "I thought it might be useful."

"Yeah," Liam said to Roxanne, "lighten up on the lad. Somebody's got to be the smart one around here."

"Every group has a smart one," Kim agreed.

Roxanne glared at them all, one by one, her mouth twitching. Then her expression softened. "Sorry, man."

Duane turned away. He looked sad now, almost miserable.

Liam clapped a hand on Duane's shoulder. "Don't worry about her." He gestured up at the huge, looming statues. "This place makes us all feel kinda small."

Kim gazed up at the statues, awestruck. "This was a long time ago," she whispered, barely loud enough to be heard.

Steven found himself staring at the Buddha statue—and, mostly, at the giant figures surrounding it. They wore a variety of clothing, from robes to crowns to ancient military uniforms. *They're all very different from each other,* he thought. *Just like us. Just like our team.*

He looked down to see a perfectly circular smooth stone. *I wonder how long this has been here, how many people have walked past it, for how many years. This place is so full of history.*

"Steven?" Jasmine touched his shoulder. "The tour group is moving along. This is our chance to slip away."

He nodded absently.

"Steven?"

He gestured up at the statues. "Jasmine," he said hesitantly. "Do you think some of the people who lived during this time . . . do you think they might have had Zodiac powers, too? Like us?"

She nodded. "Could be. And, like us, they probably

had to keep their powers secret from the rest of the world." She slapped him on the back. "Come on. Before the guards notice us leaving."

She moved off, and the others followed. But Steven remained for a moment, lost in thought. When he turned, the tour group had moved on ahead. Jasmine and Carlos were just leading the others off into a branching corridor.

"Steven?" Duane said.

Steven turned back around. Duane had stepped away, in the opposite direction from the others. He pointed, tentatively, farther down into the cave.

Steven followed him to another frieze, another clutch of statues carved into the wall. This one showed a collection of men and women in robes. They were divided into two groups, facing off against each other as if they were about to do battle.

"Look," Duane said.

Steven followed his pointing finger. Carved above one figure, the leader of the left-hand group, was a flare of energy that could have been a Dragon. And above the other leader, a chipped, worn Tiger shape rose toward the ceiling.

Steven peered closer. The Tiger leader reminded him of the etching he'd seen in the old Chinese book back in the museum. The ancient hero with mysterious powers.

Now I know, Steven thought. *I know a little bit, at least, about what those powers might have been.*

Duane took a few more steps, and Steven followed. The next carving showed the Tiger leader fallen to the ground. Dead.

"They . . ." Steven's breath caught in his throat. "Did they destroy each other?"

Duane spoke softly. "They say that, on the day this cave was completed, the people all around saw a bright flash of light that lit up the river."

Steven remembered the flash that had struck him, back in the Convergence room in Hong Kong. He remembered the cold fire lancing through him, the unimaginable sensation of power filling him up for the first time.

Then he glanced, again, at the weathered carving of the dead Tiger leader.

"People like us," he whispered.

He turned, gesturing for Duane to follow. Together they ran to catch up with the others.

CHAPTER THIRTY-FOUR

CARLOS LED the group into a narrow branching corridor, where he swiped a passkey against the rock wall. A hidden door opened to reveal a creaky, disused freight elevator.

Steven climbed inside with the others, grimacing as the elevator groaned under their weight. Carlos opened a panel and hotwired it. The elevator hummed to life, and they plunged downward at stomach-turning speed.

Steven couldn't tell how many levels down the elevator took them. But when the doors opened, he gasped at the sight that confronted him.

ZODIAC

They were in a high, wide cavern with no visible exits. One wall was dominated by an ornate statue of a dragon, its wings spread wide, stone-carved fire flashing from its mouth. Its eyes burned with an ancient ferocity.

"Will ye look at that," Liam said.

Steven felt Kim's hand clutching his hand, a little too tightly. "I, I'm not awesome with confined spaces," she said.

He turned to her and smiled. She squeezed his hand, smiled back, and let go.

This area wasn't open to tourists—the ground was uneven, the air musky and stale. Steven thought briefly of the Convergence chamber, the underground room where Maxwell had sought to harness the Zodiac power. This place reeked of the power, too; but where the Convergence hall had been a metallic, man-made room, this chamber was far older, lined on all sides with earth and rock.

Steven walked forward, almost tripping over some jagged rocks, toward the dragon carving. He touched the dragon's lower talon, the only part he could reach. The Tiger burned within him, as if it recognized a kindred spirit.

Now he could see, on either side of the dragon carving, an array of other animals. A charging ram. A crowing rooster. A snorting ox, a capering monkey. A coiled snake, slithering around the edges of the dragon's wings.

And next to the dragon: a fierce, roaring tiger.

"This place is not in the guidebooks," Duane said.

"No," Jasmine agreed. "But it's where we need to be."

Carlos was already pulling equipment out of his bag, setting up something at the base of the dragon carving. "Duane?" he called.

"This is where you pull off the big move?" Steven asked. "Where you drain Maxwell of all his Dragon power?"

"If we can do it anywhere, it'll be here," Jasmine said. "This place is called Dragon's Gate. It's a unique meeting point of Zodiac energy and, uh, ley lines . . ." She shrugged. "Carlos? Little help?"

"It's where we need to be," Carlos said.

Steven moved over to watch, followed by Kim, Liam, and Roxanne. Carlos and Duane were setting up a small machine on a telescoping tripod. They whispered to each other, fastening screws and adjusting settings on Carlos's laptop.

When they were done, Carlos pulled out the cube-machine that Duane had been programming on the airplane. Carlos hoisted it on top of the tripod assembly and twisted it into place. It hummed, its touchscreen flashing to life.

Carlos stood up and brushed cave dust off his pants. "That's it," he said. "Duane, you want to do a last-minute check of my wiring?"

Duane nodded and started fiddling with the far side of the cube. He pressed a button and two heavy metal manacles slid out on thick cables, one from each side of the machine's base.

Steven peered at the touchscreen:

DRAGON TRANSFER PROTOCOL
READY

"Okay," Steven said. "So we're all set, right?" He pointed at the screen, where a green button winked underneath the word *ready*. "Press the button, suck all the Dragon power out of Maxwell and into Jasmine."

Liam nodded. "Sounds good to me."

"Guess we're on guard duty," Roxanne said.

Kim smiled. "Can I push the button?"

Jasmine and Carlos exchanged uncomfortable glances. "We, uh, we can't start yet," she said.

Steven felt a weird, sinking sensation. "Why not?" he asked.

"Because Maxwell has to be present for the protocol to work."

Steven's eyes went wide. "Present?"

"Maxwell?" Roxanne asked. "You mean Maxwell, the most powerful dude, possibly, in all the world, who has sworn to capture us. He's coming *here?*"

"We don't know that for sure," Carlos said.

"He'll be here," Jasmine said. "He won't be able to resist this big a concentration of Zodiac power."

"Wait a minute," Liam said.

"Whoa," Kim added.

"Are . . . are you saying . . ." Steven paused. "Are we here as *bait*?"

Carlos cleared his throat. He turned away, toward the cube. Duane had stopped working, his eyes shifting warily from Carlos and Jasmine over to Steven and the others.

Jasmine looked away too. "We're all bait," she said, evasively. "Wherever we go."

"I thought we were a team," Steven said.

"We are. Of course we're a team," Jasmine said. But she wouldn't look him in the eye.

"You don't trust us," Steven said. "You don't think we can beat the Vanguard agents."

"I—I can't take any chances with Maxwell." She pointed at the machine. "This is our only chance to stop him."

"That whole pep talk you gave me. Everything you said about teamwork, about wanting us to lead normal lives." Steven struggled to keep his voice from breaking. "That was all crap, wasn't it? All you care about is destroying Maxwell. No matter who you have to hurt in the process."

Jasmine turned, slowly, to face him. "That's not true."

They stood still for a long moment. Kim, Liam, and Roxanne fell in behind Steven, facing Jasmine. She stood with Carlos under the shadow of the ancient dragon statue.

"Liam," Jasmine said. "Kim. You know I'd never hurt you. Roxanne—"

At the sound of her name, Roxanne let out a sharp, angry sonic cry. Steven clapped his hands over his ears. The whole cavern shook, and loose rock rattled down from the ceiling.

Duane walked over, slowly, to join Steven's group. Liam clapped Duane on the back.

"We *are* a team," Steven said, "whether you know it or not."

"I do know it," Jasmine said, almost in a whisper. "But the Vanguard forces almost *killed* you before. I can't let that—"

A rumbling rose up, low at first. Steven turned toward Roxanne to see if she was using her powers again. But she just looked around, puzzled, along with the rest of them.

"The machine," Jasmine said. "Carlos, protect the machine!"

As the rumbling grew louder, the ground began to shake. Rocks fell from the ceiling, small at first, then larger. Kim *poofed* out of the way just as a boulder crashed to the ground, right where she'd been standing.

"Below!" Liam yelled. "It's comin' from down there!"

Steven took a step back. The others followed him instinctively, just as the ground in front of them began to crack and split.

ZODIAC

Something rose up from the center of the room, scattering dust and rock everywhere. Steven stumbled, falling back toward the far wall.

Through the heavy dust cloud, the outline of the massive object tunneling up into the cavern became visible. Steven watched it with a sinking feeling, and he knew:

Vanguard is here.

CHAPTER THIRTY-FIVE

DUST FELL like a shroud over the cavern. Steven coughed. Through the dust cloud, he could see the Vanguard ship: a thick vessel the size of a small house, with tank treads and retractable drills protruding from the front of its body. It nosed up above the hole in the ground, coming to rest at an angle.

"Gotta admit, I'm impressed," Roxanne said. "That is an entrance."

Steven peered through the dust. He couldn't see Carlos and Jasmine anymore, or their machine. They were trapped on the far side of the room, past the huge Vanguard ship.

Kim pointed. "What's that?"

The ship began to vibrate and hum. A flat plate, shaped like a square with the corners clipped, rose up and out of the ship's hull. It started to glow.

"Oh, no," Duane said. "I think that's a—"

Steven didn't hear the rest. Suddenly his skin felt like it was on fire, burning from the inside out. He looked down at his arm, expecting to see flames. But there was no trace of a fire, no marks at all.

Steven, Roxanne, and Kim were flailing around in pain. "What is it?!" Roxanne screamed.

"A.D.S.," Duane replied, grimacing. He pointed at the glowing plate on the ship. "Active Denial System—commonly known, for obvious reasons, as a heat ray. The U.S. military uses it for riot control."

"What'll it do to us?" Kim asked.

"Nothing permanent. Except stop us in our tracks . . ."

Steven closed his eyes, concentrating as hard as he could. His Tiger form began to rise up around him, flaring with power. But then it wavered and vanished.

The pain, he thought, *it's too strong. We can't concentrate enough to use our powers!*

He looked around. Duane and Kim were on their knees now, teeth gritted in agony. Roxanne backed up, through the thick dust cloud, toward the cave wall. Liam was still on his feet, but just barely.

Steven's lapel-radio crackled to life. "—you hear me?"

He jumped. He'd forgotten the tiny radios that Carlos had issued to them.

"Jasmine?" he replied.

"I can't see you," she said. "You're on the other side of the ship. What's going on? Are you all right?"

"We're under attack," he said. "Are you feeling the . . . the heat ray, too?"

"We can feel *something*, but it's much weaker over here. Must be unidirectional." She paused. "Carlos says it's a clever way to attack you. He wishes he'd thought of it."

"I wish he'd thought of it, too!"

Steven looked up. Through the haze, he thought he saw something else moving on the hull of the Vanguard ship. Was it . . . a hatch, opening?

"I gotta go, Jasmine."

"Do you see Maxwell?" Jasmine asked.

"No. No, I do not see Maxwell." Steven couldn't keep the irritation out of his voice.

"Steven, I can't help you right now. I have to help Carlos start the power-drain procedure."

"Okay."

"And Steven? I'm sorry. I should have told you the plan."

"Yeah, okay. Later!"

The dust blew toward him now, obscuring the ship. Steven coughed and reached out for Duane, wincing with every move. He felt as if his insides were on fire.

"Duane," he said, "see if you can get near the ship, take out that heat ray."

Duane looked up, tears of pain in his eyes. "Okay," he

said, "b-but Carlos said the Vanguard tech was shielded."

"Just try!"

"But my power—"

"Duane?" Steven grabbed him by both shoulders and stared into his frightened eyes. "This is one time we *want* your power to disrupt something."

Duane smiled quickly. He coughed, nodded, and disappeared into the dust.

Steven whirled around toward the others—and found himself staring straight into the grim face of Ox.

Ox's massive fist lashed out. Steven ducked back, dodging sideways. He reached into the pocket of his cargo pants and pulled out a small electronic staff, a tiny version of the one Carlos had used to repel the Vanguard team back in Greenland. Steven clicked it on and a beam of yellow energy reached forward to engulf Ox.

"Remember this?" Steven said.

Ox just smiled. "Yeah," he said, "but we're shielded from it now. Along with the heat ray."

Steven barely saw the next punch. It slammed him backward, knocking him to the ground. He hit it hard, coughing dust. His skin still burned like fire.

Well, he told himself, *we expected that. Still, it'd be nice to catch a break once in a while.*

With an effort, he shook his head and looked up. Roxanne lay on the ground, with Horse kneeling over her. Just past them, Liam and Ox circled each other like boxers. He couldn't see Kim. She must have *poofed* away.

Under other circumstances, Steven realized, it might have been a fair fight. But Horse and Ox were both fully powered up, their energy forms blazing around them. Liam and Roxanne were trying to use their powers, but the heat ray made it impossible for them to concentrate. A spectral Ram shape flickered in the air above Liam, while a fierce Rooster struggled to stay corporeal around Roxanne's helpless form.

They've got us, Steven realized. *They've planned for this . . . planned for everything. Everything except . . .*

"We're going to need every trick," Carlos had said on the plane. "Every edge we can muster."

Steven squeezed his eyes shut, willing the pain away. He reached inside and forced the reluctant Tiger out of its cage. It radiated forth, seeking out others of its kind. Seeking its friends, its allies.

Its teammates.

Steven bolted toward Roxanne, reaching out with his hand. The Tiger power radiated forward, ahead of him. Energy flashed through the air, expanding and billowing outward.

When Steven's energy touched Roxanne, her eyes burned with sudden fire. The Rooster form flared up above her, its beak snapping furiously. Roxanne threw Horse away, breaking the Vanguard agent's powerful grip. Then she opened her mouth wide.

A fierce, powerful scream burst forth, stronger than any cry Roxanne had ever managed before. It struck the startled Horse head-on, enveloping her in an unimaginable blast of sound. Horse cried out and raised her hands to her ears. She staggered backward, colliding hard against the hull of the Vanguard ship.

Steven saw his chance and swung, punching Horse hard on the side of the head. She went down.

He held out a hand to Roxanne. She looked at him, dazed, for a moment. Then she extended her hand and let him help her up.

"Thanks," she said, coughing and holding her throat.

"You with us?" he asked.

She nodded, her face grim.

Then she turned, very fast, and pushed Steven aside. He turned, surprised, to see Ox charging toward them. Roxanne ducked her head low and cried out.

Her sonic blast struck Ox on his feet, knocking him off-balance. Steven saw his chance and leapt through the air. Ox twisted and tried to regain his footing, but he stumbled and went down.

Steven landed on top of him, punching and kicking

with the full force of the Tiger. *Don't let him get the advantage,* Steven thought. *Learn from your mistakes. Don't give him a chance!*

The battle raged for several minutes. Ox was muscular—every time one of his blows connected, Steven felt it in his bones. But Steven was faster. He landed two punches for every one of Ox's.

Finally he heard a voice in his ear: "Cannonball!"

Steven looked up to see Liam leaping through the air. Steven held up a hand, sending Tiger energy surging into Liam. The Ram form whirled and rolled along with Liam, its spectral horns slicing the air. Steven's energy flashed into him, supercharging his power, lighting him up like a full moon.

At the last minute, Steven rolled out of the way.

Liam landed on top of Ox with the full force of his steel-hard skin. Ox let out a loud gasp and went limp.

Liam rolled to his feet. "How about that," he said, smiling easily. "Immovable object wins after all."

Steven pointed toward the heat-ray projector, still glowing atop the Vanguard ship. "We've got to take that thing out," he said.

Liam reached for Ox's limp form. "How 'bout we use this?"

Steven nodded sharply. He took hold of Ox's arms, while Liam grabbed the big man's feet. Roxanne hefted his middle, and together they hurled him toward the ship.

Ox traveled two feet through the air and fell short, landing on the ground with a thud. He groaned faintly.

Roxanne gestured at the unconscious Horse. "Maybe something lighter?"

One minute later, Horse's body slammed into the heat-ray beam. The projector cracked, sparked, and split in half. One section hung loose off the ship, while the other clattered to the ground.

All at once, the pain was gone. Steven exhaled in relief, shaking out his limbs. "Vanguard *does* have the best toys," he said.

"Maybe." Liam smiled. "But I always used to break my toys."

"S-Steven?"

Kim's voice sounded scared over the radio. Steven whipped his head around, searching for her. "On our way!" he yelled. He took off at a run, with Liam and Roxanne right behind.

The Vanguard ship's entrance had piled up a mound of rock against the zodiac statues. Steven zigzagged around it and stopped short. Dog, the third Vanguard agent, stood braced against the rock pile, holding Kim tight in a vise-like grip.

"He's got me," Kim said. "I, I can't jump if I can't move!"

Liam gritted his teeth and started forward. But Steven grabbed him by the shoulder. "No," Steven said. "Like we practiced. Roxanne?"

Roxanne sucked in a deep breath and charged forward. As she drew near Dog, she let out a series of sonic

cries. Steven tensed—but this time, Roxanne's assault seemed to be silent. Steven couldn't hear anything at all.

Dog could, however. He let go of Kim and whirled toward Roxanne, grabbing at his ears. He began to howl in agony.

"I'll be a wart on my grandma's nose," Liam said. "That trick works."

"Ultrasonic cries," Steven said. "Too high-pitched for humans to hear. But *dogs* . . ."

Dog dropped to his knees, making a weak, high-pitched noise.

Liam clapped Steven on the back. "You're up, mate."

Steven charged forward, willing the Tiger power to come forth. It filled his arms, his legs, his senses. When he reached Roxanne, she backed up a step, making way for him. Dog turned, confused.

Steven leapt onto his back.

Dog reared back, howling. He reached out to grab hold of Kim. And, despite her instincts, Kim stayed put, knowing that she had to keep Dog from sprinting away. Steven grabbed him around the neck, clamping an arm around his windpipe. Dog started running, leaping around, bucking and jumping—anything that might throw Steven off his back. But the Tiger's grip was unbreakable.

Steven tugged on Dog's ear. The Vanguard agent let out a yip and turned in that direction.

"Huh," Steven said. "Steering's a little sticky . . ."

"What do you know?" Liam yelled. "Yer too young to drive!" He stepped forward and gave Steven a "Bring it on" gesture.

Steven pulled on Dog's other ear, hard. Dog spun around and took off at a run, yelping and howling. Steven held on, held on, held on . . . then leapt away just as Dog slammed into Liam at full speed.

At the moment of impact, Liam flew backward. Dog bounced up in the other direction, high into the air.

At the top of Dog's arc, Kim appeared in midair with a soft *poof.* "Remember me?" she asked. She punched him on the nose as hard as she could, then *poofed* away again.

Dog's eyes rolled back into his head. By the time he crashed to the ground, he was unconscious.

Steven ran to Liam and Roxanne. "Everybody in one piece?" he asked.

"Safe as houses," Liam said. He wasn't even breathing hard.

Before Steven could answer, Kim *poofed* in and grabbed all three of them, pulling them in for a group hug. Steven was startled, and Roxanne tried to pull away.

But Kim held on tight. "This is happening, guys," she said. "I got feels!"

"What the heck," Roxanne said. "I guess we earned this."

Steven felt a sense of pride stronger than anything he'd ever felt before. They really *were* a team, now.

Then Roxanne pulled away, pointing toward the Vanguard ship. "Is, um, is that *supposed* to be happening?"

A bright glow was rising up over the nose of the ship, piercing the settling dust. Steven's heart beat faster as he recognized the shape within the glow: a shifting, shimmering Dragon.

Kim frowned. "Is it another heat ray?"

"Or . . ." Roxanne grimaced. ". . . Maxwell?"

"No—it looks like Jasmine's Dragon," Steven said. "I think she's activated Carlos's machine."

Liam started off around the ship. "Well, let's go then. We better make sure no bloody rocks fall on her."

But Steven frowned and thumbed his radio on. "Duane?" he called. "Where are you?"

No answer. *That's not good,* Steven thought. *There might be more Vanguard agents in the ship.*

We've got to go after him. I can't abandon a team member—

Then a second, bright light caught Steven's eye. It was

coming from the very center of the ceiling, directly above the Vanguard ship. As he watched, it grew stronger, almost blindingly bright. A white-hot opening began to appear in the rock, stretching upward farther than he could see.

Liam pointed up at the hole. "That," he said slowly, "was not there before."

"And it's melty," Roxanne added. "Melty bad."

Kim turned to him. "Steven? What do we do?"

Steven looked up at the blinding light, then down to the glow emanating from Jasmine's Dragon. Two problems, both demanding immediate attention.

And then there was Duane.

Another decision, Steven thought. *And this time, I better choose right.*

CHAPTER THIRTY-SIX

JOSIE STUMBLED through the narrow, curved passageway inside the Vanguard ship, past the branching doors leading to the drill-control and weapons chambers. She punched the wall and swore softly—she couldn't believe this group of children had gotten the better of her again.

"Such language," said an oily voice from up ahead. Josie recognized it immediately: Thiago, the Rat.

CHAPTER THIRTY-SIX

Josie grunted and eased her way down into the main cockpit. It was cramped, but just large enough to hold the motley group that confronted her. Vincent, the Monkey, sat in the pilot's seat, speaking intensely in a low monotone. Next to him stood Celine, the Snake. She turned, her one visible eyebrow rising at Josie's entrance.

A smirking Thiago stood up to face Josie directly. "You combat team guys aren't making out so good, are you?" He reached down to the floor and grabbed Duane, the Zodiac's Pig, by the hair, holding him like a trophy. "I did my part. Knocked this guy right out."

"I could have just hypnotized him," Celine said. "That *is* my power, you know."

"I used my gas gun. More fun." Still holding Duane, Thiago pulled out a high-tech sidearm and squeezed a puff of gas into the air. "Pleasant oaky bouquet, too."

Josie frowned. She didn't like Thiago, and though she hated to admit it, she was a little frightened of Celine. The two of them made up the Vanguard Black Ops team, and Maxwell had assured Josie they were all on the same side. But Thiago was creepy and sadistic, while Celine seemed cold and unpredictable.

Josie turned toward the pilot's seat and gestured at Vincent—who, she could now see, was talking continuously into a cell phone. "What's he doing?"

"Status report," Celine said. "He's all business now, our Monkey."

Josie looked at her, a bit surprised. Was that a note of worry in Celine's voice?

Vincent tapped at a touchscreen, and another screen lit up with an image of Steven reaching out to share power with Roxanne. "Preliminary findings: targets manifesting previously unseen cooperative capabilities," Vincent said. He tapped again, and three portraits appeared with big red Xs through them: Nicky, Josie, and Malik. "Agents one through three neutralized."

"Hey," Josie protested.

Vincent turned and seemed to notice her for the first time. He showed no reaction, but turned immediately back to his report. "Agents one and three neutralized," he corrected. "Agent two . . . damaged."

Thiago snickered. "Damaged," he said, pointing at Josie. "That's you."

Despite her fear—and her aching muscles—Josie clenched a fist and turned toward Thiago. He flinched and shoved Duane's body away, toward the corner of the cockpit.

Vincent looked up, surprised, as Duane's unconscious form slid by him. Vincent looked slightly confused.

"That man," Vincent said, pointing at Duane. "Do I know him?"

Josie turned to Vincent, incredulous. "You fought him," she said. "Two days ago."

"Oh, yes. I was different then." A look of contempt stole across Monkey's face. "I was a fool."

Josie frowned. Vincent had been boastful and arrogant for as long as she'd known him, constantly butting into other people's business. But ever since his private meeting with Maxwell, all that had changed. Josie knew she should be happy—the "old" Vincent had been incredibly irritating. But when she looked at the cruel smile on the new model's face, a chill ran up her spine.

If I disobey orders, Josie thought, *I expect to be disciplined. A week of menial-labor duty, a demotion, maybe even imprisonment. But Maxwell has done more than that—he's changed Vincent's entire personality. Is Maxwell really that powerful?*

And if so—what's to stop him from altering all our minds?

Vincent kicked at Duane's body, just enough to make the teenager groan. "The Pig," Vincent said. "I remember him now. Payback is coming."

Thiago laughed. "I like the way you think, Monkey Boy."

Then Thiago's whole body stiffened up. He looked around, his eyes wild, as if he were caught in a mousetrap.

"What is it?" Celine asked. "What do you see?"

Thiago's beady eyes darted toward Celine, then Vincent, and finally Josie. He stared for a long time at Duane's limp form, his eyes blinking rapidly.

He can sense things, Josie remembered. *That's the Rat's power: intuition, maybe even foresight. Can he actually see the future?*

Thiago turned to look down the short passageway toward the ship's outer hatch. The hatch was out of view, around a bend. Thiago opened his mouth and spoke two words, too quietly for Celine to hear.

"What?" Celine frowned. "What did you say?"

"Someone's coming," Thiago said.

Jasmine levitated in the air, feeling the energy course through her body. The glistening Dragon shape surrounded her, its glow lighting up the entire cavern.

Carlos knelt next to the machine, adjusting switches and touching control screens. "Careful," he said. "You're tethered, remember?"

Jasmine felt a tugging on her arm. She looked down, only then remembering that one of the machine's manacles was strapped to her wrist. It glowed with power, tiny electrodes inside it feeding energy from Carlos's machine into her body.

She concentrated hard, and a faint image of the second Dragon—Maxwell's Dragon—came into view next to her own. But as soon as it appeared, it vanished again.

"Is it working?" she asked. "Are we drawing the energy away from Maxwell?"

Carlos looked up from the machine. "A little bit. But until we get to Phase Two, it won't be enough to make a difference."

Phase Two, Jasmine thought. She cast a grim glance down at the second, empty manacle, hanging loose on the other side of the machine.

"Can you handle it?" Carlos asked. "The power, I mean?"

Jasmine felt a pang of fear despite herself. "I have to," she said.

"I'm worried about you, Jaz. Back at headquarters, you almost burned yourself out. If we pull this off, you'll be absorbing *more* energy than . . ."

He trailed off. Jasmine looked down, through the halo of light. "What is it?" she asked.

Carlos was staring upward, past Jasmine's hovering form. Slowly he lifted a finger and pointed.

On the jagged ceiling, a circle of rock was glowing bright. As Jasmine watched, its color shifted from gray to red, then white.

Then the stone began to melt into liquid slag. Molten drops fell like thick rain in the center of the room. One of them struck the Vanguard ship, denting its surface with a deep hiss.

A white-hot radiance seemed to fill the hole in the ceiling. It burst through, dropping into the chamber at a measured, unhurried pace.

Jasmine's eyes, her mouth, seemed to well up with fire. She wafted back down to the ground and raised her free hand to point toward the ceiling. The Dragon's sharp energy-talon rose in unison, and it opened its mouth to spit fire.

"Showdown," she whispered.

Inside the glow, a familiar Dragon shape glowed like

a thousand suns. And at its center, barely visible through the blinding light, stood the confident, menacing figure of Maxwell himself.

"Easy, guys," Nicky said. "It's just me."

Josie breathed a sigh of relief. She reached up to help Nicky, the Dog, down into the cockpit. He was pretty banged up, his fur singed and dirty.

Celine turned to her partner, her eyes glowing with annoyance. "When you said 'someone's coming,' I assumed you meant an enemy."

Thiago shrugged. "I guess you're not always right."

Josie ignored them. "You all right?" she asked Nicky. "What's going on out there, anyway?"

Nicky brushed off his fur. "Let's see," he said. "The Tiger and his buds gave me a beat-down. I think Jasmine's up to something. Oh, and Maxwell's here."

Josie and Celine turned to him in shock. "He's *here?*" Josie asked.

Nicky nodded. "Just arrived." He didn't sound happy about it.

"That wasn't in the plan," Celine said.

A smirk played at the corners of Thiago's lips. "Maybe it was. Maybe you just didn't know the whole plan."

She glared at him. "Did you?"

Thiago just shrugged again.

Josie cleared her throat. "The question is, what do we do now? I think—"

"What do we *do*?"

They all turned around. Vincent—Monkey—stood at the pilot's console, staring at them. His eyes blazed with power and righteous indignation.

"We go help him," Vincent said. "He's our leader. We owe him everything."

Celine frowned. "Of course we have to help him," she said. "But it's a question of strategy—"

"Not me," Dog said. "I'm through."

Everyone turned to face him.

"You heard me," he continued. "Since I got this Zodiac power, I been dropped out of an airplane, frozen half to death, and bashed in the head more times than I can count. I'm out. I'm gone. All love to Maxwell, but he's gonna have to find a new whipping boy."

Thiago turned toward Nicky, a menacing look in his eye. "You think you can just *quit*?"

Nicky raised a sharp claw. "Who's gonna stop me? You?"

Josie watched the confrontation. Thiago's powers were probably greater than Nicky's—but they were less physical, too. After a moment, Thiago stepped back, holding up his hands and smiling.

Vincent stepped forward, right in Nicky's face. "You little worm," Vincent said. "After all Maxwell's done for you!"

Nicky stared at him. "Yesterday you were ready to bolt, too. You called Maxwell 'a big loud pretend-soldier pain in my butt.' What happened to you?"

"Maxwell will never let you go," Celine said, stepping between them.

Nicky shrugged. "He'll prob'ly try to come after me, I guess. But I got friends all over." He smiled. "You ever try to catch a stray dog?"

Celine didn't reply. She just stared straight at Nicky, and her eyes started to glow. A green energy glow rose above her, resolving into the image of a coiled, hissing snake. Nicky froze up, his body becoming rigid.

She's hypnotizing him, Josie realized. *Using her power. She'll make him stay, make him carry out the mission.*

Suddenly Josie knew: *I can't let that happen.*

She grabbed Nicky, wrenching him out of Celine's line of sight. Nicky shook his head, disoriented.

Celine cocked her head dangerously at Josie. "What are you doing?"

"If he wants to go," Josie said, "let him go."

Everyone froze. Josie and Celine stood face to face, both of them grim and impassive.

"And I'm going, too," Josie continued.

Vincent threw up his hands. He glared at Josie for a moment, then stalked back over to the pilot's console. He picked up his cell phone and started dictating again.

"Agents one and two," he barked, "have turned

traitor. Recommend immediate, severe sanctions, up to and including termination . . ."

Josie watched Celine carefully. The Snake woman's eyes still glowed, but not as brightly as before.

"Maxwell is out of control," Josie said. "You know what he did. To *him*." Josie gestured at Vincent. "But maybe that's okay with you. After all, you mess with people's minds all the time."

"Not like that," Celine said. Above her head, the energy-Snake whipped and lashed around angrily. "I can give people commands, make them obey me. But I don't change who they are."

"Well," Thiago said, "it seems our new power creates fragile alliances." He held up both hands and backed away, smirking slightly. "I'll leave you ladies to sort this out."

He strode past Duane's body, pausing only to give it a light kick. He ducked down and flipped open a small portal leading to a hidden passageway. Then he paused, turning back to address the others.

"One bit of advice," Thiago said. "If you defy Maxwell, you'd better have a Plan B."

Then he was gone, scuttling like a rat into his hole.

Josie and Celine stood, staring at each other, for a long moment. Nicky watched; Vincent spoke softly into his phone. Josie struggled not to blink.

At last Celine leaned forward, placing her head right next to Josie's. "Go," Celine said.

Josie pulled back. "Will you—"

"I can't go with you." Celine turned angrily toward Nicky. "Both of you, get out. *Now!*"

Josie eyed Nicky nervously. But he just took a step back, shrugging. Vincent stayed at the pilot's console, dictating his angry report.

"Come on," Josie said to Nicky.

She ushered him up into the hatchway, then climbed up behind him. The whole time, she could feel Celine's eye on her back. She half expected Celine to attack her, to grab her by the hair or club her on the back and pull her back down. But nothing happened.

As soon as they were out of the cockpit, Nicky turned to her. "S-so what's our Plan B?"

"Malik," Josie said. "We'll talk to him outside. If he's still in one piece."

Nicky nodded. Then, quick as a dog, he scurried ahead of her down the passageway.

Josie swallowed nervously and moved to follow.

CHAPTER THIRTY-SEVEN

KIM TELEPORTED to the other side of the Vanguard ship. Steven watched her vanish with a deep, sinking feeling in his stomach.

He'd made his decision. He hated to admit it, but Jasmine was right. Nothing was more important than the power-draining procedure.

He cast an uneasy glance over at the ship. *Sorry, Duane,* he thought. *We'll come for you as soon as we can.*

Then he turned to Liam and Roxanne. "Come on," he said.

He led them around the ship, creeping quietly along its hull. They passed the spot where they'd fought the Vanguard team, almost tripping over Ox's unconscious body. The other two agents, Horse and Dog, were gone.

Great, Steven thought. *More guys to watch out for—*

He stopped short, almost colliding with Kim, and Liam bumped into him from behind. Steven motioned for the group to stay low, hidden behind a corner of the Vanguard ship.

Kim pointed upward. Above, Maxwell hovered in the air, facing the huge carved dragon on the wall. He glowed brightly, chanting to himself, surrounded by his huge, raging energy form. Steven had to strain to make out his words.

"I am the Dragon," Maxwell said. "I am the storm, I am the whirlpool. I am power and patience. I forge the future."

As Maxwell spoke, his energy Dragon snapped its flaming head toward Jasmine—who stood on the ground, one hand outstretched, trying to draw the power back into herself. Sweat glistened on her forehead. Her other hand was wired to Carlos's machine, which hummed and shook, its lights flashing.

Kim pulled in a sharp breath. "Two Dragons," she said softly.

"A real battle of the bands," Roxanne said.

Jasmine's energy form raged and snarled, power

flowing from its mouth to Maxwell's. "Carlos," she gasped. "Is it working?"

Carlos popped up from behind the machine, shaking his head. "He's just too strong. He's managed to reverse the energy flow, drawing the power back into himself."

Jasmine gritted her teeth. "We *can't* let that happen."

Maxwell didn't even look down at them. "I am strong," he chanted. "I am fire, I am chaos. I am the Dragon."

Carlos stared grimly up at Jasmine. "It's gotta be Phase Two," he said. "That's the only way!"

Jasmine turned to look up at Maxwell with an expression Steven had never seen on her face before. She seemed utterly full of dread, yet resigned and determined at the same time. She turned back to Carlos, smiling sadly, and unsnapped the manacle from her wrist.

"Remember me fondly," she said.

She leapt into the air, riding the current of Dragon energy. Maxwell half turned to meet her, raised a hand—

—and swatted her across the room.

Jasmine cried out as she struck the wall, chipping one of the minor Zodiac statues. The ram's horn broke free and fell to the ground.

"Ouch," Liam said.

"Okay," Steven said, gathering his team together in a huddle. "It's up to us now."

Roxanne's eyes went wide. "'Us'?"

Steven glanced up to see if Maxwell had heard them.

But the Vanguard leader was still turned away, hovering and chanting again.

Jasmine had landed in a heap on the floor. Her energy form flickered, its shape indistinct. Energy flowed out from it even faster now.

"There's no choice," Steven said. "Roxanne, you assault him from the ground. Liam, you're with me. Kim, *poof* in above him."

Kim touched his shoulder. "I don't know . . ."

"We can do this. Remember, we're a team. He's just one guy."

"One *crazy-powerful* guy," Liam said.

"Just remember the plan. GO!"

Steven took off at a run, thinking: *I hope they're behind me.*

They were. As Steven reached for Maxwell, Liam planted himself in position, grimacing. Roxanne crouched low, aiming tight-beam sonic cries at Maxwell's head.

Maxwell whirled in response—just as Kim *poofed* in above. She perched on the head of the wall-mounted horse statue, poised to leap down.

Steven leapt up and grabbed hold of Maxwell's floating legs. He swung Maxwell around through the air, toward Liam. The Dragon energy flared bright, and Steven thought he saw a ghost of a smile appear on Maxwell's lips.

Then Maxwell simply wasn't there anymore. Steven found himself falling to the floor. He landed hard on his shoulder and cried out in pain. Dimly he saw Roxanne crash down next to him, followed by Kim.

Then Liam hit the ground, shaking the entire chamber. *That's impossible,* Steven thought. *Nothing can take down all four of us that fast!*

Then he realized: *Nothing but the Dragon.*

Steven struggled to rise, but his limbs wouldn't obey. A wave of Dragon energy covered him like a thick blanket, pressing him down against the ground.

He heard a muffled cry and turned to see Roxanne struggling beneath another wave of Dragon power. Kim and Liam were caught as well, each in a separate energy prison.

Maxwell wasn't even looking at them. His eyes were fixed on the dragon statue again, and he had resumed chanting.

"This is my place," Maxwell said. "This is my Destiny Palace. I am the Dragon, and I am born to rule."

He's so powerful he can stop us with barely a thought, Steven realized. *He knows we're no threat.*

It's over. He's won.

Then a flash of energy streaked overhead. It slammed straight into Maxwell, smashing him against the outer hull of the Vanguard ship. Maxwell flared bright, and the two energy sources slowly fused together, merging into a single blinding ball of light.

Steven was still pinned down. He struggled to roll onto

his back, squinting upward. As the energy ball moved off of the ship's hull, it drew apart, separating into two pieces again. Now Steven could see two distinct Dragon shapes, coiled around each other in a death-grip.

And inside the second Dragon: Jasmine.

"If this is your Palace," she said, "consider me the Women's March."

Maxwell laughed. "So fierce," he said. "And a historical reference, too. Extra points for that."

"You know me. Full of surprises."

She slashed out with flaming hands. He dodged them easily. "You *are* a Dragon, Jasmine. I'll give you that."

She kicked out, landing a blow on Maxwell's stomach as they tottered in midair. He doubled over, groaning.

"Better believe it," she said. She reached into her pocket and pulled out a small metallic object.

Maxwell backhanded her across the face. His hand swept through the air, leaving a trail of Dragon fire in its wake.

Jasmine cried out and tumbled backward. Her Dragon form shrieked in pain. The metal object slipped from her fingers, tumbled down, and clattered to the ground.

"A Dragon," Maxwell repeated. "But not a leader."

"Jaz, *no!*" Carlos called. He pointed at the fallen metal object—from this angle, Steven couldn't see what it was. "Phase Two!"

Jasmine raised a hand to her face, wiping away blood.

Maxwell turned away, raising his hands toward the dragon statue. "I call on the star Sha Qi," he said. "I accept the chaos, the power. I accept this—"

Jasmine leapt forward, clawing and ripping at him from behind. Her Dragon coiled around his thicker, stronger one, seeking to cut off its energy-breath. Maxwell whipped around, reaching out to throw Jasmine off—but she managed to rake her hand across the front of his shirt. The garment fell, tattered, through the air, fluttering like a dying bird.

Maxwell turned slowly to face his attacker. Jasmine reared back, ready to attack again.

Then she caught sight of his chest, and froze. It bore a long, red, jagged scar.

Maxwell hovered, drifting slowly closer to her. "Remember?" he said, gesturing at the scar. "Do you remember the day your mother gave me this?"

Jasmine said nothing.

"The day she died?"

Jasmine's lip quivered. "I remember," she said.

"She was a lot like you," Maxwell continued. "Fiery—full of power. But she never knew how to *use* that power."

He was moving closer to her as he spoke. Jasmine seemed paralyzed, unable to move. Her eyes flicked from Maxwell's face down to his scarred chest, and back again.

"And neither do you," he said.

"Jasmine!" Steven called, struggling to speak. "Snap

out of it!" But his voice was barely audible, muffled by the Dragon energy that held him tight.

"You killed her," Jasmine said, almost in a whisper.

"I did," Maxwell replied. "And you know what?"

He reached out and grabbed her by the throat.

"That was *before* I had this power."

Jasmine cried out. Maintaining his grip on her neck, Maxwell reached out with his other hand and closed it over her face. She struggled, quivering, but he held her tight.

"Relax, Jasmine." Maxwell's voice was soft now, almost kind. "I don't need to kill you. All I need to do is drain your power. In that way, you're lucky. Luckier than she was."

Jasmine let out a series of strangled cries. Maxwell's outstretched hand glowed bright, his fingers spread wide like the Dragon's talons. He seemed to be drawing more and more of her energy, her very life force, out of her body. Above and around them, their Dragons mirrored their actions, mimicking the battle being fought by their hosts.

"*JAZ!*" Carlos called out. He tossed something up at Maxwell—one of the grenades that Jasmine had used back in the Convergence room.

Maxwell didn't even turn to look. The grenade struck the outer edge of his Dragon form and bounced off, short-circuiting with a dull fritzing sound.

"No," Carlos cried. "No, no, *NO!*"

Jasmine quivered under Maxwell's grip. The sounds coming from her grew duller, quieter.

A stab of panic ran through Steven. He had never heard Jasmine sound like that before. She'd always been strong, funny, indomitable. Now she sounded as if all the fight was being drained out of her.

He glanced sideways. Liam, Roxanne, and Kim were struggling, too, held as tightly as he was by Maxwell's Dragon power. Kim tried to leap up, to *poof* away, but she couldn't get up enough momentum. Roxanne fired off a few sonic shouts against the energy barrier, but flinched as they rebounded back to her.

Up above, Jasmine had gone limp. Only the faintest energy glow surrounded her now, while Maxwell blazed brighter than ever.

Maxwell laughed. He reared his head back, and the Dragon rose up above him. Its wings seemed wider, its form more solid, its fire-breath brighter and hotter than ever before.

"Game over," he said.

Even through the haze of his energy-prison, Steven could hear Carlos's anguished cry.

CHAPTER THIRTY-EIGHT

STEVEN SQUEEZED his eyes shut, willing his body to move. He visualized the Dragon energy, the force that held him down, as a linked network of metal chains. In his mind, his hands blazed bright, sharp as Tiger's claws. He reached up and grabbed hold of the chains.

They wouldn't budge.

Frustration washed over Steven in waves. Again, he felt like quitting. *I'm not good enough,* he thought. *I can't do this. I can't escape.*

From above, a single muffled sound escaped Jasmine's lips.

Steven gritted his teeth. *I've got to do this. I've got to be good enough. If Jasmine can't defeat Maxwell, it's up to me.*

It's like I told the team: there's no choice.

He reached deep inside himself, down to his core. To the power that lay within him. It burned like ice and fire, forged from the basic forces of life. Steven dove inside, through the blazing sun of his own heart . . .

. . . and saw, once again, the serene face of his grandfather.

Grandfather, Steven cried out inside his mind. *I can't do this. I'm not strong enough.*

Yes, you are, the old man replied. *Remember what I told you. About . . . my heritage?*

You are strong because of what I gave you. And what your parents gave you, and their parents, and their parents before them.

And then, just as he had when the energy first struck him, Steven saw the great line of people. The rich and the poor, the farmers and the kings. All staring back at him, all waiting to feed him some piece of themselves, some tiny bit of strength or wisdom that would help him find his way.

Your history is your heritage, Grandfather said. *And your heritage is your strength.*

A tear came to Steven's eye as he looked at the old man's smiling face.

Thank you, Steven said.

Then he stretched out his arms and gathered up all the people, all the power, all the strength he could find. All the heart, the heritage, the memories. The things that had always been inside him, though he'd never known it before.

I summon the power of the Tiger.

The Tiger blazed bright, roaring like fire. Its flaming claws reached out and sliced through the chains that held him. Steven leapt up, free.

At that exact moment, Maxwell let go of Jasmine. She dropped toward the ground, limp and exhausted.

Steven roared, reached out, and caught her.

She twisted in his arms, barely conscious. Her Dragon form was gone. She looked normal, human, just as she'd been when Steven had first met her in Hong Kong when she was pretending to be the museum tour guide.

He started to lower her to the ground. "I got this," he said.

"Wait," she whispered. She reached out and grabbed hold of his arm. "Take that."

She pointed toward the metallic object she'd dropped minutes earlier. It lay on the ground a few feet away.

"What's that?" Steven asked.

"Phase Two."

He leaned over and picked up the object. It was a large hypodermic needle, filled with bright green fluid. With a shock, Steven realized he'd seen it before—in Carlos's lab, back at headquarters.

Above, Maxwell had turned back toward the dragon statue. His chants were louder now, his voice more commanding. "Sha Qi," he said. "This is the moment. This is the endgame."

"Hey," Jasmine said. "I . . ." She started coughing. "I was . . ." Her coughing grew stronger. A bit of blood dripped from the corner of her mouth.

Steven stared at her for a moment. She seemed drained, spent of energy, and yet she hadn't given up fighting.

"Tell me later," Steven said.

"Just do the job," Jasmine said. "Don't be a hero."

He smiled. "No promises."

Then, once again, he summoned the Tiger.

The Tiger is fast, Steven thought. *It's agile and strong. But it's more than that. It's also crafty and cunning, and its senses are sharp.*

He reached out with his eyes, his ears, his sense of smell. And something else, too—an indefinable extra sense, granted him by the Zodiac power. Growling low, the Tiger surveyed the scene:

In the shadow of the zodiac statues, Carlos punched buttons and touched screens on his machine. Jasmine had moved over to help him, and Carlos seemed relieved to see her alive. But the machine had subsided to a low hum, and the energy around it was barely visible. Carlos shook his head in defeat.

Roxanne, Liam, and Kim lay on the ground, still helpless against Maxwell's Dragon energy assault.

A stalactite fell with a sharp crack, shaking the cavern. Steven looked up past the sharply angled bulk of the

Vanguard drill-ship. Above, cracks stretched out from the hole in the ceiling. *Maxwell's arrival,* he realized. *It's weakened the whole chamber.*

And between the ship and the zodiac statues: the enemy. The Tiger's prey. Maxwell floated in midair, chanting and shining, glowing brighter and stronger with each passing second.

Fast as a cat, silent as a shadow, Steven ran to the ship and leapt up onto its hull. His hands, the Tiger's claws, fastened onto tiny dents in its surface, propelling him upward. He felt wild, inhuman, and so very much alive.

In seconds, he stood balanced on the highest part of the ship, the sharp drill-units that had allowed it to burrow its way into the chamber. Maxwell hovered just above, his face turned toward the wall. The statues stared back, the dragon and ram and rooster and tiger.

Steven leapt through the air, snarling. Maxwell half-turned—just as Steven swiped out hard, slashing him across the face.

Maxwell cried out in surprise. He lashed out, Dragon energy flaring from his hand. Steven twisted in midair, but the energy struck him a glancing blow. He screamed and spun away through the air, searching wildly for someplace to land.

Finally he caught hold of one of the carvings on the wall. He tottered for a moment, then looked down at the outcropping beneath his feet. It was a wide carving of a

CHAPTER THIRTY-EIGHT

head, cat-eyes wide with hunger, mouth bared to reveal sharp stone fangs.

The Tiger.

"Well, *that's* gotta be a sign," he whispered, smiling.

Then the Dragon energy flashed out at him again. He leapt up and swooped sideways, landing atop the ram statue.

Maxwell hadn't moved. He hovered several feet away, staring calmly at Steven from inside his raging, glowing energy cocoon. He wasn't winded. He didn't even seem upset.

"I only have one question for you, boy," Maxwell said. "Why?"

Steven gritted his teeth. "Because you can't be trusted with this power," he said.

Maxwell raised an eyebrow. "And you think she can?" He gestured down at Jasmine.

If he grabs hold of me, Steven thought, *I'm dead. He's, like, eighty times more powerful than me. I'm only gonna get one chance.*

Another blast shot out from Maxwell's hand. Steven saw it coming—too late. He tried to leap, but the energy hit him straight-on, slamming him back against the pig statue. He gasped, struggling for balance.

"You are not the Tiger I'd intended," Maxwell said, his voice still perfectly calm. "But you can still join me. I know things about you, Steven Lee. I know that a warrior's blood runs through your veins."

"Why," Steven gasped, "why would I *ever* join you?"

"Well, for one thing . . ."

Maxwell's hand swept out, and another energy blast struck Steven—in the face this time. Stars flashed before his eyes.

". . . you wouldn't have to go through *that* anymore," Maxwell said.

Steven shook his head, struggling to clear his vision. He glanced at the ceiling. It was quaking now, stalactites and bits of stone falling all around.

"But that's just a fringe benefit," Maxwell continued. "Look at the big picture. Society is crumbling. Nations, corporations—everything descends into chaos. Against this miasma, this roiling void, the powerful must band together."

Steven frowned. "You've given up, haven't you? On the, the future? The world?"

"I want to *save* the world." Maxwell held out a hand. "With your help."

He needs us, Steven realized. *All the Zodiac powers together. Me, Kim, Liam—all of us. He needs us to join him.*

"I could take you by force—bend your will to mine," Maxwell continued. "But that's not how I want it. Can't you see—"

Steven tensed his legs and leapt, straight up. He reached out, stretching his body as far as he could, and grabbed hold of the lowest-hanging stalactite. He swung his body around, scrabbling and clutching, and kicked out. His feet struck Maxwell's head, hard.

The Tiger roared.

Maxwell tumbled backward, crying out. As he crashed against the giant drills of the Vanguard ship, the Dragon form around him seemed to flicker.

Steven paused, dangling from the stalactite. "We'll never follow you," he snarled. "*Never.*"

But Maxwell was only stunned for a moment. He whipped his head up to face Steven, his eyes glowing brighter than ever.

"No," he said, "I see that you won't."

Maxwell raised his hand, and a glowing Dragon claw reached out toward Steven. The Dragon writhed, snarling, angrier than Steven had ever seen it before. Fire blazed from its snout.

Steven hissed in a breath, fighting back panic. He scrambled up the stalactite toward the rocky ceiling. But the Dragon fire flared wide, enveloping him. Slowly, the energy began to pull him down.

He struggled to keep hold of his stalactite perch, but it was no use. Maxwell ripped him free, wrenching him down through the air in a pocket of flame.

Then Maxwell grabbed hold of his arms in an iron grip, halting him in midair. He twisted Steven around to face him.

"If you will not be my Tiger," Maxwell said, "I'll have to make another."

As Maxwell stared into his eyes, something deep inside Steven rose up in primordial fear. The Tiger knew it was facing the one creature that could kill it: the Dragon.

"Wh-what are you doing?" Steven asked.

"Drawing the power out of you," Maxwell said.

Steven looked down. The energy shape around him was fading . . . and the roaring, the Tiger's constant presence inside him, seemed fainter than before.

"You can do that?" he asked.

"I've done it before, remember?" Maxwell cocked his head, a thoughtful expression crossing his face. "Oh, I can't hold it forever. Or maybe I can, now? The Dragon's power is nearly unlimited."

A strange sensation ran all through Steven. It wasn't pain, exactly—more like someone was plucking needles out of his skin, one at a time, needles he hadn't even realized were there. Again he remembered the first time the Tiger energy had made contact with him, back in Hong Kong. That had felt like a billion tiny, ice-cold pinpricks stabbing into him.

This was the opposite.

"Don't fight it," Maxwell continued. "You never asked for this power, did you? Remember how simple things were before? Remember your old life?"

Steven felt a twinge of doubt. Things *had* been simpler

back home. *Before the Zodiac power dropped this awesome responsi-bility into my lap. Before the running, the fighting, the constant threats and battles. So easy to just relax . . . to let Maxwell win, and go back to . . . to my old life . . .*

My old life. The phrase echoed in his mind. *I remember that. I remember having no purpose, no cause to fight for. Never know-ing how to act, or what I wanted.*

Or where I belonged.

"This," he croaked. "This is where I belong."

Maxwell furrowed his brow, concentrating harder. "Who told you that? Jasmine?"

"She told me about you," Steven gasped. "She and Carlos—they told me about Lystria. The city you destroyed . . . the people you murdered. Because they got in your way."

Maxwell raised an eyebrow. He seemed amused.

"You don't care . . . about anything," Steven continued. "Except your own power."

"*I* don't care?" Maxwell seemed shocked. "You're just a callow boy. You don't know anything about the Zodiac . . . about the power that lies within you, within every person on Earth."

Steven struggled harder. He couldn't break Maxwell's grip, but he needed Maxwell to think he was trying. As Maxwell pulled him close, the Dragon's flame flared bright, engulfing them both.

"You think I don't know who you are, little boy? I know more than you think. If only you'd bothered to learn," Maxwell continued. "About your parents. Your heritage. Your ancestors . . ."

Again, in his mind, Steven saw the long row of people feeding him strength. At the head of the line, his grandfather leaned in and gave him a wink.

"I know enough," Steven said.

And he stabbed out with the hypo, straight into the scar on Maxwell's chest.

Maxwell's eyes widened. He shoved Steven back, away from him. Steven executed a backflip midair, landing in a crouch on the hull of the Vanguard ship.

Maxwell stared down at the needle protruding from his chest. Its green fluid was almost gone now, pumped into his body. The Dragon form surrounding him seemed to flicker and fade.

"You like that?" Steven pointed at the needle. "It's a powerful . . . a strong necro—I mean neo—"

"Neurotoxin!" Carlos's voice said in his ear.

Steven grinned. "Neurotoxin," he said.

Maxwell scrabbled in panic at the needle. It popped free, clattering once again to the ground. But now it was empty.

Down below, Carlos stepped forward. "Chlorotoxin, to be precise!" he shouted. "Derived from scorpion's venom, but strongly enhanced by the addition of several—"

Jasmine laid a hand on his shoulder. "I think they get it," she said.

Maxwell was shivering now, trembling and shaking in

midair. The Dragon power flared, impossibly bright, and then subsided around him, reduced to a dull shimmering glow.

Liam, Kim, and Roxanne climbed to their feet. "Ace job, mate!" Liam called.

Steven smiled down at them. "Kim?"

With a soft *poof*, she appeared next to Steven atop the Vanguard ship. He pointed at Maxwell. "You want to do the honors?"

Maxwell was quivering in midair, chattering inaudibly to himself.

Kim nodded and took Steven's hands. He reached out and swung her around, back and forth. She kicked out—

—and knocked Maxwell out of the air.

He dropped fast, shooting toward the ground like a missile. Jasmine hustled Carlos out of the way just in time. Maxwell landed hard, right next to Carlos's machine.

Jasmine, Steven noticed, was glowing brighter again.

"Come on," he said, and started down the ship's hull. Just as he touched the ground, Kim *poofed* down next to him.

By the time they joined the others, Carlos had already strapped one manacle to Maxwell's wrist. Jasmine was fastening the other one to her own arm. Between them, the machine glowed and pulsed, revving up to full power again.

Maxwell's eyes stared straight ahead. His mouth moved soundlessly. He seemed paralyzed.

"That must be a pretty strong toxin," Roxanne said.

"It'd kill a wildebeest," Carlos replied. "But it's not gonna hold him long."

"Kill you all," Maxwell hissed, his lips barely moving. "All the Zodiac. Burn the Palace down and start over."

"Charming wee fella," Ram said.

"Just like Lystria," Maxwell continued. "No second chances, no warning shots. No mercy."

"He's starting to glow again," Jasmine said. "His body is already rejecting the toxin. How 'bout now, Carlos?"

Carlos flipped a switch. On opposite sides of the machine, Jasmine and Maxwell both stiffened, as if an electrical current had been shot through their bodies. Jasmine's Dragon form appeared above her, strong and fierce. Maxwell's Dragon flickered, rising up slowly. It seemed weaker now.

Maxwell lurched sideways, staring at Jasmine with an odd look. At first Steven thought it was hatred—but no, this was something different. Disappointment, maybe?

"You have no idea—what you're getting into," Maxwell said. "Vanguard has tentacles all over—all over the globe."

Jasmine closed her eyes, concentrating. Her Dragon stretched up and away from her, closing in on Maxwell's smaller, weaker-looking energy form. Energy flowed out of the Maxwell-Dragon now in a steady stream.

Maxwell staggered. "You'll be hunted forever," he said.

"*I'll* be hunted?" Jasmine laughed. "I'll be the Dragon. You'll just be another war criminal with a failed IPO."

Maxwell's Dragon spread its wings and flapped, a frantic, desperate movement. Jasmine's Dragon reared back like a snake, hissed, and lunged. It snapped its jaws, whipping and lashing, sucking the life-energy out of its enemy.

Maxwell himself stayed impassive, gritting his teeth. But his Dragon opened its jaws wide and screamed, a chilling, inhuman sound that filled the cavern.

A chill ran up Steven's spine. For a moment, he wondered if this was the right thing to do.

Kim turned to Jasmine. "Are you . . . are you taking something from him?"

Jasmine stared intensely at the grappling energy forms. "Nothing he needs," she said.

Maxwell's Dragon began to whirl around, its shriek growing higher in pitch. As Steven watched, it seemed to shrink, shriveling up before Jasmine's onslaught.

"Nothing he didn't try to take from me," she added.

The Maxwell-Dragon coughed fire, then turned its head to look straight up. It let out a final, panicked scream and vanished.

At the same moment, Maxwell collapsed. He struck the ground and lurched to one side, pulled off balance by the manacle still linking him to Carlos's machine.

Kim *poofed* in next to Steven, staring at Maxwell. "Did she kill him?"

"I think that's the least of our problems," Roxanne said.

Steven whirled to see her pointing upward. He followed her gaze—and saw Jasmine's Dragon, surging and spiraling in the air. Its fierce eyes glowed, and something that wasn't quite sound hissed out of its mouth. It seemed twice as large as before.

It turned and lunged downward, enveloping Jasmine.

When the Dragon energy struck, Jasmine arched again. Her eyes glowed, her mouth opened. Fire burst forth all around, licking and curling into the corners of the chamber.

Kim and the others shrank back. Steven just stood, paralyzed, watching the incredible display of power.

Then he felt a hand on his shoulder. Carlos stared at him with frightened eyes.

"Help her," Carlos said.

CHAPTER THIRTY-NINE

STEVEN STARED into the inferno, the fire that seemed to blaze throughout the chamber without burning anything. He focused on the Dragon, the raging Zodiac creature that was Jasmine and something else, too.

He remembered Jasmine leaping toward the Zodiac pool, reaching out for the energy beam. As she'd told Kim, back in America, Jasmine had asked for the power. In a way, she'd invited it in—but now it was threatening to overwhelm her.

Grimacing, he ran forward and grabbed her hand. The Tiger energy rose up around him. It reached out, seeking its own kind, stretching out a strong paw to help its Dragon teammate.

Jasmine turned, as if aware of Steven for the first time. She made a frantic head motion, warning him away.

"Not going anywhere," Steven said. "We can do this. Like in my quarters, remember?"

"No," she said. "Not this time. It's too much. Too strong."

The energy poured into him, coursing through his veins. It felt like fire, like sparks, like tiny electric shocks all over his body. *She's right,* he realized. *She's absorbed all the Dragon power this time. It's too much for her—too much for both of us.*

"Get away," she gasped. "Leave me."

Suddenly he knew what to do. He looked at her, gripped her hand tighter, and smiled.

"No," he said.

Then he swept his other arm wide. The Tiger whirled like a jungle cat, roaring out an ancient summons. It called out to its allies, its teammates. Its friends.

"'Bout time we saw some action," Liam said.

And then they were all there with him. Roxanne, the Rooster, her power fierce, wild, and rebellious. Kim, the youthful Rabbit, an endless font of energy and heart. And Liam, the unstoppable Ram, smiling as he fed them his strength. The Tiger guided them, led them, fed the fierce Dragon energy in tiny jolts through each of them in turn.

Slowly the Dragon form calmed, shrank to its normal size. Jasmine staggered, sighed, and dropped to her knees. She looked up in a daze, taking in each of her teammates.

"Thank you," she said.

Kim shook her head. "That was intense."

"Quite a rush," Roxanne said.

"'Ey!" Liam called out. "Look who finally showed up!"

Steven turned to look. Duane was staggering toward them, coming from the direction of the Vanguard ship.

Kim, Liam, and Roxanne moved forward to help him. "You missed all the fun," Kim said.

Roxanne grimaced. "Girl, you need to learn what 'fun' means."

The Tiger, still on alert, reached out for the newcomer—and snarled. *Something's wrong*, Steven realized. Duane seemed dazed; his movements were stiff, uncoordinated.

"Duane," he said, "are you okay?"

Duane turned glazed eyes toward Steven. "I'm sorry," Duane said.

Then he reached out and fired off his power.

"*NO!*" Carlos cried.

Behind Carlos, the machine exploded. Jasmine's and Maxwell's manacles snapped open as the blast flung them in opposite directions. The cavern floor shook, knocking Roxanne and Liam off their feet.

Dust flew everywhere. A pair of stalactites crashed to the floor.

Steven grabbed Duane by the shoulders. "Why?" Steven asked.

"Don't blame him," a female voice said. "I sort of made him do that."

Steven looked up sharply. A new agent, one he hadn't met before, walked forward out of the dust cloud. She was tall and imposing, with high boots and a cape. Her hair was swept over one eye; the other was glowing a deep shade of green.

Instinctively, Steven knew who she was: *Snake.*

"Vanguard tech is shielded from your friend's powers," Snake said. "Your little toys aren't so sturdy."

Kim, Liam, and Roxanne gathered together near Steven, waving away the thick dust.

"*Savages!*" a voice said.

Steven whirled around. Monkey stood crouched over the limp form of Maxwell, glaring at Steven with a deadly, unnerving fury.

"You did this," Monkey said. "You crippled him. A great man, brought low by the likes of *you.*"

Liam turned to Steven. "Is that the same fella we fought before?"

"He seems different," Kim said, staring at Monkey.

Snake, Steven thought. *She's the real threat here.* He turned back toward her, ready to attack—then stopped as a quake rippled through the entire chamber.

"Don't do it," Snake said. "This cavern is about to collapse."

She's right, he realized. The roof was cracking and shattering, breaking off in large chunks. The explosion had been the last straw.

"A great man," Monkey repeated. "The only person on Earth who can be trusted with the Zodiac power. Everything I am, I owe to him."

He propped up Maxwell and started leading him toward the ship. Maxwell shook his head, groggy. He seemed partially paralyzed.

"We'll be leaving now," Snake said. "Good luck getting out with your lives. If you survive, we'll see you again."

At the ship's hatch, Maxwell held up a shaky hand. Monkey paused. With great effort, Maxwell turned his head to look back at Steven and the others. When he spoke, his voice was crystal clear and full of hatred.

"You think you've won. But you'll destroy yourselves," he said. "And then you'll destroy the world."

A massive chunk of ceiling crashed down, followed by an avalanche of rock. A stalactite dropped straight toward Steven. Roxanne looked up, opened her mouth, and shattered it into powder with a sonic cry.

Kim's hand clutched Steven's shoulder, a little too tight. "Like I said, confined spaces?" she said. "Not amazing!"

The Vanguard ship's hatch slammed shut. Its engines hummed to life and it began to sink into the ground, shaking the chamber even more.

Steven motioned his team back and pointed up at the quivering ceiling. In the center of the cracked stone, Maxwell's entry passageway was still intact. "There," Steven said. "That's our only way out."

He turned toward Jasmine. She grimaced, still weak from her ordeal. But she nodded.

"Hang on," she said.

Glowing brightly, she reached out her arms. The Dragon energy fanned out, encompassing all of them: Carlos, Kim, Liam, Steven, Roxanne—even Duane, who stood dazed and disoriented, only half recovered from Snake's hypnosis. They gathered together, huddling for protection against the falling rock.

Another large stalactite cracked loose from the ceiling. Jasmine turned toward it and roared, incinerating it with the Dragon's fire-breath.

Then she closed her eyes, concentrating. The Dragon spread its wings and began to rise toward the ceiling, carrying the entire group inside its ethereal body.

She really is powerful, Steven thought.

As they drew closer to the hole in the ceiling, Steven cast a last glance down at the ancient zodiac statues. A shard of rock struck the tiger statue in the neck, severing its head. The tiger head teetered, toppled, and crashed to the ground, smashing the remains of Carlos's machine.

The stone tiger head rolled into the center of the room. It tottered for a moment, then disappeared into the huge abyss left by the departure of the Vanguard drill-ship.

"I, ah, don't think that means anything," Liam said.

Then they shot upward into Maxwell's passageway. Jasmine's Dragon energy lit up the narrow vertical tunnel, showing their progress as the rock walls sped past. Up, up they flew, clinging to each other as the cavern below crashed in on itself.

"Uh," Kim said, pointing upward. "Uh, uh, uh . . ."

Steven looked up. Just ahead, the passageway seemed to terminate in a thick round metal hatch.

"Jasmine?" Steven asked. "We're kind of heading for that hatch, like, extremely fast."

She frowned, holding her hands to her temples. "If Maxwell got through it, so can we," she said. "Hang on."

"Wait a minute, Jaz," Carlos said. "We've been traveling upward at a slight angle. If I'm remembering correctly—"

But he was too late. The Dragon opened its mouth and spat fire at the hatch. The metal burned white-hot, softened—melted—

—and then water gushed over them like a tidal wave.

Steven had just enough time to draw in a final gulp of air. *The river,* he thought. *Maxwell tunneled down from the bottom of the river!*

Then the Dragon energy dispersed, and the water

pulled Steven away. He caught a quick glimpse of Roxanne and the others, caught up in the flood, being swept back down the tunnel along with the rushing tide of river water.

But Jasmine reached out with her power and caught hold of them. With a tremendous effort of will, she pulled them all up, forcing them through the hatchway. First Steven, then Kim, Duane, Liam, and Roxanne, with Carlos bringing up the rear.

Steven shook his head, letting a few bubbles of precious air escape. He looked around at the river bed, littered with seaweed and rusting bicycles.

Jasmine's glow faded. She flailed in the water, almost floating away. Liam caught hold of her and handed her off to Carlos.

She's exhausted, Steven realized. *She got us this far—now we've got to save ourselves.*

He looked around at the group and pointed, straight up.

They began to swim. Duane kicked hard with his big legs. Liam shot upward like a cannonball. Carlos swam surprisingly fast, supporting the semiconscious Jasmine.

Steven's lungs ached as he strained to hold on to his last remaining air. *None of our powers can help us now,* he realized. *It's just us. Just seven people, determined to survive.*

Seven teammates.

He broke the surface, gasping.

The stone bridge stood a few hundred feet away, spanning the river. A couple of tourists had stopped to stare, pointing at the figures popping their heads up out of the water.

"Agggh," Liam said, spitting water. "That's not what ye want when you get up in the morning."

"Or the afternoon," Roxanne said.

Steven looked around. Duane had just surfaced, gasping for breath. Carlos was treading water, holding Jasmine's arm around his shoulder. She smiled, a weak but relieved smile.

"Kim," Steven said, suddenly frantic. "Where's Kim? Where is she?"

Liam looked around too. Roxanne made a frightened noise, a very un-sonic cry.

"Uh, guys?"

Steven looked up—and saw a very strange sight. Kim sat perched in midair, smiling down at them. She was soaking wet.

"What took you so long?" Kim continued.

Steven looked closer. Kim wasn't *really* sitting in the middle of the air. There was something underneath her . . . something that shimmered, almost invisible to the eye. Something hovering low over the river.

"It's the Vanguard plane," Carlos said. "The one they used to drop off the strike force, in Greenland. It's hovering in stealth mode."

"I *poofed* up here, but nobody attacked me," Kim said. "I think it's on automatic."

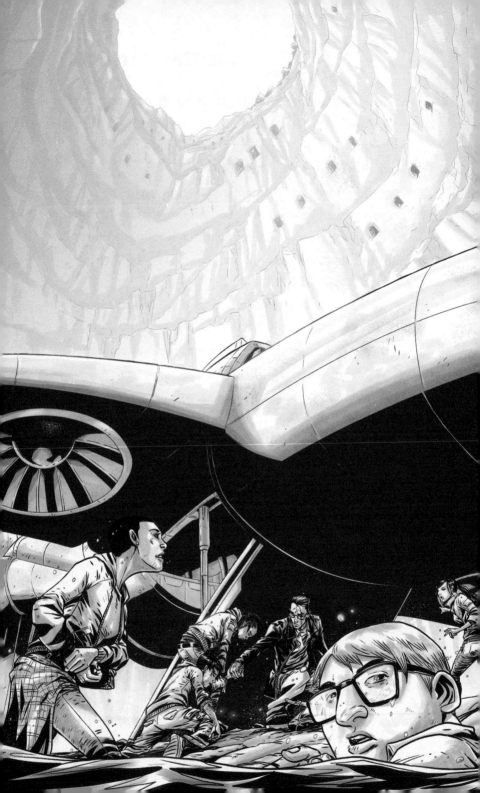

Steven motioned for the group to gather together. Liam and Roxanne splashed over closer to him, keeping their eyes on Kim. Carlos followed, along with Jasmine. Duane joined them last.

"Duane," Carlos said, "Vanguard seems to have protected their equipment from your energy-shorting effect. Do you think you can hack through that plane's security the old-fashioned way?"

Duane turned to Carlos and nodded, very fast. "It is very literally the least I can do," he said.

"Looks like we found our ride," Jasmine said. She turned to Steven, a serious look on her face. "Well, Tiger? What do you think?"

Steven looked around at the soaking wet faces, all turned to him. Then he glanced up at Kim.

"Let's go home," he said.

CHAPTER FORTY

LIAM GRABBED HOLD of the control stick with both hands. "This thing is too slow," he said. "Have y'got the voice-command circuit working yet?"

He was sitting in the Vanguard plane's pilot seat. Next to him, Duane leaned over the copilot's station, fiddling with a sprawl of wires spilling out of an exposed console. "Almost," Duane said.

"My Uncle Dez taught me to fly planes," Liam said, a lazy smile on his face. "Quite a barnstormer he was, too. One time during the war he—"

"Got it," Duane said.

Liam cocked his head at him. "Did you just say that to interrupt my story?"

Duane smiled.

Steven smiled too, watching them. *Duane actually made a joke,* he thought. *The world's full of surprises.*

Outside, they could see the Chinese countryside below. The coastline was just coming into view. Steven stood behind the cockpit, in an open area equipped with crash-seats and a large table. Jasmine and Carlos sat together at the table, talking quietly and bandaging up their wounds.

Roxanne lounged in a corner, picking idly at an old guitar she'd found in the back. "Gibson Sunburst," she said, almost to herself. "Vanguard *does* and their toys."

"All right, ye crazy plane," Liam said. "How 'bout a quick loop-de-loop?"

The plane lurched sharply upward, then flipped upside down. Jasmine swore. Steven's stomach jumped as he flew into the air, reaching out wildly for something to hold on to.

Then the plane swung around and leveled off. Steven landed, catlike, on the floor. Jasmine lurched into the table.

Liam laughed. "That's how Uncle Deke used to do it!" he said.

"Don't you mean Uncle *Dez*?" Duane asked.

Jasmine wasn't amused. She picked at a bandage covering her stomach. "Opened my wound back up," she said, wincing.

"Ah," Liam said. "Sorry 'bout that."

Steven walked up to the cockpit area. "Keep it level, you guys?" he said. "At least until everybody's patched up."

Duane nodded. He leaned in and touched the copilot's console. A tiny spout of Zodiac energy burst from his fingers.

Liam stared at him. "What was that?"

"I just told the plane not to listen to any more of your commands."

Liam sat back, chagrined. "Uncle Dez wouldn't have put up with that," he muttered.

Stifling a laugh, Steven crossed back to the table. Just then, Kim *poofed* in with a big box of bandages and first-aid equipment.

"There's plenty more in the back," she said. "Those Vanguard guys were ready for anything."

Jasmine picked out a large bandage. "Except us," she said.

Kim grinned and held up a box of pastries. "They got treats, too!"

Liam's hand was in the box shockingly fast. "So is that it for us?" he asked. "Is the whole team thing over, now that Maxwell's defeated?"

"He's not exactly defeated," Jasmine said. "Yes, we extracted the Dragon power from him and prevented him from capturing you kids. But he's still out there, and he still has his millions and at least some of his Zodiac agents and his *Carlos, what are you doing?*"

Carlos was running a large wand over her, from head to toe. "Just measuring your power," he said.

"I can't go home yet," Duane said. "I need that training you guys were talking about."

His words sound sad, Steven thought. *But his voice sounds like he wants to stay.*

"What about you?" Kim asked, looking hesitantly at Roxanne.

Roxanne gave her a half smile, then struck a chord on the guitar. "I think maybe I can make the two halves of my life fit together," she said.

Kim smiled back. "Besides, we can do more than just fight Mr. Maxwell, right? With our combined power, we could do a lot of good in the world." She stopped, suddenly self-conscious. "I—I'm sorry. That's not for me to—"

"No," Jasmine said, a thoughtful look on her face. "You're right. We've been so busy fighting for our lives . . . it's easy to forget why we're really doing this." She looked at Steven. "After all, there's more to life than just fighting the Vanguard, right?"

"If we're going to do good in the world," Steven said, "I still say we ought to have a name. All good hero groups have a name."

"Well," Carlos said, "I may not have powers, but I think I can help there. I was going to save this until we got home, but . . ."

Everyone crowded around as Carlos opened his laptop.

Steven craned his neck, watching as a simple, stylized word appeared on the screen:

ZODIAC

"Oh, great." Jasmine rolled her eyes. "What does *this* one stand for?"

A smile tickled at the corner of Carlos's lips. "It doesn't stand for anything. It's just Zodiac."

"Zodiac." Liam nodded. "Kind of on the nose, but it fits."

Kim clapped her hands. "I like it!"

Duane stared at the screen for a long moment, then smiled. Roxanne struck a triumphant note on her guitar and sang: "Zodiaaaaaaaac!"

"Steven?" Jasmine touched his shoulder. "Can I have a word?"

She led him to the far corner of the room. "I know what you're gonna say," he said. "Our teamwork was sloppy. As soon as we get back, we should set up a real training program—"

She waved him off. "Back in the cavern," she said. "When you caught me . . . I was trying to tell you something."

"Oh," he said.

"I was wrong about you. You did a great job back there. You didn't just lend physical power to the team. You made them *believe* they could win."

Steven blinked. He didn't know what to say.

"I still want you to be able to have a normal life," Jasmine continued. "But it's nice having the Tiger watching my back."

"Who wants normal?" he replied. "Normal's totally overrated."

Jasmine smiled. "Man, this is hard. I'm not used to being nice, you know? Don't tell the others." She gestured back at the table. "Especially Carlos."

"Well, you *gotta* be mean to Carlos." Steven grinned. "I mean, just look at him."

At the table, Carlos was pecking away again at his laptop.

"He's a nerd all right," Jasmine said, laughing. "But he's *my* nerd."

Steven raised his head and willed the Tiger power to come forth. It glowed above, its savage head turning to face Jasmine head-on.

"Zodiac, huh?" he said.

Jasmine looked back, very serious. The Dragon rose up, its sinewy energy-body coiling around her. It looked stronger, fiercer, more solid than ever before. When its fire-breath touched Steven's Tiger power, a flare of multicolored power surged into the air.

"Zodiac," she repeated.

They walked back over to the others. "I think training can wait a few days," Jasmine announced. "You've all earned a short vacation. And this plane can take you just about anywhere."

"Great!" Kim said. Then she frowned. "Actually . . . I can't think of anyplace to go."

"Well," Steven said, "I know where *I* want to go: back to Hong Kong. And I'd love to have some company."

One by one, the others turned to him—Liam, Roxanne, Duane, and lastly Kim. "Hong Kong?" Kim asked. "So we can see where the Zodiac power came from?"

"Not exactly," he replied. "I was thinking of the museum, not the secret sub-basement. There's a lot of stuff I didn't get to see, and I'd like to take in the rest of it." He turned to Jasmine. "If it's still standing."

"It is," she said. "But I thought you didn't care about that stuff."

Steven thought of his grandfather, of the heritage his parents had passed down to him. Jasmine was right; he'd never cared about it before. But now it gave him a warm feeling, a sense that he belonged to something greater than himself.

Then he looked at his teammates—and realized he felt something very similar toward them. They were the future, his chance to build something. His new family, built on the foundation of the old.

"I do care," he said. "I do now."

EPILOGUE ONE

THIAGO THE RAT stood in a dark, cramped cavern, scratching away at the surface of the oracle bone in his hand. *Stupid thing,* he thought. *So much slower than a holo-communicator!*

Wherever his sharp fingernail touched the bone, gray writing appeared. When he was finished, the faint message read:

**MISSION ACCOMPLISHED.
I THINK I'VE GIVEN YOUR YOUNG TIGER A CHANCE.**

ZODIAC

A massive crash resounded through the wall, shaking the ground. *That's it,* Thiago thought. *The main cavern has collapsed.* His intuitive power had allowed him to ferret out this narrow side passage, the one place where he knew he'd be safe.

The Rat's little mousehole.

At his feet, Malik—Ox—groaned and started to open his eyes. Thiago pulled out his gas gun, leaned down, and squirted another puff under Malik's nose. Malik moaned and went limp.

Thiago stared at Malik's chiseled features, his thick jaw. *You're just a little too loyal,* Thiago thought. *If I hadn't grabbed you, you might have gone along with your teammates' little walkout, formed a whole other faction. And that wouldn't have served my employers' purposes.*

You don't look like much. But sometimes one pawn can tip the whole chess game.

When Thiago stood up, a return message was waiting for him on the oracle bone.

THANK YOU. I REALIZE YOU'VE PUT YOURSELF IN A DIFFICULT POSITION. REST ASSURED THAT YOU WILL BE REWARDED.

Thiago scratched out his reply:

EPILOGUE ONE

DON'T MAKE ME REGRET THIS. IF I DO, YOU'LL REGRET IT TOO.

He stared at the bone for a long moment, but no further reply came.

Thiago exhaled, looking down at Malik's sleeping form. He was playing a risky game, he knew. If Maxwell found out about this, Thiago could wind up like poor Monkey.

He shuddered at the thought.

I hope I've picked the right side.

Then he smiled and laughed, a high-pitched chittering sound. *If not,* he thought, *I'll just switch sides again.*

After all, that's what a Rat does.

The woman sat alone in a tastefully decorated study. Every wall hanging, every book on the shelves had been carefully chosen and arranged. The final message still looked up at her from the oracle bone in her hand:

DON'T MAKE ME REGRET THIS. IF I DO, YOU'LL REGRET IT TOO.

The woman stared at the message for a long time. Then, with a quick motion, she wiped it clean with her palm. The oracle bone's surface went blank, then reverted to its screensaver: a faded picture of Steven Lee, age five, staring up in wide-eyed wonder.

A tear formed in the woman's eye.

"My little boy," she whispered. "What have we done to you?"

EPILOGUE TWO

"CARLOS, I MEAN IT. Put the wand away or I'll put it away for you, and you won't like where it ends up."

Carlos snapped the wand closed and turned back to his computer. "I'm just concerned."

"Well, don't be. I'm fine."

They had dropped the others off, and were headed back to Greenland. Neither Jasmine nor Carlos knew how to fly a plane, but Duane had assured them the autopilot could handle the flight. The idea made Jasmine nervous, but so far the trip had been smooth.

"He did good," Carlos said. "Steven, I mean."

"That's what I told him."

"Are you ever gonna tell him the whole story? About you and Maxwell?"

Jasmine frowned. For a moment, her whole body went tense. She didn't like to think about those days.

"Maybe someday," she said, keeping her voice deliberately light.

Carlos was still frowning.

"That's not what's really bothering you," she continued. "What is it?"

"I . . ." He turned and looked her in the eye. "Back in the Grottoes. The Vanguard team . . . they crumbled awfully fast."

"Our team was better," Jasmine said. But even as she said it, she knew that wasn't the whole answer.

"I suppose," Carlos replied. "But it almost seems like someone was helping us."

"Maybe I got through to Josie. She's a good person, deep inside. And she wasn't there with Snake at the end." Jasmine grimaced. "I've got a feeling our world is about to get a lot more complicated."

Carlos peered at her. "Are you *sure* you're all right? You've got a whole lot of Dragon power inside you, now."

"I can handle it. Really." She cocked her head at him. "But if you want to help me, go in the back and rustle up some dinner."

He smiled, a little flirty. "I have four advanced degrees, and you want me to make dinner?"

"I'll tell you what. Let's land this thing and meet up with the others. I've been craving dim sum for forever."

A moment later, his hands touched her shoulders. Despite herself, she jumped. He leaned in and gave her a quick peck on the cheek.

"Dim sum it is," he said.

When he was gone, she let out a deep breath. Dragon energy poured out from her mouth, her hands, up from every inch of her body. The sharp-clawed Dragon whipped around the cabin, hissing and spitting fire. Then it turned, for the first time, to gaze directly at her with glowing red eyes.

"I can handle you," Jasmine said.

The Dragon stared back silently.

"I can," she whispered.

She tried to remember what the world had looked like, before. Before the Zodiac, the Dragon, before the Convergence and the Tiger and the recruits and the power. Before . . .

Before Maxwell.

It took a lot of effort, but by the time Carlos landed the plane, she almost felt human again.

END BOOK ONE

THE ADVENTURE CONTINUES!
HERE'S A SNEAK PEEK AT THE
NEXT PART OF:

THE DRAGON'S
RETURN

STAN LEE
STUART MOORE
ANDIE TONG
DISNEY
THE
ZODIAC
LEGACY
THE
DRAGON'S
RETURN

THE AUSTRALIAN OUTBACK was a life-

less place, a wilderness of red sand and withered trees. Satellite cameras, staring down from orbit, picked up only the occasional flash of movement, a kangaroo or wallaby darting across the cracked earth.

In the midst of this desolation sat a strange, high-tech complex of buildings. The satellites couldn't see it, and it wasn't listed on any map—but it was there. It resembled a clutch of smooth white eggs half-buried in the sand, spread out in a wheel formation around the central dome.

ZODIAC

In the very center of that dome—the largest one—a man named Malosi stood waiting. He was in his mid-twenties, with gray skin, a wide face, and a nervous look in his eyes. He wore a crisp, well-pressed uniform with the insignia of the Vanguard Company on its breast.

Why? he wondered. *Why have I been summoned? Why me?*

In his hands, Malosi held a strange object. It was about the size of a softball and almost perfectly spherical except for a few dents. Its surface was bronze, tarnished and discolored in spots.

Malosi looked around. He was alone in a giant featureless chamber. The ceiling rose up to a central point; the floor was uneven, rising up and down, as if it had once been landscaped. But the only thing covering it was a thin layer of gray sand.

Malosi shifted from one foot to another. He brushed lint off of his uniform. He shifted the bronze sphere from one hand to the other.

The sphere, he realized. *It's warm.*

He looked up, startled, as a door in the far wall whirred open. He reached for his energy rifle, then realized he didn't have it on him. No weapons were allowed in the main dome.

A large, muscular figure strode into the room, action ready in boots and his own unique uniform. Malosi drew in a sharp breath. The man was Maxwell, founder and leader of Vanguard.

"Sir," Malosi said, snapping to attention.

Maxwell regarded him for a long moment with cold eyes. "It's just Maxwell," he said.

Malosi nodded quickly. "Maxwell."

Maxwell stepped forward, crossing the sandy expanse between them. His stare remained focused on his visitor. "Something wrong, Malosi?" he asked.

Maxwell had kept a very low profile for the previous year, spending most of his time there in his inner sanctum and in a secret lab. He'd left the running of Vanguard to his lieutenants, and he hadn't pursued any new military contracts. That left Vanguard's field agents—including Malosi—wondering what Maxwell's plans were.

But Malosi couldn't say that out loud.

"No, sir," he said. "Maxwell, I mean."

Maxwell stopped before Malosi. "You've been with us for four years. Is that right?"

"Yes."

"And a year ago, you were up for . . . let's call it a promotion."

Malosi felt a stab of anger. He tried to control it, but he knew Maxwell had seen his mouth tighten.

"Sometimes," Malosi said carefully, "things don't work out."

"And sometimes they do. It just takes a little longer." Maxwell gestured at the bronze sphere. "I see you have the item I requested."

"The Operator gave it to me personally." Malosi hesitated. "I have to ask, Maxwell . . ."

"Yes?"

"Anyone could have brought this to you." Malosi forced himself to look Maxwell in the eyes. "Why did you request me?"

A slight, amused smile crept onto Maxwell's lips. "Are you bored, Malosi? Tired of guarding bushes and cacti? Wondering if I've lost my fire, my thirst for greatness, along with the Dragon power?"

Malosi took a step back. "I—I didn't mean—"

"At ease." Abruptly, Maxwell turned and started toward the edge of the room. "Walk with me."

Malosi grimaced. He shot a glance at the bronze sphere in his hand, then followed. Maxwell led him past an area where the floor of the room rose up like a hill.

"Have you been here before, Malosi?"

"Once," Malosi said, still cautious. "It looked very different."

"This used to be my garden." An edge crept into Maxwell's voice. "A place of peace and contemplation, an oasis of streams, bridges, and waterfalls. But the Zodiac power ruined all that."

"The Zodiac power," Malosi repeated.

"Now this place must serve a new purpose. As must we all." Maxwell whirled around, addressing Malosi directly. "But you know all about Project Zodiac, don't you? You were fully briefed."

"Last year," Malosi agreed. "I was to be . . ." He trailed off, unable to speak the word. Malosi had spent the past year trying not to think about the power that had been promised to him and then snatched away.

"The Tiger," Maxwell said. "You were chosen to be my Tiger."

Malosi looked down, not wanting Maxwell to see the anger in his face.

"And since that time," Maxwell continued, "you've observed our Zodiac agents in the field. Snake, Monkey, Rat . . . you know what they can do. You've seen, firsthand, the power that should have been yours."

"I've been treated well by Vanguard," Malosi said stiffly.

"That's gratifying. But irrelevant."

Maxwell seated himself on a slight rise. He stared straight ahead, for so long that Malosi began to think he'd forgotten his visitor's presence.

Finally, Maxwell said: "I've made mistakes, Malosi."

Malosi cleared his throat. "That's, uh, that's human."

"Human." Maxwell smiled. "Yes. *I* am human, but the Dragon power is not. It's the greatest of the Zodiacs— orders of magnitude more potent than any of the others. It's very . . . seductive."

Malosi sat down next to his leader. "I'm, uh, sure you can handle it. Sir."

A flicker of doubt crossed Maxwell's face. He seemed to have aged recently. His eyes, his brow, his whole face looked tired.

"I've strayed from my path," Maxwell continued. "When I held the Dragon in my hand, I lost perspective.

I said and did things that I regret. And as a result, the power was lost to me."

"That . . ." Malosi paused, thinking of the Tiger power. "That's not an easy thing to live with."

Malosi looked away, lost in his own dark thoughts. He wondered how he could miss something so much when he'd never had it at all.

Then he felt Maxwell's eyes on him. When he looked up, Maxwell was staring at him with a frightening intensity.

"There is rage within you," Maxwell hissed. "The rage of the forgotten, the lost. But rage at whom?"

Malosi said nothing.

"At your father? Who walked out on you?"

Malosi shook his head. "No."

"No," Maxwell agreed. "We have ways of finding ourselves . . . new fathers."

Maxwell didn't look away. Malosi felt exposed, as if all his secrets were being revealed, one by one, under Maxwell's piercing gaze.

Then Maxwell reached into his pocket and pulled out a tattered photo. It showed a lean, athletic boy of about fourteen, with a shock of dark hair and a cocky expression on his face. The raging form of the Tiger rose up above him, roaring into the wind.

"*Steven Lee,*" Maxwell continued.

"Steven Lee," Malosi repeated.

He took the photo in his hand. It looked as if it had

been crumpled up, thrown away, and then massaged flat again.

"This boy stole what is rightfully yours," Maxwell said.

"But . . ."

"But what?"

"No. My chance—it passed me by." Malosi straightened his uniform. "Like I said, sometimes things don't work out."

"Malosi." Maxwell's voice turned dark, hard. "I am about to gain my second chance. The Zodiac powers will be mine—ours. All of them, this time."

"All of them." Malosi's eyes went wide. "Including the Tiger?"

"Oh, yes."

Malosi nodded slowly. He felt hope burning inside him, a fire he thought had been extinguished long before.

"Sir," he said, "what can I do?"

"You can start by giving me that."

Maxwell gestured at the bronze artifact in Malosi's hands. Malosi looked down in surprise. He'd almost forgotten about it.

"What is it?" he asked.

"It's called a *jiānyù*."

Malosi held out the sphere—the *jiānyù*—but only partway. Something, some instinct, made him stop. He felt that he was about to cross a line, to fall into a pit he could never escape.

"Give it to me," Maxwell repeated, "and I promise you,

the second chance begins now. For both of us."

Malosi studied the sphere. It seemed to grow even warmer, almost hot to the touch. An object of power, an ancient artifact whose significance he couldn't yet understand. Could Maxwell be trusted with it?

Then Malosi looked back down at the photo. He'd seen videos of Steven Lee in action, leaping and striking gracefully, the fierce Zodiac avatar blazing above his young figure. *That should be mine,* Malosi thought. *It's supposed to be mine.*

It will be mine.

He handed the sphere to Maxwell.

Maxwell held the *jiānyù* up to the light, gazing intensely at it. Malosi had the strange impression that Maxwell was seeing *through* the sphere, far beyond it. To the cosmos above, to the ley lines beneath the Earth. To the ancient forces that had birthed the power of the Zodiac.

"The rise of the Tiger," Maxwell whispered, "shall herald the Dragon's return."

Then he shook his head and turned to Malosi. He placed a fatherly arm around Malosi's shoulders and stared, fiercely, into the younger man's eyes.

"Are you with me?" he asked.

Malosi nodded. "I am."

Maxwell smiled, an unusually warm smile for him. Malosi felt a sudden unfamiliar surge of pride.

"Then I have already won," Maxwell said.

PART ONE
THE STORM

CHAPTER ONE

STEVEN LEE was twenty meters up in the air, descending slowly by parachute, when the truth of his situation struck him like a hammer to the head.

I just jumped out of a plane, he thought.

Steven had done a lot of bizarre things over the previous year. He'd traveled to Hong Kong, Greenland, and some strange caverns underneath China; he'd battled armed soldiers and superpowered agents, all over the world. Along the way, he'd acquired the incredible power of the Tiger.

But I've never jumped out of a plane before!

He reached down with trembling fingers and double-checked the buckle across his waist. Below, his destination lay spread out across a clearing in the desert: a multi-national school consisting of several low buildings. A rounded water tower rose up from the roof of one building.

Steven peered down. He couldn't see Kim, his team-mate, from this height. But he knew she was already on the ground.

A fierce wind rose up, blowing sand into Steven's face. He coughed and turned to look behind him. In the dis-tance, a raging sandstorm was rolling its way across the desert sand. It would be here in minutes.

And then, he thought, *it'll reach Dubai. A city of two million people.*

A sharp crack caught Steven's attention, rising above the roar of the wind. He looked down just in time to see the water tower break loose from its mountings on the roof of the school.

Steven reached across his chest and unsnapped two safety buckles. As the chute flew free, fluttering up into the air, he twisted his body and dove toward the ground.

The energy-shape of the Tiger flared all around him. Wind roared past, sweeping back his hair and spitting moisture into his eyes. The storm was growing stronger.

The water tower rolled along the roof, moving toward the edge. The school was a square, wide building, only two stories high. On the ground below, a teacher in a *hijab* was hustling a group of kids out of the building onto the playground.

The water tower was about to fall right on top of them.

Steven arched in midair, kicking out to strike the water tower on its side. It clanged loudly and rolled back into the middle of the roof. But as he bounced up and away, he saw it start to roll toward the edge again.

Inside him, the Tiger roared in frustration.

Steven reached out and grabbed a flagpole protruding from the side of the building, then used it to swing his body around. He was barely thinking; the Tiger operated mostly on instinct.

The last few children were straggling out of the schoolhouse as Steven swooped down. He grabbed up the three remaining kids in both arms and tossed them onto the playground, aiming toward a grassy area. They landed in a heap, winded but unhurt.

Steven touched down, stumbled, and looked up to see the huge bulk of the detached water tower plummeting straight toward him.

A blur of motion caught his eye. He turned to see Kim running his way. As she leaped up into the air, an energy-construct in the shape of a bounding rabbit blazed into existence around her. Steven felt her arms close around him, heard a soft *poof*—

—and then they tumbled to the ground together. When Steven looked up, dazed, the first thing he saw was the water tower crash to the pavement, exploding in a fury of water and plastic.

The second thing he noticed, as a few drops of water splashed his face, was that he was at least eight meters away from the school. The water tower had missed him.

Kim tried to climb to her feet, but stumbled. Steven reached out to help her.

"Thanks," she said. "Teleporting with a passenger . . . it takes a lot out of me."

Steven shook his head. He'd seen Kim use her power a hundred times, but he still wasn't used to it.

"Thank *you*," he replied. "You saved my butt."

She smiled that shy smile of hers. As always, it made Steven smile back.

The teacher approached, holding a girl's hand. The last of the children followed, staring at the shattered remains of the water tower. They were all between five and seven years old.

"Thank you," the teacher said. "You arrived just in time." Then she paused, frowning. "You look very young. Are you from the government?"

"Sort of," Kim said. "They called us for help."

Steven looked around. They were in the middle of the playground, near a basketball hoop with no net. On the far side of the yard, an old bus stood by a grove of brightly colored trees. Some of the kids were starting to climb aboard.

"We're here to help you evacuate," Steven said. "What's your plan?"

The teacher looked at him for a moment, unsure. A huge wind blew up, almost knocking them off their feet. Kim reached out a hand to help the woman, who kept a tight grip on the little girl's hand.

Steven looked up. The sky was dark, almost black, a roiling mass of rain and sand. It looked like a blanket of smoke, reaching all the way down to the horizon. Steven squinted and tried to make out the Zodiac stealth plane, which he knew was hovering overhead. But it was lost in the thick cloud cover.

The woman gestured toward the bus. Steven nodded, and he and Kim followed her.

"The school buildings are old," the teacher explained. "They're not safe during a storm, so we're supposed to take the kids to that old factory. It's got a shelter in the basement."

She pointed. Over the trees, past a long line of open fields, Steven could see the factory building in the distance. It was at least a kilometer away.

As they approached the bus, a young boy stuck his head out the window. "Miss Maya!" the boy shouted. "The driver can't get the bus to start!"

Kim turned to Steven. "Don't suppose you know how to fix a bus?" she asked.

He shook his head.

Sweat broke out on Steven's brow. The air was incredibly thick now, full of moisture. The wind was a constant barrage.

The boy climbed out of the bus. The teacher moved to help him, and five more kids followed, stepping down to the ground. Then another five.

Steven turned to Kim and looked her grimly in the eye.

"Fourteen kids, plus Miss Maya," he said. "We'll never make it on foot. The storm's too close."

Kim knew instantly what he was thinking. Her eyes grew wide with worry.

"Can we ask the others for help?" she asked.

Steven shook his head. "Liam's busy helping people at a half-collapsed construction site on the edge of the city. Roxanne is dealing with a traffic obstruction that's blocking evacuation efforts. And Duane has to keep monitoring from the plane."

"What about Jasmine?"

Steven shrugged helplessly. Jasmine was the Dragon, the most powerful Zodiac of all; at first she'd shared that power with Maxwell. When the Zodiacs defeated him at Dragon's Gate, Jasmine absorbed all the power. That had seemed like a good thing—but since that time, Jasmine had become very withdrawn and quiet. Steven barely knew how to talk to her anymore.

Kim grimaced. She turned to look across the fields, at the factory in the distance.

"Can you make it that far?" Steven asked.

"I'll have to," she replied. "But I can only carry one at a time."

The teacher looked at them, baffled. "What are you talking about?"

Steven cocked his head at her. "Who's your most adventurous student?"

Miss Maya turned to face the children. They stood together, eyes wide, waiting for instructions. Another gust of wind blew up, and they shrank away from the swirling sand.

"Aadab?" the teacher called.

A small girl stepped out of the group. She had dark hair and big eyes, and she looked completely unafraid.

Kim held out a hand. "C'mere, cutie."

She pulled the little girl close. Then she turned toward the open fields, staring at the factory building beyond. She tensed, clutched the girl tightly, and leaped into the air.

Rabbit energy flared around Kim. Then, together with little Aadab, she disappeared with a soft *poof.*

Miss Maya gasped. So did the whole class—except one boy, taller than the others, who stepped forward.

"Zodiac," the boy said, cocking his head to stare at Steven. "You guys are from Zodiac!"

Steven frowned. "How do you know about that?"

"My dad works for the emirate."

Steven nodded. The Zodiacs were cautious about letting the public know of their existence, but recently

Jasmine had started spreading the word discreetly among the world's government officials. That was how the Dubai authorities had known to ask the team for help.

Kim's been gone awhile, Steven realized. He touched a button on the small receiver clipped to his ear. "Kim? Rabbit? Are you okay?"

"Yeah," her voice crackled in his ear. "The girl's safe. I just needed to rest for a second. . . ."

With a faint *poof,* she reappeared in front of him.

"But now I'm ready to go again," she finished.

The students and their teacher stared at the girl who'd disappeared and reappeared out of nowhere.

Then the children all pressed forward, reaching toward Kim.

"Me next!"

"No, me!"

"Meeeee!"

Smiling wearily, Kim reached out for another child. As they vanished, the wind whipped up again. Rain began to sprinkle down.

Miss Maya gestured for the group to move up against the bus. "Everybody stay calm," she said. "We'll be safe here for a few minutes."

Then she turned to Steven with an odd, stunned look on her face. "Zodiac?"

"Zodiac," he replied.

Kim *poofed* back for another child and carried her to

safety, as well. Then another. The sky was turning very dark. Steven, the teacher, and the remaining children lifted their shirts up to their mouths to keep out the rising dust.

After the fifth child, Kim didn't come back right away. "Kim?" Steven asked over the radio.

"I'm . . . this is really hard." Her voice was crackly, exhausted. "I don't know if I can keep it up."

Steven flinched from the rising wind. "I'm sorry," he said, "but you have to."

"Talk to me," Kim said in his ear. "Distract me with something."

"Like what?"

"Anything."

Steven's mind went blank. He couldn't think of anything to say—except the one thing that had been bothering him for the entire mission.

"I'm worried about Jasmine," he said.

"Me too," Kim said. "What do you think happened to Carlos, anyway?"

Steven grimaced. Carlos was the scientific genius who, along with Jasmine, had founded the Zodiac organization. Three months before, in the middle of a mission, he'd suddenly disappeared.

For Jasmine, it was like half her heart had been torn out. She'd searched, put out feelers, called in every favor she had in the world. Nothing. It was as if Carlos had vanished off the planet.

"I don't know," Steven said.

Kim reappeared in front of him, breathing hard. She caught a face full of dust and coughed.

"I'm okay," she said. "Who's next?"

Kim took another child in her arms and turned to Steven. Her eyes were sunken with exhaustion.

"Keep talking," she said. "Does Jasmine really think Maxwell took him? Took Carlos, I mean?"

Poof.

"Uh," Steven began, touching his earpiece again. "I don't know. Maxwell—he doesn't have the Dragon power anymore. Jasmine's got it all now."

"But Maxwell still has his private army. Vanguard." She paused. "Is he gonna come looking for the rest of us?"

"He's been lying pretty low," Steven said. "But at least a couple of Zodiac operatives are still working for him. Carlos used to be able to track those guys' every move, but . . ." He trailed off, feeling helpless.

Kim *poofed* back in, grabbed another child, and vanished again.

Steven couldn't shake the dread he felt about Jasmine. He was worried about Roxanne, too—the Zodiac's Rooster. She was expecting a visit from her mother shortly after this mission. Steven had a terrible hunch that Roxanne might be planning to quit the team.

A shiver ran through his body.

"Steven?"

CHAPTER ONE

He looked up. Kim stood before him, lashed by the wind. She was breathing hard, leaning forward to rest her hands on her upper thighs.

"Nobody left but the teacher," Kim said. "And us."

"Wait!" Miss Maya yelled. She looked around, frantic. "We're missing someone. Where's Jana?"

Steven swore softly under his breath. He clenched his fists and willed the Zodiac power to rise up all around him. The Tiger's main attributes were strength, speed, and agility. But it was also finely attuned to danger, and its senses were superhumanly sharp.

Steven turned from side to side, searching the area. The energy-Tiger mirrored his movements, its deep green eyes seeing farther than Steven's own could. At last he noticed a small figure, cowering against a brightly colored flame tree down at the end of the playground.

A huge wind whipped up—the biggest gust yet—and rocked the bus. Steven, Kim, and Miss Maya backed away from the bus into the open field.

"I see her," Steven said, turning to Kim. "You take Miss Maya to safety. I'll get Jana."

Kim nodded and moved to take the teacher's hand. Miss Maya hesitated.

"Jana will be okay," Kim said. "Steven's the best."

The teacher nodded grimly. Together they leaped into the air and vanished.

Steven was already in motion, loping tigerlike toward

the grove of trees. Rain spattered against him as he ran. Behind him, the bus toppled and crashed to the ground.

The Tiger howled into the wind.

A cloud of wet dust flew into his eyes, blinding him momentarily. He waved it away, peering through the thickening rain. For a moment, he couldn't see little Jana anymore.

Then he caught sight of her again, cowering behind a tree. Its leaves were a vivid shade of red, so bright that they almost looked artificial.

The girl was only five or six meters away. But as he took a step toward her, she retreated, scurrying behind the next tree.

"Jana!" Steven yelled. "I'm here to help you!"

"Go away!" she screamed. "You're a *tiger*!"

With great effort, he willed the Tiger energy to subside. He could feel it fighting him. It wanted to be free, to protect him from the elements.

But there was a downside to the Zodiac power. Steven knew that the sight of a raging ghostly tiger was terrifying to the little girl.

"I'm just a kid," Steven called. "Like you!"

She stared at him, her eyes still wide with fear. He realized that she was the girl he had seen holding Miss Maya's hand when he first arrived.

"Come out, okay? Miss Maya is worried about you."

She shook her head.

Steven clenched his fists, frustrated. He could leap out

and grab the girl, but he didn't want to scare her any further. And he wasn't sure if even the Tiger could outrun a terrified seven-year-old.

There was a soft *poof* beside him.

"Jana," Kim called out, stepping forward. "Will you listen to me?"

Jana stood perfectly still, staring.

"I know this is scary," Kim continued. "I used to be scared, too. When this boy here"—she pointed a thumb at Steven—"when he first came to sign me up for his group, I ran away from him—how many times?"

"Three times," Steven said. "Four, maybe."

"Four times," Kim said, taking another step toward Jana. "But then I realized he was only trying to help me. Just like we're trying to help you."

A hint of doubt crossed Jana's face.

"You don't have to be afraid." Kim smiled. "I had to learn that. I had to learn to trust people."

She held out both hands. Jana took a hesitant step, then ran forward into Kim's arms.

Steven smiled. "Nice speech."

Kim smiled back at him, over the head of the little girl who clung to her. "BRB," she said, and vanished.

Kim's grown a lot, too, Steven thought. *Just like Roxanne. Do they need us anymore? Do they need me?*

A moment later Kim reappeared. She took a step toward him and stumbled.

"They're all safe?" he asked.

She nodded, then spat out a mouthful of dust and coughed violently.

"I can't," she gasped, collapsing into his arms. "I can't do it again."

He nodded, wrapping an arm around her shoulders. "Come on."

Staggering against the rising wind, he led her over to the trees. The wind raged all around them, whipping and lashing them with tiny grains of sand. Steven shrugged off his jacket and draped it over Kim's shoulders, holding the sleeve up to her mouth.

"Breathe through this," he said.

She nodded and gasped in a breath.

Steven pulled her up against the trunk of a tree. Kim slumped against it and coughed again. Then she looked up sharply, through the dust and spattering rain, at the tree. He followed her gaze.

"Those are the brightest leaves I've ever seen," Steven said. "Never thought I'd see that in a desert."

She smiled weakly.

A huge gust of wind slammed into them. Steven reached for Kim, bracing her up against the tree.

"The heart of the storm," he whispered. "It's passing over us now. We'll just have to wait it out."

She buried her head in his shoulder.

The storm grew even stronger, rising and whirling all around. Steven pulled her close, raising his shirt to his mouth so he could breathe.

CHAPTER ONE

Kim pulled his jacket tighter around her shoulders. Her presence was warm and comforting beside him. She was only trembling a little.

As they stood together, the pelting rain and sand began to rip into the brightly colored trees. Fiery red leaves tore loose and whipped all around, vivid dots of color that flashed bright and then vanished into the thick cloud of dust.

"They're beautiful," Steven said, peering up over the collar of his shirt.

Kim said something into his shoulder, but it was muffled and lost in the roaring wind.

"What?" he asked.

"I said it's just nice being here with you."

An enormous gust of wind rose up, almost blowing them off their feet. Steven closed his eyes, concentrated, and willed his power to come forth. The Tiger wasn't invulnerable, and it couldn't stop the storm. But its energy might be able to protect them, just a little bit.

The Tiger felt Kim's heartbeat even more clearly and vividly than Steven did. It roared into the wind, raging against the violence of nature. It reached out a spectral claw and swiped at the bright blood-colored leaves.

Gradually, the storm passed. The wind died down. The dust and sand subsided, leaving only a steady pelting of rain.

"You okay?" Steven asked.

"A little wet." She smiled, exhausted. "And there's sand in my hair."

He looked up. The sky was still blanketed by a gray cloud, but it was clearing fast. He could see a blurry glow starting to shine through the haze and sand.

"Look," he said.

Kim followed his gaze. As the clouds parted, they could just barely make out the tiny circling figure of the Zodiac plane. And next to it—hovering in place high in the air—was the source of the glowing light. It was too small to make out, but it was clearly a human figure. They both knew who it was.

"Jasmine," Kim said.

Steven nodded. Jasmine was the key to this whole mission—but could they rely on her? The storm was passing them by, but that black cloud looked as huge as ever. And it was still on course for the center of Dubai.

"I think I can jump again," Kim said.

"Can you carry me?"

She looked at him, pretending to be doubtful. "You're bigger than a schoolkid. But smaller than a teacher."

Steven laughed.

He looked up again. Jasmine's glow was brighter, and she seemed to be drifting toward the storm front. But she wasn't taking any direct action yet.

Jasmine was the most powerful of the Zodiacs—the only one who could take on the forces of nature. The only one who might be able to actually stop the storm.

Maybe, Steven thought.

Before Steven could speak again, his earpiece crackled. Kim touched her ear at the same time he did, and together they heard Roxanne's strained voice:

"Steven? Jasmine? *Kkkkk*-ybody? I need backup."

Kim looked up at Steven. As she reached out a hand, the Rabbit energy flared up around her small form.

"Let's go," she said.